The
POWER

JENNIFER L. ARMENTROUT

#1 *New York Times* and *USA Today* bestselling author

The POWER

A TITAN NOVEL

SPENCER
HILL
PRESS

Spencer Hill Press

Contact: Spencer Hill Press
27 West 20th Street, Suite 1102
New York, NY 10011
Please visit our website at www.spencerhillpress.com

First Edition: 2016
Armentrout, Jennifer L. 1980
The Power : a novel / by Jennifer L. Armentrout—1st ed.
p. cm.
Summary: While preparing for war with the Titans, Josie and Seth must also keep the peace between the pures and the half-bloods, while also helping Josie learn how to manage her newfound abilities.

The author acknowledges the copyrighted or trademarked status and trademark owners of the following wordmarks mentioned in this fiction: *Airbender*, Amazon, *Angry Birds*, *Beverly Hills 90210*, Big Mac, Butterball, Coke, Crock-Pot, Frisbee, Glock, Godzilla, *Good Housekeeping*, Harry Potter, Hummer, Incredible Hulk, *Lifetime*, Mack Truck, Malibu Barbie, *Mario Kart*, *Melrose Place*, One Direction, Slip N' Slide, Spider-Man, *Star Wars*, *Supernatural*, Tater Tots, The Three Stooges, Twinkies, Yukon

Cover design by Sarah Hansen of Okay Creations
Interior design by Neuwirth & Associates

ISBN 978-1-63392-057-6 (e-book)

ISBN 978-1-63392-056-9 (paperback)

Printed in the United States of America

This is for every reader
who is here to follow Seth's journey.

The POWER

1

Josie

A feather-light caress skated down my arm and over my hip. A moment passed as I stirred from the depths of sleep. Hard warmth pressed against my back, sending a series of shivers down my spine.

Only half-awake, I smiled as I blinked open my eyes. The room was dimly lit, telling me that it was way too early to be awake.

Lips brushed against the sensitive spot on my neck, just below my pulse, and another set of fine tremors danced over my skin. Muscles tightened low in my stomach.

The kiss came again, this time over my pulse, and my toes curled.

It was way too early, but who would complain about waking up this way? Not me. If I spent the rest of my life waking up like this, I'd be a happy girl. So happy.

Rolling onto my back, my sleepy grin froze as my gaze connected with pitch-black, obsidian irises. *What the . . . ?* Confusion quickly gave way to icy terror that dug deep into every cell and latched onto bone and tissue.

Oh no.

My heart kicked in my chest, pounding so fast I thought it would climb out of my chest and run out of the room.

A Titan loomed over me, his cruel lips curling into a bitter, vengeful smile. "I will find you when you least expect it," he said in a voice as suffocating as heavy smoke. "I'm always going to be right behind you. There is no—"

Jackknifing upward, I threw out my hand, prepared to deliver what was probably going to be a not-so-effective throat punch. I opened my mouth to shout, but no sound came out, and suddenly, there was nothing in front of me. Nothing.

No Titan.

I was sitting up and staring at the empty space in front of me, my heart racing. Scanning the shadowy dorm room, I found no sign of the dangerous and sickening god. Everything was as it had been before I'd fallen asleep Sunday night. TV across from the bed, turned off. The blinds covering the small window near the bathroom were slightly open and I could see the pale blue light of dawn creeping over the Black Hills, the protected portion of the forest deep within the Northern Hills of South Dakota.

My new home.

Which was sort of like my old home, Radford University. Except this University looked like something straight out of Greece during the time people actively worshipped the gods. And I was surrounded by mythical beings instead of by twenty-somethings whose greatest powers were the ability to perform tasks hungover and with minimal sleep.

Correction. *I* was a mythical being, actually, and the students at the Covenant University weren't very different from mortal students. With the exception of being descendants of gods, and the whole trying-to-kill-each-other thing they had going on right now.

But there was no psychotic Titan lurking in the shadows of my room, preparing to feed on me until I was nothing but a dried-out husk, then do other spiteful, repulsive things that I—

I wasn't going to think about.

Exhaling, I closed my eyes as I rubbed my palm over my forehead. Just a dream—a stupid dream. Titans couldn't get inside the University. Wards prevented that. The shades could, but I'd rather face a hundred souls that had escaped Tartarus than see Hyperion's or another Titan's face again.

I had no idea who the man was that I'd dreamed about, except that I knew deep in my core that he was a Titan.

"Josie?" came a rough, sleep-heavy and slightly accented voice. "What are you doing?"

My pulse kicked up again, but this time for a very different reason as I twisted around and got an eyeful of possibly the sexiest being alive.

Seth Dio—however you spelled or pronounced his last name— was lying on his side. The thin comforter was tangled low around his hips, revealing a whole lot of golden-colored skin—taut and ripped skin.

Seth had a legit six-pack. Like, not painted on, or only visible when he was flexing or doing strenuous activities. I half-suspected he was born that way, a baby with a six-pack and rock-hard pecs, doing bicep curls with milk-filled bottles. Speaking of biceps, they were extremely nice too. So were his broad shoulders and tapered waist. And his face?

God.

He was *beautiful*. Almost too much. Like his features had been carefully pieced together, a collection of perfection—which they had been. Angular, high cheekbones and full, sensual lips you could get lost staring at. Dreaming about. Well, fantasizing about. A straight, flawless nose, and his eyes . . . They were the most stunning ocher color, framed by dark, thick lashes. His arched brows were slightly darker than his blond hair—hair that he'd cut recently. I was still getting used to the shorter locks. The soft strands were buzzed close to the skull on the sides and longer on the top, sometimes straight, sometimes a mess of waves. I liked running my palms against the sides, feeling the shorter hair tickle my palms.

I just liked touching Seth in general.

Sometimes I had no idea how he had ended up in *my* bed. I mean, of course, he was there because I invited him in and wanted him there, but I don't think I was the type of girl anyone pictured with someone like him. I wasn't knocking myself. I was just being realistic. I was five feet and nine inches of uncoordinated mess most of the time. My hips would've been popular back in the fifteen-hundreds or something, when "child-bearing hips" were all the rage, and I'm pretty sure my thighs were never in style or going to be. Apparently no amount of training—kickboxing, grappling, running, defensive or offensive training—was going to tighten my stomach or trim my waistline. I wasn't thin or willowy, or graceful and demure. I was loud, could be fairly obnoxious, and I rambled.

But Seth liked me. He'd said I was his *salvation*.

And I liked him.

A lot.

I was also a demigod, Apollo's daughter, so there was that.

And Seth was the Apollyon, the product of a half-blood and pure-blood, created by the recently deceased Ares, and I was already as powerful as I could be, once I got the knack of controlling my newly discovered abilities.

His amber-colored eyes, shining like precious stones, narrowed. "Are you awake? Or is this some kind of creepy sleepwalking thing?"

My lips twitched into a small grin. "I'm awake."

"So . . ." He rolled onto his back, sliding an arm behind his head, and I sort of got hung up on watching the way his biceps flexed and rolled. "You're just sitting up and staring at me while I sleep?"

I rolled my eyes. "No."

"That's not what it looks like."

"I was actually sitting up and staring at the wall until you interrupted me."

He lowered his other hand, resting it low on his flat stomach. From my vantage point, he almost looked nude under the blanket, but unfortunately he wasn't. "That's not weird or anything."

"Whatever," I said, fixing the strap on the tank top I was wearing. "You're weird."

Those lips tipped further up on the corner. "You're hot."

I rolled my eyes again, but I was totally flattered.

His head tilted to the side. "A dream?"

The warm and fuzzy feeling of flattery faded away, and I nodded.

"You okay?"

"Yeah. I'm fine." I cleared my throat as I pushed my hair back over my shoulder. "Just a weird dream."

His stare was intent as he studied me quietly. This wasn't the first nightmare I'd had after the showdown with the Titan. And not just any Titan. Hyperion. The godly being my father had entombed thousands of years ago, and who was now loose, hell-bent on revenge. I'd somehow sent him packing when my demigod abilities had been unlocked, but he'd be back.

I knew that.

He and the other Titans that had escaped would keep coming back until we located the other five demigods, unlocked their abilities, and managed to join our abilities in order to entomb the Titans back in Tartarus.

Of course, we had no idea where the other demigods were or how we could find them. Or how we were seriously going to entomb them again. Apollo hadn't let us in on that information yet.

Though I wanted it to be the last nightmare, so badly, I knew better. Those hours with the Titan had felt like an eternity, and I tried, *really* tried not to dwell on them. I probably could use some therapy.

Wait. Could demigods get therapy? Like was there a specialist around these parts focusing on the mental health of mystical beings?

Seth's fingers brushed over my arm, drawing my attention. Our eyes met. His hand wrapped around my wrist and he dragged me down so that I was half on top of him.

Oh, I liked where this was heading.

His chest was warm under my arms and his hand was steady as he reached up, catching a few strands of my hair. He tucked it back behind my ear and his hand lingered, cradling my cheek. I lowered my mouth to his and kissed him softly. When I lifted my head, his eyes were iridescent.

"I liked that," he murmured.

"So did I." Then I remembered something super important. I hadn't really forgotten. It had just slipped my mind in the wake of the nightmare. A big goofy smile tugged at my lips. "I think you get more today."

He slid his hand around to the nape of my neck. "I think I should get more every day."

"Of course you do, but today is different."

Understanding rippled across his features, a slight widening of his eyes and nostrils. A moment of surprise, and seeing that caused pain to flicker through my chest, because he hadn't expected me to remember.

Seth expected so very little sometimes.

Pushing away the welling sadness that realization always brought with it, I kissed him again. And then once more, because I wanted to show him, I needed him to know that he had every right to expect the world. "Happy birthday."

"Josie . . ."

The way he whispered my name, so tender and potent, made my breath catch. "So, what's it feel like to be twenty-two?"

Threading his fingers through my hair, he didn't answer immediately. "Feels like twenty-one."

"That's not exciting."

He grinned again. "That's because you're still twenty and have what? About six months to go before you're twenty-one."

"You're a cradle-robber."

Seth chuckled and then lifted his head, kissing the corner of my lips. "I think that's the first time I've been called that."

"Good." I smoothed my hand over his chest, enjoying the way he sucked in a sharp breath. I loved that my touch affected him so. "I wanted to get you something, but Amazon doesn't really deliver out here, so . . ."

I really did want to get him something, but since it wasn't particularly safe for me to leave, the only option was the campus store, but I doubted Seth wanted a Covenant University mug or hoodie. I couldn't even make him dinner since I had no access to a kitchen, so I was a lame girlfriend.

Girlfriend.

I shivered.

That word still felt incredibly new. Shiny. Unfathomable. I think both of us were still discovering each other, and we were taking this slow. Like three-legged-turtle slow. Our relationship was far from perfect. There were obstacles in our path that most couples would never face, like, say, the fact we both had immortal beings gunning for us.

Then there was Seth's oftentimes disturbing past.

There was also the possibility of his future getting cut short. I refused to allow that to happen, but wasn't yet sure what I could do to stop it.

And I was also pretty sure that my father kind of wanted to murder him.

I really needed to stop thinking about all of that.

"You know what?" he said.

"Hmm?"

Folding his other arm around my waist, he rolled me onto my back and slid on top of me. His weight did crazy things to my senses—amazing, crazy things. "You've already given me enough."

My brows rose. "I haven't—"

"You have." He lowered his mouth to mine, and when he kissed me there was nothing soft or slow about it.

Seth kissed like a man coming out of an extreme drought. He sipped and he savored, drawing each kiss out of me. He was a man who thoroughly enjoyed kissing, took the scenic route and was absolutely in no hurry to get to the destination.

But I *really* wanted that destination.

You know, him and me, naked, bodies twisting together and me tossing virginity to the wind.

Seth nipped at my lower lip, eliciting a sharp gasp from me. "Mmm," he murmured, dragging his hand down my arm, catching the strap from my top. "You give me that sound."

My breaths came out in short bursts as he shifted his weight onto his left arm and rose just far enough that there was the smallest space between us. Those agile fingers worked at the straps of my top until they circled my wrists.

Cold air spread tiny bumps across my bare chest. I watched, in a daze, as he lowered his head and kissed the odd scar that remained after Apollo had unbound my powers.

Seth lifted his lashes, and I saw the smug, daring grin a second before he lowered his head again. The tip of his tongue traced the straight, five-inch line from the bottom to the top. He didn't stop there. Oh no, those tiny licks followed the two lines looping around it. He even got what reminded me of wings on either side of the strange scar.

Heat zinged through my veins as he kissed his way from the scar, discovering very, very sensitive areas. Moaning, I skimmed my hand over the shorter strands of his hair, finding the longer ones to curl my fingers around. My back arched, and he settled his hips between my legs.

"You gave me these," he said. "And they're the gift that keeps on giving."

I giggled. "You're a perv."

"I'm just speaking the truth." His mouth closed over a tip and his tongue did wicked, delightful things. "Best damn birthday gift I've ever gotten."

"Seth—"

He moved up, swiftly and with startling precision. His mouth closed over mine, cutting off my words. Wasn't complaining, not when his tongue moved along mine. Not when my chest was suddenly flattened against his. And definitely not when he did this thing with his hips, rolling them into the perfect spot that really, really made me want to bypass the scenic route and get right to the promised land.

I lifted my leg, draping it over his as I lifted my hips, following his lead. Seth moaned into my mouth, a hot masculine sound that sent a rush of sensations pounding through my body. His hips moved again, and I thought maybe this morning, because it was his birthday, we'd—

The alarm on the nightstand went off, shrill and jarring. It screamed that it was time to get up and get to training.

Seth lifted his mouth and groaned. "Damn."

My grip in his hair tightened. "We can ignore it."

"That would make me a very bad trainer if we did," he replied, his lips brushing over mine. "And I'm trying to be a very good trainer."

"It's your birthday," I reasoned. "We can get a late start."

His palm brushed over the tip of my breast. "Not a good enough reason."

"It's Monday."

He chuckled. "Josie."

"What? That's a damn good enough reason."

Seth kissed me as he pulled the straps of my top up. I was officially shut down. "You've improved in the last couple of weeks, but you still have a lot of work to do."

I started to frown. "Gee. Thanks."

Laughing, he rolled off and swung his legs over the bed, standing. He did this with such little effort and with so much grace that I wanted to throat punch him. "Get that sweet ass up and ready. Time to get to work."

I lurched out of the bed, moving like a slightly high Godzilla. "Just because you're a Pollyanna, Sethie, doesn't mean you can boss me around."

He shot me a bland look. "Apollyon, Joe. Repeat after me. Apollyon."

I grinned.

His eyes narrowed. "You drive me crazy."

Sidestepping him, I looked over my shoulder as I headed to the small adjoining bathroom. "In a good way?"

"Undecided."

"Ass."

Seth's lips curved up on one corner, making him look downright wicked. He was lucky it was his birthday, so I was going to let the whole "Joe" thing slide. I opened the bathroom door.

"Josie?"

"What?" I turned, startled to find him standing right in front of me. I still couldn't get over how quickly and quietly he could move.

"I . . ." He trailed off and then lifted his hands, gently clasping my cheeks. He kissed me, and it was sweet and tender, and so powerful. "Thank you for remembering my birthday."

And then he was gone.

Out of the room and next door, probably already in the shower, while I was still standing there, staring at the spot where he'd stood, wondering if no one had ever remembered his birthday before.

Or cared enough to.

This year, this birthday would be different, though.

2

Seth

I was an idiot to trade spending a few hours in bed with Josie for watching her accidentally set shit on fire when she was supposed to be summoning the air element.

Which was why we were standing outside, far away from any of the buildings, back near the cemetery, even though there was still a brisk chill in the air. It was only in the fifties here. Place never seemed to get that warm. Hopefully, she didn't start blowing up headstones and statues next, because I doubted that would go over well with Marcus, the current Dean of the University, who was also not a member of my fan club.

And it was also why getting our asses out of bed and training was so important. Knowing how to fight in hand-to-hand combat was important, but when it came down to facing the Titans, she was going to need to know how to use and control her demigod abilities.

Plus, Luke helped take over during the afternoon sessions, and the first time—the last time—Josie had used the elemental powers around him, she'd accidentally blown him into a wall, damn near *through* it.

Hilarious.

But painful for him.

Josie squinted as she stalked past me, heading for the straw dummy that Deacon had been way too overjoyed to help create. The thing looked like a rather fashionable scarecrow, decked out in a polo shirt and wearing a fedora.

No idea why it had a fedora on.

I didn't ask.

Crossing my arms, I waited until Josie appeared ready. Twenty hours later. She wasn't comfortable using the elements, so she paced a lot, shifted her weight, practically prancing around until she stilled.

"It's in the head," I reminded her. "You have all this power at your fingertips, but you need to fully understand that."

"I understand that."

"No, you don't."

Her hands closed into fists as she looked over at me. Her blue eyes were vibrant, very much like her father's when he was rocking irises, but when she was frustrated or angry, they reminded me of the deep blue of the Aegean Sea that surrounded the Cyclades.

They went that deep when she was turned on, too.

"I know I have the power," she argued. "Duh."

I arched a brow. "Yeah, you know you do, but you don't really believe it or trust yourself. If you did, you wouldn't be setting every damn thing on fire every time you get horny."

Her cheeks flushed pink. "I do not!"

I smirked.

"That was like once or twice." She threw up her hands. "Okay, maybe four times. I didn't this morning." A light sparked in her eyes. "Then again, maybe that just means you were slacking."

"Is that so? Me slacking?" I laughed. "Babe, if you'd been any more ready this morning, the whole damn dorm would've caught on fire."

Her entire face went red this time, but that spark in her eyes turned into a flame, and I knew her mind was back in the bed, when I was thanking her for the lovely gift of her breasts.

Josie blinked and muttered, "Assface."

"Got a new nickname for you."

"Oh. I can't wait to hear this."

Dipping my chin, I grinned as she watched me. "Anytime you get around me, you get so ready, I'm just going to start calling you Slip 'N Slide."

She choked on a strangled laugh. "Oh my God, that's terrible. If I ever hear you say that again, I might hurt you, Seth. For real."

Chuckling, I nodded at the dummy. "Tap into the wind, Josie. Feel it coursing through you. You got this."

Josie's nose wrinkled and then she focused on the dummy. Her hands closed into fists again. Her shoulders rose, and I felt it then—the small ripple of power. It flowed in the distance between us, washing over my skin. The kiss of power—of *aether* being tapped into and used—felt like stepping out into the summer sun.

Locking my jaw, I shifted my stance as I drew in a deep, steady breath and focused on Josie, only her, until the enticing wave of power dissipated.

Lightning cracked overhead. Fat, dark clouds began to form. I lifted my chin, sighing as a raindrop smacked off the bridge of my nose.

"Shoot," she muttered, shoulders drooping.

I pursed my lips as I watched the gray clouds break apart. "We're lucky," I announced dryly. "You're not going to drench us this time."

"Shut up."

My lips quirked up. "Try again."

Josie did just that. Lightning cracked again. She set the chair I'd dragged out on fire. The dummy started to smoke at some point, but then the quick shower she summoned put the fire out. The fedora was a loss.

Finally, near lunchtime, Josie got it. She summoned the element of air, lifting the dummy up and holding it there for several moments.

Each time she tapped into the *aether*, I felt the kiss of power and used every ounce of control that I had to ignore it. Being around pures had helped me build up some tolerance to the minor displays of power. And I'd experienced harder shit. For example, the erection this morning was one of them. Denying the level Josie wanted to take our relationship to was the exact opposite of easy, even when I wanted to . . . well, do right by her. Strange concept and all, but behaving myself was hard. So I got this covered.

But it was when we worked with *akasha* that I almost couldn't . . . couldn't ignore the allure.

There was nothing more powerful than that, and when it hit the air, it was like touching lightning. It called to me, sang to what existed deep inside me—this *thing* that needed *aether* as badly as a daimon did. How fucked up was that? Knowing that I shared something in common with the daimons was one of the things that kept me in check, kept this *thing* inside me locked away.

Josie was the other.

Once the dummy was back on the ground, I made her use the element of air three more times, just to make sure it wasn't a fluke. With her, you never knew.

Josie turned to me, pushing a shorter strand of blonde hair out of her face. A tentative smile appeared as she bounced over to where I stood. "I think I finally got the hang of the air element."

Truthfully, I couldn't say if she finally did have control over it or not, and we wouldn't know until she could do it several days in a row. Josie stared up at me, eyes bright and hopeful. I didn't want to piss on her parade.

"Yeah," I said, leaning down and pressing my lips to her forehead. "You did really good, Josie."

Stretching up, she looped her arms around my neck and gave me a quick, tight hug before settling back on her feet.

I stood there. Stared at her for a few moments. Like a creep. Sometimes I didn't know what to do with her. I could be touchy. Gods knew I had boundary issues. I had no problem being . . . affectionate, but I was not, under any circumstance, used to someone being affectionate *with* me. Not like this. When it was actually genuine, not forced for one reason or another, and went deeper than a physical thing.

Josie was free with the affection—the smiles and the touches, the soft kisses and the closeness.

She blew me away with all of that.

Sometimes I also wondered what I was doing with her, getting involved in a real relationship, because it wasn't exactly fair to her. A handful of months ago, I would've laughed my ass off at the prospect of something like this, but here I was, in a relationship with Apollo's daughter.

And besides all that terrible shit I'd done in my past and the shit with the *aether* that I was still struggling with, I literally had no future.

None.

Eventually, once the Titan situation was handled and I survived that, I would be going back to doing the gods' bitch work, dealing out Remediations. In other words, hunting down and destroying those who had sided with Ares against the Olympian core. And then after that? Whenever I did die, my soul belonged to Hades. There was no promise of tomorrow and no paradise waiting for me.

So doing this with Josie was selfish. Unfair. The odds were stacked against me, against us, and just like I knew Apollo was eventually going to appear at the most inopportune time, she was going to end up hurt by all of this.

But, like I said, I was selfish.

I couldn't walk away from Josie. I had tried to ignore what I was feeling for her. I had tried to leave her the day that I'd brought her here, to the University, as I'd been ordered to do, and I hadn't been able to do it. I wouldn't be able to do it.

I just hoped she didn't end up paying for it in spades later.

Despite where my head had gone, Josie smiled up at me. "I'm hungry."

A slight grin tugged at my lips. "Of course."

Josie smacked my arm. "Jerk."

Pushing the darker thoughts away, I draped my arm over her shoulders. "Come on. Let's head to the cafeteria."

"Can we grab some food and take it back to my room?"

"Sure." Considering the cafeteria was becoming more of a warzone between the halfs and pures than a place to eat, I didn't have a problem with that.

Since the very first birth of the half-blood—the child of a pure-blood and a mortal—the half-blood race was subjugated by those with pure bloodlines. It was a fucked-up caste system, reminiscent of ancient Greek times, where destinies were fated based on whether or not the blood was considered pure.

Up until recently, the halfs had it bad, absolutely no choice. The Breed Order that had been in place since the beginning stripped them of rights and prohibited the mixing of the two breeds.

At the age of eight, halfs had been brought in front of a council of pure-bloods and had been determined if they would be given the Elixir, a serum created by the gods that robbed a half-blood of all free will, and placed into indentured servitude, or if they would go into training. Some believed that training to become a Sentinel or Guard was better than the servitude, but Sentinels and Guards had notoriously short lifespans. Most didn't make it out of their mid-twenties, dying while hunting daimons—pures and halfs that had become addicted to *aether*—or from guarding the pures.

Becoming a Sentinel hadn't meant that the halfs had free will. It just meant they had been chasing the lesser of two evils.

But the rule of the Breed Order was over and gone, just like the Elixir. Halfs had all the rights of the pures, and while many pures had fully supported the change, some were not overly thrilled that they no longer had access to free labor. And there were also halfs who weren't ready to let thousands of years of injustice go.

Couldn't really blame them for that.

Some of the halfs chose to continue training to become Sentinels. Some left their posts. Others stayed. And there were even some pures, much like the saintly Aiden St. Delphi, who had risen to the occasion and were now training to become Sentinels.

Chaos had a nasty habit of sneaking up on everyone when it was least expected, and although things had been quiet the last couple of days, I doubted it would remain that way.

In the cafeteria, Josie bypassed the grilled chicken and salad bar, bum-rushing the fried foods section. My kind of girl right there. She grabbed a basket of fries and I went for the fried chicken tenders. After loading up on drinks, we headed back to the dorm, and the whole time, Josie smiled in a way I began to worry might crack her face.

I eyed her as we headed down the narrow hall toward our rooms. "What are you smiling about?"

"Nothing," she chirped, walking ahead of me.

Shifting the bottles under my arm, I found myself smiling when my gaze dropped to her heart-shaped ass. Damn. She made standard, Covenant-issued sweatpants something to dream about.

"Doesn't seem like nothing," I replied.

"Sometimes I just like to smile for no reason."

"Smiling gives you premature wrinkles."

"And resting bitchface doesn't. Yeah. I know." Stopping in front of the door to her room, she glanced over at me. "Or maybe I'm just smiling because I like being around you."

I stared at her.

The corners of her lips tipped down. "Too much?"

Slowly, I shook my head. "No. Never too much."

That smile returned in full force. "Good." She unlocked the door and said, "Just remember that."

My brows rose as I followed her and then stopped in the middle of the doorway, my jaw unhinging as I stared into the room.

"Surprise!" One—no, two or three voices shouted in unison, and I think I heard Josie giggle and say, "Happy birthday!"

I couldn't stop staring at all of the . . . balloons. Red. White. Yellow. Some were shaped like . . . *penises?* My gaze narrowed on a red one that was a good ten inches long with—yep—with balls as the base. Penis balloons. My gaze tracked down, and there was Deacon St. Delphi, Aiden's younger and definitely not as saintly brother, under the penis balloon, blond curls sticking out everywhere and silver eyes full of laughter.

"You're awestruck, aren't you?" he said, smirking. "Told you, Luke. The balloons sealed the deal."

Luke was leaning against the wall, ankles crossed. "I had nothing to do with the balloons."

"That was all me." Jerking his thumb back at his chest, Deacon smiled proudly. "All. Me."

Josie placed the basket of fries on an end table next to a small loveseat in the sitting room area. Then she took my chicken tenders and the drinks, placing them next to the fries.

She smiled weakly. "I might've, um, mentioned that you had a birthday coming up."

"Really?" I murmured.

"Cake," Deacon interjected, springing toward the coffee table. "We got you a cake."

"I also had nothing to do with the cake," Luke announced, and when I looked at him, he shrugged. "I'm pretty much just here to bear witness to your reaction."

I had no words.

"You have no idea what I had to do to get Libby to make this cake. By the way, Libby is one of our awesome cooks in the cafeteria," Deacon explained. "And I think it's a really awesome cake."

At that moment, I looked at the cake, really looked at it, and my eyes widened. "Spider-Man?"

Josie dipped her chin, unsuccessfully hiding her grin.

"You seemed like you'd be into Spider-Man."

I opened my mouth. Yep. No words as I stared at the small, round cake. Libby should go into the cake-making business, I thought, because that was one hell of an accurate representation of Spider-Man, down to the blue tights and webbing.

"Solos was going to try to come, but he's been out scouting all morning," Josie said, twisting her hands together. "But he sends his birthday wishes."

Now I was staring at her again, absolutely . . . flummoxed, and I couldn't believe I was actually using that word, but I was shocked.

"So let's eat cake before you guys have to do important stuff like train, and I have to go to class and pretend to pay attention," Deacon said, turning to the cake. Beside it were plates.

They even got plates.

Penis balloons. Spider-Man cake. And plastic plates with the words HAPPY BIRTHDAY written in multiple colors—colors that matched the Spider-Man cake.

"Happy birthday, man." Luke clapped his hand on my shoulder as he walked past me, toward Deacon. Coming up behind him, he circled his arm around the slimmer pure's waist and leaned down, kissing his neck. "I want an edge piece."

Deacon straightened, and with a grin he lifted his icing-covered pinky. Holding Luke's gaze, he sucked the white icing right off his finger, causing Luke to stiffen . . . in probably a lot of areas.

Someone was getting way lucky later.

A soft touch on my arm drew my attention. I looked down and found Josie staring up at me, nibbling on her lower lip. Made me think of me doing the same thing, and that sent a jolt of awareness straight to my cock.

"Are you okay with this?" she asked, voice low. "I just wanted to . . . you know, celebrate your birthday."

I blinked, snapping out of it. Still standing just inside the door, I hadn't said more than two words. I'd just stood there and stared. Total dick move.

"I . . . I think it is great. Thank you." Clearing my throat, I glanced over at the guys and spoke louder. Relief flickered across her face. "Thank you."

Luke nodded as he stepped to the side, a slice of cake on a plate in his hand.

As Deacon got to work slicing up the rest of the cake, I reached around Josie and gently tugged on her ponytail. When she leaned into me, I circled my arm around her and lowered my mouth to her ear. "No one has . . . has ever done this for me."

Josie pulled back, her eyes searching mine. "Done what? Celebrate your birthday?"

I shook my head. "No. This . . . this is a first."

The hue of her blue eyes deepened and then she stretched up, kissing my cheek. "It's the first of many, Sethie. Get used to it."

Closing my eyes, I pressed my forehead against the side of hers. Damn. I knew three things right then. I didn't deserve that. I didn't deserve her. And I didn't have the heart to tell her this birthday would probably be our first and our last.

3

*T*he following day, throughout afternoon training—aka beat-down time—I couldn't stop thinking about what Seth had said. It had been the same last night. I looked at him, I thought about what he said, and I just wanted to hug him.

Okay. I wanted to do other more fun things that involved more than hugging him, and we did some of those things—but not *that* thing. I was starting to become convinced that they'd end up remaking the Harry Potter movies before I got laid.

Anyway, I couldn't believe it. No one had celebrated his birthday? Not a single person, even his mother? She was a crappy mom. I'd gotten that from what he'd told me before, but to not even celebrate a birthday?

I sort of wished the woman was alive so I could kill her. What a terrible person. Or pure-blood. Whatever she had been, she was a crappy, mean person. Even with the issues my own mother had, she'd celebrated my birthday.

Mom may not have wanted me, but she loved me, and in the end, that was all that mattered.

Training wasn't horrible. Not like it had been in the beginning, when I couldn't even take a hit correctly. Now, I knew how to fall to not only avoid injury, but to quickly get back on my feet. I knew how to block punches and kicks, and had learned to deliver quite a few nasty ones myself.

I was so close to becoming a badass, killer-ninja demigod.

"You've got to use your dagger like you're prepared to kill the person you're stabbing," Seth said from the sidelines. "Not like you're wanting to poke them with it."

My eyes narrowed as I looked over at him. Okay. So maybe I wasn't a killer ninja yet. I lifted the Covenant dagger, a very sharp and deadly blade made out of titanium and designed to slice and dice, and tightened my grip on the handle. "I'm not trying to poke the dummy."

"You're poking the dummy," Luke confirmed.

I was ganged up on.

Seth stalked over to the very life-like dummy and jabbed his finger at a shallow cut in what was also very flesh-like skin. Ugh.

"This wound here," he said, referencing the cut on the dummy's chest. "Wouldn't even kill a mortal."

I frowned. "It so would."

"It would slow them down, that's for sure, but it wouldn't kill them." Luke flipped the dagger in his hand, catching it easily. Wasn't he just special. "Wouldn't even puncture a lung."

I was going to have to take his word on that.

"You know how to use this dagger." Seth lifted a hand, running it through his hair. "We've taught you everything you need. You've got the correct hold, the correct positioning. You know where to hit to take your opponent down. There's no reason for you not to use force behind it."

I started to argue, but as I stared at all the cuts on the dummy, I knew he had a point. The chest of the dummy was covered in slices and cuts, most of them, if not all of them, as deep as my finger. Those cuts were from Seth and Luke. All of mine were shallow, nicks in comparison.

I hated to admit it, but Seth was right. The idea of killing someone on purpose horrified me. I mean, thinking I could do it and wishing I could do it was totally different from actually doing it. But just because something horrified me didn't mean that when push came to shove I couldn't do it.

I would protect myself.

I would also protect those I loved.

At least, that was what I kept telling myself.

Seth glanced over at Luke. "Let's go ahead and call it a day."

"But we still have an hour," I protested.

"I know," he replied, cocking his head to the side. "You and I aren't done yet."

Seeming to get the message, Luke nodded and as he walked past me, he patted my shoulder. "See you guys later."

As the door to the training room swung shut behind him, I had a feeling I was in for a lecture.

Seth arched a brow. "You look like you just sucked on something sour. I'm not going to lecture you."

My eyes widened. "Are you sure you can't read minds and you're just lying to me?"

He laughed. "Everything you think or feel is just written on your face." Reaching over, he took the dagger out of my hand. "I want you to watch me do this."

I'd been watching him do this for weeks, but I folded my arms and I watched.

Seth held my gaze for a moment and then spun around. There wasn't a moment of hesitation. Not like there was for me, because the damn dummy looked so real. He thrust forward on one powerful leg and shoved the dagger deep into the sternum. A kill shot in under two seconds. No pausing. No last-minute weakening of the blow.

He pulled the dagger out and faced me, his amber gaze serious. "That's how you do it, and I know you are fully aware of how to deliver a killing blow."

"I am."

Stepping toward me, he lowered his chin. "But you're not doing it. You haven't done it once without being made to do it over and over again, and even then, you eventually do it out of frustration with Luke or me."

My lips pursed. I wanted to argue, but once again, he was right. And I hated it when he was right, which was way too often for me.

"There's something I need to know, okay?"

I lifted my chin, grinning slightly. "Yes, you're a sexy beast."

"I know that already," he said dryly. "But that's not what I'm asking."

I sighed. "Okay."

He held my gaze. "Can you do this?"

"Yes—"

"I don't want you to answer the question yet," he interrupted. "I want you to really think about it and ask yourself if you can really do this. Not fighting. Not using the elements. Ask yourself if you're ready to kill someone without a second of hesitation. If you're ready to deliver a fatal blow before your opponent lands a hit on you. If you're ready to be the aggressor."

Those questions left me cold. I wanted to say that I could do it when I needed to, but truthfully? The dummy swayed slightly in front of me, made of rubber and synthetic flesh. I wasn't ready to say yes, I could kill something. Well, besides animals with my car, and I still felt horrible about all of that, but on purpose?

I thought about Hyperion, and I squeezed my eyes shut. I could've killed him. Easily. The things he said and did . . . I sucked in a sharp breath and shuddered. I didn't even need to try to remember the iciness of his breath or the heaviness of his hand.

Yeah. I could've killed him.

But this? Actively killing people—er, daimons or whatever? It was different. Killing things wasn't what I was all about. It was who I needed to be to survive. I couldn't be weak. I had to be stronger than this. Strong like the female Sentinels I saw every day. Strong like I imagined Alex had been. Or was. Still is.

I opened my eyes. "Alex didn't have a problem with killing things, did she?"

Seth blinked and took a step back. Like, a legit step back.

My eyes widened. I hadn't meant to ask that out loud, and I didn't even know where that came from. Okay. I did know where it came from: my mouth, which apparently was connected to that deep, dark subconscious part of me that wouldn't shut the fuck up.

"Yeah, um, can I . . . Yeah, I didn't ask that question." My face flushed, and I hastily turned away, walking toward where I'd left my hoodie and water.

I could not believe I'd brought Alex into a conversation like this.

Seth never talked about Alex.

For obvious reasons, it was a touchy subject. I understood why. Seth and Alex had a way weird past. Being that both were Apollyons, they were fated to be together, designed in that way. But Alex loved Aiden, and I . . . I wasn't sure how Seth felt about Alex. Deacon had made it sound like it hadn't been that serious, but Deacon wasn't Seth.

Deacon was Aiden's younger brother, so maybe he only saw what he wanted to see when it came to Alex and Seth.

Seth's past was so intricately twisted with Alex's, and I knew he'd done a lot to her when he had been working with Ares, and he had come through for her when it was needed most. Hell, he had sacrificed everything for Alex's happiness. That had to mean something.

What I did know for sure was what Deacon had been super-excited about the last week or so. Due to some crazy deal with the gods, Alex and Aiden had remained in Tartarus for six months, and that time was almost up.

Alex and Aiden would be returning soon.

Bending down, I picked up the hoodie and tugged it on over my head. I grabbed my bottle of water, searching for something to change the subject to. Anything would be good at this point.

"She didn't."

I stilled, pressing my lips together. Of course she didn't. According to Deacon, Alex was the baddest of all badasses.

"She was born and practically raised in this environment except for a period of time. Alex is different than you."

My stomach twisted with a bitter burn. Ridiculous, I knew, but the acid coating the insides of my mouth tasted like jealousy. Stupid, unreasonable jealousy.

"But it wasn't easy for her, and you do have that in common," he added after a moment. "I know she didn't like it and it wore on her. It got to her."

Slowly, I turned around, clutching the bottle to my chest.

He'd moved silently and was only a foot or so away from me. "And before . . . before everything went down, she was talking about not wanting to be a Sentinel anymore. Even though that was what she'd always wanted to be. She was done with it all. The killing and the fighting."

I didn't know what to say. I didn't even know if there was anything I could say about it, because I could understand that. Who wouldn't be tired of killing and fighting?

"It wasn't easy for her, Josie, but she did it because it was her duty—she did it to protect herself and those she cared about." Seth reached around and tugged my ponytail out from under my hoodie. He draped it over my shoulder. "It's not going to be easy for you."

I licked my lips. "You don't think I can do this, do you?"

His gaze held mine for a moment and then his lashes lowered, shielding his eyes. "One of the things I like about you so much, Josie, is that you are so very mortal despite what and who you are."

A tiny flutter spread its wings in my chest. "I'm not sure if that's a compliment or not."

"It is." Lowering his head, he kissed the corner of my lips. "Come on. Let's head back and grab some popcorn. We can watch a movie before Deacon shows up and forces us to watch another season of *Supernatural*."

"I love *Supernatural*."

He smirked. "You love Dean Winchester."

"Guilty," I murmured, well aware that Seth was totally avoiding my question, but I didn't push it. Probably because I already knew his answer, what he believed.

And boy, that was one hell of a de-motivator.

I didn't say anything as Seth placed the dagger on the wall, hooking it into place among the other deadly, shiny weapons. We headed out into the main hall, past several students who were walking into one of the other training rooms. I had no idea if they were halfs or pures, but they were dressed like I was. They were Sentinels in training.

I bet they had no problem with killing things.

The afternoon sun warmed the air, but it still wasn't like the temps in Missouri or Virginia in May. I doubted it ever got really hot here, and it was downright chilly under the shady overhang of the training facility.

Walking next to Seth, I did my best to ignore the looks sent in our direction. Most people here still thought I was a mortal. For some reason, they couldn't sense me like they could with each other. I imagined it was something Apollo had done or maybe it was because I was a demigod. Not like Apollo was around to tell me. Either way, everyone stared at Seth. Everyone. All the time.

It was annoying.

I glanced over at him. The smirk was still on his lips. Yeah, he so knew everyone was staring. Instead of focusing on that, I thought about what we'd talked about the night before. Lately, Seth had this habit of asking me weird hypothetical questions. What would I be doing if Apollo weren't my father? Easy answer. I'd still be in Radford studying psychology. He'd asked where I would go if I didn't have to be here, like where I would visit. That took a little to answer, because I really wanted to think about it. I'd eventually ended up settling on Scotland, because I was fascinated with the history of the country. Each time I attempted to ask him the same questions, I ended up falling asleep before I could, or we'd end up being interrupted.

"Got a question for you," I said.

"Probably got an answer for you."

I smiled. "So, if you go could anywhere in the world, where would you go?"

He raised his brows at me. "Seriously?"

"Yes." I laughed. "You know I'd go to Scotland—"

"I know it took you nearly fifteen minutes to answer that question."

"Shut up and answer my question."

"Not sure how I can do both of those things."

I rolled my eyes. "Seth."

He smirked that sexy, infuriating smirk. "I think I would go . . . home to the Cyclades Islands—to Andros. I haven't been there since I left." He paused. "I wonder if anyone is really even there anymore. Not a lot of people lived there when I was there. It wasn't a very populated island."

If he'd told me he was secretly a huge fan of One Direction, I wouldn't have been more surprised by his answer. Based on how harsh his childhood was, I couldn't imagine him wanting to go back there. "Why there?"

He shrugged. "I don't know. I just want to see it. Kind of hard to explain."

I thought about it for a moment and wondered if it had to do with laying to rest the demons of his past. "Would you want—?"

A shout of surprise cut me off, loud and harsh. As my heart stuttered a beat, a horrific cracking sound tore through the quad, a snapping that echoed through the marble statues. A scream, high-pitched and reedy, followed. Then another. I spun around at the same time Seth stepped in front of me, shielding me from whatever was happening.

But it was too late.

I saw it.

"Fucking gods," Seth muttered.

Horrified, I smacked my hand over my mouth and stumbled a step back, blinking. I thought I was hallucinating what I was seeing, but I wasn't. It was real.

A body hung in the air, right in front of the training facility, where Seth and I had just walked out. The denim-covered legs hung straight as they swayed back and forth. A chain of some sort was right around the neck that was bent at an unnatural angle.

Someone had hanged himself.

Oh my God, no. My gaze zeroed in on the chest. No. Someone hadn't hanged himself. He'd *been* hanged.

On his chest was a piece of paper—a piece of notebook paper stabbed into the chest with some kind of knife. The words were easy to read, even with the red drenching the stomach, and hard to forget.

NO FREE HALFS.

4

A small crowd gathered quickly, their faces a blur. Nausea twisted up my insides and I had to look away. The body—the person—he couldn't have been any older than me, maybe younger. There was no forgetting his face. The slack jaw. The ghastly pallor. The open, unseeing blue eyes.

"This is so wrong," a girl said, her voice trembling. "This is so messed up."

Another girl spoke up. "Oh my gods, that's Brandon." She pushed through the cluster of people. Tears filled her eyes. "Someone get him down. Please." She twisted at the waist, toward some guy in the crowd. "Why isn't anyone getting him down?"

But Seth was already moving.

Face blank and stony, devoid of all emotion, he stalked forward, and with unbelievable gentleness he wrapped an arm around the legs, stilling the poor guy. Seth lifted his left arm, and amber light danced over his knuckles. The stream of pure energy hit the center of the chain, snapping it in half.

Seth caught the body and lowered it to the marble walkway. Without saying a word, he rose. A muscle feathered along his jaw as he studied the roof of the training facility. There was no one there now, but every being here, on this campus, was super-fast. They could've knocked the guy off the edge and been out of sight before the . . . the neck snapped.

If that was what had killed this guy. The knife in the chest could've done the job. Bile rose in my throat and threatened to come out.

"What in the hell?"

I turned toward the sound of Solos's voice. He cut through the crowd, his steps slowing as he saw the body on the ground. The tawny skin around the jagged scar on his face paled.

"Gods," he grunted, staring down.

"Someone strung him up," Seth said, his voice flat.

The first girl who spoke out stepped forward, her violet eyes wide. "Or someone used a compulsion on him. Made him do it."

A murmur rose among the small group, and that horrible bile in the back of my throat got even closer to coming out. A compulsion? Good God, I couldn't even imagine why someone would want to compel someone to do something so heinous. But purebloods did have that ability. So did Seth. The gods also had the ability. They could make a half-blood or a mortal do anything they wanted. I'd seen it with my own eyes. Even hang themselves. Or stab themselves. That kind of power was frightening.

Disturbing.

"Either way, whoever did it is long gone." Seth glanced back at me. Our gazes connected for a moment and then he turned back to the body. He said something to Solos, but it was too low for me to hear.

Solos stepped to the side, facing the group. "All right, I need everyone to get moving. Go to your classes or where you need to go, but you don't need to be here."

"Yeah, because it's a crime scene." The tall, well-built guy was dressed like me, in Covenant-issued training attire. I was betting he was a half. "Or do you guys just not care, because he's a half-blood?"

"Considering I'm a half-blood, I care." Solos shifted his stance. Guards appeared, dressed in all white, different than the Sentinels' black uniform. "You know that, Colin."

Seth turned back to the body and then tugged his shirt up over his head, leaving him in a shorter-sleeved shirt. He stepped closer to the body, carefully, respectfully, draping his shirt over the man's face.

I looked away again, pressing my lips together. This was wrong, so wrong that the word "wrong" didn't even cover it. This guy was a stranger to me, but my heart hurt and I was sickened by the implications, by what was right in our faces.

He was killed simply because he was a half-blood.

This was not remotely okay.

"You might care, but you know damn well over half of those at this damn campus don't give two shits about what has been going on yet. They aren't going to care when the gods start murdering us," the guy named Colin challenged him. "They never cared before."

"He's right," a voice said from the back of the crowd. A girl. "You know what happened to Felecia two days ago."

I didn't know who Felecia was or what happened to her.

Solos's jaw hardened. "They are looking into that. They—"

"A pure used a compulsion on her, raped her, and then passed her around," Colin returned, anger thickening his voice. "And what has happened? Absolutely fucking nothing."

Oh my God. I was really going to vomit.

"So what? No one cares, and Felecia is a whore. So whatever."

I jerked in disbelief, and Seth turned back to the crowd. The white-dressed Guards stiffened.

Several of the students stepped aside, revealing a tall, icy-blond guy. Someone muttered, "You did *not* just say that."

He shrugged. "What?" Derision dripped from his snotty tone. "You know what they say. The only good half-blood is a drugged or dead one."

Seth exploded.

It happened that quickly.

Seth flew across the walkway, reaching the guy before I took my next breath. He grabbed the collar of Icy Blond, who I was assuming was a pure-blood, and lifted him clear off his feet. Clothing ripped.

"I'm not even going to ask you to repeat yourself."

Icy Blond paled a second before Seth cocked his arm back and landed a punch that knocked his head back. Icy Blond's hands clawed frantically at Seth's arm, trying to free himself, but that wasn't happening.

Within a handful of seconds, the crowd scattered back, giving Seth—the Apollyon—wide berth. The Guards didn't even make an attempt to stop him.

"Seth," Solos warned quietly, stepping toward Seth, but not getting close.

"But I can see it in your eyes that you really believe that." Seth's free hand closed into a fist once again. "And you know what, asshole? You may be a pure-blood, and there may have been rules once upon a time that protected your dumb ass, but those rules never applied to me and what I can do to you."

I tensed, frozen where I stood.

"And they still don't," Seth added.

Another blow landed, a punch that would've shattered the jaw of a mortal. Icy Blond's lip split and blood flew as his head lolled back. Seth jerked his arm back again.

Solos inched closer. "That's enough, Seth."

He didn't listen, and for a moment I feared he wouldn't until it was too late.

Springing forward, I snapped out of my shocked stupor, raced past Solos, reaching Seth's side. Grabbing hold of his bicep with both hands, I held on. "Seth. That's enough. Let him go."

A heartbeat passed, and I thought he was going to ignore me and break the guy's skull, and while a part of me was sort of okay with that, I couldn't let Seth do it.

Slowly, he lowered his arm and let go of the pure. The guy hit the ground with a fleshy *smack* as he landed in a heap.

Well. Okay. Seth *did* let him go.

His chest rising sharply, Seth turned around. Our gazes met, and I sucked in a shallow breath. The amber hue of his eyes was bright and sharp as a winter's morning. He stared down at me, but I wasn't even sure he saw me. A shiver tip-toed down my spine as I let go of his arm.

It was like staring into the eyes of a stranger.

Seth

I was itching for a fight. A real one. Not punching the fuck out of some idiot pure-blood. That didn't cool the fire in my blood. I wanted a real fight.

"Are you going to sit down, or will you keep pacing until you burn a track in the hardwood floors?"

Unfortunately since I was in the Dean of the Covenant's office, there would be no fighting.

Turning to where Marcus Andros sat behind a huge-ass mahogany desk, there was no missing the tall and forever silent Sentinel standing directly to his right.

Alexander.

The man Alex was named after. Her father. A badass Sentinel who even I didn't screw with. He didn't speak, because the asshole Council elder who was no more had cut his tongue out years back.

I folded my arms. "What are you doing about what's happening here?"

"Nothing. I figured that was the best course of action," he replied drolly. "Just let them kill each other."

"That's what it appears to me." I kept a watchful eye on Alexander. "What happened today isn't an isolated event. Since I showed up here, they've been at each other's throats. The fighting—pures setting halfs on fire. Using compulsions?"

He rose from his seat. "I know what has been happening on my campus, Seth. Do you think I'm okay with that? That I haven't been dedicating every extra resource we have to keeping things calm around here?" He stalked around the desk and stopped in front of me. Alexander moved in tandem with him. "In case you've forgotten, I have more than half of my Sentinels and Guards safe-guarding the Covenant against the possibility of shades or Titans. You know damn well that things have gone silent where they're concerned, but that won't last long."

Of course I knew that. Shit kept me awake at night, but that wasn't what was making me want to rip someone in two. "What about this Felecia girl? What is happening to the fuckers who did that to her?"

Marcus exhaled heavily as he turned his gaze to the window that overlooked the quad. "We don't know who was responsible. She was under a compulsion. She has no recollection of who did it."

"Then neuter all the damn pure-bloods on campus."

His gaze shot to mine.

Alexander smirked, apparently approving of my suggestion.

"You think I don't want to?" Marcus's voice was low, deadly calm. "What was done to that girl was beyond reprehensible. And we are doing everything to track where she was and who could possibly have seen her. If anyone knows anything, they are not talking, either because they chose not to or because they themselves are frightened."

My jaw worked. Today was the first I'd heard about the girl and what had happened to her, and I knew—fuck, I *knew*—she wasn't the first and she wouldn't be the last. It made me think of what was done to . . . to Alex when we'd been at the Council in the Catskills. Her drink had been drugged, and well, that had been a fucking mess I hadn't exactly helped with.

Marcus turned around and picked up a mug. I imagined there was some hard liquor in that brown cup. "You could've killed that kid, Seth."

I arched a brow, wondering if the expression on my face said I had zero fucks to give, because that was exactly how I felt about killing that prick.

He lowered the cup. "And I can tell you really don't care." Sighing, he placed the mug on the desk. "With everything that is going on right now, the last thing I need to worry about is you."

"You don't need to worry about me."

Alexander tilted his head to the side and raised his brows. Without saying anything, his entire expression screamed *oh, really?*

"It's kind of hard not to worry about you, Seth." Marcus sat behind his desk. "And you know damn well why."

I laughed under my breath as I lowered my chin. To Marcus—hell, to everyone here—I was a loose cannon. They were just waiting for me to blow.

The door opened behind me, and a mini-army of Guards strolled in, keeping their distance as they made their way to where Marcus waited.

I didn't need to be told it was time for me to leave. Marcus simply tolerated my ass, and what was going down here between the halfs and pures wasn't something he wanted me involved in.

Didn't mean I wouldn't be involving myself if necessary.

I headed out of his office, out into the wide hall where Guards stood as sentries, then down the million steps I had to climb to get to his office. From there, I wasted time scoping out the walls surrounding the university. Night had fallen, and the outer walls were well-protected. For now. But shades had gotten through once before. They'd do it again.

My empty stomach grumbled. Missed dinner, but I wasn't in the mood for real food. Thinking of the leftover birthday cake in Josie's room, I headed in that direction. On my way back to the dorm, I nearly walked the same path Josie and I had earlier, bypassing going into the training facility but walking around it instead.

The spot where I'd laid the body was clean. Marble fucking spotless. No sign that anything had happened except for a single red rose that lay there.

A memorial.

One fucking rose.

Before I realized it, I'd stopped walking and was staring at the freshly cut rose. The thing would be dead in a few days, but would there be more flowers? Like mortals did at the scene of a death?

Damn pure-bloods. Anyone with two working brain cells knew there were going to be problems once the Breed Order was abolished, but this? This was. . . Yeah, there were no words. And what happened to that girl?

I hadn't been joking when I'd suggested neutering every damn pure.

"Sick, isn't it?"

Lifting my head, I twisted around and almost gaped.

A nymph leaned against the marble statue of Hera, one leg curled over the other. The same male nymph that had been outside of Josie's grandparents' house. He was still wearing the same doeskin pants, and I was almost positive the pretty fucker's chest was glittering in the moonlight.

"You lost or something?" I asked. "The woods are over the wall."

Slanted eyes focused on me. "I know where I am. Do you?"

"Uh." I paused. "Yeah, I don't even know how to respond to that."

He pushed off the statue, and in the blink of an eye he was kneeling where the body had lain. "For thousands of years, mortals and immortals have sought to kill others they believe are not like them. Even when the same blood courses through nearly identical bone and tissue." His head tilted to the side as he stared at the rose. "It was never just a mortal problem, you see. They learned it from our kind. To love. And to hate."

My brows inched up my forehead.

"It angered you, this half-blood's death." He reached out with a slender arm and ran the tip of his finger along the green stem. A second later, a whole damn bushel of roses appeared. The nymph rose and looked over his shoulder at me. "Violence begets violence."

"I'm pretty sure Martin Luther King Jr. said that."

"Wise words from a wise man," he replied, facing me. "Violence festers and turns to a bitter, infectious kind of hate, Apollyon. It spreads like a cancer, one that can only be cut out. Many here and in the world are affected by it, and these pure-bloods responsible . . . well, some may be a lost cause."

No surprise there.

"You already have that disease."

I blinked.

"It's eating away, getting closer and closer to your soul. You're walking a fine line, where you will topple into areas that are not shaded in gray. We are watching you." He lifted his chin. "*They* are watching you."

Also no big surprise there.

The nymph looked up to the onyx sky blanketed with stars. "The Titans are not the only beings they are concerned with. What's inside of you must be cut out, God Killer."

God Killer? What the hell?

I was not the God Killer. Alex had become that, or maybe still was that. I had no idea if she was still an Apollyon or a God Killer now that she had died a mortal death and become a demigod. Wasn't like email or cell phones existed in Tartarus, so I couldn't call her and ask. Then again, I couldn't imagine myself checking in with her if I could.

I stared at the nymph. "What does that—?"

Poof. That was it. The nymph was gone, and well, that was weird as shit. Obviously a warning, a really weird warning.

The roses were a nice touch, though.

I shook my head as I pivoted around and started walking, trying to shake off the nymph's random words and appearance, but that was real hard. Damn near impossible.

Stopping outside Josie's door, I glanced down at my right hand. There wasn't a blemish on my knuckles. Nothing. I was about 99% sure I'd broken that pure's jaw, and my hand wasn't even swollen.

And I was also 99% sure I would've killed him if Josie hadn't stopped me.

My gaze centered on her closed door. I knew she was in there, but I stepped back from the door.

I can tell you really don't care.

Marcus's words replayed in my head. I didn't know if he was right or not. If I would've cared if I killed that pure or not.

And I knew what that said about me.

5

Josie

"You know, I've done a lot of weird things—things you probably don't want to hear about," Deacon stated, squinting up at the entrance to the library. "But stalking a librarian is pretty weird."

I looked over at him. "As weird as doing my father?"

His eyes narrowed. "Okay. That's one of those weird things you probably don't want to know about."

I snorted like a little piglet. That was so very true. "Apollo said I should talk to the librarian here, and I'm guessing he meant that really strange woman I ran into that one day. I haven't seen her since, and none of the other staff know who I'm talking about."

Deacon brushed a curl off his forehead as he started up the wide, steep steps. "What does she look like again?"

"She was really tall—tall as Seth—and slender. She had really curly blonde hair pulled back." I paused, short of breath as I climbed the steps. Jesus. All the training, and these steps were still killer. "She was wearing these huge sunglasses, which I kind of thought was super odd, you know, being inside. Anyway, I couldn't see most of her face."

"Huh. That doesn't sound like a normal librarian. Then again, I don't really know what a normal librarian looks like." Deacon reached the top and waited for me. "You know, halfs always get freaked out around the Covenant libraries."

"Seth said something like that."

Seth.

Ugh.

He didn't show up in my room last night, which wasn't that big of a deal, but after what happened yesterday with the half-blood and then the pure-blood, I was . . . I was worried about Seth. About the way he'd looked at me like he hadn't even seen me standing there. There'd been a coldness in his eyes, not necessarily directed at me, but still unnerving. That hadn't been Seth.

Deacon stepped in front of me and opened up the heavy, titanium-plated door. The amount of money they had spent to build this place had to be astronomical.

"Luke hates this place. It's so weird that he gets wigged out in these buildings. It was the same way back on Deity Island," he explained as we stepped into the library. "Whatever it is, halfs sense something . . . *off* about these places."

I inhaled deeply, loving the musty smell of books. As far as my eyes could see, there were massive, crammed full floor-to-ceiling bookshelves. Between them were chandeliers that probably cost more than a four-year degree would.

"I wonder why they do, but you guys don't." We headed through the first row. All we'd be doing was roaming aimlessly until dinner, hoping we came across the mysterious librarian. "You all have more *aether* in you."

Deacon shrugged as he slipped his hands into the pockets of his jeans. "It's the same thing with them being able to see through a daimon's glamour. To us, the pure-bloods, they look normal. But to halfs? Daimons look like they really do, which is something straight out of a damn horror movie." He paused. "Now that you are all full demigod, I wonder if you can see through a daimon's glamour."

I wrinkled my nose. "Is it weak of me to hope I never find out?"

"No." He laughed as he knocked me with his shoulder. "It makes you sane."

Relieved he didn't think I was a giant wuss, we roamed the stacks, passing several students clustered at the large tables, their heads bent over their textbooks.

Sigh.

I kind of missed school.

And I really missed my old roommate, who'd turned out to be a furie. Erin had suffered a horrible injury by Hyperion, and Apollo—my father—said she was healing in Olympus. He'd told me she was okay, but I needed to see that for myself.

We neared the back of the library, and somewhere in a section full of books I was pretty sure were all written in Greek, the temps dropped significantly. Even in my sweater, goosebumps spread across my arms. "Did you guys know the . . . the half-blood who was killed yesterday?"

He shook his head as we hung a left, passing a series of closed doors. "No. I've heard he was a Sentinel. Was supposed to graduate this semester. Luke knows one of his friends. Said he was transferring to Vegas after this, to work near a pure community."

"That's so sad." I folded my arms across my chest. "And so damn wrong. I can't even imagine."

"Yeah," he breathed. "It had to be a compulsion. There's no other way a pure would've gotten the upper hand on someone who was practically a fully trained Sentinel. Not even a pure who really knows how to handle an element."

"I just don't understand, and it's not even because I don't get the politics around here," I explained, glancing up at the wrought-iron spiral staircase that led to the second level. "We've had the same problems in the, um, mortal world. We still do, and

I didn't even understand it then. How people can hate someone else for really superficial differences so deeply that they hurt and kill them."

Deacon was quiet as we climbed the stairs. When we reached the top, his lips were curled. "It's always been like this for our kind. For probably freaking eons, the pures have treated the halfs like shit."

A librarian hurried past us, shooting Deacon a nasty look.

He smiled as he waved his middle finger, causing me to grin. "I'm kind of surprised that the halfs aren't rebelling."

"Yet," I whispered, scanning the stacks up here. "Couldn't blame them if they did."

"Nope." His hands went back into his pockets. "Two years ago, Luke would've been put on the Elixir or killed if it got out that he was in a relationship with a pure. And you know what would've happened to me?"

I shook my head.

"I would've gotten a wink, wink and maybe a smack on a hand." His lips pursed. "That's it. They would've most likely killed Luke and secretly applauded me for getting it on with the *help*."

My stomach churned. "That's messed up."

Deacon nodded slowly. "You know what's even more messed up? That mindset hasn't changed, Josie. Not after what happened with Ares or what's happening now with the Titans. Bigotry is literally the Twinkie of human emotions. Shit will survive the apocalypse."

I shuddered, because the terrifying thing about what he said was, he was probably correct.

I was starving.

Night had fallen and Seth was currently MIA. Okay, he wasn't exactly missing in action. During training, he'd said that he'd probably be late since he was going to do some outside patrols with Solos. I had no idea what he was patrolling since there really wasn't anything out there except trees.

And more trees.

I figured he just wanted to get outside these walls, and I couldn't exactly blame him for that. While the University campus was beautiful and so much of it was still fresh and oh-so-new to me, I got restless. A lot. And I was sure it was the same for Seth, especially since he wasn't used to being confined in one spot.

But I was legit starving. My hips were about to start eating each other.

Roaming the campus by myself wasn't necessarily something Seth had warned me against, and I didn't feel unsafe doing so. The students and most of the staff thought I was some pet mortal, but I wasn't and I knew I could defend myself if necessary.

I pushed myself off the small sofa and grabbed my hoodie. Pulling it on over my head, I tugged my damp hair out from underneath, letting it fall down my back. I snatched my keys off the coffee table and then I was off.

Students lounged in the spacious, really cool lobby of the dorm, surrounding a TV that was about the size of a Hummer. We didn't have anything like that in my own dorm back at Radford. Neither did we have such great, comfy couches. I'd sat in the red one. Once. I wanted to marry it.

Of course, no one really paid attention to me as I walked out the doors that had been fixed from when the shades had gotten inside. No one really ever paid attention to me unless Seth was with me, and honestly, they were just staring at him. I was kind of like a side item, the French fries to the Big Mac.

Mmm. French fries.

I knew what I was getting from the cafeteria.

I'd probably lose weight if, for once, I ate something leafy and green or grilled, but their bacon was like an orgasm of the mouth and their fries were the really awesome shoestring kind that were so hard to find. Honestly, I think the food here was made with some kind of magic, because everything tasted better.

The night air was chilly, as usual, as I cut across the lawn and hit the pathway. The cafeteria wasn't far from the dorm, and since they'd be serving food until midnight, I was pretty confident I could get myself a plate of fries.

And maybe even a thick, juicy—

"You shouldn't be out here alone."

My breath caught in response to the unexpected voice and I spun around, immediately finding the source of the voice. Even startled, I recognized that six months ago I would've fallen over if I'd turned around that fast back then.

Ninja status halfway there.

The guy stepped out of the shadows of an olive tree—a tree that I had no idea how it was still alive in these conditions. I immediately recognized him from yesterday.

Colin.

My heart slowed down. All right, he wasn't going to be a problem. At least, I didn't think so. "I'm okay. Just heading to the cafeteria."

He slowly approached me, as if he was worried he was going to send me running in the opposite direction. "Where is the Apollyon?"

Yep. I was the fries to the Big Mac. "He's out patrolling, so I'm going to get something to eat."

"I'll go with you then."

I raised a brow. "Thanks, but that's not necessary."

"Look, I'm not trying to be domineering, but it really isn't safe for you to be out here by yourself." Closer, he passed under one of the lampposts. His black hair was shiny, an odd and, of course, majorly attractive contrast to his sapphire-blue eyes. "You saw what happened yesterday. A lot of the pures around here don't view mortals as any better than they view halfs."

See, the thing was, I wasn't a mortal. But since we were keeping that on the down low and no one seemed to sense my demigod goodness, it was my ace up the sleeve.

"If the Apollyon isn't around, then maybe you should get Deacon or Luke," he offered. "You've been hanging around them a lot."

Okay. This dude was kind of observant. Then again, everyone did think I was a mortal, so they were probably aware of who I hung out with. "His name is Seth, and like I said, I'm okay."

"All right," he said after a moment. "Can't say I didn't try."

I smiled tightly. "Good night." Pivoting around, I walked a couple of feet and realized he was right behind me. I looked over my shoulder. "You're seriously going to follow me, aren't you?"

His grin was sheepish. "I was just heading to the cafeteria myself when I saw you."

"Uh-huh."

"So, I figured we could walk together." When I didn't respond and started walking again, he easily caught up to me, keeping an arm's length distance between us. "By the way, my name is—"

"Colin," I answered, grinning when surprise flickered across his face. "I heard Solos call you that yesterday."

"Cool." There was a beat of silence. "I'm training to be a—"

"Sentinel?" This time I laughed when he frowned at me. "I just figured that was what you're doing."

He glanced at me. "The Apolly—I mean, Seth has been training you?"

I nodded.

Colin didn't respond immediately. "It's kind of odd that anyone, especially the—um, Seth would be training a mortal or that a mortal would even know about us."

A fine shiver of unease danced across my skin. "I'm sure I'm not the only mortal who knows about you all."

"True, but . . ."

"It's a long story," I said after a moment, and then I hoped he'd drop it.

Colin sort of did. "Since you're being trained is probably why you're not worried about being out here, but you've got to know that, no matter how well he trains you, you're no match for a pure or a half when it comes down to it."

Another laugh escaped me. "Is that so?"

His frown deepened and he didn't say anything as we started around the corner of a building. "And I know none of this is my business."

"But making sure I get some French fries safely is?"

He chuckled. "Well—"

A flash of reddish light lit up the quad, shooting out from the shadows. With incredible speed, Colin jumped back as the ball of light—no, fire—smacked into the building, extinguishing on contact. The smell of burnt ozone filled the air.

What the what?

"Oh, you missed." A tall guy stepped forward. "You need to work on your aim."

"Shit," muttered Colin, moving so that he was halfway in front of me.

"I didn't miss." Another voice floated out of the darkness. A spark of red light formed, casting the holder in an eerie red glow. "That was just a warning."

Then I saw the second guy, and my stomach dropped all the way to my toes. It was him—the guy Seth had knocked the hell out. Even in the poor light, I could see that his jaw was a brutal shade of purple and swollen. And there was no mistaking the fury and promise of retribution in his expression.

I could only think of two words.

Oh. Crap.

6

My heart pounded in my chest, and a sliver of fear mingled with unease as I stared at the two pure-bloods. The one Seth had punched into next week tossed around the ball of abnormally bright flames like a mortal would play with a baseball.

Keeping an eye on him, I took a small step back and to the side, out from behind Colin. Deep down, I knew reasoning with them was going to be pointless, but I had to try. "We don't want any problems. We're just getting something to eat."

"Does it look like we care what you want to do?" Icy Blond asked.

"You should," Colin challenged. At his sides, his hands curled into hefty fists. There was no missing them. "I don't think you want to piss off the Apollyon again. Messing with her will do that."

"Fuck the Apollyon," Icy Blond shot back, and the ball of flames hovering above his palm pulsed. "He's still just a fucking half-blood when it's all said and done. He isn't worth shit."

The other pure-blood shot a nervous glance in Icy Blond's direction. It didn't look like he was that on board with what was going down.

"You're a bigoted idiot," Colin spat. "And you're—"

Everything happened so fast, and I just reacted without thinking. Icy Blond cocked his arm back, and I knew he was about to let the ball of fire go. There was a chance that Colin wouldn't be able to move out of its way as fast as he had the last time. I just really didn't think.

I threw out my arm, tapping into the power coursing through my veins. Figuring that putting the flames out would render the least amount of damage, I summoned the water element. The immediate buzz of energy was magnificent. It lit up every cell in my body as if they had been starving for it. Tapping into the *aether*, well, it was like coming home at the end of the day and finally being able to take a bra off.

It was that good.

Energy burst out of me, lifting the strands of my hair. There was a second where I saw the shock flickering over Icy Blond's face, his response wholly comical. Mouth dropped open. Eyes widened. I sort of wished I had a camera to capture the moment. The ball of flames disappeared.

Of course, I blew *all of them* in different directions.

Icy Blond and his friend flew up in the air, knocked off their feet by a hurricane-force gust. Colin slammed back into the building. I'd meant to use water and that was not what had come out of me. Wind worked too, I guessed.

I winced when the two pures hit the ground a good distance away, their impact rattling the nearby trees. The wind settled around us. A handful of seconds later, the two pures were up on their feet and they were . . . they were *running*.

I felt like a total badass.

Colin stumbled to his feet, eyeing me as he gasped, "Holy shit."

Grinning, I bounced a little as I lowered my arm and turned to Colin. I watched him straighten, relieved to see that he didn't appear to be injured.

"How did you do that?" he asked, shaking his head.

"I told you I would be fine without Seth," I said.

He blinked once and then twice. "You are so not a mortal. What . . . what are you?"

I wasn't sure what I could say at this point. Colin knew I wasn't a pure or a half, and he'd just seen me use the element of air. There was only the truth at this point. I drew in a shallow breath and met his gaze. "I'm a demigod."

Seth

The moment Solos and I walked back through the inner walls, I knew something was up. Marcus was standing near the first set of tall statues. For a moment, I wondered if there were more nymphs appearing, spouting random crap, but that wasn't it.

Behind him, sitting on a bench lit by one of the lampposts, was Josie, along with the half from yesterday. What was his name? Cole? Ben? Hell if I knew.

I frowned as we neared them. Josie looked way too innocent sitting there with her hands folded primly in her lap and her knees pressed together. I don't think I'd ever seen her so . . . still. Or her face so perfectly blank.

Something was definitely up.

And why was she with Cole-Ben-whatever-the-fuck his name was?

"What's going on?" Solos asked, slowing down.

I eyed them as I crossed my arms over my chest. "I have a feeling I'm not going to like what I'm about to hear." I paused, letting my gaze slide to the half next to Josie. "Sitting a little close to her, aren't you, bud?" The guy immediately scooted to the right while Josie frowned. He moved so far I thought he was going to slide right off the damn thing.

Marcus arched a brow as he glanced back at the two on the bench. "There was an altercation between them and two pure-bloods."

I didn't care what it looked like or what anyone thought. One second I was standing near Solos, and then I was in front of Josie, kneeling down so we were eye level. "Are you okay?"

She glanced toward Marcus and then slowly nodded. "I'm fine."

Scanning every inch of visible skin, I wasn't sure I entirely believed her. Yes, she was training and she could fight, but there was this illogical fear brewing deep in my gut.

"What happened?"

Josie bit down on her lip. "Well . . ."

"She was going to the cafeteria to get something to eat," the guy said, standing. He took one look at my face and moved behind the bench, like that would help him if I wanted to do something to him. "I was heading back to my dorm when I saw her. Alone. And with everything going on, I didn't think it was safe for her to be out here and I . . ." He trailed off, swallowing hard.

"I don't think I asked you."

Josie sighed. "Seth."

"Why don't you just piss around her?" Solos suggested.

Raising a hand, I flipped him off without looking back at him. "I'm also not talking to you."

Standing, Josie punched me lightly on the arm. "Knock it off. It's not a big deal. These two guys were being jerks and one of them threw a ball of fire at Colin."

"He missed me," Colin added.

My eyes narrowed.

Josie continued as she grabbed hold of her hair and started twisting it in a thick rope. "Anyway, the one guy started to throw the ball of fire again, and I sort of didn't think, you know? I kind of just acted."

And now I knew where this was heading.

"She used the air element," Marcus explained. "They know she's not a mortal anymore."

A muscle began to tick alongside my temple. "Who are they? Besides this guy over here?"

"The two pure-bloods, who Colin was able to identify, have been rounded up, and they will be dealt with for instigating violence," Marcus stated, his voice even. "You do not need to know who they were."

I twisted toward him. "Is that so? I'm going to have to disagree."

"Doesn't matter what you agree with, Seth." Marcus paused. "I remember what happened to Jackson after he took training too far. This is my call."

My lips thinned as the blast from the past slammed into me. I hadn't thought about Jackson for a long time. Had no idea if that overconfident jackass was even still alive. He had not been a fan of Alex, and during training one day he literally stomped her in the ribs. I'd paid him back for that. Ten-fold.

"Jackson?" murmured Josie.

I shook my head. That wasn't something she needed to know about me. Hell, she already knew enough bad shit about me.

My gaze met Colin's. He held it for a moment and then lowered his. He knew who the two punks were, and I had a feeling he'd be more than happy to tell me. I was going to have a little chat with him later. "So, they know you're a demigod then?"

She nodded. "Sorry?"

"You don't need to apologize." I curled my hand around the nape of her neck and squeezed gently. "You defended yourself. You did the right thing."

"Agreed," Marcus stated. "No one was injured. If anything, she scared the two boys."

Her lips twitched at that.

"It's going to get out, probably very fast." Marcus shifted his weight as he lifted his chin. "This was bound to happen, and I don't think it's going to cause many problems. If anything, it will keep the foolish ones away from her."

That much was true, but that did mean she would be treated like some kind of prized pony, where everyone would be staring at her. I didn't want that for her.

"Well, it really isn't a big deal then?" Solos ran a hand over his head, straightening the knot of hair he'd pulled back from his face. "Here I was thinking she set someone on fire."

Josie's lips pursed. "I only *almost* did that once."

Behind the bench, Colin's eyes widened. Good. Josie was hot. Literally. After a few moments, with promises from Colin that he wasn't going to say anything, everyone split off. Solos went with Marcus to inform him of our scouting, which wasn't much of anything. There'd been no daimons nearby, but the strangest damn thing was the absolute absence of any animal or bird. That wasn't exactly normal and we didn't really know what the hell that meant.

I walked Josie back into her room, and once inside I stripped off the Covenant daggers and the titanium-loaded Glock, placing them on her coffee table.

"Are you really okay?" I asked her, tugging my shirt out of the tactical pants. "And not pretending like something else didn't happen?"

"I wouldn't pretend that something didn't happen."

Bullshit. Since I woke up in the infirmary after her demigod powers had unlocked, she'd been telling me that she really didn't remember her time with Hyperion, and I knew that was a lie.

Her nightmares confirmed that.

"Are you okay?" she asked, walking into the bedroom.

"Huh?"

She sat down on the bed and toed her shoes off. "Are you okay?" she repeated as she pulled her sweatshirt off, tossing it on the floor.

"Yeah." I leaned against the doorframe. "Why are you asking that?"

She raised a shoulder. "You were just kind of . . . distant during training and whatnot. Just making sure you're fine."

My gaze dipped to where she wiggled her toes. Last night I'd slept in my own room, needing the space to clear my head and get the residual anger out. It hadn't felt right being with her when I knew I really didn't care if I killed that kid or not.

Didn't feel right being here right now.

But this was where I was at, and I didn't plan on changing that at the moment. Leaving was what a decent person would've done.

"I'm okay," I said finally. "So, you scared those pures?"

She grinned as she nodded. "Dude, they got up and ran. And I mean, they *ran*. It kind of felt awesome."

I chuckled as I pushed out of the doorway. "Aren't you a little badass."

"I was totally a badass. Like, I felt like a . . ." She paused, her mouth soundlessly moving as I pulled my shirt over my head.

My grin was slow, indulgent, as her gaze dropped and roamed over my bare chest and stomach. I kicked off my boots, along with my socks. "What were you saying, Josie?"

Shaking her head, she blinked rapidly. "I . . . I hadn't meant to use the air element, though. I was going for water."

"Not surprised."

"Ass."

Stretching out on my side beside her, I winked. "What? Hey. At least you successfully used an element without doing serious damage."

"Oh. Wow. Is that supposed to be a compliment?"

"Sure. If that makes you feel good about yourself."

She rolled her eyes. "You're such a charmer."

"It's what I excel at best." I snagged her hand and tugged her down beside me. "On a serious note, you okay with people around here finding out what you are?"

Her nose scrunched. Gods, I still found that cute as hell. "I guess. I mean, I don't really have an option at this point. What do you think?"

"I think it will be okay." I slipped my finger under the strap of her tank top. "And if not, if you get mad, you'll just blow them all away while trying to drown them."

"Shut up," she laughed.

"Or maybe one of Apollo's powers will surface, and you'll turn them into bushes that smell like cat pee." I worked the strap down, baring the white, lacy strap of her bra. "That's what he always threatens to do to me."

"Nice." Pink flooded her cheeks and her eyes brightened with arousal. "How . . . how were things outside the walls?"

"Boring," I murmured, easing the white strap down. "No daimons or shades."

Her chest rose sharply. "That's good news, right?"

"Yeah." I moved on to the tank top again, easing it further down her arm until the cup of her bra was exposed. The heavy swell of her breast strained against lacy edging in such a mouth-watering way. "There weren't any animals, though. None. Come to think of it," I said, dragging my finger along that lace, "I didn't hear any insects either."

"That's weird." Her breath caught as the back of my hand brushed along the front of her bra. "What could that mean?"

I lifted my gaze, smiling slightly when I saw that her eyes were closed. "Not sure. Solos is going to keep an eye on it."

"Sounds like a plan." Her hand found its way to my lower stomach. I was already hard. Seemed like I was permanently that way around her, but her mere touch caused me to thicken. "I went to the library again today."

"Find out anything?" I reached around and found the clasp on her bra. With a flick of my fingers, the cups loosened.

"No," she said, her voice barely above a whisper. "I don't think I'm ever going to find her."

I drew my hand back to her front, hooking my fingers around the center of her bra. I tugged it down and the rosy, tight peaks came into view. Glorious.

Easing her onto her back, I shifted down and brought my mouth to her breast. With a sharp gasp, her shoulders pressed into the bed as her back arched. Cupping her breast with my other hand, I ran my thumb over the tight nipple. She moaned as she threaded her fingers through my hair.

"Maybe . . . maybe she doesn't exist," she said, her voice husky in a sexy way.

"You'll find her." My voice was thicker, rougher when I lifted my head, staring down at my handiwork. My lips curled up on one side. "She's got to be there somewhere."

Josie didn't respond. She was breathing hard and fast. I felt her fingers working my belt loose, and then the button. The zipper went down next and then she halted, the tips of her fingers stopped at the band of my briefs.

She was still hesitant. Like she didn't know if she was doing the right thing, which blew my mind, because when it came to this, there was nothing she could do wrong.

Not a damn thing.

I lowered my mouth to hers as I drew the briefs down my hips and then reached between us, folding my hand over hers. I pressed her palm against my length, and there was no stopping the groan. Her fingers curled around me, and my jaw locked down as raw sensation pounded through my veins. Her hand began to move. Our tongues tangled, and the taste and feel of her nearly overcame me. She quivered under me, the movement of her hand growing more confident with each stroke.

There was another part of her I wanted to taste again. Thank the gods she was wearing loose sweats, and it took nothing for me to slip my hand in them and get—

"I see your glyphs," Josie whispered, her voice awed.

A fissure of power curled down my spine. More glyphs bled to the surface of my skin, shifting and forming different symbols, a response to the presence of a *god*.

I jerked back. "Shit."

"*Seth*." Apollo's voice boomed from the living room. "You have got to be kidding me."

7

*B*lood drained from Josie's face and then rushed back up from her neck, flooding her cheeks in scarlet.

"Don't come in here!" she shrieked. Her hand tightened on my cock, which really wasn't helping things. "Don't you dare come in here!"

"Wasn't planning to," Apollo replied, and a second later, it sounded like he'd thrown himself onto the small couch.

Groaning, I eased her hand away from my dick and rolled to the side. I helped her fix her bra and top before pushing off the bed.

"You two are taking really long in there," Apollo commented.

"Really? Do you have some kind of sick sense for this?" I tucked myself back in and pulled up my zipper. Apollo was the damn God of Cock Blocking, and one of his powers was delivering blue balls. "Gods."

"It's not my fault that every time I come to visit, you're trying to get with my daughter."

"Oh my God." Josie shot to her feet and smacked her hands over her face. "This is so weird and so not cool. I'm going to need years of therapy because of this."

"You and me both," I muttered, fixing my belt.

Apollo snorted from the living room. "You could definitely benefit from therapy, Seth, and it has nothing to do with this."

Lifting my head, my hands stilled at the belt while my lips pursed.

Josie grabbed her hooded sweatshirt and tugged it on over her head. She glanced at me. "I can still see your glyphs." Her voice was low as she touched my chest with the tip of her finger, tracing the design. "It's beautiful."

I caught her hand and lifted it to my mouth. I kissed her palm. "As soon as he leaves, we're starting over."

"I heard that," Apollo said, huffing. "And it makes me want to ensure that starting over leads nowhere for you."

"Oh my God," Josie whispered.

I rolled my eyes as I snatched up my shirt and pulled it on. "Ready?"

She looked like she wanted to say no, but she nodded. She was still getting used to the whole Apollo being her dad thing. It had to be weird for her, especially since she had known him briefly as a child. He'd gone by the name Bob then. Bob. For real. And used to bring her dolls and candy. Apparently Apollo wasn't aware that he'd rate high on the "stranger danger" scale.

It also couldn't help that Apollo didn't look old enough to be her father, since he appeared to be in his mid to late twenties.

Placing my hand on her lower back, I walked with her into the living room. Apollo's large frame took up the entire couch. He was a big guy. Almost seven feet tall and broad. He looked like himself today. Blond hair. Blue eyes identical to Josie's.

In other words, he didn't look like a freak.

Josie gave him an awkward little wave. "Hey."

He smiled at her, and I was struck once more by the genuine warmth in his gaze and expression. Until Josie, I honestly didn't think Apollo had a large emotional compass. It was obvious he cared about Alex, but even then it didn't appear to run that deep.

Apollo rose fluidly. "I have not been able to visit you as much as I have wanted," he said in way of an apology for his continued absentee parenting style.

"I understand." Josie clasped her hands together. "I know being around me weakens you. And I . . . I know you're busy doing, um, god stuff."

I smirked. I was sure Apollo was busy screwing everything that walked, which was also how most of the gods spent their time, because if they were actually doing something useful, the world would end.

Then he looked at me, and his expression returned to the bored indifference I was familiar with. "Is there something you'd like to add, Seth?"

I arched a brow. "Nope."

He eyed me in a way that made it obvious he was briefly considering knocking me through the wall. "I would love to stay, but I cannot be here for very long." He turned his attention back to his daughter. "I do have news."

That was surprising. Usually he just popped in and out for no real reason whatsoever.

"Good news or bad news?" Josie asked.

Apollo smiled faintly. "I would say it is good news."

Tension eased out of her as she exhaled softly. "Well, that's good to hear."

"What's up?" I asked, folding my arms and thinking it better be awesome good news considering what he interrupted.

"It is imperative that we find the remaining demigods before the Titans do, but until recently, it would have been like looking for a long-haired cat in a room full of Himalayan cats."

Like looking for what in what?

Josie's brow wrinkled as her mouth opened, and then she snapped it shut. She gave a little shake of her head.

He continued on. "Since most of my brethren had not kept . . . tabs on their offspring, it could take us years to locate them. We do not have the luxury."

"I'm guessing you've discovered another way to locate them?"

His eyes narrowed. "Don't steal my thunder, Seth."

I rolled my eyes. "By all means, please continue then."

"Thank you for your permission," he countered drolly. "I've discovered that there *is* something that can sense out a demigod, even if their abilities are locked and hidden away."

"Really?" Josie sat on the arm of the chair next to the coffee table. "Please tell me it's not something I need that librarian for, because I'm pretty sure she's, like, left the country or something."

His lips tipped up on the corners. "She is still around, but she is . . . how do I put this? Shy? Keep looking for her. You will find her." He tilted his head to the side. "But no, you do not need her for this. What we need is another demigod."

My brows inched up. "Wait. That isn't particularly helpful. We don't have another demigod other than Josie. Unless she can sense them out."

"She can't sense them out," he replied.

"I couldn't even sense you when you showed up," she said, shoulders slumping. "Why don't I get some kind of cool internal warning system?"

"You do." Apollo turned the icy-blue stare on me. "But you're new at this and I'm going to hazard a guess here and say you were too distracted to recognize what you were feeling."

I smiled at him, the kind of smile I knew he hated.

"Oh," Josie murmured from where she was perched. "That's kind of awkward."

"Anyway." Impatience colored his tone, and of course, it was directed at me. Whatever. "An original demigod can sense other ones. They actually have some kind of internal homing signal. Has to do with the amount of *aether* and recognizing the similarity."

"Huh." Josie glanced over at me, her eyes widening as our gazes locked, and I did everything to hide my smile.

"Once we get a demigod down here, in this realm, it will take no time for the other demigods to be located," Apollo explained. "The only hold-up is getting one of them here."

"Of course," I murmured.

He shot me a wry look. "It's going to take some finagling. With the exception of our most recent offspring, demigods have been forbidden to enter the mortal realm for thousands of years. Their presence could have . . . consequences."

"Of course." It was Josie who murmured that this time.

"I do not like how similar you two are becoming," Apollo stated.

Josie flushed. "What kind of consequences?"

"Thank you for asking," he returned, and I started wondering how much longer this conversation was going to take. "As you know, all lesser beings tied to Olympus are no longer allowed in the mortal realm."

"Except for pures, halfs, and Apollyons." I paused. "And the occasional nymph and demigod."

"Exactly." The intensity of his blue eyes heightened. "If we allow one of them to come through, there's a chance that other . . . things will too."

"Like what?" Josie asked.

"You know, the occasional Pegasus or Hydra. Maybe even a Minotaur. Ultimately nothing to be too concerned with."

"Hydra?" she squeaked. "Nothing to be too concerned with. Okay."

Apollo smiled as he nodded. "I should have the release of the demigod shortly. Still waiting on Hera to sign off on it, but she's currently pissed at Zeus, and that's slowing everything down."

I decided not to comment on that. "Okay. So what demigod are we talking about here?"

His smile turned creepy, like hide-your-kids-level creepy. "You'll see." A shimmery blue light appeared over him. "Now I have to—"

"Wait just a second. Please?" Josie rose. "How is Erin?"

The shimmer around Apollo faded. "She is doing very well. I have a feeling you will be seeing her soon."

"What—"

The blue shimmer increased around Apollo and within a heartbeat, he was gone.

"—about my mother?" Josie finished, throwing up her arms as she twisted toward me. "Why does he always do that?"

"I think it makes him feel cool or something."

"Well, it is kind of cool. I mean, he can pop in and out of, like, anywhere, but I really wish he had better timing."

I snorted. "You and me both. He's the king of bad timing."

Josie smiled a little as she sat back down on the arm of the chair. "I wish he actually hung around so that I could ask him about Erin and my mom." She paused, and her shoulders slumped. "Or, you know, spend time with me."

Watching her, I tried to think of something . . . supportive to say, but what could you say in a situation like this? Her father was a dick and he was on the absentee list. It was obvious to anyone with a functioning brain that it bothered Josie. The fact that he didn't actively try to fix that somehow confirmed the first fact.

"Who do you think the demigod is going to be?" she asked.

"I don't know." I rubbed my fingers through my hair. "But knowing Apollo, it's going to be the most annoying demigod he can get his hands on."

8

Josie

J had another nightmare last night.

This time I'd been training with Seth, hand-to-hand combat. He'd taken me to the ground, except it hadn't been Seth I stared up at.

It had been the same unfamiliar face.

And he'd said the same thing he'd said in every dream. *I'm going to find you.* But this time, I was so lucky and got four extra words of warm and fuzzy. *I'm coming for you.*

I'd woken up in a cold sweat, with a scream stuck in my throat, and somehow I'd managed to not wake up Seth this time, but my entire day was off. I didn't think it was just the dream throwing me off, though.

I was also rocking some hardcore daddy issues.

And some mommy issues too.

Part of me was thrilled that I'd gotten to see Apollo yesterday, even if he'd only been there for a few minutes. I was like a sponge when it came to him, soaking up every precious second, because except for that one summer, he'd been gone all my life. I was like a puppy. Any attention was good attention. It was still hard processing that I had a dad that was in the picture, albeit not often. And even more crazy to process that said dad was Apollo, the Sun God.

There was the other half of me that was pissed every time he left, because he was *leaving* yet again. We never really got to talk. There was no chatter over coffee or lunch. Nothing personal. I'd gotten a chance to ask him about Erin but not my mom. And you'd think Apollo would, oh, I don't know, start the conversation off with news about my mother, because hello, she was my *mother*, but there was nothing.

Training had been flipped around today. Solos worked with me on the more physical stuff in the morning, which sucked, because I'd gotten used to not having my ass kicked first thing in the morning, and the day was ending outside with Seth.

And I wanted to throat punch him.

"Concentrate, Josie. That's all you have to do." He paced in front of me, obviously at his wits' end with the whole thing. "That's it."

"If that was all that it was, don't you think I'd have done that by now?" I fired back.

He shot me a look. "You're not concentrating."

"I am too!"

"That is one thing you definitely got from your father." He stopped to my right, eyes flashing. "A bird flies by and you're staring at it for the next minute, no matter what you're doing. ADD must run in the family."

My mouth dropped open. "That is not true."

"Really?" Incredulity filled his expression. "Because a couple of minutes ago, when you were supposed to be concentrating on summoning the water element, you were staring at an eagle."

"It was a bald eagle!" I argued, unsure if that was the kind of eagle I'd actually seen or not. "And it was perched on that statue."

I pointed at the gigantic marble thing. "Artemis's statue! I mean, what a coincidence."

His brows lowered. "You do realize she uses hawks, right? Not eagles."

"Oh, whatever. It was still pretty cool."

He rolled his eyes. "Okay. What about when we first started? The clouds?"

Frustrated, I threw up my arms. "It was like for five seconds and it was because the clouds looked like boobs. Giant boobs."

Seth stared at me.

"I don't like you."

He stalked toward me. "You don't have to like me right now, but you need to concentrate. You need to get better at this, because if you don't, you're never going to leave this campus. You understand that?"

Pressing my lips together, I refused to respond.

"Do you, Josie? Because if you can't summon the elements and harness them, how will you ever be able to control *akasha*? The most powerful and deadliest of all the elements." Seth got all up in my face. What he was saying was true. That also didn't mean I had to like it. "And if you can't harness *akasha*, you'll never be able to face down the Titans."

My hands curled into fists. "I know that."

"I don't think you do." His voice was low, deadly calm. His gaze met mine. "I won't let you leave here if I don't think you can actually defend yourself."

"Oh? What? You think you can stop me? Oh, my *gods*!" I shrieked.

I didn't think. I spun around and threw my arm out toward the dummy, palm open. He wanted me to concentrate? Well, I wanted to throw the damn dummy through some walls and into next year. Maybe even throw him along with it. Energy coursed through me, and the wind picked up. I opened up my hand, and I felt it—the lick of power.

A gust of wind rattled the benches as it rushed out from my palm and struck the dummy. It lifted the stupid thing up in the air, tossing it several feet backward. The dummy landed just in front of the low marble wall surrounding the cemetery, arms and legs askew.

"There." I turned to Seth, folding my arms. "Happy?"

His ultra-bright gaze roamed over me. "First off," he said, shifting back a step, "you just used 'gods' for the first time ever. Secondly, I just need to get you angry and you can do it. No problem. And finally, your eyes are glowing, Josie."

"They are?"

Seth nodded. "Glowing like Apollo's do when he wants to punch me." He walked over to where the dummy had landed, near the wall. He stood it up. "Now do it again."

Do it again? Like I was some dog learning a new trick.

"You have to do it again," he insisted, returning to his Instructor of Annoying Jerk-Face position. Legs spread wide. Arms across his chest. "You have to do it more than once, and *not* when you're just pissed at me."

My skin prickled with frustration, and anger was like lava in my blood. Screw wind, though. I was so damn sick of the dummy. Sick of not being able to do it correctly every time. Sick of my missing mom and my absentee dad. Sick of the nightmares. So over the responsibilities I never asked for.

Just sick of everything.

Like a flower blossoming for the rain, whatever existed deep inside me opened up. A chasm ripped open, like it had when I blasted Hyperion. Pure power rippled through me, and this time when I lifted my hand and opened my palm, I wasn't summoning the element of air. I tapped into the power of the gods, the energy that gave life and ended it.

Seth made a sound of surprise.

Whitish light powered down my right arm, circling like a cyclone, and then the intense white bolt of light erupted out of my palm and slammed into the dummy, lifting it back into the air again. The dummy continued to climb, higher than the trees surrounding the campus.

Akasha covered the dummy, the intensity too much for the plastic and fake flesh. It exploded with a loud *crack*, shattering into a million little pieces that rained down several feet away.

Closing my hand, I dropped my arm and turned to Seth. "There."

He was staring at me again, his gaze feverish this time, and the glyphs were out, sliding across his skin.

"And yeah, I did that on purpose, jerk-face."

Seth said nothing as he took a step toward me, but I was ready to explode like that stupid dummy. "I totally get that I need to be better at this, but I'm trying. I'm doing my best. I didn't have years and years of training. I've had months, so excuse *you* if I get a little distracted by the random eagle or boob-shaped clouds!"

His features were tight, highlighting the angular sharpness of his cheeks, and he was still coming at me with this *hungry* look on his face.

I was so not finished.

"And I know I'm going to have to be freaking awesome to fight Hyperion and the rest of the Titans. Trust me. I think about it every day," I told him, my voice warbling as tears clogged my throat. "And I try not to, because when I do, I think about—" I cut myself off, shaking my head. "You know what? Never mind. I'm going to go eat my emotions."

I started to turn away, but Seth wrapped his arm around my waist and drew me back to him. I hit his hard chest and would've bounced off if his arm hadn't clamped around me.

"Seth—"

His mouth closed over mine. I gasped into the kiss as he pulled back, lifting my feet clear off the ground. Clutching his shoulders, I was pressed between the cool base of a nearby statue and the heat of Seth within a few stuttered heartbeats. There was nowhere to go, and despite the fact that I was just yelling at him, I didn't want to go anywhere.

If yelling at Seth ended in him kissing me like this, holding me like this, then hell, I was going to yell at him more often.

I was quite happy here, even if it was out in public where anyone could stumble upon us. Then again, being in my room wasn't exactly private considering Apollo had a habit of just appearing randomly.

Seth caught my bottom lip between his teeth, and I wasn't really thinking about anything. My lips parted in response to the wicked pressure, and there was no room for anything but the way he tasted and how he felt, and I could really, really feel him. He was hard against my lower belly, and then he shifted, sliding his thigh between mine.

As his tongue tangled with mine, he moved his thigh in the perfect way, right against the bundle of nerves. Liquid heat flooded my veins and I moaned into his mouth as my hands dug into his shoulders.

"You liked that, huh?" His voice was thick and sexy, sending shivers straight down my spine and into the most interesting places.

"Yes." I nodded just in case he didn't get the message.

He chuckled against my mouth. "You know what that makes me want to do?"

"What?"

Seth's tongue traced my lower lip. "Makes me want to hear you make that sound." He moved his thigh against me, and he got what he asked for. I moaned as pleasure pulsed through me. "And again."

Oh. Oh, goodness.

His mouth was on mine again, drowning me in kisses as the arm around my waist tightened. He lowered his leg slightly, so my feet were on the ground. "Ride me," he ordered gruffly.

Heat blasted my face. Ride his leg? Oh my God, my face was burning up, but it was nothing compared to the other areas of my body. I didn't move, so he gripped my hip with his other hand and then he moved me against him. The friction was immediate.

"Seth," I gasped out, shuddering.

"Do it." His kiss was more demanding, more overwhelming. The hand on my hip guided me again, rocking me against his thigh.

I did it.

I *so* did it.

Didn't care that we were outside or that I was basically riding his thigh like someone who seriously needed to get a room. I didn't care that things had been weird in the moments leading up to this. Or that a handful of minutes ago, I was contemplating throat punching him.

On the tips of my toes, I wrapped my arms around his neck and I did what I wanted to do with no clothes between us. I rocked my hips back and forth, slow at first and then faster.

In a distant part of me, where my brain still functioned, I couldn't believe I was actually doing this out here, but the exquisite pressure building in my core obliterated common sense.

The hand on my hip glided up my waist and over my ribs, creating wave after wave of shivers. He then coasted his hand over my breast, stopping in the center of my chest.

Seth made this sound in the back of his throat, a groan that pulled me out of the haze of pleasure, because it was part aroused, but . . . but part anguished.

I started to pull back, but then he kissed me again, and I was dragged back in, back under. Our breaths were coming out in short, shallow pants in between hot and hard kisses. The tension built. My fingers dug into the nape of his neck. What felt like every nerve ending in my body stretched tight. There was a deep pulling and tugging sensation coming from several sensitive points in my body. Then it all snapped. Release coiled out from my center, and I might've shouted. It felt like I did. My throat was suddenly hoarse and there was a hollowness in the center of my chest. I didn't know if anyone heard it or if the wind whipped it away, and I wasn't even sure if I cared or not.

The release left me breathless, weak in the knees and utterly sated. If it weren't for how tightly Seth was holding me, I would have been eating the ground.

His hand trembled against my chest as he lifted his mouth from mine. The bridge of his nose dragged over the curve of my cheek and then his warm breath was dancing on my lips again. He stilled.

Seth jerked his hand back and lowered his leg so fast, I almost did fall right over. "Are you okay, Josie?"

I laughed. What a weird question. "I don't think I can feel my legs."

Seth drew back, cupping my cheek. He held me close as he lifted my head. "What?"

His eyes were doing the glow-bug thing. They were a luminous tawny color, and his glyphs were out, racing across his skin wicked fast, as if he were in the presence of a god. "Your eyes are glowing."

Seth's lashes lowered, but there was no shielding those babies. "You sure you're okay?"

"Yeah." I squeezed his shoulder, confused by his concern. "You gave me an orgasm, Seth. Not a punch to the vagina."

He blinked.

I grinned. "I'm completely fine. Except now I feel like I need a nap. And maybe some fries. Okay. Definitely some fries."

"Okay," he said after a moment, stepping back but still keeping his arm around me. "Let's go—"

"Back to the room so I can repay the favor?" I asked, touching his chest. Under my palm, his heart pounded fast. "How about that?"

Seth laughed, but the sound was off. Strained. "How about we get those fries first and then see where we're at?"

I opened my mouth to protest, but a very loud and very obnoxious yawn broke free, right in Seth's face.

"Yeah," he murmured, turning me around. "Let's get some food in you."

9

Seth

*J*osie passed out halfway through eating her French fries, and by some miracle she didn't end up face-first in the greasy basket. She was curled on her side, hands limp and open just below her chest.

I'd pulled her sneakers off for her and draped a thin blanket over her legs. A herd of Minotaurs could've performed a flash mob in the center of the room and she would've slept right through it.

Sitting on the edge of the couch, I watched her sleep like a total creeper, but I watched to make sure she was okay. That she was breathing normally. Paranoia was hitting me hard, because I knew she was okay. Tired and weak? Yes. It would pass. Maybe it wasn't paranoia. Maybe it was guilt.

It was definitely guilt.

Because I, on the other hand, was wired, chock-full of energy. Buzzed like I got after a good fight, a good fuck. Buzzed like I was every time I touched Josie.

I was wired, and I was fucking sick.

Every part of me was fucking sick, because the power lighting me up and that fucking "touch the gods-damn sky" high was borrowed. It was stolen. Fuck, it was the worst kind of thing.

I'd caved to that *thing* inside me.

When she tapped into *akasha*, it had woken up and it started paying attention. It needed and demanded, whispered to me, telling me what I could do. It remembered that I could feed off Josie without really hurting her. And I'd listened. Gods, I'd listened to it.

What the hell was wrong with me?

And it was all me. There wasn't something or someone else living inside me that I could blame.

Pushing off the couch, I stalked to the window in the bedroom and drew back the blinds. Nothing but darkness greeted me.

What in the fuck had I done?

Oh gods, I knew exactly what I'd done. I thrust my fingers through my hair. The weeks of working on the elements had been chipping away at my restraint. Fuck. And today? When she'd tapped into the *akasha*, the lick of power that washed over me had dug in deep with razor-sharp claws, opening up a need I did not want.

But could not ignore.

I knew I should've walked away. I should've ended training the first second I felt her *aether* calling out to me. Fuck. I should've ended these trainings the *first* time I found myself wanting what I should never ever want from her. There was a lot of shit I should've done, but I didn't listen.

"Fuck," I grunted, turning around as I stepped to the side. I leaned against the wall, tipping my head back. "*Fuck.*"

I'd lost control today.

When she'd gotten angry and used the air element, it hit me right in the gut. It had also turned me on, because whenever Josie got pissed, I couldn't help but find it hot. But when she tapped into *akasha*, the rush of power that permeated the air had dragged me under.

There had been no room for warnings or thoughts or seconds to consider what I was doing. I'd become a ball of action, of a thousand different things, and somewhere lust and need and want got all mixed up.

I'd wanted to *give* her pleasure.

I'd wanted to get *in* her.

I'd wanted *what* was in her.

Gods. It all got mixed up. No excuse. None whatsoever. I didn't even realize what I was doing until it was too late, until I felt the ebb and flow of *aether*, moving from her to me.

I'd fed off her.

Gut twisting, I closed my hands into fists. I'd fed off Josie, off someone who trusted me irrevocably. It was the worst kind of betrayal, and she didn't even know. She had no idea why she'd been so tired afterward. No clue to the cause behind the fact she couldn't even finish eating a basket of fries.

I'd done it, and even though I hadn't been thinking and I wasn't even sure if that was the main reason why I'd gone after her today, I still knew what had happened to her. The daimons had fed on her before we reached her grandparents' house. Hyperion had gotten her outside of their house, and even though she wouldn't talk about what had gone down when he had her, I knew he would've fed on her. After all, that was why the Titans were after the demigods in the first place. For Hyperion it was also personal. And I'd done to Josie the same thing he had.

That was unforgivable.

I had to be stronger and I wasn't. I'd failed. And if she knew what I'd done, she would be absolutely disgusted with me. I couldn't blame her for that. I deserved her repulsion and hatred.

Opening my eyes, I stared at the ceiling. I'd done this before.

On purpose. I'd had a goal, to awaken Alex ahead of schedule. It was how I learned I could feed on *aether* that way. I hadn't known that I could when it first happened. There was another time I should've done better and I hadn't.

History was always on repeat.

Disturbed, I stepped away from the wall and walked back into the living room. Josie hadn't moved. I knelt beside her and reached out, my fingers stopping a mere inch above her flushed cheek.

I didn't . . . I didn't deserve this with her.

I didn't deserve her in general.

As I stared down at her, I had to wonder what in the fuck I was thinking. From the beginning I'd known getting close to her was a bad fucking idea. I'd done shit things in my past and was sure to keep doing shit things. No future to speak of. I wanted *aether* like a damn daimon, and I couldn't be trusted.

And I had not been able to stay away from her.

I'd needed to, but I hadn't wanted to.

Need. Want. Back by popular demand.

Drawing my hand back, I clasped the edge of the cushion. Mindful to not disturb her, I bent over and kissed her parted lips. As I drew back, there wasn't even a flicker of an eyelash. Josie was beautiful as she slept on.

I rose and turned slowly, looking around the room. I knew what I had to do, and for once in my life, I was going to do the right thing.

Josie

When I pried my eyes open, my brain was full of fog and the webs of sleep clung firmly. It took a couple of moments for me to realize I was lying on the small couch. I felt like I'd slept for a billion years—a billion years curled up in a fetal position.

Wincing, I stretched out my legs and could hear the bones popping. I had no idea what time it was, but I figured if I'd over-slept, Seth would be here, shaking me awake.

Seth.

"Oh God," I murmured, placing my hands over my face. My cheeks felt hot as what we'd done in public did an instant replay, in vivid detail. A strangled giggle escaped me as I dropped my hands to my stomach. "Wow."

I turned my head to the right and remembered the fries. Holy crap, I fell asleep eating fries. When had I ever fallen asleep before finishing what I was eating?

That was one hell of an orgasm.

Totally one-sided orgasm. He'd taken me to paradise and I'd passed out on him, halfway through a basket of fries before I could do what I'd planned to do to him. Which was a lot, and definitely included getting him naked and me naked and actual *intercourse* occurring.

I rolled onto my side and squinted at the clock. Holy crap! Adrenaline shot through my veins. Jerking up, my legs got tan-gled up in the blanket. With all the grace of a demigod, I fell off the couch, my knees cracking off the floor.

"Shit," I grunted, pushing up.

It was past nine in the morning! What in the hell? Scrambling to my feet, I hopped around the coffee table, kicking my left foot free of the blanket. Why hadn't Seth woken me up? I slowed down as I entered the bedroom, tugging my hoodie off my head and tossing it aside. Obviously he felt like I needed the rest, but man, I hated being late.

Loathed it.

After the quickest shower I'd ever taken in my life, I twisted my wet hair up in a bun, shoved a million bobby pins in it, and then changed into fresh Covenant-style training attire.

The first place I headed was the room across the hall. I knocked on Seth's door, waited for a couple of minutes, and when there was no answer, I power-walked my late butt out of the dorm and toward the training arena. Since my schedule was flipped now that Luke was moving into summer classes, I figured that was where Seth would be.

It was slightly warmer outside, which felt like barely above freezing, but the sun was out, and bright, golden light reflected off the marble sidewalk.

Rounding the corner, I stepped to the side as I passed a group of students heading toward the dorms. The school year at the Covenant was similar to the University I'd attended, except they went year-round, with their class schedule changing three times over the course of a year. It ended up shortening the length of time they spent here, but I couldn't help but wonder what the point was for them. I mean, why get degrees in botany or whatever? Most of the pures lived in the communities and didn't really interact with their mortal world.

I was halfway down the walkway when the tiny hairs along the back of my neck rose. Instinct drove me to look over my shoulder. The small group of students was openly gawking in my direction. Eyes wide. Mouths hanging open. One of them, a tall brunette, was whispering to the other girl, who appeared to have lost the ability to blink. At first I didn't get why they were looking at me like they stared at . . .

They knew what I was.

Word had finally gotten out, or maybe I was just now noticing it. Either way, I wasn't sure what I was supposed to do. Wave at them? Be cocky like Seth and smirk? But I couldn't really smirk. I tried. I looked like a deranged crack addict when I did. Or just ignore them?

I settled for the latter, shoved my hands in the front pocket of my hoodie, and kept walking. It was weird, but I didn't have the brain space for that right now.

Pushing open the double doors to the training building, I hurried down the hall and hung a right, throwing open the windowless door. I skidded to a halt, scanning the room.

"Um . . ."

Luke and Solos stood together, by the mats, and Luke looked like he always did when we were training, but Solos was dressed just like him. I'd never seen Solos wearing track pants and a T-shirt.

And they were the only two guys in the room.

"Where's Seth?" I asked, walking toward them.

Luke glanced at Solos, and when the older Sentinel pursed his lips, I stopped walking. Knots formed in my stomach.

"Where is Seth, Luke?"

"I'm guessing he didn't tell you."

My heart started pounding like it did when I had to run. "Obviously not."

"This is awkward," Solos said, rubbing the bridge of his nose with his index finger.

Luke's shoulders tensed. "Seth's not going to be training you anymore."

10

"What?" My shriek echoed to Olympus, shrill and painful to my own ears. "What do you mean he's no longer training me?"

Solos exchanged another long look with Luke, and I nearly lost my shit, right then and there.

"Stop looking at one another," I demanded as anger burst out of me. A current of wind whipped through the sealed room, rattling the daggers hooked to the back of the wall. "And answer my question."

"All right." Luke lifted his hands. "Simmer down. No one wants to end up accidentally on fire. I know I don't. How about you, Solos?"

Solos shook his head.

My eyes narrowed. I was seconds away from lighting someone's ass on fire on purpose if I didn't get a better explanation, because I simply didn't understand what in the world was happening.

"I don't know what's going on. I assumed you'd fill me in," Luke explained. "All I do know is that Marcus summoned me to his office this morning and told me that your training would be changing. That Solos would be helping out with the physical stuff and that he was going to pull in someone to help you with the elements."

I stared at Luke, not sure I was hearing him correctly over the blood rushing in my ears. "What?"

Solos started talking, and I was pretty sure he was repeating what Luke said, but his words made no sense. Nothing made sense. Was I still dreaming? Was a nameless Titan going to pop out from underneath the heavy mats on the floor? I didn't *understand*. A cold numbness drenched my skin and seeped into my bones and tissues. I was flash-frozen, unable to move. I wasn't even sure I was breathing.

Something was so not right about this. I backtracked to yesterday—to the argument with Seth outside and then what happened afterward. Him. Me. Epic orgasm. Everything had been okay. Normal . . . except for those few moments afterward, when Seth had been worried that he'd hurt me.

Everything rushed back at me—sounds, voices, feelings—they all came back, snapping to the forefront.

"Where is he?" I asked, cutting off Solos.

"I don't know," he said. "Not my day to watch him."

Luke frowned. "Come to think of it, I think it's actually Alexander's day to watch him." He paused as I spun around and stalked toward the door. "Hey, where are you going?"

"I'm going to find Seth," I said, not waiting for a response.

Throwing open the door, I hung a right so I could exit through the front of the building. The first place I was going was the Dean's office. Yes, a bit crazy of me to bust up in there, but I already knew Seth wasn't in his room and that was the next place I knew to check.

I was barely aware of the bright glare of the morning sun as I hurried across the quad, toward the tall and imposing building where the Dean's offices were located. I'd only been in there once, when I first arrived, and I had the same sinking feeling I had the first time.

Two students walking down the pathway skidded to a stop when I neared them. With wide eyes, they stepped aside, allowing me to walk right down the center of the sidewalk. I really didn't have it in me at that moment to really care.

Stomach twisted in knots, I entered the main building, passing the intricate designs etched into the floor and the walls—designs that appeared to be embellished in gold. Like, real gold. Goodness. I didn't walk down the center of the lobby, like the first time I'd been in the building on the night Seth and I arrived at the University. I knew that the Dean would most likely be in his office, and that was up the ridiculous staircase. I climbed that thing like a champ, and at the very top, all the way at the end of the wide hall, I saw the Guards dressed in white, standing in front of titanium double doors.

One of them, a short-haired blonde, eyed me as I approached them. I stopped, breathing heavily. "I need to see the Dean."

"Do you have an appointment?" she asked, blue eyes icy and voice just as chilled.

I shook my head. "I don't even know how to make an appointment with him, but I need to see him."

"I'm sorry," she replied, her voice level. "But he's busy."

Of course he was. "Well, then I'll just sit out here until he's not busy."

The male Guard's dark brows knitted. "That won't be necessary. You can leave your name and we will—"

"I'm not leaving my name, or leaving in general." With each word I spoke, my voice got louder and that current of wind hit the hall, lifting the hairs around the blonde Guard's face. "So, I'm just going to plop my ass down here, right against the wall and I don't care if you have a problem with that—"

The heavy doors behind the two white-garbed guards suddenly

swung open, and the Dean of the Covenant appeared, standing in the middle. He was a tall man, the definition of sophistication. Dark brown hair groomed back from a handsome face. I could never peg down his age. He only had a few lines at the corners of his eyes and faintly graying hair at the temples.

Right now, his expression was carefully blank. "You may come in, Josie."

As I walked forward, I shot the blonde Guard a look that I would probably feel bad about later, because she was just doing her job. Marcus stepped aside, and the moment I entered the large room, my already-racing heart jumped into my throat.

Seth was sitting in the chair in front of the large desk, his back to the door. His shoulders were stiff and as straight as a board, and he didn't turn around—didn't look in my direction even though he knew I was there. The knots in my stomach tightened painfully.

"I don't think you're looking for me," Marcus said, closing the door behind him. He walked past me and took a seat behind the desk.

I shook my head. "I want—"

"Don't," Seth said.

Blinking, I stared at the back of his golden head. "Excuse me?"

"I know why you're here," he added, his voice exceptionally level. Scarily so. It was as if he could care less about what he was saying. "It's about training, and there's nothing to be discussed. It's done and decided."

My mouth moved, but there were no words as heat crept into my cheeks. Marcus—the freaking dean of the University—was watching us, watching *me*, and possibly searching Seth down to this room had not been a good idea. "I . . . I don't understand what's going on."

Seth didn't turn around, and I stared at him, totally unbelieving of what was happening. A hole opened up in my chest, split wide open, because I knew—oh God, I knew deep down—this wasn't just about training. Seth wasn't just pulling back on that.

He was pulling back on *us*.

"Solos is going to take over with Luke's help," Marcus stated, folding his hands on the desk. "He is an amazing Sentinel, and his experience will be invaluable."

I bet Solos was a badass ninja. I mean, he knew how to use nunchucks, so he had to be awesome, but he wasn't Seth. And before, Seth hadn't wanted Solos training me. What had changed?

"He will be ... perfect for you," Seth said in the same flat voice.

I inhaled, but the air got stuck in my lungs and my chest seized. "Why?" I whispered.

Seth continued to stare face forward. "It's just for the best. That's all you need to know."

All I needed to know?

"Laadan will be able to help you with the elements. She cannot control all of them, but it's the best we have right now," Marcus continued. "At least until Apollo returns. If he comes through with what Seth has informed me, then another demigod can surely help you."

"But we don't know when Apollo is returning or who he's bringing," I argued. "Am I supposed to not work on *akasha* until then?"

"Yes," Seth replied coolly. "That would be it."

"That doesn't make sense."

"It makes perfect sense to—"

"How about you actually look at me when you talk to me?" I snapped as anger shot through my system like an out of control arrow. Papers on Marcus's desk rattled. "I don't like talking to the back of a head."

"Well," Seth said, drawing the word out as he slowly twisted sideways in his chair. Cool amber eyes met mine. "I also don't like talking to the wall."

My eyes narrowed as I stepped forward. "I can totally sympathize with that, especially right now."

"This," Marcus said quietly, almost to himself. "This is so entirely familiar to me."

I didn't get what Marcus had meant, but Seth closed his eyes briefly, squeezing so hard that the skin puckered at the corners. "Exactly," he muttered.

"What is that even supposed to mean?" I threw my hands up. "Everything was fine yesterday and now it's not? I don't get what—"

"Don't make this difficult, Josie." A heartbeat passed, and his lean body tensed in the chair. "Don't embarrass yourself."

Sucking in a shallow, messy breath, I drew back as if I'd been slapped right across the face. "Don't embarrass myself?"

He said nothing, but the muscle along his jaw began to tick.

My face was burning like a wildfire. I *was* embarrassed to be having this conversation in front of the Dean, to stand here and have Seth talking to me like he was.

Like I was absolutely nothing to him. As if he was in the position to *scold* me. Embarrassed wasn't the right word. Humiliated came to mind. Hurt did too.

It was like earlier, when I was frozen in the training room. Everything shut down for a long, stretched-out moment as a deep crack lit up my chest, sharp and unbelievably real.

I swallowed past the rapidly growing lump in my throat and saw Marcus. His attention was turned to the window, and it hit me once more that we had an audience for this.

Seth's gaze shifted away from me, to the wall. I drew in another breath and it got stuck. There was nothing else for me to say right now. Nothing at all.

Squeezing my hands closed until my nails bit into my palms, I glanced at Marcus. "Sorry to, um, be a bother. The . . . the training situation is fine."

Seth's gaze flew back to mine, but I forced myself to turn around. I walked out of the room, each step stiff. I had to leave before I embarrassed myself further, because I was seconds from either screaming at Seth or crying, and those were two things I didn't want to do in front of Marcus. Or anyone.

I put one foot in front of the other and kept walking—kept going until I was all the way downstairs and then outside, the whole time my head a whirl of questions and confusion. I blindly headed toward the dorm, because there was no way I was going back to training. Not today. No way. There was a horrible burning sensation in my eyes.

"Josie."

My heart stuttered, along with my step.

"Josie!" Seth called out again, his voice closer. "Hold up."

Part of me wanted to keep going, but I couldn't. A tiny spark of hope flared to life. I turned around, stopping under the cluster of olive trees. "What?" I said when he drew near. "Did you follow me so you can scold me again?"

Seth slowed, stopping a few feet in front of me. "I didn't scold you."

"Bullshit," I snapped, latching onto the anger, because that was better than the confusion and hurt. "You scolded me in front of Marcus. Told me not to embarrass myself. Except you were the one embarrassing me."

His brows knitted. "Okay. I didn't mean to do that—"

"It doesn't matter if you meant to do that or not. You did it." I took a deep breath as I stared up at him. "What is going on, Seth? Why aren't you training me anymore?"

Crossing his arms over his chest, he didn't answer for a moment. "Like I said earlier, it's just better that way."

"That's not an explanation."

His gaze met mine and then flickered away. "It's all the explanation you need to hear."

Anger burst inside me once more and I barked out a short laugh. "Okay. You know what, I'm a grown-ass woman, and you don't get to decide what I need and don't need to hear."

"I know that, but this time, I do." His eyes deepened in hue, turning into a tawny color. "I'm not trying to be a jerk."

"Then you need to try harder," I fired back. "Because I'm pretty sure you just came out here to tell me the same lame crap you told me inside, and that's nothing."

Seth exhaled roughly as dark clouds began to roll in overhead, blotting out the sun and casting deep, unforgiving shadows across the quad. A storm was coming. "This isn't going how I planned," he said.

"How exactly did you plan this—whatever this is—to go, Seth? Everything was fine yesterday and—"

"Everything was not fine yesterday." His arms dropped to his sides as he lowered his head so we were nearly eye level. "Yesterday was one huge-ass mistake. Fuck. Not just yesterday. Everything has been."

Whoa.

I drew back again, actually took a step back from him. My mouth opened, but I'd lost the ability to form words as that fissure in my chest spread, cutting deep, and it throbbed and pulsed like a very real, raw wound.

"Everything?" That was the only word I managed.

He stared at me a moment and then looked away, cursing under his breath as he shoved his fingers through his hair. "You don't understand."

"You're right." Tears clogged my throat, and I didn't want to yell at him anymore. I only wanted this to be some kind of bizarre misunderstanding. "I don't understand. Can you . . . can you please explain it to me?"

Seth lowered his arm and looked at me. There was a wealth of secrets in those odd eyes, and I stiffened like steel had been dropped down my spine. Instantly, I knew it would be better if I hadn't asked the question. If I had just kept walking.

"I . . . I like you, Josie. I think you're great," he said, his voice flat once more, and what was in my chest just shriveled right up, like a flower left without water and sun. Everything was over. "But what we're doing isn't working out for me."

"And you're not just talking about training, are you?" I heard myself ask in a voice that was small and pitiful.

Seth said nothing, but thunder crackled in the distance.

"That's wrong," I whispered as I jabbed my finger at him. "You can't even say it."

"We're not just talking about training. I'm talking about every-thing," he said, and I flinched as that one word echoed throughout me. He looked away again, shaking his head. "Is that what you want me to say, Josie? Did that make you feel better hearing that?"

"No," I admitted, drawing in a shaky breath. "Why? Why—"

"I don't want to do this with you," he interrupted, his voice cool but his words slicing right into me. "I don't want to do any of this with you. Dammit, Josie, don't make this hard. That's enough of a reason."

The burning sensation spread to my throat and chest, and I took another step back. I didn't know what to say as I stared at him and only two words came out.

Hot tears welled up in my eyes. "Fuck you."

I didn't wait for his response, and this time, when I turned around, Seth didn't stop me. I made it to my dorm and inside my room before my tenuous hold stretched too thin and then broke. The burn intensified, climbing back up my throat as I closed the door behind me and slid down, plopping onto the floor right in front of it. I smacked my hands over my face, pressing my palms into my eyes, but that did nothing to stop the tears.

There was so much to be worried about—training, finding demigods and the librarian, my mom and Erin, the Titans, and so much more, but right then, I didn't care about any of that. My chest was split right open and my heart was torn out, left on a marble walkway by a group of olive trees. The pain was intense and consuming.

"Oh God," I whispered into the silent room.

My shoulders shook as my fingers curled against my forehead. I clamped my mouth shut, stifling the sobs that were trying to break free, but the tears came. There was no stopping them. Hot wetness slipped down my cheeks. I thought I felt the floor move under me, a tremor that rattled the furniture, but I didn't care about that either.

I didn't understand. I had no idea what had happened, but the way he looked at me, the way he talked to me, that wasn't even the Seth I knew in the beginning. This was a whole different Seth I'd never seen before.

Like the day he'd punched that pure and looked at me afterward, this Seth was a stranger to me.

The worst part—oh, God—the worst part was I knew what I was feeling. The very real pain, the bitter swelling of emotions, and the deepness of hurt were signals of something powerful and pure. Something that no longer mattered.

I was in love with Seth.

And he'd just broken my heart.

11

I was an asshole.

A huge asshole.

Nothing exactly new there, but any of the other times that I was a raging asshole, I didn't feel like total shit. And I felt like total shit right now.

Hours later, as I stood on the outer wall surrounding the campus, I could still hear the brittle emotion in her words. They whipped at me like the wind did right now, chilling my skin. I didn't have to close my eyes to clearly see the tears building in hers or to see the way she'd flinched.

Damn.

I'd hurt her. There was no denying that, but as I stared out over the dark grounds and tall pines, I knew I'd done the right thing. Lifting my right hand, I rubbed the spot above my heart. The right thing wasn't easy. Fucking sucked, but I had to do it.

There was no way I could be trusted when it came to training her. I'd proven that to myself, and if I couldn't be trusted training her, then I sure as hell couldn't be trusted being with her. Not when I now knew how easy it was to mix need and . . . well, *need*.

"What are you doing up here?"

I turned at the sound of Solos's voice. His dark hair appeared at the top of the wall as he climbed up the steep ladder. "Patrolling."

Solos stood, brows arched. "Didn't realize that was part of your duties here."

"Didn't realize that was any of your business."

His lip curled up at the corners, stretching the jagged scar that ran from the corner of his eye to his jaw. "Look, all I'm saying is that if I didn't have to be up here, I wouldn't be."

I folded my arms, turning my attention to the pines that were already starting to smell sweet.

"Especially when it's as cold as Medusa's tits up here."

Nice imagery there. "I didn't think this was your duty either since you were given a Council seat."

"Not much to do on the Council other than sit around and listen to a bunch of people argue." Solos moved to stand beside me, and I didn't even bother to hide my sigh. "You know, if I had a girl like Josie within arm's reach, I would—"

"If you don't want to be knocked off this wall, I suggest you don't finish that sentence," I stated calmly.

Solos let out a low whistle. "Well then . . ."

I spared him a cursory glance. "Any interesting updates from the world beyond these walls?"

"No shade reports or Titan sightings, but we know that isn't going to last. There have been some daimon attacks near L.A. and just outside of Vegas. I also heard that there was a surprising number near Miami. Word is it's a bunch of recently turned pures, so they're going batshit."

"What about closer?"

Solos lifted his arms and stretched, cracking the bones down his back. "There's a sizeable cell of daimons outside of Rapid City. We got a scouting team following them right now since it's too many for them to engage."

This was the first I was hearing about this. "You aren't concerned about that? It takes no leap of logic to figure out that a large group of daimons there will be heading in this direction. There isn't much else."

"We know that, Seth, but we can't take away from guarding the Covenant, not with the threat of shades and Titans looming over us." He lowered his arms. "They won't get inside these walls. Not again."

"But they can control animals. Remember last time, with the birds?" I'd been on the other side of the wall, out of their direct path, but I'd seen that Hitchcock horror come to life. "I can take out the daimons. I'll leave—"

"You really going to leave here, where Josie is? Think about it, man. Worst-case scenario is that the Titans somehow are working with the daimons, just like Ares was. This could be a trap, lure Guards and Sentinels—you—away from here for them to strike." He turned, gesturing inside the wall. "You can't tell me you haven't noticed how woefully staffed we are when it comes to Guards and Sentinels. Many have left. Can't blame them for that. Shit, sometimes I wonder why the hell I'm still here. Half of the damn Guards are pures. They can't spot a daimon to save their lives. Literally. Plus there are more half daimons now than pure ones. Those fuckers are a bitch to kill, and even we can't tell them apart. You leave, you're opening us up to a huge risk."

Hell. He had a point.

Man, what I'd give to have some newly turned daimons to take my frustrations out on. They were brutal and messy when new—at their most dangerous, as they were completely ruled by . . . by their need for *aether*.

"Want to hear something strange?" he said, and continued without my response. "When I went out beyond the walls today I heard birds and insects. The woods were alive."

"Okay," I replied. "Thanks for sharing."

Solos stared ahead. "The only time it has been silent was when you were with us."

Frowning, I looked over at him. "I have no idea how that's not just a coincidence." I paused. "Unless even the rabbits and crickets recognize how much of a badass I am." I joked, but a flicker of unease shot through me. The forest's abnormal quietness couldn't have anything to do with me. That wouldn't make sense.

"I just thought it was an interesting observation. Anyway, there's the problem between the pures and halfs," Solos continued, rocking back on the heels of his boots. "In every community, there've been issues. Just as bad as they are here."

"Not entirely surprising." My jaw worked. "By the way, did you ever hear who the pure was that went after Josie and that Colin guy?"

Solos shook his head. "No." There was a pause and I could feel his gaze on me. "By the way, Josie didn't come back to training after she left looking for you."

I said nothing.

"Luke went looking for her. Knocked on her door, but she didn't answer," he continued. "He was sure she was in there, but she wouldn't let him in. That's weird, right? They're close."

"Yeah," I murmured. My jaw began to ache as I shifted my stance. I didn't like the idea of her being alone and I sure as hell didn't like the idea of her shutting out Luke. "They're close."

"Yeah, that's what I thought."

A muscle began to throb in my temple as I looked over at him. "Remember what I told you. She really needs to work on the more brutal stuff. She's not ready to really take someone down, to make the choice to use lethal force. We've—*you've* got to get her to that point."

"I know. I didn't forget. I know where her weaknesses are." He was blissfully quiet for all of five seconds. "I don't know why you stopped training her, but—"

"It isn't any of your damn business, Solos. I'm not talking about that with you. That's the last warning you're going to get."

"Look, all I'm saying is—"

I spun on Solos, dipping low and catching him at the knees with the swipe of my leg. He hit the cement, flat on his back. Before he could move, I brought my booted foot down on his throat, slow enough to allow him to catch it with his hands, but I pressed down with just enough pressure to let him know I was so fucking done with this.

Off in the distance, I could see two Guards staring in our direction. They didn't come close as I stared down at Solos.

"I'm not sure what part of 'this is none of your business' you don't understand, but let me explain something to you." I summoned the air element when he moved his leg toward mine, pinning him down with ease. "We are not friends. We aren't going to get personal and exchange war stories. You're not going to question me, especially when it comes to her."

"Damn," Solos grunted out. "Here I thought we were buddies."

"Not even close." I tilted my head. "Do you feel me?"

Solos smirked. "I feel you, *bro*."

"That's smart." His gaze met mine. "Don't ever forget what I am, Solos."

His gaze was unwavering. "I know exactly what you are, Seth."

"Not really," I replied.

He smiled this time. Like he didn't have a boot pressing down on his throat. "I do. Whether you want to believe it or not, I do."

I glared at him. Did he realize how easy it would be for me to end his existence? Halfs were hard to kill, but not impossible. Doubted he'd survive a fall from this wall. I would. And I sure as hell knew he wouldn't take another breath ever again if I came down on his throat.

I pressed down, and his eyes widened. "You don't know what I'm capable of. It would be extremely wise to remember that."

"Duly noted," he gasped.

I held him down for a moment longer. Total dick move on my part, but wanted him to get the message. He did, and then I lifted my foot. Stepping back, I let up on the air element. He sprung to his feet, rising fluidly as he eyed me warily. "Good thing we're now on the same page."

"It's a good thing I sort of like you," he returned.

Pivoting around and facing the side, I lifted my hand and flipped him off. Then I leapt off the twenty-foot wall. Using the element of air, I slowed the descent. Hitting the ground in a crouch, inside the campus, I landed right next to two Sentinels about to walk out the gate.

"*Gods.*" One of them jumped into the other.

I smirked as I rose and then started off toward the buildings. It was early, and I was restless. Normally I'd have my hands—

Cutting that thought off, I closed my hands into fists. Even thinking about her made me want to go face-punch the statue of Hades, who would thoroughly enjoy that display.

What I'd done to her made me sick to my stomach. It couldn't be forgiven, and I should be as far away from here as possible, but I wasn't. Nope. There were obstacles preventing that. Namely, I was Apollo's bitch, and until he told me to go somewhere, I was here. Then there was the whole Titan problem and the . . .

Shit.

Who was I fooling? If I really wanted to get the hell out of here, I'd leave. Fuck Apollo and any consequences. Yeah, he was the puppeteer to my Pinocchio, but that hadn't stopped me from roaming off before. If I really wanted to, I could leave right now and head for the Cyclades. I was still here because of Josie. I couldn't be with her, but that didn't mean I couldn't protect her.

But who will protect her from you?

The whispered words stopped me dead in my tracks. They were

too real. Spoken out loud and yet inside my head. Turning around, I scanned the grounds with narrowed eyes.

Leaning against the golden statue of Apollo, arms crossed and one leg cocked, was that damn nymph. It winked at me.

"What the fuck, man?" I demanded.

Moonlight reflected off the shimmery skin as one bare shoulder rose. "I was just saying what you were thinking."

"How do you know what I'm thinking?"

"I'm special like that," the nymph replied. "So special that I'm going to point out something very important to you."

"Oh, lucky me." My gaze narrowed on him. "Why are you here?"

He raised his chin and smiled. "Does that matter?"

"Hell, yes, that matters. You came to our aid before, when we were outside these walls, but that doesn't mean I trust you or your intentions, whatever they may be." Suspicion bloomed inside me. "What is your deal?"

The nymph blinked out and reappeared directly in front of me. Impressive. Even I couldn't track its movement. "You're making a huge mistake."

Gods. Some nights just couldn't get any worse. "My entire existence is a mistake, so you're going to have to get a little more detailed about what exact mistake you're talking about."

The nymph's all-white eyes crackled little bolts of light. "Staying away from her won't save her."

Well, I was immediately proven wrong. Tonight was officially getting worse.

"And it won't save you either," the nymph added.

I barked out a harsh laugh. "There is no saving me. I know what the end game is."

"There is no such thing as finality," he replied, leaning in so when he spoke next, his cool breath moved over my jaw. "All prophecies are designed to be rewritten. No fate, no matter what is sacrificed or bargained, is final." He paused. "All the pieces are never shared."

Stiffening, I resisted the urge to draw back from the weird nymph. "You don't exactly believe in personal space, do you?"

He laughed, and got closer, which I didn't exactly believe was possible until that very moment. It was. His chest brushed mine. "I don't exactly believe you're understanding what I'm saying to you, Apollyon. You had a chance to rewrite a prophecy before, but you failed."

Everything in me stilled, right down to my heartbeat. I knew exactly what prophecy he was talking about. The one that ended in Alex's mortal death.

"You forged your own path. You listened to no one and thought you knew best. In the end, your hands were covered in the blood of the one you were entrusted to protect." The nymph's icy breath was as cold as his words. "You continue on this path, history will repeat itself, and there will be no salvation for you. There will only be an eternity of retribution and vengeance."

The nymph disappeared without sound or movement, leaving me standing there. Turning slowly, I looked around and there was no sign that the nymph had ever been there in the first place.

"Hell," I muttered, rubbing my hand along my jaw.

I wasn't sure what to think of the nymph, whether he was friend or foe, but in the end, what the nymph had said was mostly true. There *was* blood on my hands, and there was only retribution and vengeance in my future.

Josie

My face hurt.

So did my head and eyes. Actually, every part of me ached. My head was stuffy and eyes swollen from crying enough tears to fill the stupid room, and my stomach was brutally empty. I'd gone way past the stage of being hungry. It felt like I wouldn't eat again.

At some point, I'd managed to pull myself off the floor and kick off my sneakers before face-planting my bed. That had turned out to be a major mistake, because the sheets, the pillows—everything—smelled like Seth. Like the outdoors and the unique scent that reminded me of burning leaves. The tears had really started at that point, and it had been ugly. The big, fat sobs came from a deep place inside of me and they shook my entire body. I'd cried myself asleep, and when I woke up the tears started all over again. For a while, there seemed like there'd be no end in sight.

That had been Friday morning. I'd barely moved from the bed in two days, and my eyes were as dry as the desert. My hair was limp and greasy. Showering seemed like it required way too much effort.

I'd never been in love before.

I'd never had my heart broken by a guy before.

Yes, my heart had been wounded a time or two. There was this guy in high school who I had a pretty big crush on and he'd thought I was a freak. Then there'd been this dude in my history class my freshman year at Radford. I'd spent all semester crushing on him and working up the nerve to say more than a handful of sentences to him, only to find out that he was in a committed relationship, baby daughter included.

But I'd never been in love, and oh God, I was so in love with Seth. I wasn't even sure at what point it happened. The first time he'd shared a piece of himself with me? When he'd talked about his mom? Or was it when he decided to stay and train me? It could've been the first night he told me I could use him as a Pillow Pet. It could've been the night he told me I was his salvation.

Or when he had finally kissed me.

Now . . . I swallowed hard. Now he wanted nothing to do with me, and the confusion had nothing on the pain eating away at my chest.

Saturday afternoon, Luke had stopped by again. Like the day before, I hadn't answered the door. I wasn't ready to face him. Not when I wanted my mother. I wanted my grandmother. I wanted Erin. None of them were here. None of them could be.

I didn't know if the alternating sharp pulse and echoing hollow feeling in my chest were normal, but I was soul sick. I felt shattered, split in two, and I had no idea how to even begin to piece myself back together.

Rolling onto my back, I blinked open my eyes. It was Sunday evening. I was going to have to pull myself together by tomorrow morning. I couldn't hide in my room for the rest of my life. I'd need cats or something if I was seriously going to attempt that. And I couldn't do that even if the Covenant allowed animals onsite. I was important. A demigod.

I needed to finish training, and I needed to be ready when my absentee father showed back up with another demigod. There was so much I had to do, and probably would epically fail at, but I couldn't hide myself away. Because I was a mother-freaking demigod.

A demigod with a broken heart.

A demigod with a broken heart who couldn't even become a crazy cat lady, because I didn't have cats.

"God." I smacked my hands over my face. The burn was back, behind my eyes, and I wanted to punch myself in the lady parts.

I had to pull myself together. The next breath I took got stuck. Okay, I at least had to pretend to have it together.

A knock interrupted my crappy pep talk. I turned my head toward the living area, but didn't move more than that. The knock came again and then a voice followed.

"Josie, open the door."

Deacon.

Curly-haired, silver-eyed, beautiful Deacon. I sighed. He didn't have a broken heart. He had Luke, who was madly in love with him.

"I have French fries," he coaxed from the hallway.

Fries? My stomach shifted, reminding me that it did, in fact, want some food. I lowered my hands.

There was a pause. "They're fresh and that perfect mix of crispiness and softness."

Oh my, that was the *best*.

"And I have ranch dressing," he added. Slowly, I sat up and pushed a few strands of gross hair out of my face. "If you don't answer this door, I will do something drastic."

I frowned.

"I can use the fire element, which means I can melt the insides of this lock," he explained. "And I'm not that great at controlling fire. I'll probably end up catching the door on fire."

"Whoa," I muttered, swinging my legs off the bed.

"And then the fire will spread to the walls and the next thing you know, the whole dorm is burning down. Roof on fire kind of shit and Marcus will get really pissed—"

"Okay!" I shouted, standing. "I'm coming."

"Good." Satisfaction practically bloated his voice.

Shuffling to the door, I threw the lock and opened it. True to his word, Deacon stood with a bag in one hand and a bottle of Coke in the other. Eyeing the red and black bottle, I could already feel the wonderful, acidic burn in my throat. The aroma was greasy heaven. As I stepped aside, my gaze flickered over his shoulder and landed on Seth's door. An ache pierced my chest, stealing my breath.

Deacon breezed on past me, placing the bag on the coffee table, along with the bottle of Coke. Closing the door, I exhaled softly and then turned—

Suddenly, Deacon was right in front of me and his arms were around me. One second I was just standing there and the next, my face was plastered against his surprisingly hard chest, my nose buried in the loose, long-sleeve shirt. And he was hugging me, really hugging me. Not one of those lame, weak ones that made you feel like the other person was frail. No, this was a hearty one, and God . . . *Gods*, it almost broke me all over again.

"I . . ." I didn't know what to say. Tears clogged my throat again, cutting off my words and all I could whisper was, "I'm s-sorry."

"You don't apologize," he said, pressing a kiss to the top of my gross, greasy head, unlocking best friend status.

I folded my arms around his slender waist and squeezed my eyes shut. "Seth. He . . . he said everything was a mistake. We—" My breath caught. "That we were a mistake."

His arms tightened around me.

"I . . . I love him," I said, shaking. "I love him, Deacon."

"I know," Deacon said, and his hug became my everything. "I know."

12

"You've done very well today, Josie." Laadan stood with her back to the sun, her long dark hair pulled up in a neat bun. The ballerina kind of bun, which was something I couldn't pull off if my life depended on it. My hair currently looked like a bird was nesting in it. She smiled at what must've been my doubtful expression, and the smile was real. Kind. Warm. "It's not second nature to you. It's going to take some work."

Laadan always looked elegant, though. I'd seen her around the Covenant often, typically with the Sentinel who didn't speak—Alex's father. She had a timeless kind of beauty, she was a pure blood, and she had come here after the Covenant in New York was attacked during Ares's rampage. She was good people—kind and patient.

Squinting, I shrugged as I walked over the pebble-filled dirt. A dull ache throbbed behind my eyes. "It should be second nature. I'm a demigod. I should be wielding the elements like Airbender."

Her brow wrinkled. "I'm not sure what this Airbender is, but even pure-bloods struggle when they're children."

Children. When they were *children*. Exactly.

"She's right," Solos offered from where he was perched on the low wall surrounding the cemetery. "My half-sister is a full pure-blood. She controls air, and when she was little, she used to throw everything in the house around when she was in a mood."

"When she was a kid," I pointed out, knocking dust off my leg. "Not sure if you've realized it or not, I'm not a kid."

"Oh, I've realized that," Solos replied slyly.

Laadan shot him a look, but I rolled my eyes. Since I began training with him and Luke in the mornings, I quickly learned he was a careless flirt. He'd pretty much charm the pants off anything that wore them.

"You're getting the hang of it," Laadan advised, clasping her hands together, drawing my stare. She had the best nails. Neat. Trimmed into perfect ovals. Mine looked like a rat had been nibbling on them while I slept. "We've only been working together for four days and I've already seen vast improvement."

Four days? Felt like Monday was an eternity ago.

"Yeah, you haven't set her hair on fire recently." Solos smiled when Laadan and I turned to him. "What? It's the truth."

"Don't you have anything better to do?" I asked.

"Nope."

Laadan arched a delicate brow. "He should be about ready to head to the Council meeting, isn't that so?"

"Maybe."

Her smile didn't waver as she met his gaze. "I think 'yes' is the correct response."

"Fine." He hopped down from the wall with agile grace. As he strolled past me, he patted my shoulder. "See you in the morning."

"Yay," I murmured, not really able to work up the energy for a more enthusiastic response. Enthusiasm was something I was seriously lacking these days, and it had nothing to do with the headache I'd been dealing with since I woke up this morning.

Once Solos was gone, Laadan approached me and the softness in her gaze reminded me so much of my mother, of my grandmother, that for a moment, I thought the waterworks were going to get started all over again. I swallowed the tears down, pushed all the raw emotion down and closed it off.

"You really are doing well, Josie. Don't be too hard on yourself, okay?" She placed her hand on my shoulder and squeezed gently. "You've been through a lot and you've had to cope with a lot. No one is expecting you to do anything other than what you are doing right now."

Part of me wondered if Seth had expected more and that was why he . . . was no longer around.

Laadan paused, her gaze roaming over my face. "Have you been sleeping well?"

I nodded, even though that was a complete lie. At night, all alone, all I could think about was my mom, my grandparents, and Erin. Then, when my brain was bored with that, it moved on to Seth, and I spent hours trying to figure out what had gone wrong.

Last night I'd dreamt of Hyperion, and before, I'd always been able to fall back to sleep, because . . . because Seth had been there. I could let go of the horror those nightmares always brought. But last night I hadn't been able to, which was probably why my head wasn't feeling too great.

I cleared my throat. "We're done for the day?"

"We are."

We were quiet as we walked back toward the main part of campus, and as we neared the outer walkway, I noticed a lone figure dressed in all black. A Sentinel.

Alexander.

Every day for the last four days, Alexander had waited for Laadan to be finished with me. I peeked over at her. And every day, since training with her began, the minute she saw the silent Sentinel, everything she felt for this man shone on her face.

I didn't ask about her and Alexander, but that was love. There was no mistaking it.

Laadan's smile was broader. "See you tomorrow, Josie."

Smiling tiredly, I waved at her as we parted ways at the sidewalk, her hurrying to meet Alexander, and me shuffling off in the other direction.

Not hungry, and unwilling to go sit in my room and stare at the wall, I cut across the quad, heading for the gardens. I'd been spending a lot of time in there. It was pretty, and usually quiet . . . and oddly warmer than the rest of the campus.

Shoving my hands into the pocket of my hoodie, I hunkered down as the wind whipped through the campus. Only in the afternoon did it feel like the middle of May to me.

I neared the area where the half-blood had been hanged and there was a sit-in of about two dozen halfs. No one spoke, and as I lingered in the back for a couple of moments, more and more Guards appeared, keeping a watchful eye.

As far as I knew, no suspects had been found, and the half-blood's murder went unpunished. I didn't know if they'd ever find out who did it. I started to sit down, but the girl next to me stiffened and then rose. She walked to the other side and then sat down.

What the . . . ?

I froze, caught between standing and sitting. Several halfs in the back of the group were checking me out. My gaze flickered over the group, and I had the distinct feeling that I wasn't welcome. I could've been overreacting, but I straightened and started walking again. Word of what I was had definitely traveled to every nook and cranny. I'd kind of thought, stupidly so, that being a demigod would make me cool. Like, everyone would want to get to know me, because *I* would want to get to know a demigod.

Nope.

No one approached me.

Reaching the wrought-iron fence of the garden, I unhooked the gate and stepped inside, closing it behind me. Immediately, the humidity smacked into me. I unzipped my hoodie and shrugged it off, draping it over my arm as I walked deeper in the garden.

The place was stunning and downright magical.

Purple wolfsbane was vibrant and plenty, climbing the inside walls. Leafy vines wrapped themselves around smaller statues of the gods. I still had a hard time figuring out who was who. Unless it was Artemis. I knew who she was, because of the bow gripped in her stone hand.

Bright orange poppies were everywhere, crowding the en graved walkways, and so many flowers I'd never seen before, in every color the human eye could decipher. There were trees, small almond ones and larger breeds, giving the interior privacy and creating its own little world inside the iron fence.

I passed a caretaker who was grooming multi-colored roses, the kind I'd never seen outside of this garden. Some were red and yellow. Other petals were ombré, red fading into pink. Crazy. I wanted to pluck several of the blossoms and take them back to the room, but the ancient-looking caretaker looked like she'd cut me if that happened.

Finding the bench near the back, I plopped down and stretched out my legs, placing the hoodie in my lap and just . . . just sat there. Not the most exciting of all things. I didn't have to come to the garden. I could've met up with Deacon and Luke, but ever since everything had gone down, I'd been their shadow. While I knew they didn't mind, I also knew I didn't need to be their third wheel every single evening.

Deacon had been a godsend though.

If it weren't for him, I'd probably still be curled in a fetal position on my bed, smelling like week-old butt. God, he'd been amazing. He'd let me sit there and shove ranch-drenched fries in my face, then listened when I told him what had happened. Deacon commiserated with me and then he got angry with me, *for* me.

He'd offered to sneak into Seth's room at night and shave off his eyebrows, and while there was a part of me that would've loved that, I advised him against that idea.

But Deacon didn't have any answers nor did he understand Seth's sudden one-eighty, but in a way, he hadn't seemed all that surprised.

"You're going to have to fight for that guy," he'd said.

I'd shaken my head, taken aback by the idea and thoroughly confused. "I don't think there's anything to fight for."

And how could there be? It had been so easy for Seth just to cut off everything with me, without so much as a reason or warning. How could you really care about someone when you could walk away from them that easily?

I'd asked Deacon that, and again, he really didn't have an answer.

Neither did I.

I loved Seth. I was *in* love with him. And I hurt so bad that every night, my pillow turned into a tissue, but I wasn't going to beg Seth. I was feeling pretty pathetic, but that was a hard pass. I had my limit.

Or at least that was what I kept telling myself every time I passed his room or when I thought I saw him on campus. Like yesterday, when I was leaving the garden, I thought I saw him when I stepped out, but when I looked again, no one was there. I had seen him on Tuesday, talking to Luke as they were walking toward the main Council building. I wanted to give chase, to corner him, and demand to know exactly what had happened— what I'd done to initiate this change in him.

Because I had to have done something.

That was the only thing that made sense. I just had a hard time figuring out what it was. Could he have just gotten so frustrated with me, because I wasn't getting the hang of using the elements, that he started thinking I was weak? I knew Seth valued strength. Without having ever met Alex, I knew that was what had drawn him to her, besides the freaking Apollyon connection thing. Or was it because the relationship sometimes felt . . . one-sided. Like what had happened on Friday, after training. It had been all about him giving me pleasure and nothing for him. Should I've been more aggressive in my attempts to please him? I didn't know. I'd never been in a relationship before. What did I know? Seth could've just grown bored.

Or maybe he'd found someone else.

A slice of pain lit up my chest. God, it was possible. There were so many beautiful girls here—willowy and flawless, stunning pures and halfs. Seth probably had a damn fan club on this campus and there was no shortage of willing partners.

He could be with someone else now.

He could've already been with someone. Someone stronger, more experienced and who didn't lurch around like Big Foot after six beers—

Cutting off those thoughts before I ended up wailing like an angry baby, I forced my thoughts to other things. Before I headed back to my room, I needed to swing by the library and do my daily stalking—

Something snagged my attention, and I looked to my right, seeing nothing at first. I wasn't even sure what I—*there*! Leaning forward, I squinted as I stared through the thick leaves, swearing I saw something . . . shimmer? Glitter maybe? What the . . . ? I scooted forward on the bench. A handful of seconds later, I saw it again. I had no idea what I was seeing. The leafy vines climbing up the statues and spreading from one to another were thick and tall—taller than me, but something was behind them. I was sure of it. Whatever it was, it was flesh-colored. Bronzed and it—

"What are you doing?"

Jerking back in surprise, I straightened as I lifted my gaze. So focused on what I was seeing, I hadn't heard someone approaching me. I hadn't expected anyone, to be honest. No one seemed to ever come into the garden, but now I was staring at Colin.

"Nothing." I glanced back at the vines. No movement. No glimmer. Whatever was there, it was gone now. My gaze shot back to the half. I hadn't seen him since the night with the two pure guys. "What are you doing? Following me around again?"

His brows rose. "Um. No. Not really. I actually come in here once a week. It's a good place to chill and clear the mind after training."

"Oh." Warmth poured into my cheeks. This was awkward. "I . . . uh, haven't seen you in here before."

"It's a pretty big garden. You could roam around here and never run into anyone, but that doesn't mean others aren't in here." Colin lifted a hand and ran it through his black hair. He lowered his arm as he glanced around. "Do you come in here a lot?"

Holding my hoodie in my lap, I shrugged. "Sometimes."

There was a beat of silence. "Like I said, it's a good place to think."

"Yeah," I murmured. Goodness, I was a stellar conversationalist. It was kind of embarrassing, but I was just so . . . so drained—physically, mentally, and definitely emotionally. I mustered up some energy though. "So, you come in here . . . to think?"

Colin nodded and his brows knitted as the balmy breeze stirred the leaves. "I started coming in here a while ago, after Ares first came here." He paused, glancing at the bench. "May I?"

I nodded.

He sat down beside me, resting his arms on his thighs. "My uncle on the pure side of the family used to be the Dean here. Pretty cool guy. Didn't go along with all the bullshit politics, and my older brother was one of his personal Guards." Clapping his hands together, he tilted his head to the side, gaze trained forward. "Ares got into the University disguised as another Covenant Instructor. He killed my uncle and brother in seconds. Literally ended their lives in seconds."

"Oh my God, I'm sorry." I blinked as I swallowed hard. "I know it doesn't change anything, but I really am sorry to hear that."

"It's okay." His lips kicked up in a faint, sad smile. "Sorry works, because you mean it. Anyway," he said after a moment. "My uncle loved these gardens. Walked every evening in them. Coming in here is like . . . like being close to him, you know?"

"Makes sense," I whispered. If I was still around anything that reminded me of my grandparents, I'd be there every day.

He straightened as he stared down at his hands. "I never did thank you for that night."

"Thank me for what?" Genuinely curious, I looked over at him.

Colin grinned again. "You stepped in, stopping things before they could get really ugly. Those pures could've done some damage and I would've been forced to defend myself. Even though the laws have changed, the mentality that pures can do whatever they want is still there and that they are better than us—that their lives matter more."

"That's stupid," I stated. "And I don't think Marcus would've allowed them to do whatever they want."

"He might not, but there's a lot of people here that would've protected their asses and hung me out to dry if I'd done something to them. But you scared them off. Had them running." He laughed. "You scared me a little bit. Wasn't expecting that."

My brows rose.

"Anyway, thanks. I figured you all were trying to keep what you are quiet and you risked that. Thank you."

I didn't know what to say, so we sat there in silence for a couple of moments.

"So . . ." He bit down on his lip as he stared ahead. "Are you going to tell me to leave now, or would you like the company? I mean, I can be quiet and sit here, stare at some plants."

A begrudging smile formed on my lips. Honestly, I wasn't up for much conversation, but what else was I really doing other than staring at some plants and feeling sorry for myself?

So I took a deep breath and said, "You can stay."

"Huh." There was a pause and those midnight blue eyes met mine. "Do I have to be quiet and stare at plants?"

I coughed out a laugh. "No. You don't have to do that."

"Good," Colin replied. "Because I have all these questions about you I've been dying to ask, you know? I've never met a demigod before. You cool with that?"

Was I? I shrugged. I had a feeling Colin was going to be disappointed with my answers considering I'd never met a demigod either, and I really didn't consider myself one. "Sure. Whatever you want."

Seth

I was in full creep mode.

Which wasn't any different from the last four days that I'd been keeping an eye on Josie. Some would probably call it stalking. I would call it making sure she was safe.

The last couple of days, she'd gone to the garden after training with Laadan. Today had been no different. She'd headed straight for the enclosed area and I followed like I had every other time.

Deep down I knew I didn't need to do this. Wasn't like she was going to be attacked by a rogue rose bush, but I didn't like this. Her going to this quiet place, sitting for an hour on a damn bench, staring off into nothing, looking . . . looking so damn sad, it took everything for me not to go to her. Cross the small distance between us and pull her into my arms. Comfort her. I didn't want this for her.

There was a lot I didn't want for her. Namely my fucked-up ass.

Staying away from her wasn't easy. Every night I fought against the draw to go to her, and practically every night ended with my hand on my dick and the image of her branded in my mind.

Sick thing was I wasn't sure what was constantly drawing me to her more—her, or what was *in* her. Maybe a mixture of both. It didn't matter.

Josie didn't have to be here. She could be with Luke and Deacon. There was no reason for her to be alone.

I passed the ancient caretaker who was probably older than the dirt she was digging around in, my steps soundless as I followed the now familiar path. Josie never knew I was here. It would stay that way. I would remain in the background, waiting until she left, and then I would make sure she got back to the dorm. Then I—

Josie's soft laugh stopped me dead in my tracks. "It's not really that exciting," she said. "I hardly know what I'm doing most of the time."

What the hell? I stepped over a low stone wall, going where no man had probably gone before. Careful not to trample the cluster of peonies, I unlocked a whole new level of creepiness by peering through the thick vines at her. My gut immediately tightened.

What the fuck?

Sitting on the bench beside her was not Luke or Deacon. It was that guy again, the one that had been with her when she'd used the air element. Colin was his name.

"It's still awesome," he said, and, *oh yeah, real fucking awesome.* His entire body was twisted toward her. "Your father is Apollo. That's pretty amazing."

My jaw locked down. What was she telling this douche? She didn't know him. *I* didn't know him.

One of her shoulders rose as she fiddled with the sweater in her lap. She was always moving some part of her body. Fingers. Legs. Feet. "I guess so. I've only seen him a couple times. He's busy doing . . . god stuff."

Colin shook his head. "What about your mother?"

My eyes narrowed as Josie really started twisting the sweater between her hands. "She's not here," she replied after a beat of silence. "I mean, she's with Apollo. With everything going on with the Titans, it's not safe for her here."

"Understandable." He finally looked away from her, and that was a good thing, because I was beginning to think those blue eyes would look excellent on the ground, lying among the damn peonies. "I was kind of lucky, you know? My mom was mortal, and she knew the truth. My father—a pure-blood—loved her. He didn't care that she was mortal."

I didn't give two shits if his mother was Hera.

Behind me, a throat cleared.

Looking over my shoulder, I spied the ancient, knocking-on-death's-door caretaker. I could barely see the face under the wide brim straw hat, but I could feel the disapproving glare in every cell of my being.

I stared the caretaker down until the little body threw up its arms and shuffled off, muttering under its breath in what sounded like ancient Greek.

Whatever. I turned back to Josie and Dickface.

"My father was . . . he tried to keep the relationship hidden. He would leave the community and visit me and Mom every weekend—always a long weekend. Friday through Monday. When I was younger, I didn't realize we were different. Mom was always honest about what Dad was. I didn't realize that he had another family in his community—a pure one. Wife. Another son. I think my mom knew. I'm pretty sure she did, and I don't think she cared. She loved him that much that she didn't care that when he left us, he went to another family, one that his kind approved of."

"Oh my gosh," Josie murmured.

Colin was quiet for only a damn moment. "When she got pregnant with my older brother, things changed. My father ended up moving in with us. For a couple of years, I guess we were like normal mortal families. At least it felt that way to me."

Now Josie was staring at him and I could see the sympathy all but pouring out of her. Fuck me. "What happened?"

Colin glanced up at the sky. "I was young. Daimons tracked my father home one night. They got hold of my mom and killed her just for sport. My father was able to stop them from getting to us, but my mom . . . she died defending my brother and me. She wasn't trained or anything. She knew what they were, and she went down fighting. Because of her actions, it gave my father a chance to fight."

"Sounds very brave."

"She was brave." He smiled faintly.

Josie looked like she was seconds away from pulling him into a bear hug. "I'm so sorry."

"Thank you." He turned to her. "Anyway, that's some depressing shit right there and you look like that's the last thing you need right now."

Oh, like he knew what she needed right now? The hand at my side closed into a fist. I was going to rip out Colin's tongue and shove it up his ass. Possibly an excessive reaction, but what the fuck ever, it was going to make me feel real good.

Her hands stilled. "Is it that obvious?"

Colin tipped his head back. "Ah, you just look . . . like you could use a friend."

Josie pressed her lips together and didn't respond. I tensed, preparing myself for her to agree. She did need friends. Luke and Deacon were great, but the more the merrier or some shit.

Though, couldn't she find another chick? I was moving before I realized what I was doing. Stepping back from the vines and onto the walkway, there was a moment when I could've done the right thing, but nope. Apparently I could only half-ass one right thing. I was stalking right toward them.

"I haven't seen you with the . . . with Seth." The words were quietly spoken, but oh, I heard them. "It's weird. Usually, I don't see you without him and—"

"And I'm right here."

Josie squeaked as her head swung toward me. Her eyes, those endless eyes, widened in surprise. "Seth?"

I stopped in front of them, eyeballing the little punk bitch on the bench. "You say my name, Josie, like you aren't sure who I am, but considering how you normally scream my name, I'm a bit surprised."

"What?" she gasped, and I could tell she was locking up. "What did you just say?"

"I think you heard me," I replied, my attention focused solely on the tool. "This is the second time I've found you like this. Third time's not going to be a charm."

Josie's chest—that remarkable, lovely chest—rose sharply. "This is not really happening," she said. "This is not seriously happening right now."

"Whoa." Colin raised his hands. "I don't know what you think is going on here, but it's not."

"It's not?" I laughed, the sound biting and harsh as I told myself to stop and walk away.

"Colin, you don't need to respond to any of that," Josie said, cheeks pink. "Seth can be delusional—"

"Look, delusional or not, I don't have a death wish," Colin said, shaking his head. "I'm not trying to get with what's yours."

"Yours?" Josie repeated slowly. "*His?*"

"Good to hear," I said smugly.

Colin lowered his hands to his knees. "I think she's a pretty cool girl, and I like talking to her." He looked over at her. "I like talking with you and this has been great—"

"Oh my God." Josie squeezed her eyes shut. "This *really* cannot be happening."

"I mean, I want to hang out with you and—"

"You should've stopped talking while you were ahead," I advised, stepping toward him. The toes of my boots brushed his. "Because, you see, I don't like—"

"Colin doesn't care what you like." Josie shot to her feet, dumping the sweater to the ground. "And I don't even know what you're doing here. Did you follow me in here?"

Well . . .

I turned to her. Our eyes locked, and damn, it was like a punch right through my chest wall.

Colin rose and stepped aside. "Obviously, you two need to talk." He paused. "I'll see you later, Josie."

Much to my amusement, she barely acknowledged the guy with a nod. Her gaze was on me, and while she was angry, pissed really, she couldn't look away. Neither could I.

"Did you follow me in here?" she repeated, and when I didn't answer, she slowly shook her head. "You did, didn't you? Have you been following me since—?"

"It's not what you think." I stepped back.

Josie blinked rapidly. "You don't know what I think! I just want you to answer—"

"You need to be more careful," I interrupted.

"More careful of what?"

I gestured to where Colin had walked off. "Of trusting random people. You were telling him about Apollo." Okay. My reasoning sounded lame to my own ears, but in for a penny . . . "And you were talking about your mother—"

"Oh my God! You were totally eavesdropping on us. What the

hell, Seth?" Anger tightened her features, and because there was obviously something wrong with me, I hardened. A pissed Josie was a very hot Josie. "You ended things with me without even telling me why. I haven't seen you in days, and yet, here you are, listening to me talk to another guy?"

"I wasn't listening," I said, and immediately I realized how stupid that stance was going to be. "Not for the reasons you're getting at."

Her eyes narrowed. "That's bullshit, Seth, and you know it."

"This is stupid." Mainly, I was stupid. I took another step back. "I don't even know what I was thinking."

"I don't know what you're thinking either. God, I wish I did, but I do know what you're feeling." She raised her hand and pointed at me. "You're jealous."

"Jealous?" I laughed. "Of him?"

She rolled her eyes. "Yes. Of him. Because why else would you be hiding in the garden listening to us?"

Shit.

I really didn't have a good response to that.

"I shouldn't have been," I said after a moment. Bending down, I picked up her sweater and held it out to her. "I should've just left you guys alone."

Her lips parted, drawing my attention. It took no amount of effort to remember how they felt. Tasted.

I was getting harder.

She drew in a deep breath and briefly closed her eyes. "You treated Colin like crap and he didn't deserve that. That wasn't cool, but I'm . . . I'm glad you are here, right now."

"Come again?"

Josie's fingers found the end of her ponytail. She started twisting the length. "I don't want to argue with you. Can we . . . can we talk? I mean, I want to talk to you. I think it would be good if we did and—"

"It won't be good."

Her brows knitted. "It can't be any worse than this." Her voice cracked on the last word and she quickly looked away, dipping her chin. "I . . . I miss you, Seth. I really miss you, and I lo— I just miss you so much."

My hand tightened around her sweater. The words *I miss you too* burned through my tongue, scalded my entire body.

Her glistening gaze drifted back to mine. "Nothing?" she whispered, and then she let out a shaky laugh. "I just . . . want to understand what I—" Her voice shook. "I just want to know what I did wrong."

What she did wrong? Shocked into silence, I could only stare at her. She thought she'd done something wrong? That this was on her? She hadn't done a damn thing wrong. She was an angel.

Thick lashes lowered. "Okay. All right." When she reopened her eyes, she was looking down. "I . . . Um, I have to go . . ." Josie's voice trailed off and then she was hurrying away, rushing down the walkway and disappearing behind the vine-covered statues.

And I was standing there, holding her sweater in my tight grip when I wanted to be holding her.

13

*W*hitish-red flames crackled over my knuckles, spitting tiny sparks into the air above my hand. I stared at the fire, a little awed over the fact that this was something I could create out of thin air and that I could actually control it.

And well, that was pretty damn amazing.

I wasn't going to think about the fact that it had taken three weeks of working with Laadan to get to this point where I was now an official firestarter. Three. Long. Weeks.

Laadan was an excellent teacher and incredibly patient, even when I'd singed her eyelashes on more than one occasion. Deacon had been helping out on and off, and he wasn't as terrible as he'd made it seem. Deacon could control fire. Marcus had been right. Working on controlling one element helped with the other three.

Two days ago was the last time I'd incorrectly summoned the wrong element, but that had been a fluke. I'd been distracted, because as I stood in front of Laadan, focusing on summoning the element of earth, I'd seen Seth on the closest walkway.

I'd accidentally knocked Laadan over.

Seth . . .

My chest ached and the flames faded out. I'd barely seen him since the day in the gardens. I couldn't believe I'd even tried to talk to him after he'd been such a jackass, but I'd been desperate to know what had gone wrong between us. Sort of still was. What had I done wrong?

But he kept away and I didn't give in to the urge to visit him. I'd thought that the pain would lessen as each day passed, but it hadn't. The hurt was just as raw and brutal as day one.

But I was . . . I was going about my life. I was mastering the elements and I was getting really kick-ass at the whole hand-to-hand fighting thing, able to stand on my own against Solos and Luke. I hated myself for thinking this, because it was so lame, like the lamest of the lame, but Seth would've been proud if he'd seen how I'd taken Solos down yesterday, sweeping his legs right out from underneath him.

I'd done a little dance.

I'd looked like a chicken with its head cut off, but I'd rocked that dance and I was going to rub it Solos's face every chance I got.

After practices, I avoided the garden. What once had been a brief respite from all the crap now made me feel uncomfortable, like I needed to bury my face in a pillow and never resurface. But Seth hadn't scared off Colin.

Glancing over to where he sat, legs stretched out in front of him and his back against a tree, he was intent on whatever he was reading. On the other side, Luke was studying and Deacon, well, he was not even pretending to study. While Luke held the textbook open, pressed against his chest, Deacon had his head in Luke's lap. For a few minutes, he'd napped. Now, every couple of seconds, he flicked his fingers off the back of the textbook. Luke had either the concentration of a cobra or the patience of a saint, because he hadn't punched Deacon yet.

I looked down at the textbook I'd swiped from Deacon's room a few days ago, after we did our daily librarian check. It was *Myth and History 101*, a true account of their history, which was pretty much a Lifetime movie with cheating couples who were immortal and had superpowers. Every one of the gods pretty much hooked up with anything that walked, and I mean, anything that walked.

Anything.

I shuddered just thinking about the section on my father. Good *gods*, I was traumatized. Like there had been this nymph who literally turned herself into a tree to get away from Apollo.

Turned. Herself. Into. A. Tree.

Then there was this poor guy who got turned into a bush or something, and that's not even the worst of it.

Not even.

My father put the "who" in whore.

Speaking of less traumatizing things related to Apollo: he hadn't shown up since appearing when Seth and I had . . . I cut the thought. There was no news. So no demigod bloodhound, but oddly, I was beginning to be able to sense the difference between pures and halfs. It was something that had started off as a barely noticeable ripple of energy, like a warmth I felt whenever I was around a pure-blood. I didn't feel it around Luke or Colin or Solos. I'd mentioned it to Laadan and she felt that it was some of my demigod powers starting to kick in, slowly but surely, and she'd said there'd probably be more. Since I was sensing the *aether* in the pures, I wondered if eventually I would be able to find the other demigods. At this rate, I might have to, since Daddy Dearest was MIA.

The *aether*-sniffing thing was pretty cool.

But weird, really weird.

Things were rather calm, though. Actually, that wasn't necessarily true. Things were calm for me. Everyone pretty much gave me a wide berth. Only a few brave souls came around when Colin was hanging out with us. They'd chat with him while trying to inconspicuously stare at me. Other than that, no one really seemed to be all that interested in having a demigod on campus.

What was going down between the halfs and pures, on the other hand, was not calm. From what I gathered there had been no leads on who had killed the half-blood or who had been responsible for the horrific things done to that girl, Felicia. Colin believed that the powers that were—the campus council—hadn't tried hard even though half of the Council was made up of halfs. It was one of those things you didn't want to believe, but had to accept as being true, because it was.

There had been two more rallies in the last week, with halfs calling for serious investigations into what was happening at the campus and in other communities. Deacon and I had joined Colin at the last one, and so far everything had remained peaceful. Probably had to do with Marcus and a crap-ton of Guards having been present.

Staring out over the quad, the division between the two sides was painfully obvious.

Since it was actually warm outside—not hot, just warm—a good portion of the school was hanging on the main quad, stretched out under the afternoon sun or playing a really weird version of Frisbee where they weren't actually touching what looked like a much heavier and dangerous disc.

Halfs were grouped together on the other side of where we sat, closest to the dorms. It was a Saturday, and only a few were in their black training attire.

We weren't the only ones who had a mixture of halfs and pures. There were other small groups clustered around us that had a mixture. I liked them.

My gaze tracked the silvery disc as it zoomed across the quad. A pure jumped up, throwing his hand out. The disc stopped before it reached his hand. The pure flicked his wrist and it flew back across the quad.

Why couldn't they just, I don't know, catch and throw it like normal people? Pain zinged behind my eyes.

Closing my eyes, I rubbed my temples with my fingers. The dull ache that had come and gone every day over the last week was back. You'd think with becoming a demigod I wouldn't have to deal with things like headaches or periods. That would be nice.

"If you fall asleep again, I'm going to get a marker and draw a mustache on your face," Luke announced.

Colin chuckled. "I hope that happens."

"I'm not asleep," protested Deacon. "I'm being all observant and shit."

I continued rubbing my temples.

"Observing what?" Luke asked.

He huffed. "Look at me, noticing stuff that a trained Sentinel doesn't notice."

"I'm not really a Sentinel anymore," Luke reminded him.

"Yeah, and I'm really not lying here thinking about getting that bag of weed and smoking it."

I smiled tiredly.

"You're always going to be a Sentinel, no matter what you say," Deacon continued. "Anyway, see the group of pures over there?"

Opening my eyes, I looked over to where Deacon was pointing with his bare feet. There were five of them. All dudes. Two of them were fooling around with the Frisbee disc of doom.

"What about them?" Colin asked, closing his book.

Deacon rolled onto his side and shifted down so his cheek was resting on Luke's thigh. "They're up to something. They keep whispering and going over to the red-headed dude." The red-headed dude was throwing the disc to the blond dude on the other side of the quad. "I've been watching them. Each time they throw that damn thing, they're getting closer and closer to the halfs over there sitting with their backs to them."

Colin set his book aside and leaned forward, bending one leg. "Good catch, Deacon."

"Like I said, I'm observant."

Luke snorted.

Shutting my eyes again, I increased the pressure on my temples. I had a bad feeling about the disc of doom.

"Oh crap," muttered Colin. "I hope I don't get threatened again."

I started to frown, but my lips froze as I felt the shiver of awareness dance down my spine. A new sensation I'd felt several times in the recent days, but only once before, and that was when Seth had been nearby, waiting to speak with Solos after training.

And Colin's reaction also made sense if it was Seth. Threatening the guy appeared to be a rather favorite pastime of Seth's, and that was the only pastime I was aware of. I'm sure he had more fun ones, kinds I didn't want to think about.

And that made the ache in my temples increase.

My heart started pounding as I kept my gaze focused on the grass between my legs. Wasn't like Seth was actually going to come over here. He was avoiding me just as hardcore as I was avoiding him.

"Are you okay?"

Air in my lungs halted at the sound of Seth's voice. Three weeks since the last time I'd really heard him speak. Three. Long. Weeks. I hadn't forgotten his voice, but my memories did no justice. The slight accent was still there, hinting at some exotic background.

"Josie?" he asked.

"She's gone mute," Deacon quipped, and I heard him sit up. "Luke didn't tell you that in your daily check-ins with him?"

Oh my God.

Heart pounding, I slowly lifted my head and my chest clenched when our gazes locked. Muscles tensed in my legs and the fight or flight response kicked in. I wanted to get up and run off. Weak, so very weak, but I'd been doing everything in my power to avoid Seth since the day in the garden.

Seeing him hurt.

Having him standing in front of me just killed me.

God, Seth was beautiful, so beautiful. Looking at him now, with the slightly arched brows a darker blond than the unruly strands atop his head, and the full lips, I had to wonder if I'd been smoking meth thinking he and I actually made sense. That he'd been that seriously wrapped up in me. My personality was only going to carry me so far.

Geez. Listen to me. I needed some daily affirmations or something.

The right eyebrow rose further.

Speaking would be smart. "Headache."

He blinked. "Headache?"

Since I'd spoken one word, proving I was not in fact suddenly struck mute, I nodded.

Looking over at Luke, Seth's brows furrowed together. "You haven't mentioned she'd been having headaches."

I frowned and found my voice. "Why would he? Not like you'd care anyway."

Seth's gaze shot back to mine and his eyes narrowed. Maybe no one else had heard that? "I care," he stated, the two words punctuated clearly.

Awkward silence descended around us as Seth and I stared at each other. How weird would it be if I jumped up and threw my arms around him, clinging to him like a needy octopus? That would be weird. And pathetic. What about jumping up and punching him in the nuts? Also weird. And violent.

Colin stood slowly, drawing Seth's attention as he brushed off the back of his jeans. "You again," Seth stated.

"Yep," Colin replied without looking up. "Me again."

"Yay," murmured Seth.

I sighed. "Did you need something?"

Seth's attention shifted back to me. "Do I need something to walk over here?"

My fingers curled inward. "Yeah, I think you do."

"I missed them together," Deacon said, bending his knees and resting his arms on them. "They're so warm and fuzzy, don't you think? So cute."

Seth ignored them. "I didn't realize I needed a reason to say hello to my friends."

"You have friends?" I shot back, and then sort of felt like a bitch immediately afterward.

His eyes narrowed. "Friends as real as yours."

The very personal dig stung as I shot to my feet with a quickness that surprised us both.

"You're an ass." I bent over, picking up my borrowed book. Seth was quick, snatching it out of my hands. "Hey!"

Stepping back, he turned it over in his hands and his brows flew up. "Really? *Myth and History 101*? Are you reading this for fun?"

"So what if I am?" I made a grab for the book, but he sidestepped me. "Give it back."

"Maybe *I* want to read it for fun."

I stared at him. "Are you twelve or something?"

"I was wondering the same thing," Luke said, and Seth shot him a droll look. Deacon was grinning like the Mad Hatter.

Seth smirked as he lifted his gaze to mine. "Actually, come to think of it, reading this for fun is practically the lamest—"

"Oh, shit!" Colin shouted, his eyes widening as he stared across the quad.

As Seth and I turned, I reached over and ripped the book from his hands just as I caught sight of the disc of doom winging over the pure. Someone shouted, but it was too late. The Frisbee on steroids slammed into the back of a girl's head with a sickening crack, knocking her over. She hit the ground, red mixing with her blonde hair. The people sitting around her flew to their feet. Several crowded around her. The book slipped from my fingers as the red-headed pure who'd controlled the disc laughed. The guy actually *laughed*.

One of the halfs from a nearby group stood and hit the ground running at full speed. He was as fast as a cheetah. One second he was by us, and the next, he was tackling the red-headed pure to the ground.

Chaos erupted.

It happened so fast, one side converging on the other, that scuffles broke out everywhere around us within a matter of seconds. Deacon sprung to his feet, right beside Luke just as a pure fell into Colin. They went down in a tangle of punches and kicks.

Oh man, someone was going to end up on fire.

Seth was suddenly in front of me. "You need to go back to the dorm now." He took hold of my arm and spun me around, toward Deacon. "Make sure she is—"

"Are you freaking serious?" I tore my arm free from Seth. "I can fight and I—" My words were cut off as he shoved me to the side and snapped forward, catching a pure in the chest with a solid swipe of his arm, knocking him back.

Seth looked at me pointedly. "You can do what again?"

"I can fight, you giant jackass of jackass proportions." Spying a pure who was going all firestarter a few feet to my left, I lifted my arm and opened my hand. Summoning the element of water, I grinned when lightning cracked overhead and a white glow surrounded my palm. Power left me, but it was *akasha*. As the bolt of energy streamed out, it turned into a jet of water. The liquid slammed into the pure, knocking him over, head over feet. Closing my hand, I spun around to Seth and lifted my middle finger. "How's that?"

He arched a brow as he spun, catching a half-blood that had stumbled backward. Righting the younger kid on his feet, Seth gave him a gentle push. "You're going to want to stay out of this."

I was going to have to agree with Seth on that.

Things had escalated quickly, and there was no way I was staying out of it like I had done that day in the cafeteria, while innocent people had gotten so horrifyingly injured.

It wasn't something I even thought twice about, and maybe later, I would look back and be a little shocked by how quickly I got in the middle of it, but right now, it was instinct.

Pures didn't fight fair. That was for sure.

A pure had a half pinned against a tree with the air element. Leaving Seth's side, I stalked up behind the pure. Clapping my hand on her shoulder, I spun her around. Surprise widened her eyes and she dropped the half-blood.

"That's not very nice," I told her.

Her lower lip trembled, and when I let go, I figured she was going to run off. She didn't. Throwing out her hand in my direction, I knew she was going to summon the element.

"Not smart." I caught her arm and twisted as I stepped behind her, bending her over as I did exactly how Seth and Solos had trained me in the beginning. I shoved my leg between hers and wrenched to the right. Down she went.

As she scrambled off, I lifted my head just as a pure guy bum-rushed me. Like, legitimate rushing at me like a linebacker. A moment of trepidation seized me and then I shut it off. Sidestepping the massive dude, I dipped down and kicked out, sweeping his legs out from under him. He fell backward, hitting the ground with a fleshy *thud*.

Spinning around, I saw the guys. Deacon had his phone in his hand, snapping pictures with a smirk on his face while Luke had two pures, one in each hand. He brought them toward each other, knocking their heads together. Colin had a cursing pure restrained on the ground and Seth . . .

Seth power-bombed a pure into the ground with one arm.

Whoa.

That was hot.

A hand snagged my ponytail, jerking my head back. I cried out, more in anger than in pain. I caught the slender arm and twisted around, bringing up my leg. I slammed my knee into the flat stomach of a pure. She dropped my hair and doubled over as I jumped back.

"Are they insane?" I asked, dodging a ball of flames that smacked into the tree above Deacon's head. "I'm a demigod. For real?"

"And I'm the Apollyon, and yes, they are just that dumb." Seth darted around me, catching a pure by the shoulders and taking him down to the ground. He raised a fist. "Really dumb."

"Not dumb," the pure spat back. "Pure. We're pure and we're going to keep it that way. And you might be the Apollyon, but you're nothing but a dirty fucking—"

Seth's fist ended that sentence. Blood and spittle flew. "Bigotry is dumb, you know, just in case you didn't realize that yet."

The pure didn't hear him, because he was knocked out. Part of me couldn't believe that this was happening. I turned and jumped to the side, narrowly avoiding a punch to the face.

"Gods," I snapped, more than irritated.

Coming at me again, the pure lumbered forward, blood trickling out of his nose. He got all *Fists of Fury* on me, swinging with enough oomph to do some damage, but that wasn't going to happen.

I wasn't the same Josie who walked into the University months ago.

I was part-badass-ninja.

Catching his hand, I used his momentum and body weight as I ducked under his arm, taking him with me. I flipped the dude, laying him out flat on his back. I bet he was seeing stars. Or maybe Greek minotaurs. Whatever.

"Damn." Seth stared at me.

"What?" I shook my arms out as I straightened, tossing my ponytail back. "Did you think I've just been moping around and not getting better?"

Okay. I'd been doing a lot of moping in my alone time, but he didn't need to know that.

His lips twitched and his gaze dipped a fraction of an inch. His features tightened, and I recognized that expression. Hungry. Starved, really, and something inside me, something just as hungry and something entirely stupid, responded. My lips parted. Seth took a step toward me.

A punch of unnatural power rippled through the air. My gaze locked with Seth's. The hue of his eyes burned a bright tawny color. "Is it a god?"

He shook his head as he scanned the quad. "I don't know what it is. I haven't sensed . . ." He trailed off, eyes widening. "What the . . . ?"

I spun around in the direction he was staring and my mouth dropped open. No more than ten feet away, double doors appeared. Like, literally out of thin air, and it was an ancient-looking thing. The frame was a silvery material I assume was titanium, and the rest was a smooth bronze.

Those fighting near it scuttled back, staying a good distance away. There were symbols all over the doors—ancient lettering that reminded me of the letter "F" and a really weird peace sign that also looked like a stick person. I tried to decipher the meanings, but I was too distracted to give my newfound ability the time. There was a Romanesque helmet on each door, and underneath each was what looked like a crudely drawn three-headed dog. I jerked, realizing what those etchings symbolized.

The doors swung open and cool, musty air billowed out over the grass. The green blades curled into themselves, rapidly fading to a dull brown as the heavy breeze pulled back into the gaping blackness. Two faint forms appeared.

"Oh shit," Seth muttered.

I tensed, preparing myself for a horde of Titans or shades. Maybe even rabid bears or over-excited, spitting llamas. That's not what came through the door.

A girl did.

She looked to be close to my age, maybe a year or two younger, and pretty wasn't a strong enough word to describe her. She wasn't very tall, but the tight jeans and tank top showed off a body that was somehow ripped and curvy at the same time. Long chestnut hair fell in waves down her shoulders and over her chest. Her eyes were a warm brown and her full, rosy mouth perfectly complemented her heart-shaped face. The girl was gorgeous in a wild, unfettered kind of way.

She wasn't alone.

Beside her was a tall, dark-haired man, and Good Lord Almighty, he was . . . wow. He was taller than Seth, but not as broad, with dark brown, almost black hair, and eyes that were a startling shade of gray. His face was near perfect—high cheekbones, straight nose, and an expressive mouth. He was wearing jeans and a regular shirt, but for some reason I thought he looked like he'd be more comfortable in the garb of a Sentinel.

Behind them, the door folded into itself, collapsing until nothing was left except for the astonishingly good-looking couple.

"Well . . ." The girl looked around, dark brows arching as a half was lifted into the air and tossed past them like a football. Her lips were pursed. "This is super unexpected."

"Not entirely," the man beside her said as his silver-eyed gaze landed on us, settling on Seth as the girl stepped forward.

Deacon shouted over the melee, his voice filled with joy, and out of the corner of my eyes, I saw him start toward them. Despite all the crazy going on around us, the beautiful man smiled in response, flashing even, white teeth.

Understanding seeped in as a brawling half and pure got close to the newcomers. Throwing a punch, the half knocked the pure back several feet. He bumped into the new girl and turned, flames flickering over his busted knuckles.

Her reaction was wicked fast.

The girl's arm shot out and her hand landed on his shoulder. She spun him around as she dipped low, kicking out with her leg. She caught the pure just below the knees, taking his legs out from underneath him. As the now-dazed pure fell forward, she slammed her palm into his back. Static burst and crackled into the air, and the pure flew forward, landing in a moaning, twitching heap facedown several yards away.

Damn.

In complete control of every muscle in her body, the girl straightened fluidly. The whitish light faded from her right hand. Her lips curved into a half-smile that was vaguely familiar as she knocked a strand of long brown hair out of her face. "Hey, Seth."

Seth was nearly immobile as he stared at the twosome. Glyphs bled to the surface of his golden skin, piecing together and changing so fast I had no idea what the runes were saying, but the taut set of his features said it all.

"Alex," he breathed.

14

*M*y skin buzzed. Blood pounded. Pulse accelerated. Energy poured into me as if I'd taken a jolt of caffeine straight to the heart. The glyphs, the mark of the Apollyon, were doing a fucking happy dance on my skin in response to Alex.

In response to the *Apollyon*.

Shit.

Oh shit.

The connection was snapping to life, waking up like a sleeping cobra, and it was there, between us, preparing to strike. The entire world zeroed in on this girl. The thing inside me, that felt like a part of me but something else entirely, was roaring like a freight train.

Without warning, a piece of knowledge floated among my thoughts. *I can use her. I can use them.* The moment those thoughts hit me they almost faded from my grasp. Like a word you couldn't place, but waited on the tip of the tongue. Ever since I Awakened, that had happened on and off. For the longest time I didn't understand why, just thought I was spacing out, but I realized it was from when I Awakened and what had happened. It was the same thing that happened to Alex. Thousands of years of information downloaded, passed down from every Apollyon from before. There was tons of crap I knew, but didn't always realize since the knowledge existed in the back of my subconscious.

But now those odd thoughts, even as concerning as they were, faded away like leaves in the fall.

Alexandria Andros stood in front of me. It was really her. Flesh and bone, but she looked nothing like the last time I'd seen her. Her hair was longer, like it had been when we were first introduced at Deity Island. The hairline scars that had covered every inch of her skin were gone. Scars from when Ares had literally broken every bone in her body. Because she wore a sleeveless shirt, I could see that the tags on her arm and neck were also gone.

It was more than the physical. The emotional weight she had carried was gone, lifted from her shoulders. Those whiskey-colored eyes were *happy* and full of laughter. Years of pain washed away, as if none of it had ever happened, but it had happened.

I had happened.

Seeing her like this, though, carried some measure of relief. I had planned on never seeing her again. That had been ideal, because . . . well, who wanted to come face to face with the person they'd gotten killed? Because that was what had happened, and knowing what I did helped me ignore what was going on inside me.

Alex had died a mortal death, because of me.

But she looked good. She looked great, actually. And she appeared happy.

She wasn't the only one who was overjoyed.

Deacon had launched himself at Aiden—Aiden *saintly* St. Delphi—nearly knocking him backward, over a fallen pure. The brothers hugged, oblivious to those fighting around them. Other than their eyes, they absolutely had nothing in common.

Which was why I liked Deacon.

Aiden pulled back, clasping the sides of his younger brother's face. "Look at you," he said, voice thick. "Are you actually growing a beard?"

Deacon's laugh was hoarse. "Yeah, right. Hair doesn't grow on this pretty face."

"More like baby face. Gods," Aiden said, wrapping an arm around his brother's neck, dragging him back. "I've missed you."

"Same," Deacon muttered as his shoulders trembled.

I tensed when Alex started walking toward me. She halted when I shook my head. Her lips pursed, and for a moment I thought she would do what she wanted, because that was the Alex I knew, but she surprised me. Alex turned back to the brothers. She joined them, and they opened up, pulling her into a group hug. A second later Luke was with them, and even over the angry shouts, I could hear Alex's happy squeal. Reunited at last.

I turned from the happy reunion and searched for Josie, finding her immediately. She was standing off to the side, staring at Alex with wide eyes, apparently unaware of the smoke billowing from the burning olive tree behind her. I couldn't even imagine what she was thinking, but good sense told me she knew exactly who the newcomers were. Alex squirmed her way out of the group hug and scanned the quad. "What in the hell is going on, guys?"

I followed her gaze, spying Colin taking down another pure. I smirked. "Everyone is just getting close to one another. You know, love taps and all."

She arched a brow. "Uh-huh."

"Things aren't good between us right now," Luke explained as he stepped back, draping his arm over her shoulders. "I'll explain later."

Alex squinted and started to frown as she stared at someone. "Is that . . . Boobs?"

Turning to where she was staring, a strangled laugh crawled up my throat. Leave it to Alex to notice her nearly immediately. "Yeah, that is."

"Huh." Alex glanced at me, brows raised, and it didn't take a rocket scientist to figure out the giant leap she was making. "Interesting."

Not really.

Shouts calling for the fights to stop echoed through the quad. Guards and Sentinels rushed in, breaking up the remaining fights. Good to see they had such a sense of urgency in getting their asses over here. A lone Sentinel broke free though, his tall body going rigid.

"Dad!" Alex shrieked and then took off, running at full speed toward the man. He opened up his arms, and she all but tackled him. She face-planted his chest and the older man picked her up off her feet.

Seeing that, yeah, it got me in places I didn't even know I had. I'd never met my father. Only knew that he was long since dead. Alex grew up thinking that her father had passed when she was a baby, but that hadn't been the truth. He'd been hidden away at the main Council in the Catskills, and it was only right before Alex and I faced down Ares that she got to finally meet her father.

They had a lot of time to make up for, and I'm sure the last time they were topside hadn't been enough.

Alex threw her head back and laughed as she grabbed her father's hand. She all but dragged him over to where Aiden stood with Luke and Deacon. Then, unsurprisingly, Solos was suddenly with them. The whole gang was back together.

Except for all the ones who'd died and didn't come back as demigods.

Gods, my skin was crawling and not in an unpleasant way, but in a familiar way I'd hoped I wouldn't experience again, and that could only mean one thing.

Tucking her hair back behind one ear, she glanced over at me. Our eyes met, and I knew she was feeling it too. Oh yeah, that happy little buzz that tasted of *aether* was there. Shit on shit-covered bricks.

How had I not been paying attention to the time that had elapsed? Oh, right. My mind had been focused on a different girl. I should've been prepared for this. Prepared for the very real possibility that we'd . . .

Fuck.

That we'd still be connected.

Had it been too much to hope that wouldn't be the case?

Scrubbing my hand through my hair, I turned and checked on a pure who was lying facedown. I knelt, checked for a pulse and found one. Pures were notoriously hard to kill, just like with halfs, but it wasn't impossible. They could be seriously injured. I looked up, seeing the girl who'd been struck by the disc being carried off on a stretcher. A hard-enough knock to the head could still do some damage, just like it would to a mortal.

I rose and immediately my attention focused on Josie. She was still standing where she was, her arms wrapped around her waist as she watched Alex and Aiden. Slowly, her gaze trekked over to me. Her throat worked on a swallow as she pressed her lips together.

My feet were carrying me over to her before I even knew what I was doing. I stopped in front of her. "Are you okay?"

Josie nodded. Her gaze roamed over me and then drifted beyond my shoulder. Her voice was barely above a whisper. "That's . . . that's her, isn't it?"

"Yeah." I faced the happy little group. Alex was doing some kind of dance with Deacon. My lips twitched. "That's her."

She was quiet for a moment. "She's so beautiful."

I glanced at her sharply.

"I mean, not that I expected any less," Josie was quick to add.

"It's just that I . . . I don't know, I just didn't know what she looked like. But look at how happy all of them are! It's . . . I'm rambling, and God, wasn't all of this just crazy? The fighting? It was like East Side versus West Side. Marcus really has his hands full." She kept going, a mile a minute. "I hope that girl is okay. Do you think she will be? I mean, that would've killed a mortal. Like, dead on arrival kind of dead. And half of them didn't even seem aware that a freaking door appeared out of nowhere and—"

"Whoa." I touched her arm. Electricity danced from her skin to mine. I tried, and failed, to ignore it. "Slow down, Josie."

Her gaze dropped to her arm and then flicked up. "I'm not going fast."

I raised an eyebrow.

"Whatever." She stepped to the side, and my arm fell back as she stared at the group again. "Shouldn't you be over there?"

I coughed out a dry laugh. "Uh. No."

"Why?" Her nose wrinkled. Cute. Dammit. Still so cute. "I'm sure they would like to, I don't know, hug you and stuff. You did so much for them. You did everything for them. You—"

"I did what I had to do for them. What I shouldn't have had to do in the first place," I cut her off, unable to listen to her making me sound like I'd done something heroic. "They wouldn't be where they are now if it hadn't been for me."

"You're right." She straightened out her arms and looked me head-on. "They wouldn't be standing here, being all immortal and stuff if it hadn't been for the sacrifice *you* made. And I hope, or at least I'm hoping, they recognize that. If they don't, then they aren't worth what you gave—"

"You don't know what you're talking about," I snapped, uncomfortable with what she was suggesting, and uncomfortable with everything that was going down. *Everything.* "That's the problem here, Josie. You only see what you want to see. You have no fucking clue what you're talking about, especially when it comes to them—to *her*. So just drop it," I said, slicing my hand through the air between us, "because it's none of your business."

She paled as she stepped back, folding an arm across her stomach. Thick lashes lowered, shielding her eyes. "No," she said, her voice reedy. "I'm seeing everything now, but you're right. Them. Her. They aren't any of my business." She took another step and then turned, her voice pitched low. "I'll see you . . . around."

Dammit.

My anger had risen to the surface, like water boiling over, and I'd lashed out like the dick that I was. None of this was her fault and she meant well. Josie always meant well.

Things with her were messed up, but she didn't deserve this shit from me. Keeping my distance from her the last three weeks had made me experience serial-killer levels of asshole, but she, of all people, didn't deserve this.

I started after her, but I didn't get very far. Marcus finally appeared. Happy reunion number five million took place, and before I could sneak off, and by sneaking off I meant following Josie, I was surrounded by what Deacon had dubbed the Army of Awesome.

While Marcus dealt with the latest civil breakdown, we ended up in one of the large conference rooms in the main Covenant building. I had no idea what I was doing there, but every time I tried to leave the room, someone asked me a question.

Namely that someone was Alex, who was sitting on the leather couch, squeezed in between Aiden and her father. Deacon was perched on the arm, beside Aiden, and Luke was sitting on the ottoman. Solos was leaning against the wall, grinning. Everyone was happy.

Not that I wasn't, but I didn't want to be in this room with them, so I stayed by the window, watching the Guards escort pures and halfs back and forth. But my attention kept wandering

back to who was sitting on the couch. Out on the quad, I'd managed to ignore it, but I couldn't seem to stop it now. Every fiber
of my being was aware of potent *aether* emanating from the two
demigods, but it was more than that. The long-dormant cord was
thrumming to life, and I was doing my best to—

"Why do you keep staring at me?"

Realizing I was, in fact, staring at Alex, I blinked. Awkward.

Aiden leaned against the cushion on the couch, tossing his
arm along the back. "Good question."

I shot him a bland look before focusing on her. "You look like
. . . like you did when we first met."

"I do, right?" She lifted her hair in both hands and wiggled the
ends. The last time I'd seen her, her hair was much shorter. Ares
had gotten hold of it, lopping it off with a knife. "Apparently
when you die, you get doused with Scar Begone or something."

Jaw working, I looked away from her. *When you die . . .*

"Not that she really died," Aiden intervened quickly, always
the mediator. "But when you enter Tartarus the correct way,
you're kind of . . ."

"Reassembled?" Alex said with a laugh. "Caleb is the same way.
So are Olivia and Lea."

The names of those who had perished echoed in my skull.

"How are they doing?" Luke asked.

"Great. Caleb and Olivia are together, just like they were, um
. . . here. Topside. And we've played *Mario Kart* with Persephone
a couple of times."

Alexander's brows rose at that.

She giggled. "She gets mad when she loses, though."

"And when she gets mad, that usually means Hades is going
to be in a worse mood than usual." Aiden grinned a little as he
glanced at Alex. "We make ourselves scarce when that happens."

"Sounds like fun," Solos said, but his tone was the complete
opposite.

"It's really not that bad. Pretty much whatever you want is there," Alex replied, leaning her head onto her father's shoulder. "But we miss you guys. Sucks that we have to wait six months and we aren't allowed to communicate with anyone topside during that time. Feels like forever to us down there."

Her father turned, dropping a kiss to the top of her head.

Aiden leaned forward, his gray eyes serious. "So, we've heard about what's going down with the Titans." His stare landed on me, and I thought it was ironic how they couldn't communicate with us but they seemed to know what was going on somehow. "Any updates?"

"Not really." I folded my arms. "Hyperion was out of commission for a while, but I'm sure he's back or will be soon. Apollo is supposed to be bringing a demigod back with him to help locate the other ones so they can entomb—"

"Other demigods?" Alex frowned. "Demigods like Aiden and me?"

"You don't know about that part?" I asked.

Aiden shook his head. "This is the first time we're hearing about anything demigod-related."

"Why am I not surprised you guys only got half of what is important?" I sighed, pressing my shoulders against the wall. "I'm going to give you the version for dummies."

"Gee, thanks," Alex replied. "Otherwise, we might not be able to process it."

I smirked. "When I was created, the gods knew something was going on and that there was a chance that we'd connect and one of us would turn God Killer on them, so they took precautions."

"Man." Aiden slid a hand over his face. "This is going in so many directions."

"The gods came down to earth, got it on with various men and women, and produced twelve demigods. *Born* demigods. Not made ones like you two. You know, *real* demigods," I pointed out, and Alex rolled her eyes. "The gods locked their abilities, basically turning them into sleeper demigods. Of course, Hera ended up killing some. So did . . . so did Ares. Six remain. The Titans got hold of two of them, but Apollo said that one of the original demigods would be able to find the other three. If we get the six of them together, then their abilities will automatically unlock."

"The Titans have two of them?" Aiden asked.

"They're feeding off them," Solos added. "It's how they're getting their powers back."

"Oh my gods," Alex whispered. "Feeding off them? Like daimons?"

"Basically." Solos pushed off the wall. "We have no idea what condition they are in or even where the other three are. We're waiting on Apollo, and you know how he takes his time with stuff."

"Did you know Ares was taking out demigods?" Aiden's gaze latched onto mine.

I resisted the urge to flip him off. His suspicions were warranted. "Contrary to popular belief, I didn't know everything Ares was up to. I didn't know about any of this until Apollo told me."

"We didn't think you knew everything," Alex threw out, but yeah, didn't quite believe that.

Aiden glanced at her and then his attention flipped back to me. "Hold on a sec."

"Holding," I murmured.

He ignored that. "You said that there are six demigods alive. Two were with the Titans and you needed to find three more. Shouldn't it be four more? Or did I forget how to count?"

"Yep. You forgot how to count," I replied dryly.

Aiden looked unimpressed with my comment. I thought it was pretty astute. "Do we need to find three or four of them?"

"I think it's cute how you've inserted 'we' into this." I smiled tightly.

"We're up here for the next six months," Alex stated slowly, like I needed the time to comprehend. "So, duh, we're going to help while we're here. This isn't a vacation for us."

I was going to throw myself through a wall.

Aiden nodded in agreement. "So, there are—"

"Oh! Holy shit balls." Deacon jumped up from the couch and looked around the room, the corners of his mouth turning down. "Where is Josie?"

"Hell," Luke grunted as he too glanced around, like he was going to find Josie hiding under a chair or something. "Did we forget her? She's not still out on the quad, is she?"

Yes, I wanted to tell them. *Yes, you totally forgot about Josie.* "She went back to her room."

Deacon's brows furrowed together. "Why did she do that?"

Well, let me count the reasons . . .

"Who's Josie?" Alex asked, confused.

"Uh . . ." I looked over at Deacon. "You want to do the honors? I know how much you love awkward conversations."

A wide smile broke out across his face. "Of course, especially when I'm not the center of the awkwardness."

Luke snorted.

"So!" Deacon clapped his hands together as he faced Alex and Aiden. "Did you guys happen to notice a certain girl out on the quad when you did your magic doorway thing?"

Aiden glanced at Alex. She raised a shoulder. "There were a lot of people out there that I hadn't seen before." She paused. "I noticed Boobs, though."

I slowly shook my head.

"Um, that's not who I'm talking about. Anyway," Deacon said, his gray eyes light. "She's pretty tall. Well, taller than you and everyone is practically taller than you, Alex. Has long blondish-brown hair. Kind of weird hair."

"Awesome hair," Luke added.

Alexander frowned silently.

"She does. It's like an array of colors. One moment it looks completely blonde. The next it's long brown and then it changes again. It's very cool," Deacon continued, and I had to agree with him on that. "And when you see her, you're going to think, wow, this girl looks familiar. You won't be able to put a finger on it at first, but it's going to nag at you and then, when it hits you, you'll—"

"Deacon," Aiden warned. "Who is Josie?"

His brother pouted for a second and then sighed. "Fine. She's a demigod. Like, a born demigod. Powers unlocked and all, and she's super-cool and really nice." His gaze slid over to where I stood and his expression turned sly. "Isn't that right, Seth?"

I eyed him. "Right."

"You're forgetting the best part." Solos walked past the couch, sending me a long look. "Which god she came from."

Aiden seemed to get what wasn't being said first. His eyes closed as he rubbed his fingers along his brow. "Gods."

"What?" Alex looked at him and then at me. "Whose kid is she?"

"Apollo's," Deacon answered, his smile going up a notch when Alex's gaze flew to him. "Yep. Josie is Apollo's daughter."

Her mouth dropped open.

"And that kind of makes you and her cousins? I guess?" Luke frowned. "I don't know what exactly, but it does make you two related. Somehow. I don't know how, but she does have some of your mannerisms. It gets really weird sometimes."

Alex twisted toward her father, and he nodded. She didn't move until Aiden curved his hand over her knee, then she whipped back around. Her mouth moved wordlessly for a few seconds. "Holy crap. I . . . I don't know what to say."

"That was pretty much our response at first," Luke sympathized as he hooked one leg over the other. "Seth brought her to the Covenant."

Alex's brows flew up. "Oh, really?"

"Apollo put him in charge of her safety," Solos added, voice roguish as he jerked his chin in my direction. "And he takes her safety very seriously."

"Huh." Aiden tilted his head to the side.

"You see, Hyperion was gunning for Josie. Seth made sure she got here, and some shit went down, but Seth kept her *real* safe," Solos continued. Next time, I wasn't going to stop when I had my boot on his throat.

Alex eyed me intently. "I feel like I need to say thank you. I mean, she's family. Which is kind of weird. And actually," she paused as she scooted forward, "there's a lot I need to thank you for." She glanced at Aiden. "A lot that *we—*"

"That's not something we need to do." I was off the wall in a nanosecond. "I've got to go."

I didn't wait for a response. I stepped out of the room and headed through the relatively empty lobby. The door didn't swing shut behind me.

"Seth."

Fuck me.

"You keep walking," Aiden said. "I'll keep following."

Of course.

Tipping my head, I swallowed a mouthful of curses before I turned around. "What do you want?"

Aiden walked up to me, and for a couple of moments, we just stood there, nearly toe to toe, neither of us speaking. How many times in the past had we ended up in this stance? More times than I could count. Usually we'd be seconds away from going at each other's throats. We did not have the greatest past together, but the last time I'd seen him . . . I saw a man who was broken.

Now I saw a man who was whole.

"There's a couple of things I need to tell you, and then there's something I need to ask you." Aiden lowered his chin as he spoke.

"I know you aren't exactly thrilled that we're here, but Alex has been waiting to see you since she found out what you did. I know you don't want to hear it, but I'm going to say it, and the next time Alex goes to say it, you're going to let her do just that."

I opened my mouth, but he went on. "We owe you everything and we know that. And I know you don't want to hear this, but thank you. Thank you for what you did for us."

Mouth clamped shut, I fixed my gaze on the wall.

"We won't forget that," he added, and then after a pause, "even if there are days—months, and probably years—where I wish I could forget that."

I huffed out a laugh as I looked back at him. "I really don't like you, Aiden."

His lips twitched. "Good. Because I still don't like you either."

"Perfect." I started to back up. "Anything else, Saint?"

"Yeah. Just one more thing." Aiden's eyes turned gunmetal gray. "Are you still connected to Alex?"

"Why don't you ask her?"

"I'm asking you."

I drew in a deep breath. There was no point in lying. "Yeah. Yeah, I am."

15

"This is kind of weird," Colin stated as he stared out over the nearly empty cafeteria. "It's like a ghost ship. Well, maybe a ghost cafeteria."

Holding my plate of bacon and bottle of apple juice, I had to agree that this was weird. Normally there were a lot more students in the cafeteria on Sunday morning. Right now, I could count on both hands how many were actually in the room, and they were pures.

Pures who watched us warily as we sat at a small round table near the windowed wall overlooking the statues of the eleven remaining Olympian gods. I could feel their stares as I screwed the lid off my juice.

What was also weird was that Luke and Deacon were normally waiting for us in the lobby of the dorm or, if one of us was late, they were already in the cafeteria. Luke was an earlier riser, meaning he'd drag Deacon out of bed even if the boy was half-asleep.

They weren't here.

Of course, it sort of made sense. Deacon was probably spending time with his brother. They might even end up here. And from what I gathered, Luke was super close with Alex. The whole gang might walk in at any moment. So it made sense, but it was also just weird, because we were missing people.

And Seth?

Seth had stopped coming to breakfast the day he'd stopped training me. I was still getting used to it.

"You think everyone is in hiding?" Colin asked, scooping up his egg whites. Ew. Who just ate eggs without the yolk? The yolk was the best part. "Or was there a massive party last night and we weren't invited?"

"And everyone is hungover now?" I smiled as I picked up a slice of bacon. "It's possible."

He snorted as he rested his elbow on the table. "We're just that uncool."

I was feeling pretty uncool and in desperate need of a pity party, but I didn't know Colin well enough to be comfortable with me turning into a whale-sized baby in front of him. "Probably has to do with the fight yesterday. Maybe people don't feel entirely safe right now."

"True. I like the idea of there being a big party, though." He chewed his eggs. "Or it could be the fact we now have two more demigods roaming around campus."

The yummy-tasting bacon turned a little sour in my stomach.

"You guys are like mogwais fed after midnight," he continued.

I cracked a smile at that. Though none of us were as cute as a mogwai.

Colin finished off his eggs and then moved on to his whole-wheat toast. All the butter in the world dumped on that bread wouldn't make it taste like anything besides cardboard. "So, do you know those two? Aiden and Alex?"

Shaking my head, I put my bacon down, no longer hungry, which was a crime when it came to bacon. "No. Yesterday was the first time I'd even seen them."

"Man, they are like legends." He shook his head, and there was no mistaking the awe creeping into his tone. "They actually *are* legends among our kind."

"Really?" I murmured, staring at my pile of bacon.

Colin munched on his toast. "I never actually formally met them, but I was here when they first came, before they left to fight Ares. The fact that they did that willingly is freaking beyond amazing. I mean, who would want to fight the God of War?"

Not me, but that was no big surprise.

"They're pretty badass," he went on, and I swallowed a sigh. "I might have a crush on Alex."

I slowly lifted my gaze to his. Seriously?

He flushed. "I mean, not in *that* way. I'm smart enough to realize Aiden would kill me. I have a respect crush on her. She's badass. She left to fight Ares knowing she wasn't going to walk out of the battle."

How fast could I haul butt out of that cafeteria?

"That took major balls." He paused, frowning at his half-eaten toast. "Well, it took major ovaries. She had no idea that Apollo, your father, had given her ambrosia. Or at least that's the legend and she . . ."

Colin's praise party faded in a dull hum that matched the ache behind my eyes. I knew my irritation was unreasonable, and I also knew exactly what the source of my anger was.

Jealousy.

My skin should have been green by then. Seeing Alex yesterday had totally confirmed what I always believed about her. She was literally everything I wasn't.

How in the world could Seth have ever been interested in me after sort of being involved with someone like her?

It wasn't her fault. Hell, the girl didn't even know I existed. She was batting in the major leagues and I was still trying to get into the minors. My irritation and frustration were all on me.

I was woman enough to admit that.

After breakfast, I parted ways with Colin even though he was all about us going for a run or something—and who in the hell did he think I was, that I was going to voluntarily do that? Ha. I went to the library, trolled around in there for hours with no luck, and then finally moped back to my dorm.

I stopped at my door and turned to Seth's. Chewing on my lower lip, I willed the door to open and for Seth to step out. I don't even know why I wanted that. He'd made things pretty clear yesterday. He'd made it clear weeks ago.

Turning around, I walked into my room, went to the bedroom, and picked up the old picture of me with my grandparents and mom. I wished I could crawl back in time and commit the moment to memory, because I didn't remember the hours leading up to it or after it.

None of us had second chances.

Well, except Alex and Aiden. And Seth. And me, in a way. A lot of us had second chances, but we didn't get to pick what they would be.

Based on my appearance, it was around the time of middle school. I was so freaking chubby, a total butterball, and the pattern on the paisley shirt didn't help. But I was smiling. So was Granny. And Papa. And Mom. It had been a good day.

Placing the picture on my nightstand, I wiped the back of my hand under my eyes. My cheeks were damp, and I wasn't sure what or who I was crying for. All I knew was that I'd been crying a lot lately, and I hated that crying made me feel weak.

What in the hell was so weak about it? Like that was the worst thing I could be doing right now. I mean, I could be engaging in self-harm or risky behaviors. I could be shit-faced or high as a kite. Nope. I was weepy, and I had a feeling there were people out there who probably thought going out and picking fights or drinking until they vomited was better than having a good cry.

On second thought, drinking until I didn't know who I was sounded good right about then. I just . . . I really didn't want to . . . feel anything. I missed my family. I missed Erin, and as much as I wanted to turn Seth's nuts into a punching bag, I missed him—the him from *before*.

God, his words still stung, but I saw the truth behind what was driving them. I'd probably seen it before, but hadn't wanted to truly acknowledge it.

Plopping onto my back, I stared up at the ceiling. Seth's sudden change of heart sort of made sense now. He had to have known it was getting close to when Alex would return. There was no way he hadn't. Not with the kind of bond they had. He had to have known she was coming.

I'd seen the way he'd stared at her yesterday.

And when I left the quad, Seth hadn't followed. He stayed there with them, with her. That wasn't jealousy talking. That was just reality.

Even though Alex and Aiden had the kind of love poets rambled on about, there had been something powerful between Seth and Alex. Deacon had said so himself, something practically unbreakable.

I always thought his reluctance to talk about Alex had to do with his guilt, but now, I knew there was more to it. Seth wasn't over Alex and whatever they shared.

And that sucked.

Because I couldn't compete with someone who was a legend. Someone Seth had given up eternity for.

I was in love with someone who was still wrapped up in someone else—someone who was a freaking legend among their kind.

A knock on the door drew me out of my thoughts. Sitting up, I swung my legs off the bed and stood. I hoped it was Deacon or Luke or both of them. Deacon would watch *Supernatural* with me and everything would be right in the world, at least for a few hours, and I wouldn't feel like I . . . like I was forgotten.

Opening the door, I came face to face with Alex.

Holy crap.

Startled, I took a step back as I felt my mouth drop open. What was she doing here? Was she at the wrong door? Oh my God, what if she was at the wrong door and had meant to knock on Seth's?

I was going to punch her.

Okay. She could probably kick my ass, so I would punch her and run.

She clasped her hands together as she looked up at me. "Hi," she said. "I know we don't know each other, but I was wondering if you had a couple of minutes to chat?"

Struck dumb, I stepped aside. Would I seriously refuse her? Uh. No. Alex walked in and closed the door behind her. I faced her, having no idea what in the hell was going on.

Standing in front of her, as close as we were, I felt like—like Bigfoot looming over her. A blonde Bigfoot. I could legit pick her up and put her in my pocket.

"I'm Alex An—"

"I know who you are." The moment those words left my mouth, I cringed. Icicles could've formed in the room. "I mean, I know who you are. Everyone knows who you are."

Her brows lifted. "That's kind of creepy."

I snapped my mouth shut.

"Not that you're creepy for saying that. It's just that I'm not used to everyone knowing who I am." She paused, wrinkling her nose—and *oh my God*, my eyes widened. I did that. All. The. Time. "Well, people kind of knew who I was before the whole 'rise from the dead' demigod thing, but it usually wasn't anything good."

"Oh," I murmured, still staring at her.

A half-smile formed on her lips. "Anyway, you're Josie."

I nodded slowly.

Alex laughed, the sound husky and warm. "Well, duh. You know who you are."

I nodded again.

"This isn't coming out right," she said with another laugh. "I wanted to meet you. I hear there's something we have in common."

"We've both been with Seth?" I blurted out, and holy shitballs, I did not just say that.

Her brown eyes widened slightly as her mouth formed an O.

I totally just said that.

"Oh my gosh, I mean, not that you've *been* with Seth, like *with* him. I haven't even actually *been* with him in *that* kind of way." Heat scalded my cheeks. I wasn't even sure if Seth and Alex had gone *there*, but I was seriously hoping that they hadn't because that would be yet one more thing she had going for her that I didn't.

Ugh. I couldn't even believe my brain was spewing out these kinds of things.

"I meant that we have him in common and that's all I was trying to say," I finished lamely.

"Um. That's not what I was going to say," Alex said, blinking slowly as she reached up, tossing her hair over her shoulder. "I was going to go with us both having Apollo in common."

"Ah. That . . . that makes more sense." Walking around her, I dropped onto the cushions of the love seat, suddenly exhausted. The epic diarrhea of the mouth was tiring. "Apollo. Yeah, he's, um, something else, isn't he?"

"Yeah," she drew the word out as she sat in the small chair. "I want to talk about Apollo, but let's back up a second. You and Seth are . . . together?"

My face was going to melt right off. Tongue twisted, I had no idea what to say, because we weren't together anymore, and Alex was the absolute last person I wanted to be discussing this with. But it was my fault for letting my mouth strip down and do a jig.

Alex's lashes lowered, but the intensity of her stare could still be felt. "Okay. I know you don't know me at all, but you're going to learn pretty quickly that I'm super blunt, and I feel like I totally need to get this out in the open, because I didn't know we had more in common outside of Apollo. And I'm going to probably punch someone for not filling me in on that."

Oh geez. I squeezed my eyes shut.

"You know that Seth and I—"

"I know what you guys are," I cut in. "I know a lot about what happened. Deacon filled me in and Seth . . . he talked a little about it."

Her gaze sharpened. "Okay. Then did Seth explain that he and I kind of were seeing each other only for, like, a hot second?"

I shifted uncomfortably. "Well, we didn't really get into that kind of detail."

"I see." She paused, glancing down at her hands. "Seth and I never got together like that."

Something did a wholly inappropriate happy dance in my chest.

"We did fool around a couple of times," she added, lashes lifting, and that something stopped dancing and whipped out Covenant daggers. "But Aiden was my first and he will be the only one."

Oh. That something slowly lowered the daggers.

"Don't get me wrong. I cared about Seth—I still do. Things are . . . weird between us. Complicated isn't even a right enough word, and if you really know what happened, you understand that, right?"

I nodded. "I do."

Alex held my gaze for a moment and then reached up, wrapping her hands around the middle of her hair. "Seth and I never went that far." She started twisting her hair, and *oh my God* again, I did that all the time too. This was so weird. So weird. She twisted her hair into a rope. "But you two . . . ?"

"No. I mean, we were seeing each other, but not . . . not anymore."

She eyed me closely. "Were you guys serious?"

"Yes. I mean, I thought so. I . . . uh, I really cared—" I cut myself off, looking away as I shook my head. "None of that matters."

"I think it matters if you were actually dating Seth and he didn't have sex with you."

My attention swung back to her sharply.

"The Seth I knew would pretty much hump a tree if there was a hole in it," she said, and my nose wrinkled. "And he was never serious about anyone."

"I don't think that really makes me feel better about not having gone there with him," I admitted, and when she opened her mouth, I continued. "Look, what he and I were at one point doesn't matter now."

"Yes. It does." She stopped twisting her hair. "As long as I knew Seth, he didn't get involved seriously with anyone. Like, no one would've been under the misconception that it was serious if it wasn't. Seth didn't do relationships."

Seth apparently still didn't do relationships, and as jealous as I was when it came to Alex, she wasn't the problem. She was in love with Aiden, but that didn't mean Seth hadn't harbored those kinds of feelings for her. It was obvious that he had.

And still did.

And I really did not want to be talking about this with her.

Scrubbing my temples, I tried to come up with a way to say that without being completely rude to the myth, the legend known as Alexandria Andros.

"You really don't want to talk about Seth with me, do you?" she asked.

I glanced over at her, frowning. "Can you read minds?"

Alex tipped her head to the side and laughed. "Nope. But I feel you. I just want to say one thing. I hope that things aren't really over between you two, because Seth . . ." She sat back, exhaling softly. "Seth is . . . he deserves some happiness."

Tears immediately rushed my throat and burned the back of my eyes. I believed the same thing, but I wasn't his source of happiness. I didn't even know what I was to him, but it wasn't that.

"I haven't talked to him. He's avoiding me. I'm not surprised," she said, and then let go of her hair. The thick strands were slow to unwind. "Sorry. You don't want to hear about that."

I sort of, kind of wanted to hear about her and Seth and his avoidance, even though I didn't, but I was a glutton for punishment, so I did.

"So." She scooted forward, dropping her hands to her knees. "Apollo is your father, and he's kind of like my great-great-great-times a million grandfather, so we're kind of, like, related in a really weird, this shouldn't happen in real life sort of way?"

I laughed, unable to help myself. "Yeah, something like that, I guess."

Alex smoothed her palms over denim-clad knees. "So, Deacon and Luke were saying you had no idea what you were until Seth showed—"

An ear-piercingly shrill alarm sounded, silencing Alex. My head jerked up, and Alex was on her feet, her hand snaking around her back. A second later she held a dagger in her hand. I had no idea where she'd gotten it from. Thin air? A nifty hidden pouch? It didn't matter, because I knew what the blaring horn meant.

The Covenant was under attack.

16

*P*acing the length of my room, I tried to work off the pent-up restlessness that was crawling through my system like an army of fire ants. I'd already run five miles, boxed with Solos, showered—rubbed one off in the shower while my mind conjured up a stream of things I'd done with Josie and things I'd never gotten the chance to— and I still couldn't sit still.

Not when I wanted to be across the hall. Not when I wanted to go find Colin and remove his balls with a dull dagger, centimeter by fucking centimeter, because I knew he'd gone to breakfast with her this morning. Wasn't the first time, but usually Deacon and Luke were with them, and that made it different.

And not when I knew Alex and Aiden were roaming this very dorm.

I could feel Alex.

She was a faint hum in the back of my subconscious, like a light far off in the distance, visible but not bright. It was nothing like it had been before, much more muted and a hell of a lot more tolerable. Thank the gods I couldn't feel what she was feeling, because damn, I would need to give myself a lobotomy. Or she and Aiden weren't currently screwing like an Olympian god after a dry spell and that was why I wasn't feeling much. Gods, I hoped that wasn't the case. If I started feeling what was going on with them, I was going to have to—

Sirens blasted, breaking the silence and spinning me around. The shrill sound was all too familiar, and I snapped into action. Vicious excitement replaced the restlessness, and I knew just how screwed up that was, but right then? Oh yeah, I could use a fight. Yesterday in the quad had been child's play.

Grabbing the Glock loaded with titanium bullets, I hooked it into the holster and fit it around my thigh. I snatched the daggers off the dresser and headed out the door, not even bothering with grabbing a shirt.

I came to a complete stop as Josie's door swung open.

What in the holy fuck were Alex and Josie doing together? For just a few seconds, the three of us were literally frozen, staring at each other as the sirens blared overhead.

And then Alex broke the silence.

"Really?" she said dryly, eyeing me with a smirk. "You're going to fight with the awesomeness of your six-pack as a weapon?"

I arched a brow. "Yeah, you know, I was going to test out the whole abs of steel theory thing. The gun attached to my thigh and the daggers in my hands are just props. Mainly for show. Don't want to take away from the gloriousness that is my body, though."

Her smirk flipped into a grin. "Whatever." She started forward. Up ahead, a tall figure stepped out in the hall, and light glinted off the titanium daggers in his hands. Aiden. Of course their room had to be close to mine.

Of. Course.

My gaze shot to Josie. "What do you think you're doing?"

She was in the process of closing the door when she frowned. "I'm going to help—"

"You are going to help by staying safe in your dorm and not answering the door to anyone but me or one of the guys."

"I can fight," she insisted, her cheeks flushing pink. "You saw me yesterday. I know what—"

"Do you hear those sirens?" I lifted my chin to the ceiling. "This isn't a fight between halfs and pures. That means something has gotten inside that shouldn't be inside."

Her blue eyes deepened to storm clouds. "I know that. I can—"

"Do you remember what happened last time?" I stepped to her, my chest and stomach clenching at the memory. "I'm not going to end the night searching you down and finding you like I did last time."

Blood drained from her face. "And last time, I was taken from *your* room. You know, the safe place!"

Well. Shit. She had a point. I shook my head. Time was of the essence here. "Then you don't answer the door unless it's me."

"Seth—"

"Just stay in your room, Josie. You'll be safe there."

"I don't see you telling Alex to stay in her room," she fired back. "Nor did Aiden seem to stop her."

"That's because I know Alex can hold her own." And truth? I also wouldn't lose my shit if Alex got hurt. Josie? I would go nuclear on this gods-damned Covenant and level the place.

Josie stepped back, bumping into the door, and I could tell I'd said something very, very wrong to her. I wasn't quite sure what it was. I'd said a lot of bad shit to her recently, but I didn't have time to really question it. She turned around stiffly and went back into her room.

At least she was staying put.

Hooking the daggers on to the belt, I took off down the hall. When I hit the lobby, I spotted Colin standing with a group of halfs. I started to order him to keep watch over Josie, but I trusted that she'd only open the door for me. I didn't trust that of Colin.

He was a young half, susceptible to compulsions, and I had no idea what was going on out there.

Bursting out the front doors and into the cooler evening air, I made my way past the small army of Guards. They had already begun setting up a line in front of the dorm.

I stopped, grabbing the collar of one of the older Guard members. His eyes widened with surprise as I lifted him up on the tips of his toes. "Try actually defending the students this time. If this line is broken when I get back, I'm not going to be happy, and that means you're not going to be walking for the next week or month. Feel me?"

The older man swallowed hard and nodded. Letting him go, I sure as hell hoped, for his sake, he got the message. Last time, the possessed Guards and Sentinels had gotten right into the dorm and right to Josie.

That knowledge ate at me as I forged forward. After what had happened that night, I'd told myself I wouldn't put duty before Josie, and I was doing it again. A ball of dread settled in my stomach like lead. The nymph's words floated through my thoughts as I cut across the quad, heading for the walls. Was I going down the same path again?

Up ahead, I could see Sentinels racing forward. Smoke billowed from the vicinity of the main wall and spilled into the courtyard. Shadows moved inside the dense smoke, and from a distance it looked like a macabre dance. In about ten seconds, I caught up to Alex and Aiden, and it was more than a little bizarre falling into step beside them. As we drew closer, the scent of burnt trees and something far more pungent filled the air.

Aiden glanced over at me. "Lose your shirt, man?"

Back in the day, that question would've opened the door for the perfect comeback, one that usually involved Alex. Now? I lifted my hand and flipped him off. "Anyone know what's going—?"

A white-garbed Guard staggered out of the smoke, the front of his outfit splashed with red. His throat was torn open, revealing the pink, congealed tissue and shattered bone. The Guard went down on one knee and then crumpled.

"Daimons," Alex said, flipping the dagger in her hand. "Or a mountain lion."

Reaching to my side, I unhooked one of the daggers. "I'm going to go with a daimon."

"That's a relief." Alex slowed her step. "Because I really don't want to kill a kitty."

I paused long enough to look at her. She tossed a grin in my direction.

Aiden moved ahead, throwing up a hand, stopping us. "Hold on a second." He moved his arm, holding his palm out toward the thick smoke. A slight ripple of power sparked. Wind picked up behind us, turning into a heavy, churning gust. The stream moved over the courtyard, lifting the smoke and blowing it back.

Holy shit, there were daimons everywhere, and the titanium gate was open. A few bodies littered the ground and as the wind settled, I realized all those still standing were halfs, which explained why no one had summoned wind yet, and on the ground . . .

Shit.

Dead and/or dying pures.

Some still being fed on, like a scene straight out of a zombie horror.

Aiden looked over his shoulder. "Being able to control all the elements has its bennies."

Huh. Look at Aiden, being all demigod and stuff. "Cute," I said, stepping over a fallen Sentinel. "But can you still fight?"

Alex snorted as a daimon lifted its head from the neck of some damn pure who should've never been out here, thinking he stood a chance. The daimon was a half. There were no razor-sharp teeth or creepy-ass black eyes. The male looked normal. Well, with the exception of the blood pouring from its mouth and the skin stuck between its teeth.

Daimons were such messy eaters.

They chewed and bit to get at the *aether* in the blood and they weren't exactly particular about what area they went for. This one was as cliché as the last one. Had gone straight for the throat. Daimons were drawn to pures because they had more *aether*.

The male tilted its head to the side and sniffed the air. A slow smile split across its gruesome face, and a second later it sprang to its feet. Behind him, several daimons turned toward us.

But demigods and an Apollyon? We were chock-full of *aether* goodness and our appearance was like ringing the damn dinner bell.

"Can I still fight?" Aiden asked, smirking.

Flipping the dagger in my hand, I rolled my eyes. A second later the half daimon rushed Aiden's back, and in the last moment, Aiden spun, kicking his leg out. His booted foot caught the daimon just below the knee, the impact shattering the bone. The daimon went down, and oh yeah, that fucker was going to be out for the count. It started to climb back up, but Aiden caught it in the chest, with a dagger.

Daimons who used to be half-bloods didn't implode in a shimmery dust. When they died, they died like the rest of us. A pile of flesh and bone that looked like any number of dead bodies. This one fell backward, eyes clouding over.

"Yeah," Aiden said. "I can still fight."

"Lucky us," I drawled, moving forward. "What would we do without you?"

However Aiden responded was lost in the shrill, annoying-as-hell scream of an oncoming daimon. It was a pure, and this one looked jacked the hell up. Skin leached of all color. Eyes nothing but black pits. Teeth like a damn shark's.

And it was time to play.

Meeting the daimon head-on, I slipped under its widespread arms and popped up behind it. Landing a kick in the back, I jumped on top of it as it fell, then slammed the dagger deep into its back. The daimon froze and then imploded like a mini-glitter bomb.

I threw myself into the fight. Could've taken that dumbass out with one jab, but nah. I needed to work out the pent-up frustration. I needed to get it out of my system.

So I toyed with them. Pure daimons I took out with a dagger quickly, but I waited for the halfs that were turned—the ones who were trained Guards and Sentinels. They knew how to fight. I went hand-to-hand with them, exchanging blows until each punch started knocking around the bitter emotions gnawing away at my heart. Every so often I caught a burst of power— Alex or Aiden using the elements—and each small surge of energy fueled me.

I turned, coming face to face with a female half with blood smeared across her mouth. One eye was gouged out, probably from coming face to face with another Sentinel. Real attractive.

Grinning, I lowered the daggers.

The half daimon opened her mouth just as blood burst from her chest. The pointed end of a Covenant dagger appeared and then retracted, and the half daimon dropped.

Solos stood behind her. Scratches cut deep into his left cheek. "Sorry. I owed her that." He gestured at his cheek with the bloody end of the dagger. "Not looking to have a matching set."

"No doubt." Wiping my arm across my forehead, I glanced down at my chest. Flecks of blood covered me. "What the hell happened?"

"That cell outside of Rapid City grew—shit." Solos dipped down as a daimon launched itself at him. He rose, slamming the dagger up. "As I was saying," he said, shaking out his damp hair. "Fucking pure Guards couldn't tell when they came to the gate—they were turned Sentinels. Let them right in and then the rest came out of the woods."

Over his shoulder, Alex delivered a powerful roundhouse kick, knocking the teeth out of one of the daimons. "What about the outer walls?"

"Overrun." He grunted, catching a daimon and tossing him my way. "Complete loss, man. Complete loss."

Catching the daimon with one hand on the shoulder, I introduced chest to dagger. Glitter bomb ensued.

"Oh, shit," Solos said.

I lifted my head, unable to figure out his expression as he wiped at the blood on his face with the back of his hand. Yanking the dagger out, I spun around and jerked to a stop. Nearly fell the fuck over. No way. My fucking eyes were deceiving me, because there was no way Josie was standing right in front of me.

Josie

My grip tightened on the dagger I'd picked up from the . . . the man in white. The man who lay unmoving on the ground with his throat absolutely ripped apart. I could see his trachea. I didn't even know what a trachea looked like, but I was pretty sure I could see it. Or his larynx. It had only been after I walked past him that I realized he had daggers and I needed daggers.

I felt bad poaching the dagger from him, but it was heavy and warm in my hand as I forced myself forward, knowing I was making the right choice. I was not a weakness that needed to be hidden away.

I was a mother-freaking demigod.

Like a real demigod, not a ready-made microwave dinner like Alex and Aiden. I was, like, a casserole that took all day to be slow-cooked in a Crock-Pot kind of demigod.

I could fight.

I was not weak.

I could hold my own.

As I stared at the bodies on the ground, some moving or crawling, and some with the pallor of death seeping into their skin, I wasn't entirely sure this was wise, because I . . . I'd never seen anything like this. It was a war zone. Shouts rattled my bones. The metallic scent of blood mingled with smoke. Cries followed my footsteps as my heart pounded.

This wasn't training. This was real. This was what these people lived under the threat of.

Smoke plumed from burnt patches in the soil. I could see Alex and Aiden, fighting side by side, a dynamic duo—an extremely attractive and agile dynamic duo—and further up, there was a half-naked Seth, standing beside Solos. I twisted to the right, my heart stuttering in my chest. *Something* stared at me.

Something as white as a sheet of paper, with all-black eyes and teeth that looked like they belonged on a demonic dog.

Holy crap, what in the hell was that? I stumbled back out of surprise and then understanding struck me. A daimon—holy crap, that's what a pure-blooded daimon looked like! I could see a daimon for what it was now, and oh my *gods*, they were not pretty.

It sniffed the air like a dog, legs tensing. Then the thing launched off the ground like it had rockets under its feet, coming right at me.

Darting to the side, I spun around as its bare feet kicked up loose soil and dirt. The thing twisted and shot toward me.

This isn't training. This isn't training.

Air froze in my lungs as I planted my left leg behind me. *I'm not weak.* The daimon landed right in front of me. *I can hold my own.* I sprang forward, using my back leg to propel me. Pulse pounding, I held tight onto the dagger as I whipped around the daimon. Our arms brushed, and I dipped down, swiping out with my legs.

The daimon went down, sprawling onto its back as I popped up. Instinct took over, and I raised the dagger. I didn't think as I brought it down, slamming it into the chest. The dagger went through the torn shirt and into the chest cavity as if the daimon's skin was made of water. There was little or no effort behind it. I couldn't believe it. The dagger went clean through, nearly to the ground.

It jerked, back bowing, and then imploded in a shower of glittering dust. It happened so fast I nearly fell forward, catching my balance before I stumbled through whatever was left of the daimon.

"Holy crap," I whispered, and then coughed out a startled laugh. I did it. I totally did it, and Seth—he thought I couldn't do this, take out a daimon. But I did it!

Empowered by my proven badassery, I headed toward the group, where they were still fighting the remaining daimons. Seth took out a daimon, and like the one I got, it exploded into a strange shimmer. My gaze connected with Solos's.

"Oh shit," Solos said.

Seth spun around, and I swear he almost fell over. Shock splashed across his face, and then his eyes went luminous, a deep burning tawny.

Uh-oh.

Bare-chested and speckled with blood and God knows what else, Seth prowled toward me. "Please tell me I was knocked over the head and I'm seeing shit, because—"

A blood-curdling scream raised the hairs all over my body. I spun around, and inhaled sharply. A female Sentinel rushed me. Blood covered her face like a gruesome smear of red lipstick. Her blue eyes were unfocused, glazed over. There were no daggers in her hands. She shrieked again, and a part of me knew she wasn't friendly, but she didn't look like the—

"Josie!" Seth shouted, springing forward, and it all happened so fast.

Stepping into her attack, like I'd done before, I started to dip down to take her legs out, but she spun on me, forcing me back a step. Her arm cocked and she screamed again, swinging like a pro—like she knew exactly how to deliver a debilitating blow. I dodged the blow and thrust my arm back, about to shove the dagger forward, but I . . .

I hesitated.

Oh my *gods*, I froze for a second. Wrong, totally bad move, but she looked like any other Sentinel. She looked mortal. *Human*. Not some deranged Greek creature hell-bent on gnawing on me like a chew toy.

A dagger exploded out of the center of her chest, cutting off her chilling scream. Blood sprayed the front of my shirt. I didn't move, couldn't, as she fell forward, and all I heard was the sickening suctioning sound of the dagger being yanked out.

Alex stood there, her wavy hair a wild halo around her. "Were you going to hug her or something?"

"I'm done," Seth growled.

I had no idea what Seth meant, but he sheathed his daggers and then stepped forward, raising his right arm. An amber glow surrounded his bicep as the glyphs rushed to the surface of his skin. The light, the color of his eyes, wrapped down his arm like a shining cord. Energy filled the air as he summoned *akasha*.

Seth was deadly and quick with dispatching the remaining daimons. Spinning as fluidly as any trained dancer, he moved his arm like he was tossing a baseball, hitting each remaining daimon wicked fast. The moment the amber light hit them, they ceased to exist. There a second, gone the next. Nothing, not even a shimmery dust. Same for the half daimons.

"Well, that works too," Alex said dryly, "but less fun."

Seth's expression was locked down as he faced us, walking back to Aiden and Solos. He said nothing as he curled his hand around mine, the grip tight but not painful. Our eyes met.

No words were necessary to convey the message.

I was in so much trouble.

17

*N*ever in my life had I wanted to lock a woman up in a titanium-encased room with an army of Hades's Guards. Actually, that wasn't entirely true. I'd wanted to do that a time or two with Alex, something Aiden would've been a hundred percent behind.

But it was different this time, because it was . . .

It was Josie.

"You guys got this handled from here?" I asked.

Aiden glanced down at where my hand was wrapped firmly around Josie's. "There isn't much left to do except . . ." He glanced around, frowning. "Clean up."

"We got this," Alex confirmed, her gaze darting to Josie. She shifted her weight from one foot to the next. "You okay with this?"

I cocked my head to the side. Did she legit just ask Josie if she was okay with *this*?

"Yeah." Josie started to turn away but stopped. She extended her arm, offering the dagger. "I, um, took this from a Guard who . . . didn't need it anymore. It's not mine."

Solos looked up from where he was checking out a fallen Sentinel. "You take out a daimon with it?"

She glanced down at the dagger and then nodded, surprising me. "Yeah, I . . . I took out a daimon with it."

"Then it's yours," he said, sighing as he rose, brushing his hands off on his pants.

"Oh," she whispered, and for a moment I was sort of struck stupid by the fact that she had managed to kill a daimon. And as I stared at Josie, her expression said she was also a bit surprised by it too.

The dread that had formed in my gut earlier now churned viciously. Completely stupid, but there was a huge part of me that didn't like that she had killed a daimon, that she was even in the situation where it had to go down. Damn stupid. Because Josie had been created to be a weapon. There'd be a lot of killing in her future.

"Well, there you go." I steered Josie around. "Check you guys later."

Josie grumbled something under her breath when I started walking, tugging her along with me.

"Seth, this isn't—"

"Not yet." My voice was a low warning. "I don't really trust myself to speak to you right now."

Her gasp of outrage was audible as I led her around a dead daimon. "I think you're completely overreacting!"

"And I think you don't understand the words I just spoke to you."

She tried to pull her hand free. She didn't get anywhere. "You do realize that I've been training to fight? And that I'm a demigod? Oh, yeah, that's right! You haven't been around to know—"

"*Gods*," I stopped suddenly, causing Josie to stumble. I caught her other arm, steadying her. "Do you have any idea what I felt when I turned around and saw you standing there with a damn dagger in your hand?"

Her gaze searched mine intently. "But that's my duty."

"I don't care." And the moment the words were out, they were the damn truth. "You're not ready for this." I dropped her arm and gestured to the mess around us. "And you could've been hurt. Or worse yet, this could've been a trap and one of the damn Titans could have been blowing through the Covenant right now, and if that had happened again, I would've—" I cut myself off, unable to go there. My heart felt like it had stopped when I saw her, and it still felt like it was trying to recuperate.

"You what?" She sucked in a soft breath. "Why do you even care? You—"

"You don't get it." Twisting around, I started walking again, pulling her along behind me. We made it past the main Covenant building before she spoke again.

"You don't need to hold my hand."

I shot her a look. "Apparently I need to. If not, who knows where you might end up?"

"I'm not a child," she spat. "I don't need a babysitter."

I snorted. "Yeah, I beg to differ on that account."

Josie tried to pull her hand free again. The end result was the same as before. "You lost your hand-holding privileges, Seth."

"Holding hands is a privilege?"

"Damn straight it is." Her hand squeezed mine until the bones in my hand started to grind together. "Especially with me, and if I remember correctly, you said you were done with me."

I sighed. "Josie—"

"And you told me not to embarrass myself," she continued, her voice rising as we passed a group of Guards. "You've said that you didn't want to do *any of this* with me anymore. So, you don't—"

Stopping suddenly, I faced her as I pulled her to me, chest to chest. I wasn't thinking as I cupped her cheek with my free hand and tilted her head back. Not a single thought occurred when I lowered my mouth to hers.

I kissed Josie.

She stiffened against me, and I marveled at the softness of her lips, the sweet taste of her mouth. Fuck. It had been weeks since I'd held her like this. Kissed her. Tasted her. Her chest rose sharply against mine, and in the back of my head, I knew this wasn't right. My chest was covered with blood. So was hers. People moved around us, and I'd hurt her once before, in ways she didn't even realize.

None of that stopped me.

The tip of her tongue touched mine and the punch of arousal nearly took my knees out from under me. I groaned into her mouth as I slid my hand back into her hair. The kiss deepened, and it was a nearby shout that brought me to my senses. I lifted my mouth from hers, leaving a hairsbreadth between us.

"What . . . ?" she murmured.

My lips brushed hers as I spoke. "It was the only thing I could think of to get you to stop talking."

Tension locked up her muscles. "That . . . that is really wrong."

Yeah, she was right.

Drawing back, I realized how lucky I was that she hadn't stabbed me with the dagger she now clenched in her right hand.

Lips tingling, walking was a bit harder now, but I kept hold of her left hand, and she was quiet. Kissing worked. But at what cost? I shouldn't have done that. I'd hurt her again.

And I was as hard as a titanium dagger.

Gods.

The dorm came into view, thank the gods, and the Guard I'd threatened on the way out looked relieved when I passed him by without introducing his head to his own asshole. Lifting my free hand, I tapped into the wind element and opened the doors for us. The act didn't draw attention from the halfs and pures congregating in the lobby, separated by a—oh shit.

I stopped short. So did Josie, and she stared at the same thing I did. A very new addition to the lobby, in the form of three statues. Each of them was about seven feet tall, made of pure marble. They looked like three angels praying, hands folded demurely under their chins and wings tucked close to their backs. Expressions serene for now, but I knew if that stone started to crack, the looks on their faces would be far from that.

"What . . . what are those?" Josie breathed.

"Furies," I said. "A problem we really don't need right now."

Josie blinked. "Furies? Is Erin in there?"

"I don't think so. Probably three of her million sisters." I led her around the statues, giving them a wide berth. "They appear whenever the gods are displeased with something. They serve as a warning even though they are entombed for right now."

"A warning?"

"That if whatever is going down that has them pissed off doesn't stop, they'll release the furies, and these kind aren't going to be like Erin. They're going to rip through everything and everyone in their paths." As we walked through the lobby, she was craning her neck to stare at them. "My guess is the gods are pissed about what's going on between the halfs and pures, but that may be giving them too much credit. Not like they ever cared before."

Josie was quiet as I led her down the hall, and when we came up on our rooms I made a split-second decision and brought her into my room. I let go of her hand the moment the door closed. She halted just inside the sitting area of the room. "What am I doing in here?"

Good question. "Just stay put for a few moments, then I'll take you to your room."

She stared at me balefully as I stalked past her. Damn. A pissed-off Josie was still an incredibly hot one. The hardness wasn't going down anytime soon, which was whatever, because I was a walking hard-on anyway. Once inside the bathroom, I grabbed the towel and ran it under the tap. Wiping the blood off my chest, I walked back into the main room, finding her where I'd left her.

"I'm surprised you actually listened."

"I . . ." She faded off as her gaze tracked my hand and the towel before looking away, focusing on what appeared to be my shoulder. "I didn't stay because you told me to."

"Of course not," I murmured.

Her nose wrinkled. "I stayed because I think we need to clear the air between us."

"Is that so?" I tossed the towel onto the back of the chair.

Josie stepped away from the door and placed the dagger on the coffee table, then stepped back, wiping her right hand on the side of her jeans. Then, slowly, her gaze lifted to mine. "I know what happened between us."

My stomach clenched. "Josie—"

"No," she stated the word so strongly, so firmly that it caught my attention. Silenced me. "You're going to listen to me, because I deserve that. Do you understand me?"

I totally understood that my dick was pressing against the zipper of my pants at a very inappropriate time. Jaw working, I nodded.

"At first, I didn't understand. I was shocked, because I thought . . ." She swallowed hard before continuing. "It doesn't matter what I thought, and I want to get one thing straight. I'm not telling you any of this because I expect pity or any real explanation. I'm telling you this because we're going to have to work together. We're going to be seeing each other around, and I don't want to worry about things being weird and awkward."

"Okay."

Her eyes flashed. "And we need to establish some boundaries—rules about what you can and cannot do with me and how you will speak to me."

My brows inched up my forehead, but I kept my mouth shut, because the hard glint to her eyes told me she sort of wanted to cut me.

"All right?" When I nodded, she exhaled roughly. "I know you're still . . . um, hung up on Alex."

I stared at her a moment, unsure if I'd really heard her correctly. Okay. I did hear her right. Maybe she was joking. Based on the seriousness with which she delivered it, I was going to go with the fact she was being serious.

She lowered her gaze as she twisted her hands together. "I mean, obviously you're still attracted to other people. Duh, but I get that what runs deeper is reserved for her."

"Wait. What?" I said, snapping out of it.

She moved back and sat on the edge of the chair. "I mean, it totally makes sense now, and I feel like an idiot for not seeing it before. I get that you're in . . . in love with her and—"

I laughed. I couldn't help it. Holy shit.

Her eyes narrowed. "I don't think this is funny."

"It kind of is, trust me."

"No, it's not." She popped to her feet, and at her sides her hands balled. "You can stand there and laugh, because you're either a jerk-face or in complete denial, but I saw the way you looked at her—"

"The way I looked at her?" Incredulous, I stared at her.

"When she first showed up on the quad, you stared at her like you—you never expected to see her again."

"Because I really was hoping not to," I admitted, brows furrowing.

"I totally understand that. I mean, trust me, I get it." Her arms folded across her stomach. "Seeing someone you want and can't have—"

"That's not the reason, Josie. I am not in love with Alex." I stared at her a moment. "I was never in love with her. It wasn't like that between us."

"You're saying there wasn't anything there? That you felt nothing for her?" she challenged.

Part of me couldn't believe we were having this conversation. Turning away, I shoved my hand through my hair, clasping the back of my neck. "Of course I felt something for her, but it wasn't that. It wasn't what she felt for Aiden or he felt for her."

"Maybe you don't even realize it," she said after a moment, her voice quiet. "But I see it. I get—"

"I don't know what the hell you're seeing." I whipped around, chest rising heavily. "It has nothing to do with her—with Alex! It has nothing to do with you."

Closing her eyes, she shook her head as she turned her cheek, and there was a second where I realized that if I let her believe this, everything would be easier, but that's not what I did.

"Gods, Josie. Do you really think I see you and her as the same? Alex is Alex and my past with her is in the past, but you—you are *everything*."

Her blue eyes were so big they nearly swallowed her face. "I'm everything? If that's the case, then I don't understand. Why wouldn't you want to be with me? Why would—" Her voice cracked, and I hated that, and couldn't stop myself. I stepped toward her, but she held up her hand. "How could I be everything to you when you broke my heart?"

"What?" I stopped. Everything stopped as I stared at her.

Josie shook her head as she pressed the heel of her hand

to her chest. "I can't be your everything. You would be with me. You would, and I wouldn't be feeling like this. My heart wouldn't be broken." Eyes glittering like sapphires, she took a step back. "If I was everything to you, you'd love me as much as I love you."

18

Josie

Oh my God.

My words echoed in the silence, bouncing back and forth between us. I couldn't believe I'd said that out loud. What was I thinking? I had no control over what I was going to say.

I was going to punch my own mouth.

Seth tilted his head to the side as he stared at me. "What did you just say?"

Taking another step back, I glanced at the door. Could I make a run for it? Seth could definitely catch me, but right now, he probably didn't want to.

"Josie?"

My heart stuttered at the raw quality of his voice. I wanted to deny that I'd uttered those words, but I couldn't. How could I when it was the truth, and it wasn't like I could take those words back. I couldn't.

Lowering my hand, I drew in a shallow breath. "I love you; I'm in love with you."

Seth jerked like I'd punched him. "You can't love me."

My mouth dropped open. "There you go again! Telling me what I can do and not do! Telling me how I feel. Stop doing that."

"But I . . ." He shook his head. "I'm at a loss to what to say."

"Well, that's a first," I said dryly, but the fact he had no idea what to say stung as if I'd stepped on a hornets' nest. "I don't even know why I told you that. Not like I haven't embarrassed myself enough when it comes to you. I don't even know why I'm in love with you. You're an ass. And I have shitty taste in—"

"Stop." He shot in front of me, moving so fast I didn't see him until we were face to face. "Please just . . . I . . . I don't know what to say, Josie."

I winced, feeling what he was saying all the way to the core. "That . . . that says everything, Seth, because if you don't—" My voice cracked, right along with what was left of my heart. "If you don't know what to say, then that's it."

"You don't understand." His voice was low. "I don't understand anything." Heart aching, I stepped to the side, but Seth followed.

"Please, just let me go. We can forget we even had—"

He clasped my cheeks in a gentle grasp. "No one has ever told me that before."

"What?" I whispered after a moment.

His eyes were wide, slightly dilated. "No one has ever said they loved me or were in love with me, and actually meant it."

I couldn't believe that. Not even his mother? Yes, that was a different kind of love, but then I remembered how his mom was and once again I found myself wishing she was alive so I could bitch-slap her into eternity. But to live the years he had, and to never experience any kind of love wasn't just wrong, it was sad. I wished it wasn't so.

Seth's hands slid down my neck, stopping where his thumbs pressed against my pulse. "But you . . ."

I had a choice here. I recognized that. I could save face and let this go. I could pull away and walk out of this room, but I was hurting for myself and despite everything that had gone on between us, I was still hurting for him. Maybe that. "But I love you."

Seth's hands shook—*his* hands. Hands that were always so steady in battle, but they trembled now, touching me. "I don't deserve that from anyone, but especially from you." Voice rough and heavy, he searched my face intently. "That is a precious gift that I . . . that I am not worthy of."

I sucked in air. Oh gosh, that hurt. Hearing him say that tore me up, ripped me right apart, and it struck me then. I knew why he had backed off. Him pushing me away had nothing to do with Alex or with me. It was because of him, because of how he believed he deserved nothing more than punishment.

That he sincerely believed that the only thing he had was to atone for his past sins.

Tears pricked my eyes as I folded my hands over his wrists. I had to prove what he believed wasn't true.

Prove that he was the total of everything he'd done and not just the dark things he was ashamed of, and I would do so, because I loved him and accepted him for who he was, for all his faults. That was what love meant.

Love fostered courage.

Stretching up on the tips of my toes, I braced myself, gripped his wrists tighter and leaned in, kissing him softly. He stiffened and then tried to pull back, but I followed, the whole time my stomach twisting and fluttering like a hundred hummingbirds had taken flight.

"You're wrong," I told him, settling back on my feet. "You're so wrong about so much, Seth."

Thick lashes lowered, shielding those extraordinary eyes that held a wealth of secrets. I lowered his hands and started walking backward, toward his bedroom. I didn't let myself think of what I was doing, what I was about to initiate.

"You deserve me," I told him, and he didn't argue. He appeared to be struck silent. "I've told you that before, in this very room. I wasn't lying then. Nothing has changed. You deserve me."

He flinched once more. "Josie, I—"

I silenced him with a kiss and I threw everything I was feeling into it, every ounce of love and hope and all the hurt I felt when he'd pushed me away and all the ache his words created now. I kissed him like I would never do it again.

"You're worthy of love." My pulse was all over the place as I pushed him back and down on the edge of the bed. "You're more than worthy of my love."

Seth watched me with bright eyes as I placed a knee on either side of him and climbed into his lap. I lowered myself down and I felt him, hard and straining against the rough material of his tactical pants.

Letting go of his wrists, I took a deep breath and grabbed the hem of my soiled shirt. I pulled it off over my head before I lost the courage. Seth's chest rose with a sharp inhale as I let the material fall to the side.

He said nothing, but his hands landed on my hips. I took that as a positive sign.

Fingers trembling, I reached behind and unhooked my bra. I held my breath as the straps slipped down my arms and then fell to the floor. Wasn't like he hadn't seen all of this before, but I was never the initiator and I'd never felt more vulnerable in my life. My newfound courage would falter if he pushed me away now.

Seth didn't move for several moments, and then his eyes closed. My heart skipped a beat. He lowered his head, pressing his cheek against my breast. The slight stubble along his jaw abraded the sensitive skin, causing me to shiver.

"You . . . you are truly a goddess," he said, his hands sliding off my hips to my lower back. "Sometimes I'm not entirely convinced you're real."

My lips parted on a soft inhale. "I'm real."

"You feel like a dream." He turned his head slightly, nuzzling the hollow between my breasts. "Like I'm going to wake up one day and realize none of this was ever real."

I cupped the back of his head, threading my fingers through the short strands of his hair as I lowered my chin, kissing the top of his head. I didn't trust myself to speak then because I was afraid I'd start crying and that would really deter where I was trying to go with all of this.

"Or that this," he continued, lifting his head and looking up at me, "will turn into a nightmare and you will end up hating me with every fiber of your being."

"Never," I promised, sliding my hand to his cheek.

His eyes glowed. "And you can be so sure of that, Josie?"

Instead of answering, I found one of his hands and brought it to my breast. My heart pounded so fast that I feared demigods could have heart attacks.

Seth's gaze dropped to his hand, and when I let go, he didn't. He drew his thumb over the tip, eliciting a gasp from me. "What are we doing?"

I thought it was pretty obvious. "I want you."

He groaned as if he were in pain. "Not as badly as I want you."

I shivered at his words. "Then have me."

A long moment of silence passed between us, and I had no idea which way he was going to go with this. Sex wasn't a cure-all. I'd progressed enough in my psychology studies to know that, and hey, I had some common sense, but it was the most . . . perfect way for *me* to show just how much I did love him.

Seth's gaze lowered, a moment passed, and he said, "I can do this."

I didn't really understand what he meant and I didn't get the chance to ask either, because he stood suddenly, lifting me into the air like I weighed nothing and I sure as hell weighed something.

Gasping, I held onto his shoulders and wrapped my legs around his hips as he turned around so my back was to the bed.

One hand fisted my hair and he dragged my head down so our mouths were lined up. "Are you sure?"

It was crazy. We'd barely talked for weeks and when we did, we'd argued. I didn't think my first time would be like this. Maybe after dinner or a movie or after snuggling, but none of that mattered to me. *Seth* mattered to me. Proving to him that love was a gift which he was worthy of mattered to me.

I closed my eyes. "I've never been more sure."

Seth had me.

One second he was holding me and then he was kissing me, his tongue tangling with mine, and there was no slow build-up. Our teeth gnashed together, but I didn't care. He let go of my hair and both hands gripped my hips. He lifted me away from him and in a split second my back hit the bed.

And he was on me.

It was rather impressive how quickly he got my pants off, even when they'd gotten hung up around my sneakers. My panties came next and then his boots and pants. He stepped away long enough to grab a condom out of the nightstand, tossing it on the bed beside us.

Seth stood at the end of the bed, his erection jutting out, so thick and hard that for a moment I felt a nugget of trepidation. This . . . this might be a wee bit painful.

Worth it.

But painful.

He reached down, wrapping his hand around my foot. "There isn't an inch of you that I don't want to savor." He drew my legs apart, baring everything, and I fought the natural urge to hide myself. "Not a single inch of skin that I don't want to taste."

"Oh. Oh my . . ." That was all I could say. My brain broke.

One side of his lips kicked up, proving that the Seth I knew was still there. That cocky half-grin was as infuriating as it was sexy.

I watched, muscles tightening low in my stomach, as he came at me from the foot of the bed. He started at my ankle, kissing and licking his way up my leg, lingering at the surprisingly sensitive spot behind my knee before continuing up my thigh. My breath was coming out in sort-of pants, and when he reached the crease of my thigh, he ran his tongue along the crease, creating a rush of dampness. Then he started all the way down on the other leg.

He made a sound against my inner thigh, like a purr, and then he nipped at the skin. My hands fisted the comforter and my hips rolled. Seth moved up, dropping those hot, wet kisses over my belly and then my breasts. His fingers and then his tongue moved on the hardened nipples, and it wasn't long before I was grasping the back of his head, my body moving restlessly, wanting and seeking oh-so-much more.

"Seth," I urged, grabbing his arm and trying to pull him down on me.

"I'm savoring." He worked his way back down, his tongue dipping into my belly button. "Patience, Josie."

I was breathing heavy. "I'm out of patience."

He chuckled against the fluttering section just below my navel. "We're going to have to work on that."

"No," I protested. "We do not need to work on that right now."

Seth paused just over the space between my thighs and lifted his head. The slow grin that tugged at his lips sort of made me want to kiss him . . . and punch him. "You sure about that?"

"Yes."

One brow rose as he curled a hand around my thigh, spreading my legs further. "Now, Josie, you know what they say."

"I don't care what anyone says right now."

"You should. Good things come to those who wait."

A laugh caught in my throat. "I've waited. You've waited. It's time for the good things."

Seth's gaze dropped. "Damn. I so agree on that."

He dipped his head and my back arched as a strangled cry erupted from my throat. Good *gods*, I couldn't breathe as he teased and tasted, nipped and sucked. There was no room for thinking, only feeling, and with each thrust of his tongue, my body rose. Moans escaped me. Desire pounded through me, mixing with something far deeper. Emotion swelled in my chest, and when he lifted his head again and pierced me with those amber eyes, I knew there would never be anyone else for me.

"There has only been you," I told him even as warmth splashed across my cheeks. "There will only *be* you, Seth."

His features sharpened and then he surged over me, that hungry near-haunted gaze fixed on mine. I trembled as he reached for the condom. I ached as I watched him roll it on.

He held my stare as he reached between us, easing a finger through the gathering wetness. "This is mine."

It wasn't a question. Oh gods, that was a statement, but I nodded, because it was his. I was his. Like my skin was branded with his scent and aura, I was *his*.

He circled his fist around the base of his erection. "This is yours."

I was more than thrilled to hear that.

Seth brought his mouth to mine, his tongue delving, matching the thrusts of his finger and then his fingers, quickly working me back to the point where I felt like I would explode into nothing. He pulled away just before, and I whimpered, but then I felt him, just the tip, pressing against me.

My heart pounded wildly as his gaze found mine once again. "I don't want to hurt you," he said, voice hoarse as he moved his hand away. "It's the last thing I want to do."

"I trust you."

Skin puckered between Seth's brows as he squeezed his eyes shut. He didn't move, and I wasn't even sure he breathed. He was going to pull back. I sensed it, and I couldn't let him do that.

Gripping his hips, I lifted mine before I could really think about what I was doing. A gasp punched out of me as I stretched around him.

Seth groaned as the muscles in his arms bulged. "Gods, Josie, I'm trying to take this slow."

"I don't want you to take it slow."

His laugh was strangled. "You're going to kill me."

My heart pounded fast. "I don't want that."

"I know." He slid a hand down to my thigh, lifting my leg slightly. The arm beside my head trembled as his intense gaze searched my face. "I need . . . I need this to be perfect for you."

I licked my lips. "It . . . it already is, because it's with you."

Seth's forehead dropped to mine as a shudder rocked his body. Neither of us moved or spoke for what felt like a tiny piece of eternity, and then he kissed me softly, and there was something infinitely sweet in the way his mouth moved over mine. The hand on my upper thigh shook once more and then his hips thrust forward, all the way.

Air lodged in my throat, pushing out the soft cry as my fingers dug into his sides. A dart of pain shot through me as I squeezed my eyes shut, giving way to a burning sensation that wasn't exactly painful. I didn't know how to describe it. Adjectives failed me. There was a deep pressure inside me, neither uncomfortable nor entirely pleasant.

Seth shifted his arms and his elbows dug into the mattress as his large hands cradled the sides of my face. Deep inside me, only his chest moved against mine and only his thumbs glided over my cheeks. Tears burned my eyes, but not from pain, because it really wasn't that bad. Oh no, there was a deep and tender emotion swelling in my chest.

"Josie?"

Throat dry, I swallowed and opened my eyes. My breath caught again at the sight of him. His face was tense and those amber eyes were luminous, so bright they'd outshine any star in the sky. He was waiting for me, making sure I was all right, and nothing could set me more at ease. "I'm okay."

"Thank the gods," he grunted, voice strained.

Seth began to move then.

He flexed his hips, pulling out slowly. The pull, the friction of the act, sent my pulse skittering. My muscles locked up. He smoothed his thumb along my lower lip. "Relax. I need you to relax, okay?"

"Okay," I whispered, forcing myself not to be so . . . so stiff.

He pushed in again, seated deep, and I was pretty sure my nails were scratching his skin. With a moan that sent shivers down my spine, he lowered his mouth to mine. He held himself still again as he parted my lips. The kiss started out slow, leisurely, as if he had all the time in the world, and I got a little lost in that kiss. The burn eased off, but the pressure increased, becoming a pulse that demanded more.

I tentatively wiggled my hips, stopping when a harsh groan brushed my lips.

"You don't have to stop," he said. "You want to move, *agapi*, you move. You do exactly what you want, because there isn't a damn thing you can do wrong."

Agapi.

Love.

A word I wouldn't have understood before the demigod abilities had been unlocked, but I did now.

The endearment warmed me, and I did want to move. So I did. I arched my hips, moving them in a small circle. The act sent tiny coils of pleasure radiating out from my core, and Seth remained still, his forehead against mine as I grew accustomed to the feel of him.

Growing bold, I dragged my hands up his back and down, over the tense muscles of his lower back and further south. He made that sound again, and when he tilted his hips, it was my turn to moan.

Seth shifted his weight onto one arm as he moved his hips, sliding back and forth slowly and then faster, deeper. His hand cradled my hip, steadying me as he thrust forward, eliciting a sharp cry of pleasure from me.

He shuddered at the sound. I gripped his shoulders as I wrapped my legs around his waist. A rough curse burst from him as he went deeper. He moved in a rhythm that drove me crazy and was not enough and too much at the same time.

"Seth . . ." My hands spasmed over the muscles flexing and rolling along his spine. "Oh, *gods* . . ."

His back bowed and his lips moved down my throat and further, to the tip of my breast. I jerked, back arching, and that pace he was setting picked up, became feverish. Molten lava flowed in my veins as bolts of biting pleasure shot out.

"Gods," he groaned; his mouth was near my temple now and he was moving so fast, his hips slamming into mine. "This," he said, dragging his hand down my belly, to the place between my legs, just above where we were connected. "This is what I want. Nothing else. No one else."

"Yes," I gasped out, and I might've repeated the same word over and over, in a way that would've been embarrassing if I cared at that moment, but I didn't.

Seth was doing things with his fingers I didn't even know were possible.

He was everywhere—his hands, his mouth—on me, in me, and it was too much. I couldn't keep up. I didn't need to. My head was spinning and the intensity of the bliss building inside me heightened to the point my hips jerked clear off the bed.

I threw my head back, screaming his name as everything came apart. Release exploded and it was shattering, lighting up every cell, and the pleasure rolled out in tight, sensual shockwaves, obliterating my senses. I heard myself tell him that I loved him and I told him in a crazy, abandoned way, in a voice I didn't recognize.

Seth's restraint broke. No longer holding himself back, the pump of his hips lost all rhythm as he shoved his arm under my lower back. He lifted me up, sealing me tight to him as he ground against me, sending another wave of exquisite pleasure. He extended his other arm, up my back, holding me off the bed as his hips pounded forward. His strength was overwhelming. He held me up and he took me like I . . . like I wanted to be taken. The moment was incredible, like nothing I'd ever experienced before.

Then he was on me, pressing me down into the mattress, not an inch of space separating us as he kissed me hard. His hips jerked once and then twice, and then I could feel him pulsing.

Seth said my name against my lips, and it felt like forever passed while our hearts slowed and the sweat cooled on our skin. "Are you okay?" he asked.

"Perfect," I murmured. "So perfect that I can't . . . even move or think."

He chuckled and then he finally moved. He lifted his head and pressed a kiss to my forehead and then my brow. He dropped a kiss on each eyelid and then the tip of my nose before he found my mouth, and *gods*, when he kissed me it was the sweetest, tenderest thing ever. It spoke those three words I'd said, but he hadn't. That kiss said it all and more.

Not only did it say love.

It spelled hope.

Seth

Lying on my side with Josie tucked to my front, I told myself over and over again that I could do this with her.

But I had to do this right.

Josie snuggled against me, wiggling her bottom against my groin, and fuck, I'd been hard since she fell asleep, and each time she moved it sent a jolt straight from my dick to my spine. Curling my arm around her waist, I held her tighter, unwilling to wake her.

She was worn out, falling asleep minutes after I had gotten rid of the condom and brought a warm, wet cloth to her, washing away the evidence that there had been no one else before. Not that I needed to see that to know, but gods, there was a knot in the base of my throat that wasn't easing off. I wanted to worship her all over again.

Sex had never been like this. Nothing in my life had ever been like this. Everything from the moment I'd met Josie had been a new experience for me. She was truly a miracle and even the simple act of lying beside her soothed me.

I was awake, but my body was at ease. My mind was a different story.

I can do this.

I'd been so close to telling her what I'd done, and the guilt from keeping that secret from her churned my stomach, but I . . . I could rectify that.

I can do this.

Gods, there was no other way for me. I had to control myself. I had to make sure I never allowed myself to get to the point where I took from her what was never mine to take. I could never allow myself to feed off her again.

Josie loved me.

Holy shit.

I dropped my head, pressing a kiss to her bare shoulder. Josie *loved* me. Not a single part of me doubted that. I didn't deserve that gift, but I could . . . I could be better for her. I could be worthy of her love.

That was what I had to do.

I *would* be worthy of her love.

Because she was more than worthy of that. She deserved more than that, and I would give that to her. There would be no room for anything else, because after this—after having her, after knowing that she was mine—there was no way I could stay away from her.

So I would do right by her.

Even if it killed me.

Kissing her neck, I smiled when she murmured something that sounded distinctively like "cupcakes" under her breath. I was surprised it wasn't "bacon" since I was sure she dreamt of that stuff. I kissed her cheek and then settled my head on the pillow.

Josie wiggled again, and I swallowed a groan. I wanted her again, but this, the quiet moments between us, with both of us lying together were fucking bliss. There were no other words for it.

Never would be. This was a piece of beautiful paradise, something I would treasure when it came time to pay my dues.

But a cold voice whispered, sending unease down my spine. *Will it last?*

19

In the middle of the night, I woke up, and this time I wasn't selfless. I was hard and nestled against the curve of her ass. I had no idea what time it was or what was going on outside these walls, and I really didn't care.

Everything was focused on the soft body in my arms.

I was going to wake up Josie in the best possible way.

I coasted my hand over her waist and then her hip, my fingers dipping between her thighs. I found that spot, dragging my thumb over the tiny piece of flesh. Her thighs parted and her moan was sleepy. I shifted my hand, sliding my finger inside.

Grinning in the dark, I forged a path of kisses down her neck as I rocked my hips forward. She was starting to move against my hand in a slow restless circle. Her breaths picked up and I felt the moment she came fully awake. Her head kicked back against my chest and her hand fluttered to where mine played between those pretty thighs.

"Seth," she moaned, her voice husky. "That . . . that feels amazing."

"It's going to feel even better, sweetheart."

Her chest rose sharply as I curled my other hand around her breast, finding the hardened nipple. She was sensitive there, and as I worked the little nub between my thumb and finger, her hips moved wildly.

I rolled away long enough to reach inside the nightstand and grab another foil packet. I broke records getting that condom on. Josie started to turn, but I stopped her. Curling my body behind hers, I slid my hand down her side to her thigh. I lifted her leg, draping it over mine.

"I . . . I don't know what to do," she admitted.

"Shh. You just being right here is doing everything." I kissed the space below the nape of her neck. My heart pounded wicked fast. "I'll take care of the rest."

Lining our hips up, I entered her from behind, careful to take it slow, because I wasn't sure if she was sore or not, and she'd stiffened at first, relaxing after I held still. I gave her time to adjust and then worked my way in, inch by inch, until I was seated.

"Oh my gods," she gasped. "You feel . . . this feels different."

I brought my hand back to that bundle of nerves just above where we were connected. "Better?"

"Yes." A soft, feminine sound left her as I withdrew slowly, to where only the tip was left in, and then I slid back in. "Deeper," she murmured. "This is so much deeper."

"Wait until I get you on your knees." I started rocking faster, moving my thumb and finger over her center in tune to my thrusts.

"Oh gods."

"You're going to love that." I groaned as she thrust that ass back against me. "Fuck. I think you love this."

"I do," she moaned, grasping my arm.

Her soft moans and my harsher grunts soon filled the dark room, and the sounds of our bodies coming together heightened the tension building inside me.

A gnawing ache stirred in my gut and spread to my chest. A very different kind of hunger took root. It would be so easy to just have a taste—a small, insignificant taste. I'd just have to move my other hand from her breast and I could—

No.

Shutting that part of me down, I focused on how she fit me like a glove, how she rolled her hips back against my thrusts with abandonment. I focused on how her movements were slightly awkward and untrained, and how that was so much fucking hotter than anything. I focused on her love and her trust until that ache receded and the only thing I felt was her and not what was in her.

It wasn't easy, but I did it, and hell, there was no way I was going to last long. I wanted to. I wanted to stay deep inside her for fucking hours. She was so damn tight and hot that she branded me, and yeah, this wasn't going to last long.

A powerful release rolled down my spine, and when she found hers her body contracted around mine in a way that tossed me right over the edge, burying my face into the side of her neck as I came. Like the one earlier, the release fucking wrecked me. It was never-ending, and by the time my pulse slowed down, I wasn't sure I could ever move again.

"You all right?" I murmured against the back of her neck.

"Yeah," she replied, reaching back and running her hand over my hip. "You're not going to break me."

The thing was, if I wasn't careful, I would do that.

Knowing that gave me the energy to take care of the condom, and when I returned to the bed, I tucked her against my front again. She was out before me, but I quickly followed, dozing off despite where my thoughts had gone. When I woke again, a handful of hours later, it was dawn, and I was going to wake Josie again, but this time with the second best way possible.

With a plate of bacon.

Easing away from Josie, careful not to stir her, I slipped off the bed. In the dusky light streaming in from the window, I found a pair of sweats and slipped them on. I grabbed a Henley off a pile of clothing and walked into the bathroom. I quietly brushed my teeth and scrubbed my face before heading back out into the bedroom.

I got hung up staring at her for a moment.

Curled on her side, the comforter had slipped down to her hips, and a whole lot of peachy skin was on display. So was a dusky pink nipple, peeking out beside the arm folded across her chest. She was a damn goddess lying there, but it was the absolute peacefulness in her expression as she slept that held me immobile.

I never wanted to see her look any other way.

And I knew that wasn't going to be possible. There was a lot we had to face, but I was going to lessen any blow coming at her.

Moving to the bed, I picked up the comforter and pulled it up, covering her. I leaned down and kissed her softly on the cheek. I straightened and with my shirt in hand, I slipped out of the room. Out in the hall, I pulled the Henley on over my head as I walked toward the lobby. The place was silent, as it was too early for the students to even be up on a Monday morning, and after what happened yesterday evening, I doubted there'd be classes. I neared the lobby, a shiver of awareness skating over my skin, and I knew it wasn't entirely empty.

I slowed my steps, frowning as I spotted Alex standing a few steps away from the entombed furies. She didn't look over at me when she spoke. "This is weirdly familiar, isn't it?"

"Yeah." A whole lot of shit was weirdly familiar. "Was kind of hoping I wouldn't see these bitches again."

Alex smiled slightly.

I stopped, running my hand over my chest. "Why are you up so early?"

"Haven't really slept yet. Been helping with clean-up," she explained, and I imagined that if I was a better person, I'd feel bad about not helping.

But I didn't.

Not at all.

I looked around, expecting to find Aiden. "Where's your shadow?"

"He's still at the wall with Solos. The gate was damaged during the attack, so they're staying out there until it's repaired."

"So responsible," I murmured.

Alex faced me. For someone who hadn't slept, there wasn't a shadow under her eyes. "Solos didn't make it sound like the University's been having a lot of daimon problems, so the attack of such a sizable grouping is pretty bizarre."

"Not really." My gaze flicked back to the statues. "We have a bunch of pures here. A lot of halfs. An Apollyon. And three demigods. We have so much *aether* that . . ." My jaw worked. "That this place is like a damn buffet."

"Good point. And it's not like they don't know this place is here."

"Nope."

"And what about these lovely ladies?" she gestured at the furies with one arm. "Solos is thinking it has to do with what's going on between the halfs and pures."

"What else could it be?"

Her gaze met mine and she raised an eyebrow.

She meant me.

Lowering my chin, I coughed out a laugh. "I've been behaving myself, Alex." Sort of.

"That's good to hear." She paused. "Can I say something without you running off or interrupting me?"

My lips quirked up. "Depends."

"I'm being serious." Alex wound her hands around her hair, twisting it in the same manner Josie did whenever she was nervous, and man, that was weird to see. "I've never gotten the chance to thank you and you won't let me, so please let me just say thank you."

I opened my mouth, but snapped it shut as Aiden's words resurfaced. I kept quiet, not because of him, but I figured the sooner I allowed Alex to apologize the quicker this would be over.

Alex drew in a deep breath. "Thank you for what you did for Aiden and for me. You sacrificed your mortal *and* afterlife for us."

Turning my head to the side, I cracked my neck. Standing here, listening to this . . . No words.

"But I also want to thank you for that day," she said quietly.

"What day?"

A moment passed. "When we fought Ares. I didn't get a chance to thank you for staying with me when . . . well, you know what."

"Gods." I squeezed my eyes shut, but that didn't stop the rush of memories of that day. They plowed into me with the force of a freight train. Her standing in front of me, tears streaming down her face as she begged me not to leave her, to hold on, and I did. I held her until she was no more. "Alex, you shouldn't—"

"I said thank you and I mean it. Thank you from the bottom of my heart, but I . . ." She cleared her throat, and then without any warning, she sprang forward and wrapped her arms around me.

I was as still as the furie statues.

Alex squeezed me tight. "Thank you," she whispered against my chest, and then bounced back, putting distance between us. "I still want to throat punch you from time to time."

I laughed hoarsely. "Yeah. Trust me. I still want to throat punch myself too. And Aiden. I've always wanted to throat punch him."

She chuckled softly as she turned back to the furies. "How's Josie?"

My attention sharpened at the change of subject. "Why do you think I would know how she is? And by the way, why were you in her room yesterday?"

Alex's lips curled up. "Well, to answer your second question first, she and I are kind of related, so it made sense to go meet her. To answer your first question, your second question kind of gives that away."

I narrowed my eyes.

She sighed. "And I talked to Luke a little bit ago. He said you two were together, but . . ."

I said nothing at first. It wasn't like I was ashamed of my relationship with Josie or that it was weird to talk to Alex about Josie after my past with Alex. I mean, yeah, it was awkward, but we'd been inside each other's heads more than once, so whatever. But Josie was . . . she was precious to me and that made me wary of what I said and who I said it to.

But this was Alex.

Rubbing at my chest again with my palm, I sighed. "Josie is good. She's asleep right now."

"Huh." There was a pause. "In her bed or . . . ?"

I rolled my eyes. "Mine. Alex. Mine."

"*Huuuh*," she stressed that word this time. "So, I'm guessing you two are . . . ?"

"Together? Yes. We're together. Look, I'm heading somewhere. I'll be out on the wall, probably in the late morning or early afternoon." Done with this conversation, I started toward the door, but she stopped me by calling out my name. "Yeah?"

Alex lifted her chin. "You okay, Seth?" she asked after a moment. "And I mean, are you really okay?"

Those statues of the furies stood between us, a symbol of how not okay things could get, because I knew Alex didn't think their presence had anything to do with what was going on between the breeds. And maybe they didn't. Maybe what I had done, what seemed to breathe inside me, with me, had brought them here. And maybe I was about to lie.

Either way, I nodded. "Now . . . I'm okay."

Josie

Walking the first row of skyscraper-sized shelves, I trailed my fingers along the dusty spines. I really didn't expect today's library stalking to be different from any other day, but Seth was meeting with Marcus and Solos about the attack, and I needed to get out and move around since I really didn't want to bum-rush whatever meeting Marcus was hosting.

I had a feeling that if I didn't leave Seth's room and was there when he returned, I'd never leave. That didn't sound like such a bad idea, but there was still so much to be done.

My mind just wasn't on those things, and maybe that made me a bad demigod, but whatever. The last fifteen or so hours had been . . . life-changing in the most amazing way. Maybe I was being silly and girlish, but what-the-fuck-ever. Yeah. What-the-*fuck*-ever. Love and living were just as important as fighting and surviving, and being girly equaled being awesome, so . . .

Glancing down at the marbleized floor, I bit down on my lip, but it didn't stop the grin from spreading across my face. Last night and this morning, and then again, before I left had been absolutely . . . oh gosh . . . mind-blowing, and I had really been missing out on the whole sex thing.

Wow.

Though I was glad Seth had been my first, and he would be my last. There was no doubt in my mind.

I crossed into row number two of the stacks, feeling flushed as I thought about what Seth and I had done. Warmth seeped through my skin and traveled through my veins. He was insatiable, and I was totally down with that.

But as great and awesome and fantastic as the sex had been, the giddy grin on my face had nothing to do with that.

Agapi.

Yeah, it had a lot to do with that. It had to do with him calling me sweetheart. Had a lot to do with the hope swelling in my chest. Had a lot to do with everything that was and wasn't said between us.

And okay, the sex played a factor. I mean, come on. He picked me up and held me off the bed! Whoa. And he'd brought me a plate of bacon this morning.

Bacon.

I was so going to marry this guy, whether he knew it or not. And marriage could totally be in our future, because we were going to survive the whole Titan gods thing and I was going to find a way to get him out of the hands of the gods, now and for eternity. I knew who could do that and I had a plan, fostered this morning while I'd showered and it was a pretty damn good—

"Hello."

Startled by the cool, oddly accented greeting, I stepped back and lifted my gaze from the floor. The first thing I noticed were black heels. Pointy-toed and spiked. Like the kind of spiked heel I would look like a baby giraffe in. My gaze tracked up thin calves and over a tight pencil skirt in charcoal. The white blouse was tucked into the skirt, and ruffles traveled up the center of the woman's slim waist and chest.

Blood-red lips were pressed together, forming a thin line, and dark sunglasses, huge ones, covered her eyes. Like before, her hair was pulled back in a tight bun, but I could tell that her hair was super curly. Excitement flooded me as I stared at the tall, slender woman.

The librarian stood in front of me.

20

fraid the librarian would disappear if I blinked, I gaped at her. "I've been looking everywhere for you for, like, weeks, and that probably sounds super weird, but—"

"I know you've been looking for me," she replied coolly, her chin lifting a fraction of an inch. "But you were not ready to find me."

Any doubts I'd had that this librarian was normal, or whatever the closest thing to normal was around here, faded away. And the fact that she knew I was looking for her was more than just a little creepy, but I had to play it cool. I didn't want to scare her off or say the wrong thing. My father had told me to find her, and that meant she had to be very important.

"There is something you need to see." She pivoted around smoothly, not even waiting for me to agree to follow her. She lifted a hand and with a flick of her wrist motioned me to follow. "Come along, now."

Trepidation walked alongside me. I had no idea where we were going or what she was, but I was relying on the fact that my father had told me to find her. So I was hoping she wasn't going to kill me.

"So," I said, clearing my throat as I followed her. "How did you know I was ready now?"

"I sensed the bloodletting," she replied, gliding ahead. I wasn't even sure her feet were touching the floor, because her heels made no rapping sound. "That has changed things."

"Bloodletting?" I frowned. The tiny curls pinned back in a bun almost seemed to . . . vibrate. Or squirm. I blinked. I was totally seeing things. "What does that mean?"

She looked over her shoulder. The sunglasses shielded her eyes, but the flat press of her lips was not exactly warm. "You are no longer a virgin, correct?"

I tripped over my feet. Throwing out my arm, I knocked a book off a shelf in the process of steadying myself. The heavy tome smacked off the floor. "What?"

"You engaged in fornication? There was penetration of—"

"Oh my God, I totally get what you mean. I don't need an explanation." My face burned. "How do you . . . ?"

"I can sense these things."

I almost asked how, but figured this was one of those things I didn't want to ever know about. "I . . . I don't know what is weirder. Talking about this with you, or the fact you can sense that."

Her laugh was like falling glass, brittle and frail. "If you think that's weird, I worry if you have the mettle for what awaits you."

It took me a moment to realize what mettle was, because seriously, it was the twenty-first century and no one really used words like that anymore. "I'm not afraid."

I couldn't see those eyes, but I had the distinct impression that I should have been grateful for that. "We'll see."

She faced forward, her strides long and quick as she led me under the staircase, stopping in front of one of the doors that

Deacon and I had seen. She opened the middle one and walked through.

Hoping I didn't end up on an Olympian AMBER Alert, I walked through and into a narrow, brightly lit hallway. The librarian stepped around me, walking ahead, and again, the curls of her hair moved. Wiggled?

I shook my head. "By the way, my name is—"

"Josephine Bethel. I know."

"Of course," I muttered. "I mean, you know I'm not a virgin anymore, so . . . Anyway, I don't know your name." *Or how do you walk in those heels with no sound.* I didn't say that last part out loud.

She stopped in front of a . . . wall. I looked around, seeing no doors. Nothing. My gaze flew back to her. Oh geez, I was so going to end up on an Olympian missing person's report.

"My name? Your father did not tell you?"

I shook my head.

She laughed again, and this time, she smiled. Full red lips parted, revealing *fangs.*

Holy crap.

Like legit canine fangs, vampire style.

I stepped back, pulse kicking up as I suddenly wished I'd brought the dagger with me. My next thought was that I didn't need a dagger, because I was a demigod, and I had a whole lot of badass skills. But she had fangs, and they weren't even like daimon shark teeth. My mind raced through the myths book I'd been reading.

She tilted her head and there was something very, very snakelike about the movement. "You do not know who I am?"

Goosebumps rushed over my skin as I stared at her. The sunglasses. The tight, coiled hair that seemed to move. Fangs. Snakelike movements. My gaze dropped to her feet. How did her heels make no sound? That was potentially the least important clue, but the *sunglasses*? Could she be . . . ?

No.

No way.

I swallowed hard. "Why are you wearing sunglasses?"

"Would you prefer I removed them?" She reached up, hooking a finger around the arm of the sunglasses. "Most would not."

"No," I said quickly, lifting my hand. "That's not necessary."

A close-lipped grin appeared.

I drew in a shaky breath. "You . . . you're not . . . ?" I couldn't even bring myself to say it, because saying it out loud sounded so crazy. I mean, a lot of things I once thought were just some insane old myths were actually very real, but this . . . No way.

"Are you asking if I'm a Gorgon?"

My heart dropped into my stomach.

"Once upon a time, I was something very different. A priestess in Athena's temple, but then Poseidon found me." Her smile faded, and one of the tight curls that rested along her temple swayed and then stretched. The tip of the curl wasn't a tip.

Oh my *gods*.

The tip was the head of a tiny *snake*. My eyes widened as it opened its mouth and hissed, revealing a forked tongue. The librarian was Medusa.

"He took from me what was never his, and Athena, being the goddess of reasoning and intelligence, turned me into a monster." Her upper lip curled as she snorted. "Great judge she makes. I was punished for Poseidon's actions."

"That's so wrong." I didn't know what else to say.

"That's the way the gods are," she replied.

I couldn't believe what I was seeing—who was standing in front of me. "But I thought you . . ." Oh man, how did I say this? "I thought you were killed."

"By that little punk bitch? Perseus? Please." Medusa laughed. "He couldn't fight his way out of a pack of declawed kittens without his daddy Zeus stepping in."

I opened my mouth, but I really didn't have any response to that.

"You are so incredibly naive." She tweaked my nose with cool fingers, causing me to blink. "It's cute. Not flattering cute. But cute."

My brows lifted. Did Medusa just tweak my nose? What was this life?

"There are myths and then there are truths. Perseus decapitating me is obviously a myth. People needed a hero then. The gods gave them one. Well, namely Zeus gave them one, most likely to anger his wife, considering the little demigod was his bastard offspring." The tiny snake curl hissed before it settled against her cheek. "But Perseus tried to fight me. He did not succeed."

It took me a couple of moments to find my voice. "What are you doing here, in the Covenant library?"

"A form of punishment." One shoulder rose. "I have anger management problems."

"Oh," I murmured.

She turned sideways. "When my skin turns green, it's not a good thing."

That . . . that made sense. Kind of like the Incredible Hulk. "And . . . um, your eyes? Do they turn people to stone?"

"You'll know the answer to that in a few moments." Turning back to the wall, she waved her hand.

The air in front of the bare marble wall appeared to ripple. Electricity filled the air, dancing along my skin. The wall warped and then split up the center, peeling back. A wooden door appeared with vertical slats held together by dark metal. Hinges creaked as it opened.

"Your father told you to find me, because I'm not a librarian, Josephine." Medusa glided through the door. "My punishment was to become *the* Guard, what every Guard has been modeled on thereafter. Used to be treasures I kept safe, riches of untold proportions. Sometimes it was an important person, an entity that would be fated to become something great, and now . . . this."

Taking a deep breath, I followed her into a large chamber. A shudder rolled down my spine as I looked around. Torches placed every couple of feet along the walls burned, casting a soft, dancing glow on dozens and dozens of stone statues.

Not just regular statues. But people. Some stood tall. Others cowered. Hands and arms shielded faces on many. Weapons were clenched in hands. All had horrified expressions on their faces, etched forever in stone.

Yep.

That part of the myth was true. Medusa's eyes turned people to stone.

I hurried past them, not wanting to look at them too long. Medusa walked through an archway and down another hall. The walls in there were covered with the same glyphs I'd seen on Seth. Marks that stood for invincibility, courage, strength, and power.

And those glyphs shimmered on the marble walls just like they did on Seth's skin.

"Come now," Medusa called as she approached a door that was silver. In the center was a lightning bolt. "It is time."

"Time for . . . ?" I trailed off as she opened the door. All I could do was stare.

Sunlight, beautiful and bright, shone down on a grassy meadow full of vibrant purple and blue flowers. Trees rose into skies as blue as my father's eyes . . . when he had eyes.

As if compelled, I walked forward and through the door, into . . . I don't even know what I was walking into, but I knew it was no longer in the same realm as the library. The air smelled sweet, a scent I couldn't place, and the breeze was warm, toying with the strands of my hair. I inhaled sharply as I slowly turned around. Energy was heavy here. I could feel it coasting over my skin, seeping into my bone and tissues.

"Where am I?" I asked.

"You are at the entrance of one of the gateways to Olympus." She turned, spreading her arms wide. "This place and others like it must be guarded at all costs. If the Titans or if the God Killer ever discovered this gateway, they'd be able to enter Olympus."

"God Killer?" My mind raced through what I knew about the two Apollyons and how a God Killer was created. Alex had become the God Killer, but it was assumed—I guessed—that when she died her mortal death, she was no longer the God Killer. It was why she had to die in the first place. "There is no God Killer."

"Hmm," she murmured. "Is there not?"

I looked at her sharply, but before I could question her a sudden flash of light cut across the clearing, momentarily blinding me. When it receded, I gasped and clasped my hands over my mouth.

In the meadow, a couple of feet in front of me, was the most beautiful animal I'd ever seen. Taller than me and broad, the horse shook its white coat as it swished its tail back and forth. It was a proud and strong creature, one I'd never seen before.

Large and graceful wings arched from the horse's sides, sprouting just above powerful forelegs.

"Oh my gosh." I reached out toward the Pegasus, and then immediately yanked my hands to my chest. "I want to touch it. Can I touch it? I can touch it, right?"

Medusa looked at me, a single brow rising above the dark sunglasses. "If he doesn't want to be touched, he will let you know."

Probably by kicking me in the face, but it would be worth it. Slowly, as if under a spell, I approached the magnificent creature. My heart pounded as it lowered its massive wings and shook its head, tossing the heavy mane around its neck. Slowly, I placed my hand on its side. Muscles bunched under my palm, but the Pegasus didn't dropkick me as I ran my hand along its strong back.

A knot formed in my throat. I don't even know why, but I wanted to cry. I mean, this was so much better than visiting a llama farm or something. I was legit touching a Pegasus. "He's . . ." I swallowed. "He's beautiful."

Medusa stayed back. "He is."

"What is he doing here?"

"They always come when there is activity at the gateways," she explained. "Pegasus are curious creatures, sometimes even social. Their blood has a paralyzing quality to it, used by the nymphs."

"I've seen it in action." My voice was shaky as the awe-inspiring creature drifted away from me, walking toward the trees. I wanted to follow, maybe give it a hug, but I didn't want to push my luck. "Will more . . . creatures come?"

"I do not think we'll be here long enough for that." She waved her hand again and the ground began to shake.

I spread my legs, bracing myself as the earth trembled. The Pegasus appeared unfazed as it grazed nearby. Pulse picking up, I looked down. Flowers shook. Soil erupted, kicking small pebbles into the air. Twelve shimmery columns appeared, forming a circle around Medusa and me. As the glow faded, there were twelve stone busts sitting on pedestals.

"These are the Twelve." Medusa walked forward. "They represent the Olympians On each embodiment is their icon, what the children of the gods will need to defeat the Titans."

Holy moly. I turned, my gaze glancing off each of the busts. This was why Apollo had told me to find the librarian—find Medusa. She was guarding the gateway and the icons.

Spying my father's, I walked over to the stone bust. A small golden harp, about the size of my hand, dangled from the neck.

A harp.

Not even a legit-sized harp.

For real.

Artemis had a bow. Poseidon a trident. A spear rested in front of Athena. An unlit torch stood in front of Demeter. Hades's bust wore a helmet, and I had a . . . harp. Well, there was a seashell in front of Aphrodite, so I figured it could be worse. But between a seashell and a harp, I had no idea what to do with either.

Seeing the icons that would never be touched was sad. Zeus's scepter would never be picked up. Neither would Ares's shield. I didn't know their children, but the loss was heavy in the silence.

"So many lost lives," Medusa murmured, picking up on the nature of my thoughts. "And many more will be lost."

I shivered, not because her words scared me but because I knew they were true. Drawing in a deep breath, I reached for the golden harp. As my fingers neared it, the tips hummed as if my body recognized the importance of the symbol.

"Now is not the time," Medusa said, startling me. She was directly beside me. "Once you take that icon, it cannot be given back."

"Okay." I looked at her. "My powers have been unlocked—"

"And taking the icon will give you more *aether* than anything that walks the mortal realm." The curls on her head vibrated and more tiny snake heads appeared. Creepy. "You will be extremely powerful, and even more useful in the hands of the Titans and to others."

I assumed she meant daimons.

"When you have found the other demigods, bring them back here. That is when you must take the icon." Even though I couldn't see her eyes, I could feel them holding mine. "You must be careful of who you trust, child, of whom you have given your heart to."

I stiffened.

"Power is the most alluring of all vices. It corrupts and destroys," she said, her voice shifting low. "And it is the most hidden of all transgressions."

A cold chill radiated down my spine. "You're talking about Seth."

"He is not what he seems," she said, and a snake snapped at the air. "The Apollyon has committed acts of great treachery."

"I know." My hands curled into fists. "I know what he's capable of. And I know who he used to be and who he is becoming."

Her head turned slightly as an owl hooted from the trees, and Medusa sighed.

"Of course. *She* is coming."

"Who?"

Medusa stepped back as the wind picked up. The curls thickened all along her head and then sprang free. I gasped. Snakes of all sizes formed, hissing and striking at the space. I tried not to stare or freak out, but then the owl called out. I blinked and without any warning, a tall woman stood in front at the edge of the clearing.

Brown hair fell in waves to her waist, covering her chest, which I figured was a good thing. Her white gown brushed the grass and was as transparent as glass.

She was not a waxer.

"Athena," hissed Medusa. "How nice of you to join us."

My eyes widened. I might've stopped breathing.

The goddess shot Medusa a silencing glare as she approached me. I didn't know what I was supposed to do. Bow? Get on my knees? I didn't do that when Apollo came around, but this wasn't my father. This was the goddess Athena, who apparently punished victims of sex crimes and turned them into monsters. She was in front of me before I could do anything, and I was staring into all-white eyes.

"This," Athena spoke, lifting her hand. She held a vial with a bluish-red liquid in it. "This is for you, child of Apollo."

Uh . . .

Athena held the glass vial out to me. "It is the blood of a Pegasus. You know what it does."

This was the most bizarre day of my life, and that was saying something.

Slowly, I lifted my hand and closed it over the vial. My skin brushed Athena's and a jolt of electricity shocked me.

Athena's lips curled up on one side.

I glanced down at the vial. This would definitely come in handy, especially since it worked against the Titans.

"There is something you must know," Athena said, and her voice seemed to carry on the wind. The sound was everywhere. "Medusa guards this gateway and these icons, but her power to turn man to stone does not work against deities."

"Unfortunately," muttered Medusa.

Athena ignored her. "She will not be able to stop the Titans or even a demigod, and especially not the Apollyon."

My head jerked up. I hadn't known that. I assumed Medusa's freaky eyes worked on everything. I also didn't like the way Athena tacked Seth onto that like he'd be the biggest threat. Seriously? Like, maybe the Titans were the ones they should really be worried about, but I understood their trepidation when it came to Seth. He'd sided with Ares and gone against them in a plot to overthrow the mortal realm and Olympus. That was going to take a while for them to get over.

"You will need the toxin," Medusa warned, drawing my attention back to her. Thankfully, her hair had returned to normal. "But not for whom you expect."

21

*R*estless, I shifted where I sat on the couch and wondered for the hundredth time how in the world I'd ended up sitting next to Alex and Aiden while they tried to keep their hands in their own laps.

I'd been sitting here first, when it had just been Solos, Marcus, and Alexander discussing the issue of the breached gate and the attack last night. Aiden had been there also, but he'd done the dark and brooding thing, leaning against the wall until Alex showed up with Deacon and Luke.

They'd brought lunch.

Laadan even appeared before heading off with Alexander to do things that would probably traumatize Alex. Of course, once I started thinking about those kinds of things, my mind wandered to Josie and to all those kinds of things I'd rather be doing in that moment.

And that just made shit real awkward sitting next to Alex and Aiden, because with her this close, I was picking up on what she was feeling. Not as strongly as I used to, when it had gotten to the point where it felt like we were virtually the same person. I could pick up the barest trace of emotions, almost like a word that was forgotten as it reached the tip of the tongue. There was a faint, warm sensation of arousal and the bitter tang of dread. A very odd combination radiating off of her.

That also meant she could probably feel mine, so I really needed to stop thinking about finding Josie and seeing how many times I could make her scream my name.

I shifted again, spreading my thighs.

Alex glanced over at me, her cheeks slightly flushed. *Great.* I rubbed my finger along my brow as Deacon reached across the round table and swiped a handful of Tater Tots out of Luke's carton.

"Do you think classes will resume tomorrow?" Deacon asked, stacking the Tots on his plate. "I guess I should've asked Marcus when he was here."

"They'll probably have a service for those who fell during the attack," Solos said, walking over to the table. He flipped the chair around and sat down, resting his arms on the back of the chair.

Deacon's fingers stilled over the Tater Tot snowman he appeared to be building. "Gods," he murmured, sitting back. "I would like to go just a couple of months without having to go to a funeral service."

That didn't seem likely.

I glanced at the door. Josie had gone to the library again, but I was thinking she should be done by now. I'd told her where I was going to be, so she knew where to find us. Part of me wished I'd gone to the library with her.

"It's weird," Alex said as she picked up Aiden's hand. I had no idea what she was doing, but it looked like she was massaging his fingers or something. "We see so many people entering Tartarus on a daily basis, so you think we'd be accustomed to it, you know?" She shook her head as she stared at Aiden's hand. Her fingers moved over his. "But I'm not. I guess it's different down there, because you know they'll be happy, but I'm . . . I'm just rambling."

"It's okay." Aiden leaned over, kissing her temple. "We don't have services down there."

"Makes sense," Solos said, lips kicking up. "Everyone's sort of already dead."

Alex rolled her eyes.

"Do you ever think we could visit?" Deacon asked, grabbing a packet of ketchup. "I mean, I'd like to see—"

A sudden shot from outside interrupted him, then a loud bang, like a crack of thunder. I shot up, right beside Alex. Aiden made it to the window first.

"Gods," he said.

We were on the first floor, toward the back of the main Covenant building, and the window overlooked a decent portion of the north quad, which gave us a bird's-eye view of a pretty decent throw-down between groups of halfs and pures. The crashing noise had to have been from the shattered statue closest to the building. They'd managed to knock that thing over.

"Ouch," Alex murmured as a half landed an impressive roundhouse.

My lips pursed as a pure tapped into the air element and tossed one of the halfs into a group of about five others, knocking them over like a set of bowling pins. "Well, that escalated quickly."

Solos sighed, dropping his head onto the table. "Gods, is it wrong if I just pretend I have no idea what's going on outside?"

Reaching for a Tater Tot and finding them gone, Luke frowned as he glanced over at Deacon's plate. "Marcus is planning on putting that curfew in place, starting tomorrow, I think, but that isn't going to stop this."

"Nothing is going to stop this." Alex pressed her hands to

the window. Her breath fogged the glass. "This wasn't what I wanted—what *we* wanted."

Alex and Aiden were pretty much responsible for the Breed Order being disbanded and the removal of the Elixir. Did they really think everyone was just going to go along with the new way of life?

Guards began to fill into the quad.

"I'm going to find Josie." Pivoting around, I stalked across the room and threw open the door. I turned to the right and took two steps.

Josie was walking down the center of the lobby, her high ponytail swaying with each step. Relieved to see that she wasn't out in that mess, I crossed the distance between us, and two different needs sprung alive inside me. I focused on the right one, the one that mattered.

"Seth—"

Circling one arm around her waist, I clasped a hand along the nape of her neck and pulled her to me. My mouth was on hers in a nanosecond. She tasted of mint as I lifted her up onto the tips of her toes, bringing her hips into contact with mine. Her breathy moan made me harder, which seemed impossible until now. She looped an arm around my neck as she pressed her chest to mine. How quickly could I get us somewhere private? There was a supply closet to the right. Various conference rooms.

"Really?" Solos walked past us, shaking his head. "Don't get her pregnant in the lobby, Seth."

"Oh my God," Josie groaned, dropping her face on my shoulder.

I flipped Solos off. He laughed as he headed outside. Curling my hand around her ponytail, I pressed my mouth to the space just below her ear. "I was actually thinking of making use of that closet over there."

Josie laughed softly. "I've never done that before."

"Figured as much." I nipped at the fleshy part of her earlobe, drawing a sharp gasp out of her. "And just so you know, I am more than willing to introduce you to semi-public sex."

"Seth," she whispered. "You are terrible."

I dragged my nose along the side of her cheek. "Look, I'm just letting you know that I'm all about sexual education. We need to discover what you like and don't."

"So helpful of you."

"That's me." Drawing back, I kissed her nose. Our gazes met, and I smiled without even thinking about it. Felt strange. Felt good. "Glad you're here. Did you run into any problems outside?"

"No. They weren't even paying attention to me." She stepped back, lowering her arm. "And it looked like the Guards had them under control."

"Good." I reached for her hand and saw she was holding something. "What's that?"

Her eyes filled with exhilaration as she opened her hand. A vial of some kind of dark blue liquid lay in her palm. "Blood of a Pegasus."

I looked up. "How did you get that?"

"Athena."

"Come again?"

"You heard right." She rocked back, seconds from bouncing. "I found the librarian. But she's not a librarian. Not really. I mean, I guess in some weird way she is, but you're not going to believe what I saw, who I saw and then I found— "

"Whoa. Slow down there, Mighty Mouth."

Her nose wrinkled. "Mighty Mouth?"

"Kind of sounds sexual. Like your super power would be sucking—"

"Seth," she snapped, eyes narrowing.

"But I meant you're talking so fast I can barely pick up what you're saying."

Josie shook her head. "Sure you did."

I winked. "How about we take this convo to that room back there? Practically everyone is there." I took her free hand, but she didn't budge. I searched her face. "You okay?"

"Everyone is there?"

"Yeah. Luke and Deacon, and Alex and Aiden." I paused. "You know they can be trusted with this, right?"

"Of course," she replied quickly. "I just don't want to intrude."

I stared at her a moment. "Intrude?"

"Yeah." She slipped her hand free as she glanced down at the vial. "I mean, it's been six months since they could all hang out, and I don't want to intrude."

I didn't know if I should laugh, hug her, or shake her. Pressing the tips of my fingers under her chin, I lifted her gaze to mine. "Okay. There's a couple of things you need to understand."

One eyebrow rose. "Oh, really?"

"Yes. Really," I repeated. "Alex and Aiden are back for the time being. It's weird. Trust me. And to be honest, you know how I feel about being around them, right or wrong, but you have no reason to feel like you're intruding. You're not."

Her lashes lowered and she sighed. "I know. It's just . . . they are such close friends and none of this is important right now, but I guess . . . I'm socially inept when it comes to these things."

"That makes two of us then."

She laughed softly and looked up. "Awesome."

"You don't ever have to worry about them. Hell. Given some time, Alex is probably going to become your best friend."

Her eyes widened and she winced. "I don't know about that. I mean, there's the whole Apollo thing and then the whole thing with you, and that's like sharing way too much weird stuff."

"Josie." Chuckling, I lowered my mouth and kissed her. "You are . . ."

"Amazing?" she supplied.

"I was going to go with crazy, but amazing works too." I laughed when she smacked my arm with her free hand. Luckily, not with the vial of Pegasus blood, because that would've sucked. "You ready?"

"Yeah. Just one sec." Pink spread into her cheeks. "There's something I need to tell you first."

"Okay."

She stretched up and over, speaking in my ear. "I love you."

Fuck. Muscles locked up. Heart picked up. Skin hummed. And that closet was looking more and more like a place we needed to investigate.

Josie kissed my cheek and then settled back. "I thought you should be reminded of that." Taking my hand, she squeezed gently. "Ready?"

Those three words struck me silent as I led her to the room the crew was in. They were three words I wasn't used to hearing. I didn't think I'd ever be.

Everyone was pretty much where they'd been when I left, except the cartons of food were closed and Aiden was sitting while Alex stood next to Deacon and Luke.

"Found her." I shut the door behind us, keenly aware that everyone in the room noticed our joined hands. I was . . . weirdly proud of that. "And she has something very interesting to share."

Josie waved her closed hand at everyone, and one quick glance showed that her face was a shade somewhere between red and fire-engine red. She focused on Deacon. "I went to the library and I finally found the librarian."

"What?" He slapped his hands down on the table, rattling

empty water bottles, his expression crestfallen. "Are you kidding me? The one day I don't go and you find her?"

"Librarian?" Aiden asked, leaning forward.

Josie caught him and Alex up on the whole vague Apollo message to find this librarian. "I saw her today. She's not the only thing I saw." Whirling to face me, excitement practically poured out of her. "Oh my gosh, I forgot to tell you. I saw a Pegasus today. Like a real, live Pegasus, and it was amazing. I got to touch it. It liked me. I think. I mean, it didn't kick or bite me."

Aiden cocked his head to the side, his brows lifting. The dumbfounded look on his face was pretty priceless.

"Are you high?" Deacon asked, and then laughed. "Because if so, I want whatever you're smoking."

His brother turned and looked at him.

"What?" Deacon shrugged, sitting back in the chair. "That sounds like some good shit."

"I wasn't high." Josie slipped her hand free and walked over to the table. She put the vial down. "This is blood of the Pegasus."

"You bled the Pegasus?" Horror etched into Alex's expression.

"Geez! No. It didn't come from the one I saw. At least, I don't think it did." Josie frowned as she stepped back, standing next to me. "Athena brought it."

"Athena?" Luke eyed the vial and then carefully picked it up, turning it over in his hand. "Like, *the* Athena?"

"Yes. And the librarian is—you guys are never going to believe this, but she's Medusa. Like snakes in the hair and creepy eyes and everything," Josie explained in a rush, and now I was staring at her with the same expression as Aiden. "Apparently Perseus never killed her. That was a lie."

"Man," Deacon murmured. "I could've seen Medusa. This is so fucked up."

Aiden shot him a look. "I think it's probably a good thing you *didn't* see her."

"It probably is. I get the impression she's not too keen on the menfolk," Josie said as Alex walked back to the couch. Aiden leaned back and she dropped down in his lap. "She took me to the door under the stairs, which sounds kind of creepy, and into this weird hallway where she made a door appear out of thin air. There was this chamber full of stone dudes."

"Medusa," Alex repeated, slowly shaking her head. "And a Pegasus?"

Josie nodded. "I found the icons and the—" She frowned. "I found the icons. I know how to get to them once we find the other demigods."

"They're in the library?" I asked.

"I don't know. The place they're kept in is kind of accessed through the library, but I don't think it's actually there," she explained, glancing at the vial as Luke placed it back on the table. "Athena appeared then too. She gave me the vial. I guess it's for . . ." Her brows pinched. "I guess it's for the Titans since it works against them."

"It works against everything," Luke said. "Would kill a mortal if it even came into contact with their skin."

"This is good news, though," Aiden said as he looped his arms around Alex's waist. "We know where the icons are. At least that's one thing marked off the list."

"It is." Josie glanced up at me and she smiled. "Now we just need to know where the other . . ." Her eyes widened. "Glyphs," she whispered.

I felt the presence of a god a second before energy rippled through the room. Two shimmery pillars appeared next to the table, and a second later Apollo was standing there.

He wasn't alone.

Beside him was someone I'd never seen before. Some dude a little over six feet tall, and as wide as a damn linebacker.

"I've brought you guys someone," Apollo said. No hello. Typical Apollo. Just popping in with random strangers with no greeting whatsoever. Such a douche. "Everyone meet Hercules."

Everyone stared.

Apollo smiled as his all-white eyes gave way to blue irises that matched Josie's. "Yes," he said, "*that* Hercules."

22

J'd thought earlier that today was the most bizarre day of my life, and I had not been wrong. It just went from crazy-weird straight to insanity-land. I'd seen Medusa, Athena, and a Pegasus today.

And now I was staring at my father, Apollo, who was standing next to Hercules—*that* Hercules.

My brain sort of emptied out, which was probably a good thing, because I'd been stressing since I'd left the library. Medusa's parting warning was more than unsettling. I had a feeling they'd given me the toxin with the idea that it wasn't just for the Titans. Knots of unease had formed in my belly. It wasn't that I believed that I'd ever have to use it against Seth, but it was the fact that they thought I'd have to.

That was what bothered me.

"Holy. Shit," murmured Deacon, breaking the silence.

I blinked once, and then twice. Hercules was still standing there, a smirk on his well-formed lips. The demigod was striking. A head full of blond, wavy hair. Eyes as blue as the morning sky, and his muscles had muscles. They strained the white shirt he wore, and even his thighs bulged in a way that made me think the seam of his jeans would explode at any given minute.

"I see you all know who I am," Hercules said. "Not that I'd expect anything else. After all, I am *the* Hercules."

My brows rose.

Seth snorted.

"Hercules is a dick," Apollo stated, and the demigod shrugged his shoulders. Obviously that wasn't the first time he'd heard that. "But he's the only one Zeus would allow out of Olympus. He will be able to locate the other demigods."

"Because I'm that awesome," Hercules replied.

Apollo sighed as he rolled his eyes. "And as I said, he's a bit of a dick."

"A bit of a dick?" Seth murmured, his gaze moving from the tips of Hercules's boots to the top of the blond head. "A small dick?"

Oh my God.

Alex smacked her hand over her mouth.

"You'd like to find out, wouldn't you?" Hercules replied.

Seth snickered. "I don't need to go on a search and find mission to discover what's already obvious."

Oh. My. God.

The demigod stepped forward. Empty bottles on the table rattled. "I've heard about you, Apollyon. I've heard *all* about you."

"Oh my," whispered Deacon. He elbowed Luke with glittering silver eyes. Aiden and Alex stood.

Apollo folded his arms. "You two will be making out soon, I see."

"I'm not surprised," Seth replied, ignoring Apollo. One side of his lips kicked up. "After all, I am *that* Apollyon."

"Something to be proud of," Hercules replied.

Well, this was going downhill fast.

Seth lifted his chin. "At least what you've heard about me is true. You? Mostly myth, right? I bet Daddy makes sure everyone thinks you're a big, bad—"

"No," snapped Apollo as Hercules raised his hand. A white glimmer danced over the demigod's knuckles. "You cannot hurt the Apollyon."

Seth's smirk grew to epic proportions. "Damn straight."

"Oh, don't get me wrong, Issues Boy," he said, and Seth scowled. "Herc here can hurt you, but I'm telling him not to. The same goes for you. I need both of you to behave."

"That's no fun," pouted Hercules.

"Wait." Deacon's gaze bounced back and forth. "Can we call you Herc?"

The demigod looked over his shoulder. "Everyone else does."

"So cool," murmured Deacon, silver eyes wide.

I felt like I needed to sit down.

Apollo glanced over at the couple standing in front of the couch and he smiled, warming the ethereal beauty of his face. My chest squeezed. "It's been too long since I've seen you two," he said. "Both of you look very happy."

"We are," Aiden responded.

Next to him, Alex let out a little squeal and then she shot forward. Apollo chuckled as he opened his arms wide, welcoming Alex. He hugged her. She hugged him. The squeezing in my chest increased.

I stiffened and then forced myself to not have any reaction. I shouldn't have one in the first place. This was . . . sweet. They obviously hadn't seen each other in a very long time. Casting my gaze away, I focused on Herc. He was watching Apollo curiously, as if he'd never seen the god hug anyone before. The demigod's gaze slid to mine. I looked away and saw Seth watching me. I smiled at him, because I didn't have a reason not to smile. Everything was cool.

Everything was not cool.

Reaching up, I flipped my ponytail over my shoulder. I don't know why it bothered me. Okay. I totally did. Apollo hadn't even greeted me. His *daughter*. I was just standing over here like a doofus.

Aiden clapped a hand on the god's shoulder and said something too low for me to hear as Alex drew back. She smiled up at Apollo, and I exhaled very slowly. Time to pull the big-girl panties up. Things were weird between Apollo and me, and Alex had known him for a long time, like really known him. I only knew the fake Apollo and the real Apollo, and I could literally count on both hands how many times I'd seen him.

Seth folded his arm over my shoulder, and I kept that smile plastered across my face. "So, what's the game plan?" I asked, focusing on Herc.

Turning toward us, Apollo eyed the arm around my shoulder, and I silently dared him to say something about it. "It's fairly simple. I see you've found the Librarian. Otherwise I'm not sure how you would have a vial of Pegasus blood."

"I did." I kept my voice level. "I also found the icons."

"Perfect. I knew you would." His smile was brief, not nearly as enormous as it had been when Alex squeal-tackled him. "Now, all we need are the demigods."

"And that is where I come in. It's why I am incredibly useful." Herc looked around the room, as if he was making sure everyone was focused on him. Over his shoulder, I saw Luke roll his eyes. "I can sense other demigods—"

"Yes," Seth cut in, sounding bored. "We know. Your super-special spidey senses allow you to sniff out other demigods."

His eyes narrowed. "I *am* super-special."

Aiden closed his eyes as he scratched his fingers through his dark hair. Beside him, Alex bit down on her lip.

I stepped in before the conversation derailed. "But how are we going to use that now? Can you sense where the demigods are now?"

Herc smiled as he checked me out, and he didn't even try to hide it. His gaze lingered in areas that made me feel like I was standing there nude. "Why don't you and I take this conversation—"

"Do you want to die?" Seth asked casually. "For real this time?"

"I wasn't talking to you." Herc winked at me, and I couldn't tell if this dude was for real or not. "I'm not sure if you know this or not, but I've slayed many beasts—the Nemean lion, the nine-headed hydra, a fire-breathing Cacus. I could keep going—"

"Please don't," Apollo said with a sigh, and I placed my hand on the back of Seth, balling my fingers around his shirt. "No one cares."

Herc snorted. "Everyone cares."

"I kind of care," Deacon suggested. "I mean, I want to hear about the nine-headed—"

"Shut up, Deacon," Aiden said.

Looking over his shoulder, Herc grinned. "We'll talk later."

Deacon beamed.

"I didn't bring him here first," Apollo explained. "That's what's been taking so long. I took him around the whole damn globe—"

"It was a lot of fun," Herc added.

"It was horrible," Apollo replied stoically, and my lips twitched. "We were able to find the locations of three of the demigods—ones not captured by the Titans. We couldn't locate the captured ones."

"Huh. Not so special then," murmured Seth.

Luke choked on what sounded like a laugh.

Apollo's irises disappeared, replaced by fathomless white orbs that spit tiny bolts of light.

"Uh-oh," whispered Alex.

"One of the demigods is in Canada, near the city of Thunder

Bay. Another is located in a small village called Pluckley. It's in Britain. I'm sure you've never heard of it."

"Actually," Luke drawled, "it's supposedly one of the most haunted villages in all of Britain, so that's kind of ironic that a demigod . . . Okay," he said, eyes widening when Apollo faced him with a less than impressed pinch to his face. "Never mind."

"The other demigod is in southern California, in the area of Malibu," Apollo continued. "I don't care which one you start with first, but those are the three who need to be found." There was a pause and he turned to me. Or at least I thought he did. I couldn't tell since he didn't have normal eyeballs. "I must leave. I will return when I can."

Then Apollo—my father—was gone, simply disappearing as if he was never there. Gone without so much as a handshake.

Let alone a hug.

And before I could ask him anything about my mom or Erin.

Seth

"Herc is sort of a douchebag."

"Sort of?" I laughed as Josie and I walked across the north quad. The only sign of the earlier fight was the missing statue. "He's a giant bag of dicks. Small dicks, too."

She laughed as she scanned the grounds. The late-afternoon sun was already beginning to fade and the warmer temps were dropping. "He seems very full of himself, but if he's able to lead us to the other demigods then we need to tolerate him."

"I can't make any promises."

Glancing over at me, she grinned. "You think Solos is going to be able to make use of the Pegasus blood?"

Solos had shown back up after Apollo had left. Once he got

past the unexpectedness of finding Hercules, Josie had shown Solos the vial. The older Sentinel was going to lace weapons with the toxin. Not the Covenant daggers, though, since that was way too dangerous. He was going to use the blades that were shaped like icicles once released. At least with them, we didn't have to worry about accidentally nicking someone.

"I've never been to California," Josie said, arms swinging at her sides. "I'm glad we picked there first. Is it wrong that I'm kind of excited?"

"No. Why would it be?"

Her shoulders rose as she glanced up at the sky. "Because it's not like we're going on vacation. I know it's going to be dangerous out there, or it could be. We have to convince some random person that they're a demigod."

"That's probably going to go over well," I remarked.

She laughed again. "Yeah. Plus, there's so much going on. The issues with the halfs and pures. I haven't heard anything about my mom or Erin. We have no idea how to find the demigods that the Titans have captured or what's happening to them, and I—"

"I get what you're saying. We've got a lot to deal with and focus on, but that doesn't mean you can't enjoy life a little."

"Huh." Her lips pursed.

"What does that mean?"

Josie stopped and turned to me. The wind tossed a few strands that had escaped her ponytail across her cheeks. "It's just strange coming from you."

I arched a brow. "What's that supposed to mean?"

"I don't think you live life by that motto." She poked my chest with her finger. "I don't think you've really been enjoying life until recently."

Opening my mouth, I started to argue that, but what in the hell could I say? She was right. "Touché."

Her grin spread as she pivoted back around and started walking again. "I really wish you'd seen that Pegasus. Seth, it was amazing."

"It's just a horse with wings."

Gasping, she shot me an arched look over her shoulder. "I don't think we can be friends anymore."

"That's okay. I have no intentions of being just friends with you."

Josie rolled her eyes. "Are you going to start training me again?"

"Why not?" I could do the hand-to-hand stuff, but the elements? I really didn't think I should be pushing it. "But we're leaving in two days, so that's going to make training hard."

"True."

We didn't talk for a few moments as we neared the dorm, and I figured we wouldn't have a lot of alone time in the next two days. Right now, Deacon was fanboying all over Hercules. Man, I felt for Luke, who looked like he wanted to gouge his own eardrums out and throw them on the floor, stomping on them, when we left. It wouldn't be long before everyone reconvened to make plans for our trip. There was something I wanted to talk to Josie about.

"Hey." I caught her hand and hauled her back to me. "You okay?"

"Yeah. Of course." She placed her hand on my chest and tilted her head back. "Why do you ask?"

"Really?"

Her nose wrinkled. "Really."

"Okay." Guiding her off to the bench, I sat and tugged her into my lap. She tensed for a moment and then relaxed. "I saw the way you looked when Alex and Apollo saw each other."

Josie's eyes met mine for a moment and then skittered away. I wasn't having that. I caught her chin, forcing her gaze back to mine. She sighed. "Was it that obvious?"

"No." My gaze searched hers. When Josie had locked up earlier, watching her father get all friendly with Alex, I found myself wanting to hit Apollo with *akasha* for the hundredth time. "It wasn't noticeable."

"But you noticed."

I looped my arm around her hips. "That's because I'm always watching you. If you knew how much, you would probably think it was creepy."

"Seth," she laughed.

"Truth? I stared at your ass the whole way to this bench."

"Oh my God." She shook her head. "You're ridiculous, Sethie."

"I'm honest." Sometimes.

"Yeah . . ." Another sigh shuttled through her. "I just . . . He barely even addresses me, you know? And I never get to ask him anything. He pops in and out without any real discussion. He seemed . . . he seemed really happy to see Alex. Like they hugged and I . . ."

I wanted to hurt Apollo.

She exhaled roughly. "I don't have my grandparents anymore. Or my mom, and he's my father, but he doesn't act like it. I just feel like I'm an orphan sometimes. I mean, I really am."

"I feel you," I said. Josie leaned in, resting her cheek on my shoulder. I lifted my arm, folding my hand around the nape of her neck. "You're not alone in that. I understand."

"You do," she murmured.

I smiled slightly as I looked down at her. Those beautiful eyes were closed and long lashes fanned her upper cheeks. Then she lifted her head. Curving her hand along my cheek, she raised her mouth to mine.

The brush of her lips against mine was tentative at first, nothing more than a sweep of her lips, but it hit me hard. I knew she felt the swift reaction to her. There was no hiding what was pressing against her ass or how my hand tightened along the back of her neck.

"I like kissing you," she said. "Thought I'd share that."

I caught the corner of her lip, nipping lightly. "Well, whenever you want to do that, have at it."

"Any time?"

Tilting my head, I took the kiss deeper, and Josie eagerly met it. It was like we weren't even sitting outside, where anyone could walk right up to us. It didn't matter. She squirmed in my lap, restless and seeking more. My hands joined in, sliding down her body, stroking over the curves waiting under her clothes. I wanted to explore her. Wasn't going to happen right then, though.

Sensing Alex, I pulled away. "We're about to have company."

"Huh." Josie blinked and then shifted her gaze over my shoulder. "Oh. That is so weird."

I said nothing as I shifted on the bench, turning Josie so her legs dropped between mine. I expected her to get up and put some distance between us. I wasn't sure if she was okay with the very obvious state of our relationship being out there given . . . well, given my past with these two.

Aiden's steps slowed as they approached us. Clearly, the expression on my face was not exactly a welcoming one. "Sorry," he said, looking up to the sky. "We don't mean to interrupt."

"But you're going to?" I replied.

"Yeah." Alex's grin was weak. "We just left them. I'm not sure how any of us are going to survive long in Herc's presence. He's a giant douchebag."

Josie giggled. "That's what I said."

"Great minds think alike." Alex's smile warmed. "We just want to make sure you guys are okay with us going along with you all."

"Of course," Josie said, leaning back into me. She wasn't getting up or moving away from me. Not a single part of her was . . . ashamed or worried about what anyone thought.

Damn.

"Good," Alex replied.

I smoothed my hand over Josie's hip. "Not like we really had a choice if we said we didn't want you two going along."

"Nope," Aiden responded with a smirk.

My gaze met his. "Just like old times."

There was a pause and those gray eyes burned silver as he said, "Hopefully not."

23

"*Y*ou can't stop me," Deacon stated firmly, probably in the most serious voice I'd ever heard him use. "I'm a grown adult."

Aiden took a deep breath, but it didn't help. "I can stop you. Easily."

"I'll like to see you try."

Watching the two brothers argue was like having front-row seats at a tennis match. I had no idea who was going to win. Deacon wanted to go with us to find the other demigods. Aiden was not having it.

"You don't want to see me try." Aiden was sitting on the couch inside of the room he and Alex were sharing, which was actually a pretty decent-size room. Bigger than mine or Seth's. It had a real living room—an actual couch, two papasan chairs, and an ottoman that Alex was sitting on. I honestly had no idea how I'd ended up here.

After Alex and Aiden found Seth and me on the bench, the four of us had walked back to the dorm. We entered their room, and while I'd been gaping at the size of the thing, Seth left to go find Solos. He'd said he'd be back.

That was an hour ago.

I was really hoping he hadn't run into Hercules, because I was sure that wouldn't end well at all.

"You probably think I want to go with you because of Luke." Deacon stood in front of the couch, his cheeks flushed with frustration. "It's not because of him." He glanced at Luke. "No offense, babe."

"None taken," Luke said from the other side of the couch.

"But I also would like to take a moment to point out that he is also missing classes to go on this demigod scavenger hunt."

"That's different," Aiden reasoned calmly. "He's trained, Deacon. You know that. This trip could be dangerous."

"I know that, and it's not like we haven't had this conversation a million times. I get that you want to protect me. I appreciate that, but I'm not a kid anymore."

My gaze connected with Alex's as she winced. I totally got where Deacon was coming from. I also understood why Aiden wanted him to stay here, where it was measurably safe. We had no idea what would happen out there.

"I know you're not a kid, Deacon."

Deacon shook his head. "You don't get it. I know how to protect myself, but it's more than that. I don't get to see you for half a year, Aiden. That's six months. You're unreachable to me," he said, and his voice dropped. "It's like you're dead."

Luke leaned forward as Aiden winced.

Aiden said, "Deacon—"

"No. You need to hear this. Both of you do. I'm happy that you guys are okay. That you're going to have eternity and you're together, but it's not easy on me," he said, eyes glistening, and I felt like I shouldn't be here to witness the very raw pain Deacon was expressing. "I miss you, and this is my time. I have six months to see you. That's it before you have to go back. And who knows how long this is going to take? You could be gone the entire six months. I want to see you. That's fair."

His brother lowered his gaze as he shoved his hand through his thick hair. He didn't say anything as Luke rose, walked over to where Deacon stood, and wrapped his arm around Deacon's shoulder, drawing him to his chest. He kissed the top of Deacon's blond curls.

"Damn." Aiden dropped his arm and looked up. "I didn't think of it that way."

"Of course not," muttered Deacon. "That's why you need me around. I think of all things."

Aiden laughed hoarsely and then glanced over at Alex. She smiled reassuringly at him, and it was so apparent that those two were on the same page, as if their minds and souls were linked.

Would Seth and I ever get to that stage? Would we have a chance? I sucked in a short breath and forced it out slowly. We would have that opportunity. I had a plan. Not the greatest. I just needed Apollo to hang around long enough for me to put that plan into action.

The door opened and, as I looked over. Hercules strolled in. His upper lip curled. Distaste was clearly etched into his handsome features. "Even this room is small. Why is everything so small here?"

"It's a dorm," Luke explained, and I had to give him credit for even trying. "Things are kind of small in dorms."

I thought about my dorm back in Radford. "And this is actually bigger than—"

"This is not big," Herc cut me off, and then lifted his arm, flexing his bicep. "*This* is big."

I opened my mouth, but yeah, I had no words.

"But why do you all have a better room than me?" he asked,

looking around with a critical eye. He gazed at Aiden. "I mean, who are you, anyway?"

"Well." Alex popped up from the ottoman. "I'm hungry. You want to go get some food with me?"

Several seconds passed before I realized she was talking to me. I stood slowly as she walked over to the door, sending me a look that warned I better hurry. I did.

Once out in the hall, she lifted her arms and shook her fists at the ceiling as she stomped her feet. Full tantrum mode.

I grinned.

"Oh gods, I can't even deal with that guy," she said. "It's only been a couple of hours and I want to gouge his eyeballs out with my toenails."

"Toenails?"

"Yes," she seethed. "Because they are blunt and it would hurt more, after I delivered a kick to his stupid face."

I laughed as the image formed in my mind. "He's definitely a jerk."

"I'm not even surprised that Apollo managed to find the most annoying demigod," she said as we walked down the hall. "Besides the fact that he has impeccable timing, he has a superpower when it comes to finding douchebags."

The fact that Alex was aware of how bad Apollo's timing was made me think of how she'd discovered that. We reached the crowded lobby. Several students standing near the furies gawked openly at her as she strode toward the door. Night had fallen.

"Wait." I caught up to her, keeping my voice low. "Isn't there a curfew?"

Alex snorted as she opened the door. "Yeah, but it doesn't apply to us."

My brows flew up as we walked out of the door and, sure as hell, walked right past the Guards enforcing curfew. They said nothing. Not even when Alex wiggled her fingers at them.

Alrighty then.

"I hope there's still something to eat in the cafeteria," she said, glancing over at me. "By the way, I'm almost always starving."

"Same here." I wished I'd had my hoodie with me. The wind was still cool, even in June. "They will probably have some cold food out. They normally do overnight. Someone keeps it stocked throughout the night."

"Cool." We walked a few moments in silence and then she said, "Are you good with everything? Leaving for Cali and what we might face out there?"

I nodded and immediately stopped myself from reading more into what was definitely a harmless question. "I am. I mean, I don't know what exactly we might come across, but I've . . . I've faced a Titan before."

Her lips pursed. "I'd heard. You took Hyperion out."

"Kind of," I said as we followed the walkway, eerily alone on the quad. "I just put him out of commission."

"After being . . . alone with him," she added quietly.

I glanced at her sharply. She was staring straight ahead. I didn't respond.

"You know I fought Ares, right?" she asked.

"Yes."

She wet her lip and then stopped walking, facing me. "Ares didn't just kick my ass and he didn't do it quietly. He . . . he broke me for a long time, in a way that I wasn't sure I'd ever really recover from." Each word she spoke was painfully blunt and obviously wasn't easy for her to speak. "I don't know what happened when you were with him. No one has said anything, but I know how . . . I know how evil works."

Closing my eyes, I looked away and swallowed. There'd been no nightmares the last couple of days. I was hoping they'd stay away. Total textbook avoidance, but I really didn't have the time for a mental breakdown.

"Anyway," she said. "I'm just putting this out there. If you want to talk about any of that stuff with Hyperion, I'm here."

"Okay." I cleared my throat as I flipped my ponytail over my shoulder.

Alex smiled a little, a small one that kind of made me feel bad for being upset earlier about her and Apollo.

As we stared at each other, realizing that we had yet another thing in common, a very tenuous bond formed between us. It was frail, brand spanking new, but we'd both looked into the eyes of . . . evil and were standing here despite it.

"Sooooo," she drew the word out as we started walking again. "You and Seth . . . ?"

Oh my, that was going from one awkward conversation to another.

"Looks like things have changed since the last time we talked." Alex laughed then, and the earlier somberness washed away, as if she had practice moving on quickly from terrible, horrific things. "Which was what, just a day ago?"

"Yeah." I laughed along with her. "Feels like weeks, right?"

"That's how it always is when stuff is going on." She hopped up on a low wall and walked on the edge. All right, I was back to not liking her, because I would've fallen right off that like a three-legged llama. "So, it seems like you guys have worked things out."

Part of me didn't want to talk about this, but my tongue started moving as always. "I think so. Yes," I corrected myself. "We've worked things out."

At least I thought we had. We hadn't had a chance to really talk. We were together, but sitting down and actually having a conversation about the state of things was probably a good idea.

When she didn't respond, I looked over at her. Her expression was blank as she walked the wall.

"He doesn't think he should be happy or have anything good in life," I told her, and maybe I shouldn't have said any of that, but

I wasn't sure if Alex really got the kind of place Seth had been existing in, what he was *living*. "Some of it has to do with what he had to do. After what went down with Ares, the gods used him to hunt down and kill those who sided with Ares. He was basically their assassin."

Alex's lips parted. "I . . . I really didn't know that."

"And I know all about the things he did when he was working with Ares. He hasn't forgiven himself for that. Not that some of those things he'd done or been a party to even warrant forgiveness, but he . . . he's stuck, and it's not right," I said, stopping when she came to the edge and peered down at me. "I know there are things you probably will never be able to either forgive him for or forget about."

She cocked her head to the side. "Sometimes I've completely forgiven him. Other times I still want to punch him."

"Understandable." I met her gaze.

Several moments passed and then Alex turned her gaze to the sky. Her shoulders rose. "I worry about him."

"You—"

"I worry about what he's capable of," she added, and I tensed. "I know that's not something you want to hear and please know it's not . . . it's not coming from a bad place. Seth is . . . he gave up everything to make sure Aiden and I had forever. There is good in him, so much good, but . . ."

I thought about what Medusa had said. "But what?"

Her lashes lowered, shielding her eyes. "There is so much darkness in him."

"I know," I whispered. "But he can find the light."

Alex said nothing.

"He deserves a real life," I insisted. "He deserves a second chance."

"Agreed." She jumped off the ledge, landing nimbly beside me. "I mean, Seth has issues, but he deserves happiness. He really does."

"I'm going to make sure he has that," I told her, and I wanted to scream it from the mountaintops.

Alex's eyes widened as she stared at me. "That's pretty hardcore."

I shrugged. "It's true."

There was a pause. "You love him, don't you?"

There was no hesitation. "I'm in love with him."

24

With a hammering heart, I tried to hold still, to do exactly what Seth had ordered me to do, but this was pure torture.

Blissful, crazy, delicious torture.

Seth's calloused palms glided up my inner thighs and around to grip my rear. I stared at the top of his bowed head. Part of me couldn't get over the fact that *he* was on his knees in front of *me*.

Tension ebbed and crested, and I bit down on my lip as his tongue moved along the seam of my thigh. He was killing me. Slowly. Like he'd killed me that night before, when he finally returned from meeting with Solos and we snuck back to his room. We didn't get a lot of talking done then. Our tongues and mouths had been busy with other things. We didn't have a lot of time alone today either. Not when we had to spend the majority of the day preparing for the trip in the morning.

My hips twitched as his tongue moved closer to where I really, *really* wanted his tongue to be.

"Don't move," he commanded in a rough voice that sent a shiver racing across my skin.

At my sides, my fingers spasmed with the need to bury them in his hair and guide that wonderful, and somehow still incredibly annoying mouth over just a few inches. "I'm not moving."

"You're moving." He kissed my inner thigh. "Restraint is an acquired skill."

I glared at the top of his head.

"One that I haven't really mastered." Lashes lifted, and air lodged in my throat as our gazes connected. "Which will be sort of obvious in a few seconds."

His warm breath danced over where I wanted him so badly. I held my breath. He moved his hands, using his thumbs to open me up.

"Oh gods," I whispered.

His tongue skimmed along the heated flesh, wringing a tight gasp from me. He moved to the other side, avoiding the center, and he kept licking and tasting until my legs shook.

"Ambrosia could not be sweeter than you," he growled, and then his tongue delved in. He lapped and sucked, and I couldn't keep my hips still. There was no way. I moved against his mouth.

There was a stuttered heartbeat and then his mouth closed over me. Crying out, I let my head fall back as he suckled deep and hard. I fell right over the edge, into waves and waves of shuddering pleasure.

Suddenly, I was flipped around. A hand landed on the center of my back, guiding me over. My hands hit the bed and my arms shook as Seth gripped my hip with his other hand. I was still coming when he entered me from behind.

This position was new, and holy crap, I'd never felt anything like it. He was in and in deep, and moving, pounding. His strokes were hard and fast, knocking my hair forward and in front of my face. My arms gave out, but before I could fall forward, I was lifted up once more. He moved me, controlled me with an ease that was overwhelming.

And hot.

Really, really hot.

I was on my back and my legs were over his shoulders and he was in me, plunging and retreating, and the tension was spinning tighter and tighter again.

Seth's striking face was a mask of determination, jaw hard and lips thin. His eyes were an incredible, luminous tawny color. My hips buckled and my back arched as he drove in, over and over until the tension broke apart once more, taking him with me. He stiffened, kicking his head back as he groaned out my name. Veins jutted out in stark relief as he pulsed deep inside me.

When he lowered my legs and eased out, he climbed over me, kissing my lips. I had a hard time mustering the energy to do much more than lie there as he disappeared to take care of the condom. I hadn't moved by the time he returned.

Seth was all okey-dokey about that.

He stretched out beside me, tossing his arm and leg over me. He drew me close and every part of us was touching. Both of us were nude and sweaty and it was freaking perfect. In moments like this, it was easy to let myself think, dream, that he and I were just normal, like any other couple in the world.

His hand grazed my breast. "I was thinking . . ."

"I didn't know you were capable of that," I teased.

He chuckled. "Sometimes." That wandering thumb of his found the hardened tip. "But I was wondering if there was any way I could convince you to stay here while we head to California."

That knocked me out of my pleasure-induced haze. I turned my head toward him. "Come again?"

"You don't really need to be there. Hercules, the legendary Bag of Dicks, can find them without you," he explained as my eyes narrowed. "We can bring the demigods back here, to you, where it's safer."

"Besides the roaming packs of daimons, potential shades and Titans, and halfs and pures fighting constantly," I pointed out.

He raised his head up, propping his cheek on his fist. "Yeah, but the Covenant is warded against Titans."

"For now."

"But you'll still be safer." He smoothed his thumb over my nipple, but that wasn't going to distract me. "I just don't want you in a dangerous—"

"Don't say it." I lifted my hand, placing my fingers against his lips. "I get it, Seth. I really do. You want me to be safe. I want you to be safe, but you know that you can't keep me here. Eventually I'm going to have to fight the Titans." My heart rate kicked up at the thought even though my voice was level and calm. I sounded so mature and accepting of my future that I thought I sort of deserved a basket of chicken tenders or something. "That's going to happen."

A muscle thrummed along his jaw, but he kissed the tip of my finger. I smiled at him. "We don't even know what's going to happen out there. Probably nothing but really awkward conversations with some person who has no idea we're about to tell them they're a demigod."

"Yeah, I figured that would be your response, but I had to try."

"And that's the only reason why I'm not throat punching you right now," I paused, smiling sweetly, "with love."

His lips curved up on one corner. "Can you make me a promise though?"

I waited. "Yes. I promise to forever use you as my Pillow Pet."

Seth chuckled. "I'm glad to hear that, but that's not what I was asking about."

I giggled. "Okay. What?"

There was a pause. "If we run into any problems, promise me that you'll stick close to Alex and Aiden."

Unsure I heard him correctly, I looked over at him again. "What?"

"If anything goes down, you'll stick close to them," he repeated. "I know you've been training. I know you can fight and you're using the elements. I'm not saying this because I doubt your ability to fight and hold your own." He paused, brows furrowing together. "Even though I sort of suggested that earlier, but I was being a dick because, well, I'm a dick."

I snorted.

"But I just want you to stick close to them, okay?" he finished.

I really had no idea where to start with this. "Why would you tell me to stay close to them and not you?"

His hand stilled on my breast. "I can get a little . . . out of control if a fight turns bad."

My brows inched up.

"I just don't want anything to blow . . . back on you," he added as his lashes lowered. "I couldn't deal with being the reason something—"

"You're not going to be the reason." I placed my hand on his cheek, lifting his chin so his eyes met mine. "And I know you're never going to hurt me."

A muscle flickered along his jaw. "How did I . . . ?"

When he trailed off and didn't finish, I ran my finger under his lower lip, smoothing out the skin. "How did you what?"

Those eyes met mine again. "How did I get so lucky with you?"

"Good question," I murmured.

He laughed, but the light sound quickly faded, as if it was never there. "I know that sounds stupid, saying something like that, but I . . . I never expected you, Josie. Not once did I ever think any of this was going to happen." He paused, dragging his hand down, over my stomach. "I've never been in a serious relationship."

"And this is serious?" I asked, wanting to squeeze my eyes shut.

"More serious than I've ever been about anything in my life," he said, and there wasn't a part of me that doubted what he said. He shifted his palm against his cheek. "But you know that this . . . this won't last."

Ice drenched my skin.

"No matter how badly I want it to, and I do, Josie." His eyes closed briefly. "I want it more than anything, but I made a deal, and at some point they will come to collect."

"And I'll be there to stop them," I stated.

His eyes flew open. Surprise flickered over his face. "Josie—"

"If I have to fight every god, including my father, to get you out of that deal, I will." Determination filled me. "That's a check you can take to the bank and cash."

"Wait. Did you just say that's 'a check you can take to the bank?'"

Heat hit my cheeks. "My granny used to always say that."

Seth looked at me a moment and then dipped his head to mine. He didn't kiss me, just rested his lips against the curve of my cheek. "You are still so very mortal."

"And you still like that about me?"

"Yes." He kissed my cheek then, sliding his hand further south. He cupped me, squeezing. "I also really like *this* about you."

"Perv."

"Believe it." His hand drifted away though, and he grinned as he stared down at me, but that smile didn't reach his eyes.

"You need to learn to trust yourself more," I told him, patting his cheek. "Like start some kind of daily affirmations or something."

"Oh yeah, Joe, I'll start doing that in the morning. Immediately."

"I won't tell anyone." I grinned.

"Whatever." He laughed as his hand drifted across my belly.

Relieved that he was joking and laughing again, I let my gaze roam over his striking face. His lashes were lowered and the corners of his lips were curled up on one side. As I watched him, I thought about what Alex had said earlier. I pushed those thoughts aside and another thought surfaced, something I'd forgotten about with the arrival of Hercules and . . . well, Seth being Seth . . .

"Hey," I said, and his lashes lifted. "Do you think it's possible that Alex is still the God Killer?"

One eyebrow rose. "No. It was why the gods insisted that . . . that she had to die a mortal death. That way, she would no longer be the God Killer."

I frowned. What in the heck was Medusa talking about then?

"Why are you asking that?"

I shrugged. "Just wondering."

Seth curled his hand over my hip. "Alex isn't the God Killer. She's still an Apollyon somehow. A demigod and an Apollyon."

My frown increased. "How can she be both . . . ?" I trailed off as I realized what that meant. My stomach seized. "Are you two still connected?"

His gaze flicked up to mine. "Yes."

Every muscle locked up. I lay there, unable to move. I couldn't think around the knowledge that Alex and Seth were connected, joined in a way that I could never fathom, couldn't—

"Josie." His hand left my hip and curled around my cheek. "Alex and I are connected still, but not like it was before. No-where near as powerful."

I drew in a shallow breath as I grabbed his wrist. My stomach churned, and I felt like I might vomit. "Are you just telling me that to make me feel better about it?"

"No. I swear. I can barely pick up anything from her and when I do, it's faint." He dipped his head and kissed the tip of my nose. "Trust me, I'm not overly thrilled about it, but compared to before, it's not a big deal."

Not a big deal. I kept repeating that, over and over, but knowing the man you loved was connected to another woman on a mystical, cellular level was totally a big deal!

Seth smoothed his thumb along my lower lip. "It doesn't affect us, Josie. Never has. Never will. What I have with you—"

"It's okay." It had to be, and I could be cool about this. Alex was in love with Aiden, and Seth cared about me in a way he never cared about someone before. I knew that. I turned my cheek and kissed his palm. "It's okay."

He slid his hand off my cheek and gripped the back of my neck. "You sure?"

"Positive." I let go of his wrist and placed my hand on his chest, feeling his warm, hard skin. Honestly, I wasn't all that okay, but I had to deal with this, and maybe after we found the demigod in California, I could have a minor freak-out session.

"You ready to do this? It's going to be a long-ass day," Seth said after a few moments. "Over a twenty-hour ride between here and Malibu."

"Yeah." I stretched, wiggling my fingers and toes. "But I refuse to be in the same vehicle as Hercules."

"Cosign," he replied. "Fucking cosign."

25

Seth

*S*hit rolled downhill the moment we all were standing by the outer wall, preparing to climb into two Covenant SUVs.

First off, it was too early, and Josie and I hadn't spent the night sleeping and being all responsible, getting rest or anything. Maybe dozing here and there, but definitely not being *restful*.

More like ridiculously active.

But the things she said last night, about fighting the gods, including her father, weighed on me. Fighting those twisted fuckers usually ended with someone being dead or getting turned into some kind of sedentary object for their enjoyment.

I didn't want her fighting for me.

And I also didn't want the faint connection between Alex and me to bother her. I couldn't blame her for being upset though. Honestly, I admired her for how she was dealing with it.

The second thing that warned me this trip was going to be full of potholes was the fact that Deacon was out here. Why in the hell he was tagging along was beyond me, but he was not going to be my problem.

"I call shotgun," Hercules called out.

And there was the third and final giant pain in my ass. I turned around, squinting as I stared into the glare of the morning sun.

"Oh my gosh," murmured Josie, her wide eyes moving from him to me. She did a double take. I couldn't believe what I was seeing.

Hercules was dressed like me. Sporting faded jeans and a gray Henley pushed up to his elbows. He had a cup of coffee that smelled like . . . vanilla and mint?

"We're wearing the same shirt," he pointed out with a smirk.

"Except I'm wearing it better," I remarked.

Josie made a soft choking sound as the demigod tilted his head to the side, expression perplexed. "That's not possible. You do not have the body that I do. I'm a ten."

I stared at him, brow rising. "Are you for real?"

"Am I not standing here?" Hercules chuckled, lifting the coffee cup. "I know. I know. Seeing me, *the* Hercules, is hard to believe, that such a legend could be—"

"I know this part is hard to believe," I said, reaching down and clasping Josie's hand. "But I don't care, and if you could, like, I don't know, eat shit and shut the fuck up, I'd be forever grateful."

I pulled Josie around to the back of the SUV, letting go of her hand to throw open the hatch. Slipping her bag off her shoulder, I tossed it into the back and added mine with it.

"I think he likes you." Aiden leaned against the bumper.

Alex snorted as she walked by.

I snatched the aviator sunglasses off his head and slipped them on. "I'd also like it if you'd eat shit—"

"Seth." Josie smacked my arm and then smiled apologetically. "Sorry. He's not much of a morning person today."

"Would've never guessed that." Aiden folded his arms. "I was thinking we'd stop near Vegas for the night. That'd leave us about five hours and get us to Malibu sometime in the afternoon, depending on when we leave."

Luke stopped by, his gray beanie pulled low. "We just need to keep our eyes open for daimons. We'll be super-close to a huge colony out there."

I nodded.

"We got this." Alex bumped her hip against Aiden's. "Nothing like taking out a few daimons to break up the boredom of a long drive."

"Like old times." Aiden lowered his head, kissing her. "But let's try not to have a repeat of that."

"True." Luke backed off, walking over to where Deacon was rummaging through the back of the SUV, which reminded me of something.

I grabbed my bag and opened it. Reaching inside, I found the slender tablet and pulled it out. "You forgot this."

Josie's eyes lit up with excitement. "Ah, I totally forgot my e-reader. Awesome." She popped forward, kissing my cheek as she clutched it close to her chest. "Thank you. I'd go crazy without this."

"That's sweet," Alex teased, punching my arm. "You're such a sweetie, a big old ball of sweetness."

"People are really annoying this morning," I grumbled.

Alex laughed as Aiden dragged her over to the other SUV. "It *is* very sweet of you," Josie said, stepping back from the rear door. "Thank you."

"Uh-huh," I muttered.

Marcus appeared outside the wall, flanked by several Guards. He spoke to Aiden and Solos first, and then frowned at something Hercules said. Only gods knew what it was. Probably something about the size of his muscles.

I turned, brushing the dust off my hands, as Marcus and crew made their way over to us. The dean smiled tightly at Josie and then those cool emerald eyes landed on me. "We'll be waiting to hear from you all once you arrive in California and locate the first demigod."

I nodded as Marcus spoke to Alex and Aiden. The game plan was to take the demigod to the University and then head to Canada. Bending over, I picked up another duffel bag. This one was loaded with enough guns and weapons to bring Homeland Security screaming down on us. Several of the blades inside were wrapped and protected after being dipped in the Pegasus blood.

Which made flying a bit tricky.

We could use compulsion on a few mortals, but all of TSA and everyone nearby? Yeah, that would be a pain.

"You'll be seeing us again, sooner than you expect." Hercules paused long enough to slug down some coffee. "It will take no matter of time for me to zero in on who you're looking for."

"That's good to hear." Marcus's tone was bland.

"All right. We're ready to head out," I announced before Hercules could launch into a massive speech on how awesome he was.

Hercules tossed his cup aside. It hit the ground, breaking into four large sections. A vein popped along Marcus's temple as Hercules headed for our SUV. "I'm riding with you guys."

Solos stopped, bag in hand, and veered around sharply, heading for where Aiden stood.

"Oh, no," I called out, smacking my hand on the rear door. "You're going with us, buddy. Oh yeah, you're going down in a ball of flames right along with us."

Josie giggled as Hercules yanked open the back passenger door. The SUV shook and groaned under his sudden weight.

"You aren't going to be laughing in an hour," I warned her.

Prowling around to the back of the SUV, Solos tossed his bag in. "You're lucky I like you."

I closed the rear door. If I was going to have to deal with

Herc-The-Dickface, I wasn't going to suffer alone. Oh no, my kind of misery demanded company.

Alex darted over to her father as I walked around to the passenger side of the SUV and opened the door for Josie, who already had her nose buried in her e-reader. She barely looked up as she murmured her thanks. Shutting the door, I turned and caught Aiden's gaze.

He wasn't exactly smiling. That damn look was on his face, one I'd seen a dozen times, usually back then, before Ares. Before Alex Awakened on her eighteenth birthday. The same look he gave me whenever he saw me with Alex.

Like he trusted me as much as he did a daimon starved for *aether*. Didn't blame him either. He wasn't like his brother, who seemed to see puppies spewing rainbows in everyone. He wasn't like Josie, who didn't know me back then. Who only knew the Seth *she* wanted me to be.

He stared at me like he knew I was wearing a mask and he was waiting for it to shatter, revealing what truly existed underneath.

Is it possible that Alex is still the God Killer?

What an odd question for Josie to ask. What an odd thing for me to think about right now.

Aiden pivoted around, hand clenching the car keys as I closed the door behind Josie. Solos got in the back, and once I was behind the wheel I pushed Aiden out of my thoughts. I reached into my pocket and pulled out the disposable phone we'd gotten the night before. I placed it in the cup holder.

Behind me, Hercules lurched forward, grasping the back of my seat. "You know, this is the first time I've been in a SUV. Apollo just kept popping me around every place, so please don't ruin my first experience with less than stellar driving."

I clenched the steering wheel.

"You haven't been in the mortal realm in a while, have you?" Solos asked.

"No, but I've been watching a lot of TV and movies. I know all about California," he explained sagely. "I watched all the episodes of the old and new *Beverly Hills 90210*, *Melrose Place*, and *Laguna Beach*."

This guy was not for real.

I glanced over at Josie. Her lips were pressed together as she stared down. A second passed and she peeked up. Her eyes danced with amusement.

Solos sighed. "This is going to be so much fun."

"Oh, everything is fun when I'm around." Hercules's knees knocked into the back of my seat as he leaned back. "This one time, when I was ordered by the gods to . . ."

I could only think of three words.

Fuck. My. Life.

26

"*Y*ou should drive, because I'm going to end it all. Once we're on the freeway, I'm going to jump out of this vehicle and throw myself in front of a Mack truck."

Josie's laugh cut off her yawn. "That's a little excessive."

Adjusting the sunglasses I'd stolen from Aiden yesterday morning, I smirked. "I do not think anything is excessive when it comes to him."

"But that won't even kill you."

I sighed. "Yeah, but I'm pretty sure it'll knock me unconscious for the time being."

She laughed again and glanced out the window. Heat rolled off the cracked asphalt. The temps were nothing like South Dakota. "Oh, geez."

"He's still with that woman, isn't he?"

"Yep."

We'd arrived in Vegas last night, about an hour or so before midnight, picking a hotel far from the strip, where only the dazzling and flashing lights could reach us. Of course, the moment

Hercules's feet touched the pavement, he was off. Kind of couldn't blame him. The last time I'd been in Vegas had been with the Titan Perses, and if you looked up the definition of drunken debauchery, there would be a picture of Perses and me.

This time was different.

The flashing neon lights, the alcohol, the girls and the hyped-up atmosphere held no allure. Once I'd closed the hotel door behind Josie and me, I didn't reopen it until this morning.

Like an old man, ball and chain included, and I was fucking a-okay with that.

But Hercules obviously had had a rough and interesting night.

He showed up this morning smelling like a distillery, wearing the same clothes as yesterday, except the Henley was torn and he must've forgotten to button his pants. And he wasn't alone.

Hercules literally tried to convince us to allow some chick who was wearing cut-off jean shorts and a bra to come with us. Not going to happen. I looked over, past Josie. Now he was impregnating the chick's mouth with his tongue.

Gods.

"Huh," Solos said, tipping his head onto the back of the seat. "Good thing demigods can't get STDs."

"I'd be more worried about what he'd give her," Josie commented.

True dat.

Finally, he hauled his huge ass into the SUV and, thank the gods and all their screwed-up glory, he passed out the moment we hit the freeway that fed into southern California and stayed that way the rest of the trip, proving that the gods sometimes smiled down on us.

Josie

California was shiny.

Well, at least southern California was. The sun was . . . everywhere. Big and round in the endless blue sky, glinting off the roofs and windshields of the nonstop stream of cars barely moving on I-405. Waves of heat rolled off the asphalt, and even with the air conditioner on full blast, the warmth was creeping into the vehicle.

Six hours in the car was painful and the windy mountainous roads with Seth behind the wheel had me thankful more than once that I was a demigod, but the place was . . . *gods*, I'd seen nothing like it before. The peaks and bluffs were vast and beautiful, and I wanted to stop at one of the many look-out points, but figured no one would appreciate that.

I'd rolled down the window and the roaring warm air lifted my ponytail and washed over my skin as we'd raced up Kanan Road. The moment we crested the last hill and the ocean came into view, I almost forgot about what we were here to do.

The sea was endless.

A shade of blue that grew deeper and brighter the closer we got. I'd never seen the ocean before, and it went on, until it faded into the sky. I'd never felt sand between my toes or the white frothy tips of an ocean's wave. Being here, finally, was surreal.

And all I could think about was where Malibu Barbie would live.

After grabbing a quick lunch, we ended up stopping at an older, retro-style motel along the Pacific Coast Highway, creatively named the Malibu Motel. Unloading our bags and the massive number of weapons didn't take that long. The inside of the motel kind of reminded me of the one Seth and I had stayed at before, except we weren't in the honeymoon suite this time.

Based on what Hercules had discovered with Apollo, we figured we'd find Poseidon's offspring somewhere in Malibu, but the
place wasn't particularly small and there were people, lots of . . .
really attractive and thin people.

We hit the area of Paradise Cove in the afternoon, and while I
was thrilled to get sand between my toes, I wished I'd had some
shorts to pack. Sweat was already accumulating in places sweat
should never gather, but the sun felt good on my skin. It seemed
like it had been way too long since I'd actually felt warm.

Plus, I felt like an ogre around these people. A big, hairy ogre.

The first day searching was a fail on many levels. We didn't find
who we were looking for. We nearly lost Hercules to a group of
bikini-clad girls multiple times, and we had to drive further out
from the coast to find a store that sold shorts my thighs would
actually fit in.

Sigh.

And then the shorts were a mistake. Seth said I looked hot, and
later, in our bed that creaked, he showed me how hot he thought
I looked in those shorts, but while I was out on the beach, my legs
were so white they were blinding.

Dusk was quickly giving way to night when we stopped to grab
dinner at The Beach Café. Seated inside at a large table, I couldn't
help but wonder if any of the patrons, the very mortal patrons, noticed anything *off* about our group. Besides the fact that our group
had an extraordinary amount of attractive people—not like that
was anything rare in L.A., but did they feel anything strange?

Could they sense at all that demigods, the children of demigods, and the Apollyon surrounded them? Like a weird vibe in
the air or just that sensation you sometimes get that warns you
something isn't right?

I knew I never felt anything when I was a normal mortal. I'd
believed that Erin was totally who and what she said she was. I
had no idea she was a mortal creature known as a furie.

Other than the waitress openly gawking at the guys, she didn't seem to realize that she was surrounded by mythical creatures as she took our drink order.

I went with a Coke. Most went with water . . . until it came to Herc's order. He eyed the menu. "I'll take a gin and tonic."

The pretty waitress, who I'd already assumed was in the L.A. area to be an actress, because I assumed everyone there was there to act or model, blushed. "Can I see an I.D.?"

My eyes widened. I.D.? Hell. There was no—

"Honey, you already saw my I.D.," Herc said as he glanced up. His gaze caught and held the waitress's. Tiny hairs rose on my arm as a *push* rolled across the table, a flicker of recognizable power. "You know I am of age."

The waitress blinked slowly and then said, "How about an appetizer?"

Holy wow.

I'd never get used to seeing a compulsion used, and even though it was over something so minor, I didn't like it. "You shouldn't do that."

Herc looked at me like he couldn't even fathom why I suggested that. "I want a drink, so I'm getting a drink."

"But you don't need a drink," I reasoned, curling my fingers along the edges of the laminated menu. "Compulsions shouldn't be used for something so . . . so trivial."

He raised an eyebrow. "Why not?"

I glanced around the table. Alex looked seconds from face-planting the menu. Aiden was staring at Herc with a mixture of morbid fascination and distaste. Solos was actually checking out an older blonde woman who looked like she belonged on House-wives of Whatever. Luke shared Alex's expression, and Seth, who was beside me, looked like he wanted to punch the demigod, but that was no different from the moment they crossed paths.

Deacon was the only one who actually watched Herc with favorable interest.

"It's not right," I explained. Slowly. "You're messing with her head. That is wrong."

He shrugged. "She's just a mortal."

"Just a mortal," I repeated dumbly.

Seth draped his arm along the back of my chair. "Don't waste your time, Josie."

"Nothing with me is a waste of time," Herc stated, and I joined Alex, wanting to face-plant the table.

"Anyway," Aiden cut in smoothly. "Today was a bust," he said, keeping his voice low. "While it may not seem like we're in a time crunch here, the longer all of us are in one location, the more likely we're going to run into problems."

"Not just with the Titans," Solos agreed, still focused on the older blonde woman. "But we'll have daimon problems before we know it."

"I'm not worried," Herc replied.

Seth smoothed his hand along my back as the waitress returned with our drinks and we placed our orders. Aiden got a burger without buns, and I felt like that was a crime against nature.

"Worried or not, we need you to find the demigod, not the girl in the skimpiest bikini," Alex pointed out as soon as the waitress disappeared. "Even though you do seem to have an impressive talent for that."

So true.

Herc smiled proudly. "You all need to have faith."

"I have faith," Deacon commented. "All the faith."

"I like you," Herc stated, and Luke inhaled through his nose as he widened his eyes. "Why? Because you recognize how awesome I am."

"Fuck me," Seth muttered under his breath, and then louder, "Can you just not talk? At least until the food gets here?"

Herc frowned as confusion flickered across his face. "Why would I not talk?"

"Okay." I smiled brightly and continued before Herc could. "So the plan for tomorrow is to keep looking here, in the same area?"

Aiden nodded. "Malibu is only about nineteen miles. He has to be around here somewhere."

I thought about walking nineteen miles and almost wished Herc was talking about himself. The conversation shifted, though, to what it was like in Tartarus for Alex and Aiden, and we lingered well after the food arrived and was consumed. All of us listened to them, even Herc, and I wondered if it was possible to get a tour of Tartarus without being, well, you know, dead. I'd kind of like to see the ball of fire that turned into a dragon that Alex described.

The vibe was good as we headed back to the Motel. Herc was chill, which helped everyone in terms of patience and happiness, but as we neared the Motel a strange feeling hit me as I stared out the window, focused on the dark waters of the ocean.

The roof of my mouth dried. Tiny balls of dread formed in my stomach. A great sense of foreboding washed over me, so strong and insistent that I tensed in my seat. I glanced at Seth. He was focused on the road. Herc and Solos were quiet in the backseat.

My temples pounded as I faced forward in the seat. Nothing was going on, but I couldn't shake the feeling that the peacefulness felt by everyone wasn't going to last.

The dry spell when it came to nightmares ended that night.

I'd had another one.

The same as before. The unfamiliar Titan was there, this time in the car Seth had been driving. He'd appeared in the backseat and this time he told me something that chilled me to the very core, three words that followed me as I showered and got ready for the day.

Dig a grave.

That's what the unknown Titan had whispered in my nightmare. *Dig a grave.*

Needless to say, that sort of freaked me out.

We hit up Paradise Cove again; this time Aiden, Deacon, Luke, and Solos stayed back, which left the rest of us to start the needle in the haystack search. I wasn't so confident that we'd find him as we drove along Cliffside Drive.

Hercules was confident, though. "He's here. I can sense him."

"Is it like a disturbance in the force?" Seth quipped, glancing into the rearview mirror.

I grinned. *Star Wars* reference for the win.

"Actually, yes." Hercules nodded seriously.

Seth looked like he was going to gouge his own eyeballs out.

"He's here. I can feel him." Herc shifted in the seat. "You need to pull over. Now."

"Give me a second." Finding a place wasn't easy. It took several minutes, and Seth ended up parking near some overlook. "All right. Let's do this."

Seth opened his door, and I hopped out, stretching as I walked over. "Whoa. The view . . ."

"It's amazing." Alex joined me. Near an edge of a bluff stood an overlook obviously created for the view.

And it was stunning. A breeze washed over my already-warm skin as I stared down at the sand and ocean. The area was rough. Waves high. Black spots in the water, appearing and disappearing every few moments, turned out to be surfers.

Wait a second . . .

Seth walked up behind me and pulled the back of my shirt down. "Your gun was showing."

"Oh. Awkward." I turned to Herc. "You sense Poseidon's son here?"

The demigod nodded. "Yes. He's definitely out here."

"Here" was Point Dume, a small community on a bluff, over-looking a strip of sand and the rocky ocean below. A place popular with surfers, by the looks of it.

"Do you think his son is a . . . surfer?" I asked, staring back out over the cliff. A shadowy blob rose up, coasting a wave. "I mean, he is the son of Poseidon, so that would . . ."

". . . be really cliché," Alex suggested. "But would make sense. I mean, his abilities are locked up, but that doesn't mean he wouldn't have some sort of affinity for water. Did you have anything that, looking back, reminded you of Apollo?"

Not that I knew of, but knowing my luck, people probably thought I was creepy or something.

I started to respond, but Herc was walking off. Alex sighed as she caught up to him. Seth waited for me, his eyes hidden behind the sunglasses he'd taken from Aiden. I was grateful I'd picked up a pair during my depressing shopping excursion last night.

We quickly encountered an obstacle—a large metal gate that blocked the paths leading down to the beach.

"Looks like the beach is private," I noted, briefly turning into Captain Obvious.

Seth stepped around and placed his hand near the lock on the gate. The surge of power was faint, but a second later, the gate unlocked. He gave it a little push and it swung open.

Where Seth's hand had been, the metal was melted.

"Well," I said. "That solves that."

I followed behind them, unable to shake the feeling that we were trespassing. I didn't vocalize that sensation, because it was such a mortal thing to feel. I mean, what would anyone do if they caught us? Try to arrest us?

Oh no.

Heart skipping a beat, I thought about the fact there was a Glock shoved into the back of my not very attractive, size-too-small shorts.

"I can practically smell the money," Alex commented as we started down one of the steep dirt trails that led to the beach. "You think the guy we're looking for lives in one of those houses?" There were massive houses all along the bluff. The kind of homes that could fit an entire football team in them. Mansions of all shapes. I bet there were celebrities who lived here.

Oh my God, what if Poseidon's son was a celebrity?

Hercules moved swiftly down the trail, and I was surprised I didn't tumble down the path, knocking everyone out of the way like a sling-shot Angry Bird.

The moment we hit the beach, Hercules hung a right. Up ahead there was a cluster of guys standing among surfboards that were stuck upright in the sand. Some were wearing board shorts. Others had wetsuits half-on, pulled up to their lean waists.

Alex's steps slowed even though Hercules was stalking past them. "I have a feeling we're not welcome here."

"Understatement of the century," I murmured as one of the taller guys broke free from the group. His damp blond hair curled across his sun-kissed forehead.

"Hey," he said, reaching Alex first. "What the fuck do you think you're doing here?"

Alex looked at him and laughed—laughed and kept walking. The surfer dude didn't think that was funny. He grabbed her arm, and that was all it took.

She spun on him, capturing his arm. Yanking him forward, she used his body weight against him. Thrown off-balance, he stumbled, and Alex dipped under his arm, twisting it back behind him. "Didn't your mama teach you not to grab girls?"

"What the—?"

"Wrong answer." Alex twisted his arm and flipped him. The guy hit the sand on his back, his expression absolutely dumbfounded. "I'd stay down if I were you."

Shouts rose from the group of surfers. They started toward us, their bare feet kicking up sand.

Seth faced them. "I wouldn't do that if I were you."

All of them—all six of them—skidded to a halt. Whatever those guys saw in Seth's face had them backing up like scolded puppies.

He chuckled. "Smart idea. Have a nice day, fuckheads."

"God." I stared at Alex as we started walking again. "You're a ninja."

She shrugged, and she kind of looked like one in her black tank top and shorts. Of course, she looked super-cute. Not like a blonde ogre. I glanced back at the guys. They were crowded around the dude still laid out on the sand. Had Alex seriously injured—

"There he is," Hercules announced.

My head whipped around. At first, all I saw was Hercules, but then, several yards ahead was a lone guy coming out of the ocean, a surfboard lifted over his head. Waves lapped at his knees and then his calves. Within moments, he was on the beach, biceps flexing.

This guy looked like a demigod.

Tall and lean with a tightly ripped stomach, his dark hair was slicked back from a classically handsome face. Skin bronzed and eyes that were an odd mix of blue and green, he smiled and nodded when we neared him. He looked about my age.

At least he didn't seem like he was going to cuss at us.

I had no idea how this was going to go down. It was something

we'd talked about during the ride down here and over dinner yesterday. Breaking this kind of news was going to get crazy.

"You sure it's him?" Seth asked in a low voice.

Hercules chuckled. "I have never been wrong."

"That's not entirely reassuring," Alex muttered, and then gave
the guy a little wave. "Hi!"

"Hey. Saw you guys had some problems up there," he said,
lowering the board and shoving it in the sand. He smiled at Alex.
"That was hot, but you guys should be careful. If you're not a local,
you're not going to be very welcome here."

"Thanks for the heads-up," Seth said, stopping beside me. "But
we're actually looking for you."

The guy's brows flew up. "Me? I'm sorry." He took the four of
us in. "I don't recognize you guys, and I think I would."

"I'm Hercules," Herc said, spreading his muscled arms wide as
he smiled. "Yes, *that* Hercules. I've come from Olympus to find
you—you, the son of Poseidon."

My mouth dropped open. Oh my God.

"Tactful," muttered Alex as she turned sideways, placing her
hands on her hips. "Gods."

The guy stared at Hercules and then laughed. "Man, you're as
high as balls, aren't you?"

Hercules frowned as he glanced over at me. "I don't even know
what that means."

"It means you're an idiot," snapped Seth. He shook his head.
"He's not high. He's just . . . socially inept."

Hercules turned to Seth, scowling.

"We really need to talk to you," Alex jumped in. "It's very important and we've come a long, long way to find you."

"Look, I'm not sure what's going on here," he said, looking
over his shoulder. "But I've got to go." He started to lift the board.
"I'll see you—"

"Wait. Please." I stepped forward, and surprisingly he stopped. "I know what he said sounded completely crazy—"

"No, it didn't," Hercules snapped.

"Dude." Seth placed a hand on Hercules's shoulder. "Can you like, keep it quiet for a minute? Just a minute."

The demigod mulled that over. "Maybe."

I drew in a frustrated breath. The demigod part was out of the bag, so it was time to go full crazy on the poor guy. "What he said is true, though. My father is Apollo. I'm a demigod, just like Hercules, who is that Hercules." I jerked my chin at Alex. "She's also a demigod. Not like you or me, but she's one too."

His light eyes slid from me to Alex. She smiled tightly at him. A moment passed. "Yeah," he said, drawing the word out. "This is where I end the conversation and bow out politely."

He started to turn again, but I shot forward, grabbing his arm. His head whipped around, and I decided showing worked better than telling. I lifted my right hand and summoned the element of fire. Energy coursed through me and, in a heartbeat, flames danced over my knuckles.

"Look down," I ordered quietly.

He hesitated a moment and then his chin dipped. He jerked back, but I kept hold of his arm. "Holy shit, your hand is on fire!"

Several people nearing us slowed, and Seth moved closer, blocking their view. "I'd put that out before I have to put everyone under a compulsion."

Nodding, I shook my hand, dispersing the flames. "As a demigod, you can control fire."

"Holy shit," he repeated, staring at my unblemished skin.

"But that's not it," Alex added. "You'll be able to control wind and earth, and I bet you already are super-familiar with water, all things considered."

Blood drained from his face as he lifted his gaze to mine. "Your hand was on *fire*. Like, legit fire."

"Not really, but kind of." I glanced over at Seth. "We can explain it all to you. I promise."

"That's not normal," he reasoned. "That is some serious, not-normal shit right there."

His pupils were dilating, swallowing the bluish-green hue, and that couldn't be a good sign. Nope. Not at all.

"A minute is up," Hercules said, crossing his arms. "Do I still need to stay quiet?"

"Yes," Seth and Alex replied at the same time.

Hercules sighed. "You guys suck."

"We would like to talk more with you." I kept my voice low and level. "Is that okay? Because we really need to explain . . ." I trailed off. A weird scent tickled my nose, one that did not belong oceanside.

The scent was dank and musky, rich as fresh soil after a heavy rain. Tiny hairs rose over my skin.

Seth cursed, hands flexing at his sides. "We've got shades."

27

Seth

We didn't have the greatest plan when it came to how we were going to break the news to Poseidon's son, but seriously? Just blurting out what was going on? Hercules was a fucking giant pain in the ass, but right now he wasn't our biggest problem.

The scent of the Underworld surrounded us.

Adrenaline spiked through me as I scanned the beach, not seeing anything out of the norm. Surfers were crowded nearby. Girls in bikinis walked, but a shade could be in any one of them. I wasn't surprised. Things had gone way too smoothly on this trip. This was the risk I knew we faced, because if there were shades, there were Titans.

"We need to go," I said, grabbing the guy's arm as my gaze met Josie's. "Right now."

He dug his feet in. "I'm not going anywhere with you—with any of you."

"We're not going to hurt you," Alex reasoned, which was hilarious considering this guy had just seen her singlehandedly take down a guy a foot taller than her. "We're here to protect you."

"From what?" He yanked on his arm, but he wasn't going anywhere.

"From the Titans who want to drain you dry," Hercules replied, and for a very brief second I entertained the fantasy of dropkicking him upside the head. "They will turn you into a shell of who you used to be."

"What?" the guy's voice pitched up, and panic flooded his already pale face.

"Jesus," muttered Josie, and the scent of the Underworld increased. "We will explain everything. I promise you, but we need to get you out of here."

"I'm not going anywhere with any of you. I'm going—"

"Yes. You are." Done with this, I pulled out the gun as I shifted, blocking my hand as I pressed the business end of the Glock against his lower back. "Don't freak out. I need you to stay calm, but what you feel against your back is exactly what you think it is."

Josie's eyes widened.

"Oh God," the guy gasped with a shudder, and for a moment I thought he might pass out.

"We don't have time for this. You'll thank us later, trust me, but right now I need you to start walking."

The guy didn't move.

I sighed. "What is your name? Mine is Seth. Queen Kung Fu is Alex. You already know who the steroids guy is. That is Hercules, and the beautiful blonde standing in front of you is Josie. What's your name?"

A moment passed. "G-Gable."

"Okay, Gable, we're going to walk up this beach and then up to the road. We're going to put you in our car, and then we're going to leave the place, hopefully without incident," I explained slowly, clearly. "You don't want any incidents, do you?"

"No," he said.

"Perfect. Now you're going to start walking." A second later, he started walking. I glanced over at Alex. "Call Aiden and let him know we found him. Tell him we'll meet them over at the motel."

"On it." She reached into her back pocket and pulled out the throwaway phone as she walked ahead, watching the beach as she dialed Aiden's phone.

Josie worked on assuring Gable of the fact that we didn't plan on shooting him in the back while Hercules actually became sort of useful as he picked up the surfboard and flanked us.

Escorting Gable toward the trails, I kept an eye out for any strange behaviors. People were watching us, mainly because I was super-close to Gable. No one saw the gun, and we needed it to stay that way.

The walk up the trail wasn't as fast as I'd hoped. Gable stared at Josie as she continued to talk softly with him, explaining what was happening. I don't think anything was getting through to the guy. Every so often, his arm trembled.

At the top of the hill, the SUV came into view, and still no sign of a shade. Josie placed her hand on Gable's other arm. "Everything is going to be okay. We're going to take you to meet our friends. They're . . . um, excited to meet—"

Gable suddenly spun on me, twisting so that he could work his arm out of my grasp as he dipped low, muscles tensing. He shot back up, aiming his elbow for my nose.

Awesome defensive move. Boy took some classes. That move would've taken me down.

If I weren't the fucking Apollyon . . .

My movements were too fast for him to track. Blocking his arm before it could connect with my face, I knocked his elbow away and then slammed my hand into his shoulder. He fell back into the side of the SUV. His eyes flew wide, and before he could recoup, I was in his face, gun shoved into his side.

"That's not possible," he said, chest rising and falling rapidly. "No one can move that fast. No one—"

"No one who is mortal," I said, getting my face all up in his. "I'm going to be a nice guy for once and pretend you didn't just try to break my nose, but you get one free pass from me. That's it. After that, I don't give a fuck who you are or how important you are. I will lay you out and it won't be pretty."

Gable's chest stopped moving. On the other side of the SUV, Alex opened the door. Hercules was at the rear, eyeing the vehicle and the surfboard he carried.

"Seth." Josie leaned into me, and I inhaled deeply, catching the scent of the shampoo she'd used this morning. Shea butter. There was something calming about that. "He's scared. He has every right to be."

I met Gable's stare. Very little of the bluish-green eyes was visible. "He should be scared."

"That's not helping," she replied, and then she faked a smile like only she could. "Gable, I really need you to calm down and work with us here. We're not going to hurt you. If we were, he would've already done it."

Gable's frantic gaze swung to Josie. "Are you holding me for ransom? Because if you need money, I can get it. You don't have to do this."

"Gods," I grunted, shaking my head. "We're not holding you hostage."

"Hey!" Gable jerked as his focus shot over my shoulder.

I glanced over, just in time to see Hercules step to the edge of the overlook and toss the surfboard over the cliff like he was throwing a football. I *almost* laughed. Almost.

Hercules turned around, seeing all of us staring at him. "What? It wasn't going to fit without doing . . . stuff to the seat."

Gable snapped out of it, and a different kind of horrified expression flooded his face. "My board! What the fuck, man? You just threw my board over a cliff!"

"We'll get you a new one that Hercules won't smash," Josie promised, and I snickered at that. "But we need—"

Wind picked up, and there it was again. Musky. Dank. The smell of death. Shit. Josie sensed it too.

"We need to go." Alex jogged around the front of the SUV. I pulled Gable away from the back door. She threw it open.

Gable twisted in my grip, but I got him turned around, prepared to throw him head-first into the car if necessary. I started to lift him up when a dark, oily heaviness permeated the air around us. I looked over my shoulder.

An older man came up the trail, looking like any guy who would be out on the beach for a stroll. Loose khaki pants, white T-shirt, and sandals. A silver watch glinted off his wrist. The stench of death was strong, but he was still too far away to tell if he was a shade or some guy out for a walk.

"Everything okay up here?" he said.

"Don't," I heard Alex warn Gable in a hushed whisper.

Josie spoke up. "Everything is fine. Thanks."

"I don't know about that," the man replied. "Doesn't seem like it's okay." He started toward us, steps purposeful and precise. "Seems like something is going on here."

My eyes narrowed as Josie tensed beside me. The moment he got close enough to see his eyes, I cursed. They were watery, washed out, and devoid of most color.

The man was possessed by a shade.

"Hercules," I snapped.

Thank the gods, he got the message. Head bowing, the massive lump of flesh and muscles charged forward with a smirk.

Knowing what was up, the shade stepped back. "You stupid cattle," it spit. "Give it up now. My liege will make it painless—"

Hercules slammed his fist into the man's jaw. Bone cracked. The impact spun the man around in a full, perfect circle. He started to go down, but the man jerked once and then twice. Mid-fall, his back arched and his mouth dropped open.

He let out a horrible screeching sound, like metal grinding on metal, and the black smoke poured out of its mouth, flooding the sky.

"Holy shit." Gable fell back against the side of the SUV. "*Holy. Shit.*"

The black smoke spiraled like a mini-tornado before arching down sharply. Hercules grabbed at it, his fingers going through the smoke. It shot across the side of the road, zig-zagging like a damn snake. Then it was out in the road, dodging traffic until it was no longer seen.

"We really need to go before anyone questions that or the dead guy." Josie opened the passenger door. "Like, for real."

Good call.

"You saw that?" I asked Gable, and when he didn't answer, I tapped the side of his face. He blinked rapidly. "We aren't messing around here. You get me now? That thing was after you."

"Me? I-I don't understand. I'm not anything special."

"*I'm* something special. You're kind of special." Hercules sidled up beside us. "But I already told you. You're the son of Poseidon, and the Titans want you because they can feed off you."

"Oh," Gable murmured, dazed. "You did tell me that."

"Yep." Hercules smiled.

Gable wasn't struggling as I shoved him into the back of the SUV. What he'd just seen had sucked the fight right out of him. Alex was on one side of him, Hercules was on the other.

I caught Herc's attention. "Keep him under control."

He one-finger saluted me.

Rolling my eyes, I shut the door and as I passed Josie, who was getting in, I smacked her ass. Yeah, not exactly the most appropriate time, but I wasn't the most appropriate person. Her head whipped around, and I winked. She shook her head as she got in, closing the door behind her. A second later, I was behind the steering wheel and then easing out into traffic.

It wouldn't take long before someone saw the body. We were going to have to ditch this car and lay low.

"You hanging in there?" Josie twisted around and asked.

Gable looked up and slowly turned his head left, then right. "Dude, that was . . . that was some *Supernatural* shit right there."

Alex choked on her laugh. "Man, Deacon is going to love you."

"What is *Supernatural*?" Hercules asked, frowning.

"You watched *Laguna Beach*, but not *Supernatural*?" Alex scowled at the demigod. "Man, that is just wrong on so many different levels."

As they went back and forth, my attention flipped between the road and the back seat. We had Poseidon's son, but that shade was still out there, and where there was one, there were more.

And then there were Titans.

Josie

If Gable wasn't already thoroughly overwhelmed, bringing him to a motel that I was sure had witnessed a ton of overdoses and one or a hundred sex-for-money acts a week, and then introducing him to the rest of the crew, tipped him all the way over the edge.

All of us crammed into a small motel room that smelled of mothballs. Solos was standing by the window, forever on lookout. Next to Alex was Aiden, leaning against the faded green wall. He'd taken the SUV and ditched it, returning with a white Yukon he'd said would not, under any circumstances, be reported as missing.

He'd used a compulsion.

Something I had yet to try. Mainly because it still didn't feel right to mess with someone's thoughts. I kept that opinion to myself, though, because I was sure that it wouldn't be welcome. I'd probably be laughed at a little.

Deacon and Luke were sitting on the floor. Brave guys. Seth was lounging in front of the door. Somehow, and no one wanted to look a gift horse in the mouth, Herc was asleep, his snore drowning out conversation every couple of minutes.

Gable sat in a worn chair by a small, scuffed table, and I sat on the edge of the bed. He'd listened to everything we had to say, giving him an introduction to the whole world of pure-bloods and half-bloods. Everyone helped out, touching on the war with Arcs and everything that had gone down worldwide because of that. I explained, as best as I could, the whole "you're a demigod, but your powers are locked and we need to defeat the Titans" thing.

His wide, startled gaze roamed through the room, and when I had a feeling he was starting to not believe us again, everyone in the room who could control the elements gave him a little show.

Hours went by as we answered his questions. Well, as the other people answered his questions, because, unsurprisingly, I didn't know the answers to some of what he was asking.

Gable seemed to calm down and he was digesting everything. When a lull occurred, broken only by Herc's snores, I leaned forward. "I know this is overwhelming. I was in your situation not too long ago."

"Yeah." He nodded as he scrubbed his fingers through his hair. "It's . . . God, I don't even know what to say. You know, my mom never talked about my dad." He laughed, dropping his hand. "I always thought it was because he was some wild one-night stand or something. I mean, she moved on. Multiple times. Marriage is business for her."

Seth arched a brow.

"I wasn't even sure he was alive," Gable said, slowly shaking his head. "And I've got to be honest, a lot of this is hard to believe. I get what you're saying. I even understand it, but I'm still having trouble processing it."

"That's understandable." Deacon grinned up at him. "We grew up in this world. You didn't."

Gable opened his mouth and then closed it. "And you're a-a pure-blood?"

"Yep. Technically, we're called the hematoi, but that's the snob version of pure-blood," he replied.

"And he's a half-blood." Gable nodded at Luke, who gave him a thumb's up. His gaze moved over to Alex and Aiden. "And they used to be a pure and a half, but . . . now are demigods." When he got a yes from them, he looked at Solos. "And he's a half-blood?"

"That's what I am."

Gable looked at Seth, brows puckered. "And you're the Apot-polla?"

I laughed. "Wow. That's not a version I've heard before."

Seth sighed. "Apollyon."

His lips moved as he silently pronounced it, and I had a feeling he was still saying it wrong. "So . . . what do we do now?"

"We take you back to the University in South Dakota, where you can be protected and trained until we locate the rest of you guys." Seth pushed off the door and walked across the room. Gable tensed in his chair. "It's a lot to swallow and you probably have an awesome life here, but that life is going to change. It has to."

Seth wasn't really good at the motivational speeches.

"You're very important, not just to us but to the entire world," Aiden said, obviously seeing the alarm swelling in Gable's gaze again. "You have a higher calling, Gable."

I shot Seth a look as he turned around and rolled his eyes.

"You will save not only the world, but the Olympians. Not only that, but once your abilities unlock, you're going to be immortal,"

Aiden continued. "So your life you have here, right now, is just a speck. You'll be able to come back to it, at least for a while, but there . . . there are bigger things waiting for you."

Immortal.

Something I didn't really think about as I watched Aiden's little pep talk smooth over Gable's ruffled edges. I was immortal. Unless someone cut my head off? No. According to Seth, that wouldn't even kill me. It would hurt, but I guess my neck would reattach. Only a god or another demigod could kill me.

Or Seth.

Or a Titan.

Oh my God, why was I even thinking about that right now? My train of thought had derailed massively, but I was immortal. Seth wasn't. If the gods left him alone, he would age, and then once he died, he would be indentured to Hades.

How had I not really thought about that until now? Granted, there were a ton of things going on that had distracted me, more pressing items to think about. So now I needed to figure out how to get him out from under the gods' thumbs, get his deal undone with Hades without it affecting Aiden, and make sure he was immortal.

It had to be doable.

I mean, Apollo had made Aiden immortal, right along with Alex. So it was possible, and I was his daughter. He did it for them. He had to do it for me. I nodded to myself, because that helped cement my belief that there was no way he would refuse my request.

"What do you think, Josie?"

I blinked and twisted toward Alex. "I'm sorry. I dazed out. What?"

Alex's lips curved up at the corners. "Instead of staying here tonight, Gable says he has enough room at his place for all of us. Then we'll start to head back in the morning."

Glancing back to where Hercules was sprawled across the bed Seth and I were sharing, I cringed. The middle of the already weak bed sagged. "Sounds like a plan to me."

Waking Hercules up and getting him to his room to gather up his stuff took longer than it ever should've, but the guy slept like the dead. For only a handful of minutes, Seth and I were left alone. We quickly packed up our things, shoving them into the oversized travel bags. When we were done, I dropped mine on the bed and started to turn, but Seth walked up behind me, wrapping his arms around my waist. He didn't say anything, just skated his lips down the side of my neck.

Closing my eyes, I leaned back as I settled my hands on his arms. His warm breath and hot mouth had me yearning for more than a few stolen minutes.

"Do you think this is smart?" I asked. "Heading to Gable's house?"

Seth hesitated and lifted his head. "I don't know. Part of me thinks it could be a bad idea. We don't know this guy, but it can't be any more open and risky than staying in this place. The shade has spotted him. They'll be out looking for him. Only good thing is they can't know where he lives. Or they'd already have gone for him."

"True." Turning in his embrace, I looped my arms around his neck as I rested my cheek on his shoulder. "This has been surprisingly easy."

"Yeah," he replied after a moment. "And that's what worries me."

28

"What did you say your mom does for a living?" I asked.

Gable glanced over at me as we walked up a fancy stone driveway, the kind that has different colored pavers lined up to look like cobblestone. His smile was sheepish. "She used to be an actress, back in the late eighties, early nineties. Not anyone you'd know, probably. Did a lot of B-rated stuff."

That B-rated stuff must've opened a lot of doors, because Poseidon's son lived in a mansion. One of the huge houses we'd seen on the bluffs, overlooking the beach and ocean below. The place was a massive stone estate, several stories, complete with some fancy foreign car parked in front of the porch and double-glass doors.

"Was she in porn?" Hercules asked, and when we all looked at him, he shrugged massive shoulders. "What? We get porn in Olympus."

"But not *Supernatural*?" Alex asked. "That doesn't even make sense."

Hercules squinted. "I must check out this *Supernatural*."

"Is your mother here now?" Aiden glanced over at Solos. If she was, this could be awkward. Of course, they'd break out the compulsion, so they probably weren't that worried about it.

Gable shook his head as we walked up the wide set of stairs and then across a covered porch. "She's actually in Europe with her latest husband." Stopping by the doors, he tapped his fingers along a small black box. It beeped three times and then flashed green. He opened the door, and cool air rushed out. "No one is here."

"Not even servants?" I asked.

He laughed. "We don't have servants that live here. We do have cleaners that show up every other day, but it's just me right now. And you all."

"How locked down is this place?" Solos immediately went into security mode, scanning the atrium-style room.

"Like Alcatraz," Gable replied, walking forward and around a round table with a beautiful fern sitting in the middle. "Once the alarm is set, no one is getting in without us knowing. We also have motion detectors inside and outside the house that can be turned on. I can hit the inside ones once everyone is down for the night."

Directly in front of us, a huge spiral staircase led upstairs. To the right appeared to be some kind of library, and then there was a living room. I was afraid to touch any of the stuff. The furniture looked like it cost more than my college tuition did.

"Nice place," commented Luke.

Seth didn't say anything as we followed Gable through a dining room with a massive table and really cool-looking chairs with high gray-cushioned backs. Considering that he'd grown up wealthy, he was probably used to a place like this. All of these guys were used to it. After all, just experiencing their University told me that their society practically rolled around in the money.

Seth actually hadn't said much the whole drive over here.

I was sure he just had a lot on his mind. It didn't help that we were roughly in the same area where we'd spotted the shade.

When I thought about the shade, I thought about the poor man that had crumpled to the ground with a broken jaw. I knew that, once possessed, there was no saving the mortal, but knowing that didn't make it any easier to really deal with. That was another life lost, and for what? Did the man even know what happened to him? Would his family be looking for him?

I sighed, rubbing my fingers along my right brow. The dull pounding of a headache was back again after being gone the last couple of days. It was weird. I was a demigod, so I figured headaches shouldn't plague me. The only thing I could think of was that maybe it was tied to my lack of sleep.

We followed Gable into a beautiful kitchen, complete with Shaker-style white cabinets, marble counters, and a gorgeous gray backsplash. The island could seat six, and the eat-in kitchen featured a table nearly as big as the one we'd passed in the formal dining area.

"Is anyone hungry?" Gable walked around the island.

"We're always hungry," Deacon replied. "Always."

Gable smiled at that as he turned to the double-door fridge. "I think I have some frozen pizza I can pop in the oven." He paused, glancing over his shoulder at us. "Or we can order out."

"I don't think that would be wise," Aiden replied, leaning against the island. "Frozen pizza is cool."

Gable hesitated and then nodded. "Cool." He pulled out two frozen pizzas, turned on the double oven, and then faced us. "I can show you guys around if you want."

"Yes." Solos appeared in the kitchen doorway. "I want to check the place out."

I glanced at Seth, but he was watching Gable like a hawk. All of us shuffled back out into the atrium. The tour was surprisingly quick. A movie room was behind the staircase, like a real movie room, complete with a projector and a popcorn machine. Adjacent to the theatre was a billiards room. Aiden lingered at the pool tables. I found that funny, because I really couldn't picture him playing pool. The dartboards had caught Deacon's eye. Alex was checking out an arcade game. Looked like it involved shooting asteroids or something. The wall sported a TV as big as the one in the living room. We'd briefly lost Hercules outside by the lit pool. Upstairs there were more than enough bedrooms for everyone. I stopped counting at six. The strategically placed cameras throughout the house impressed Solos and Aiden.

Rich people took security seriously.

Seth and I ended up in a guest bedroom that looked to have been decorated by a professional designer. It was a tranquil mix of pale blue and white. Reminded me of the photos in *Good Housekeeping*. Granny was a huge fan of that magazine.

Everyone was either in their rooms, dumping their stuff, or downstairs, where Gable was putting the pizzas in the oven. Solos was sticking close to him.

I watched Seth place our bags on a pale blue bench in front of the queen bed. "You don't really trust Gable, do you?"

"It isn't anything personal." He walked over to a matching dresser, dropping his stolen sunglasses on the top. "We don't know him. Anything about him. And he's handling things pretty damn well."

"Too well?"

He raised a shoulder. "He's downstairs making pizza for us. A bunch of strangers who just told him that we're descendants of Greek gods."

I dropped down on the edge of the bed and sank into its softness. "Good point, but after I got my initial freak-out over and done with, I went along with you."

He walked over, stopping in front of me. "You also got to sleep off a lot of the shock."

"And I used you as my Pillow Pet—"

"And drooled on me."

I rolled my eyes. "I did *not* drool on you, but the point is, that yes, this is a lot to swallow, but it's not impossible to process and deal with."

"Hmm..." He knelt in front of me, wrapping his hands around my calves.

Cocking my head to the side, I smiled slightly. "What are you up to?"

"Nothing." He kissed my right knee and then my left. "Okay. I'm up to something. Thinking about breaking this bed in."

"Oh my gosh," I laughed, slipping my fingers through his hair. "You have a one-track mind."

"At least it's on a fun track, right?"

"Yeah." I slid my fingers out of his hair, down his cheek. Tipping his chin up, I studied his face. He was strikingly beautiful, unreal in a way, but there were so many layers to him. So much more than a sculpted face and body.

He turned his head, kissing my palm. "You doing okay?"

I thought of the nightmare from last night. "Yes. Of course."

Those startling eyes met mine. "You've been rubbing at your brow and temple a lot. What's up with that?"

Damn. He was observant. "Just have a minor headache. Not a big deal. I think it's just lack of consistent sleep."

"Then maybe you should rest," he offered, kissing my palm again. "I can grab some slices and bring them up to you." He started to rise.

I stopped him. "I'm not sleepy. I swear I'm fine."

He appeared to consider that. "What were you thinking about earlier?"

"When?"

"At the motel. You were completely in a different world," he explained.

Bending forward, I kissed his forehead. "I started to think about something really random."

"You? Thinking something random?" He laughed when I leaned back and smacked his arm. "Never would've guessed that."

"Ha. Ha."

"So what were you thinking about?"

"About the fact that I'm immortal and you're not," I explained, grinning when his brows inched up. "But I'm going to fix that."

His mouth moved wordlessly for a moment. "How . . . how are you going to fix that?"

I grinned at him. "I know Apollo can do that—make you immortal. He made Alex and Aiden immortal, so it's totally possible."

"Yeah," he said slowly. "It's possible, but that was different for them. Apollo isn't going to make me immortal."

Undaunted, I continued. "Oh, he will. And he'll also make sure that deal you made with Hades is null and void if he wants me to help take down the Titans."

Shock splashed across Seth's face. "What?"

"I've been thinking about it for a while. They want me to help them. They need me, actually." Feeling pretty smug, I moved to kiss him again, but Seth pulled back. He rose. I frowned. "What?"

He stared down at me like I'd sprouted a boob out of the middle of my forehead. "You're going to try to negotiate with the gods?"

"Well, with my father—"

"Who is a god, Josie. You cannot negotiate with them, not even Apollo. They will turn every deal and flip it back on you," he said. "I've seen them do it, and your father is no different."

That wasn't exactly what I wanted to hear, but I wasn't surprised. "If they want me to stop the Titans, they will do this for me."

"You're insane," he whispered, backing up.

"Geez. You're welcome." I pushed a loose strand of my hair back. "Look, I'm going to do something. There is no way I'm going to allow them to continue using you and then take over your afterlife. Nope. Not going to happen. So just accept it and move on, because I'm hungry."

Seth gaped at me. "I am not worth that kind of risk, Josie."

Anger flashed through me. "Would you please stop saying that? I hate it when you say that."

"Why?" Frustration filled the air. "Because it's true. Is that why?"

"It is not true, Seth."

He laughed harshly. "You have no idea, Joe. That's the problem. It isn't your fault, but you have no idea."

"Well, that's not insulting or anything."

"I don't mean it to be, but it's the truth. You're willing to put yourself in a very precarious position when you don't know what I'm capable of, but *I* do, Josie. I know exactly what I'm capable of."

I forced myself to take a nice slow and even breath. "Seth—"

"No. This conversation is over and done with. You're not going to make any crazy deals that backfire in your face." He waved his hand as if he was signaling the end of this conversation, and that was a big oh-hell-no. "I made my bed and I'm going to roll around in it."

I waited a second. "Are you done yet?"

His eyes flared a bright ocher.

"Just wanted to make sure, since you think you can tell me what I can and cannot do. Guess what? You can't. And you know what else? I understand that because of what you did in your past, you think you're not worth me—"

"In the past?" Seth laughed again, the sound cold and hard. "You think I'm talking about that shit with Ares? How about a couple of weeks ago?"

"What . . . what do you mean?"

Seth stared at me a moment and then he spoke a shattering four words. "I fed off you."

"What?" I whispered after what was probably an entire minute of trying to process what he'd said. There was no way he said what I thought he said, because it didn't make sense.

He turned sharply, stalking away from the bed, giving me his back. "Fuck. I should've told you before . . . before you gave yourself to me, but I'm a fucking selfish bastard. You heard me right, Josie. I fed off you—off your *aether*."

My lips moved, but my tongue forgot how to form words. Shocked, I sat there as an icy shiver danced down my spine. Goosebumps raced over my skin. Seth had fed off me?

"That's the kind of . . . of *thing* I am."

Lifting my gaze, I saw him drag his hand through his hair. His fingers spasmed around the strands, tugging them briefly before his hand dropped to the nape of his neck.

"I have a . . . a problem. I've had one for a while now, and I tried . . . I'm trying not to be that person, but it's *in* me, and it comes out. I know it's going to again, and when it does, I don't care who I hurt—what trust I break. In that moment, I don't care who I'm hurting. Even you." The raw edge to his words cut deep. He turned slowly, his chest rising sharply. "I don't want to be that person. Gods, not with you, but I am."

Suddenly, he was in front of me, clasping my cheeks. My heart jumped in my chest. "Every day I want you, Josie. I want *everything* about you. I see you and I want to get between those thighs and spend a lifetime there. I want to get so deep in you that you can't tell where you end and I begin. I want to taste you and fuck you until I don't know anything else. Constantly. I want more than that. Not going to lie. I want to hold you."

I couldn't breathe as his gaze held mine captive.

"I want to be with you. I want to spend every day with you. Every hour, down to the last fucking minute and second," he said, his voice rough. Cutting. "But that's not all I want. What's in you? The *aether*. Fuck." His eyes closed briefly and when they re-opened, they burned with unholy light, shocking me. "I want that just as badly. Yeah. I want that. I *had* that when you were coming on my knee."

My heart pounded fast. His words created a mixture of disgust . . . and God, lust. That was there, too, responding to his words. There was something wrong with me. There was something definitely wrong with him.

"I cannot be trusted," he said, holding my chin so I couldn't look away, so that I had to hear and see those words. And I saw his words. I heard them. "And you know what? You're the only one who doesn't see it. You think Alex doesn't? That Aiden doesn't? They do. That's the kind of person you're willing to anger the gods over. That's the kind of person you're willing to make a deal for and give up gods know what for." Dropping my chin, he straightened, letting his hand fall to his side. "I am not worth that."

Seth walked away again, and the numbness faded. Emotion rose inside me, as violent as a hurricane battering the shoreline. Hurt exploded in my chest just as fury burned red-hot in the pit of my stomach.

"How many times?" I asked.

There was a pause. "Does that even matter?"

"How many times?" I shouted this time, not caring if anyone heard me.

His head fell back. "Just once."

I let that sink in. I wasn't sure if that changed anything or not. I wasn't even sure what I was supposed to do with this information. The back of my throat burned as I stared at his rigid back. I couldn't even really think. "When?"

Seth didn't answer for a moment. "I did it the . . . the last day I trained you. When we were arguing and then . . . making out. I lost control and fed off you."

My mind raced back to that day. "I don't understand. I didn't feel anything. The last time I was fed off of, it hurt."

His spine seemed to stiffen even more. "It doesn't always hurt. It can be done so that it doesn't."

I sucked in a sharp breath. He'd been all over me that day, and I had . . . I shook my head, so . . . so freaking numb. And suddenly, it made sense. Why he'd pulled away immediately afterward. It wasn't just because he thought he wasn't worth it, but also because he'd done something wrong, horribly wrong. To me.

And he'd never fessed up to it. Not until now.

Seth had fed off me.

I shot off that bed like a rocket. He faced me just as I reached him. I didn't even think as I cocked my arm back and punched him right in the stomach. Seth doubled over with a grunt.

"That," I said, shaking as I forced myself to step back. "That is for feeding off me."

"Gods," he gasped. "I deserved that."

"How could you?" I demanded, hands clenching into fists again. "How could you do that after knowing Hyperion had—he had done that to me?"

"I . . ." He didn't finish that statement, because what could he say?

I wanted to hit him again. I wanted to kick him. *Gods,* I wanted to whale on him. Tears filled my eyes as I continued walking back, until I bumped into the bench. I wanted to . . . I wanted to shake him and I wanted him to never have told me what had happened. "Why didn't you try harder?"

He straightened and he sounded like he'd swallowed glass when he spoke. "I didn't realize what I was doing at first. That

. . . that doesn't make it right, but as soon as I did, I stopped. That's why . . ."

"Why what?" My voice cracked.

Seth looked away. "That's why you weren't hurt. You were just tired."

"Just tired," I whispered, remembering falling asleep while eating. My legs shook and I sat down heavily on the bench. I tried to make sense of this. "So you stopped when you realized what you were doing."

"That doesn't change the fact that I did it."

Did it? Or not? I had no idea. Nothing to base this on. I mean, it wasn't like he'd cheated on me or had been abusive in the way normal people were, but this was a betrayal. This was a big deal.

I smoothed my hand down my face, shaken. "I want you to be honest with me. You only did it once?"

Seth nodded.

"And that's why you stayed away from me after that?"

Another nod.

I squeezed my hand, placing it against my chest. "But you haven't done it since we . . . since we got back together. Why?"

"I . . . I never want to ever hurt you or . . . take from you what is not mine." He went to the door and leaned against it. Slowly, he shook his head, and in that moment, I'd never seen him look so young and vulnerable. So *human*. "And I decided that night we came together that I wouldn't ever do it again, and if I did . . ."

"What? What would you do then?"

Lips thin and pressed together, he closed his eyes again. "I would make sure you'd never see my face again."

Anger beat out all the other emotions once more. "Oh, instead of, I don't know, coming and talking to me about it? Letting me help you? Us working together—"

"Working together on what, Josie? You think you can help me with this, with this thing inside of me?"

I snapped my mouth shut even though there was so much I wanted to say, that could be said. I could've told him no. That this—that becoming better and doing better—was all on him. I could've told him yes. That I could help him. I could support him making right . . . right choices. I could be aware of when it was becoming too much for him. I could tell him that I wanted to throat punch him. I could tell him that I still loved him.

And I did.

But I didn't.

Because I was furious. My skin practically split with the anger. Because I was hurt. The ache was in my chest, spreading and swelling, because . . . dammit. Because I was revolted. I expected better from him, and he had betrayed that expectation and trust. He'd done to me what Hyperion had done to me. That made me want to hurl.

Lowering my gaze, I pressed my balled hand against my forehead and forced the knot in my throat to ease back.

"So." His gravelly voice broke the silence. "This is it?"

I didn't say anything. All I could think about was that night he said he was afraid that everything would turn into a nightmare and that I would hate him forever. He'd been living with this secret for weeks, like a sword of Damocles hanging over his head.

Several moments passed and Seth then said, "Out of everything that I've done, what I did to you was the worst. You were a gift to me, and I fucked that up. That's on me, and I'm so incredibly sorry." He paused, and I squeezed my eyes shut. "There's nothing more in this world I'm—"

A sudden shout from downstairs cut him off. I reacted out of instinct, springing to my feet as Seth spun around, throwing open the door. There was a loud crash, raising the hairs on my arms. Everything with Seth was pushed aside as we rushed from the room.

29

Seth

*F*eeling gutted, I left the room, rushing out into the long hallway. At the end, Deacon was coming out of the room he was sharing with Luke, his expression pinched with concern as he tugged a clean shirt on over his head. He joined us as we hit the steps.

I was sick to my stomach, even though I'd done the right thing by telling Josie, and discouraging her from making a deal she'd regret.

Shit. I'd tasted fear the moment she said she planned on making a deal with the gods for me. They would've flipped it back on her so fast her head would be spinning. There was no way I could allow her to do that.

So I did what I should've done weeks ago, when she'd told me that she loved me. I'd told her the truth, exposing who and what I really was to her. If she never spoke to me again, I wouldn't be surprised.

But I couldn't focus on that right now. I had to compartmentalize, shut down the turmoil. There'd be time later to dwell in that shit, roll around in it.

Our feet pounded off the hardwood steps of the stairs. The foyer came into view. I saw Hercules's massive ass first, and then Aiden. He had a Covenant dagger in his right hand.

"What's going on?" Josie asked, her voice hoarse. The muscle along my jaw tensed.

"He's . . . he's dead," murmured Gable.

Not seeing whoever he was talking about, I stepped down into the foyer and found Gable standing nearly under the stairs. His face was as white as a daimon's. Not a good sign.

"Who's dead?" Deacon walked past Josie, joining Luke where he stood off to the side, near the entrance to the living room. Or the sitting room. One of the dozen needless rooms in this house.

"Look outside," Alex replied as she strolled in from the kitchen area, the duffel bag of weapons clenched in her hand. She placed it on the floor, just behind the table in the middle of the atrium.

My gaze tracked the length of the atrium to the double doors. There were glass panes, and in the center of the left door I could see a rough circle of spiderweb fissures in the glass. The cracked glass was smudged with what looked like a mixture of blood and some other kind of fluid.

Then I looked down. The porch light was on, casting a yellowish glow on the prone body. I could make out sandals, pale white legs, and dark shorts.

"He k-knocked on the door," Gable said, lifting a hand and thrusting it through his hair. He tugged on the ends. "When we came out here to see who it was, he saw u-us through the glass and . . ."

"He decided to introduce his face to the glass door, total zombie style." Luke pulled a Glock out of the bag. "There was a shade in him. The moment he hit the ground outside, the shade came out and took off."

Shit. "That's not good."

"Nope." Aiden's shoulders tensed. "I think it was scouting."

"It?" whispered Gable. "That's Mr. Nanni. He lives d-down the street."

"He don't live anywhere now," Hercules responded. "That's a dead Mr. Nanni."

Aiden pivoted around, jaw tight as he pinned Hercules with a look. "Not helping."

The demigod shrugged. "Whatever," he muttered, cracking his knuckles.

There was a pause. "Nothing can get through that glass, right?" Gable asked. "It's reinforced."

"Reinforced glass didn't mean shit," I replied. "That won't even stop a daimon."

"W-What's a daimon?" Gable asked.

"Quick and dirty explanation?" Deacon turned to him. "They used to be pures and halfs, and they became addicted to *aether*— that's the substance inside of all of us that makes us who we are. Not good."

His wild gaze flew back to the window. "Are there daimons outside now?"

Aiden laughed dryly. "If only we could be that lucky."

Thunder cracked overhead, rattling the house, and yeah, that was a bad, bad sign. Especially when there was no lightning.

"And it doesn't look like we're going to get lucky," Solos said with a sigh.

Gable looked up at the ceiling. "Is it going to storm?"

"Not the kind of storm California needs." Alex flipped a dagger in her hand as she walked up to Aiden.

Kneeling by the bag, I pulled out a dagger and then a slender stake. I looked up. Josie stood there, hand out. My gaze connected with hers, and I looked away, jaw working. No doubt she was thinking about me. About what I'd done. I was no better than a fucking daimon. Just not as messy.

I handed her both of the weapons I held. "The slender one is dipped in Pegasus blood," I reminded her.

She said nothing as she took the blade and then reached for the dagger. I held onto it, forcing her to meet my gaze.

"Are you ready to do this?" I asked. "There can be no hesitation. Something is coming, and whatever it is, we're going to need to take it out. If you're not ready, you need to hide."

Her blue eyes darkened. "I'm ready."

I hesitated for a moment and then let go. I grabbed the same weapons and then rose. Outside, the wind was picking up, and from the glass doors we could see the palm trees bending under the weight and force of the wind.

"What the hell is coming?" Deacon asked. "Storm?"

Luke laughed. "Again. As if we could get that lucky."

I stayed close to Josie when she walked forward. She might want to stab me with one of those weapons, but my priority was her. In all honesty, I couldn't give a fuck what went down with Gable at this point. My goal was to make sure that after whatever was coming our way, she was still standing.

Everyone else was on their own.

Like they were trained, a line was formed several feet back from the door, blocking Gable. Instinct had driven Josie to stand on Solos's other side. She hadn't been schooled in this kind of technique, how to form a line against an enemy. There hadn't been enough time to drill years of training into her. I flanked her, fingers tense around each weapon.

Thunder boomed overhead, deafening as it shook the paintings on the walls. Somewhere in the house, something fell over and crashed. A loud *crack* followed, and a palm near the driveway broke in two.

Something stirred outside. My eyes narrowed as the wind continued to pick up in one area, near one of the SUVs. It spun and spun in a small area, like a mini-tornado.

"What ... what is that?" Josie asked.

"Gable," Aiden said, his voice level. "You need to hide right now. No matter what, you do not come out unless it's—"

The cyclone shot forward, aiming straight for the doors. I prepared for it to come right through the glass, but it stopped before it connected, spinning in one spot. The cyclone was over seven feet tall and as wide as a person. I had a really bad feeling about what was inside that air mass.

"Um," Deacon murmured.

A heartbeat of silence passed and then, clearly, the sound of the front door unlocking could be heard.

"What the ... ?" Alex trailed off as the series of clicks stopped.

"Security systems fail," I muttered.

The glass doors swung open and the cyclone shot inside. Wind whipped out as the cyclone slowed, unfolding until a figure became visible inside.

"This isn't a friendly," Solos said, stepping forward on his right leg as his arm cocked back. "No need to wait." He let go of a dagger.

It flew through the air, hilt over blade, and went through the mini-tornado, embedding deep in the center. The moment it made contact, a rush of air burst out. A sonic boom knocked all of us back, like we were nothing but bowling pins.

I landed on my ass next to Josie. The Covenant dagger fell from her hand, skidding across the floor. She cursed, rolling onto her side as she scrambled toward it on her hands and knees.

"Really?" A deep voice boomed through the house, and I turned sharply. The tornado of doom was gone and in its place was a man. A very tall man with a head full of brown hair and shoulders bigger than Hercules's. "You threw a dagger at me?" He tipped his head back and laughed as he reached down, grabbed the hilt, and then yanked the dagger out. He dropped it on the stone floor of the foyer. "This is going to be easier than I imagined." Then he opened his eyes. They were all black.

The man before us was a Titan.

"Oh my *gods*," Josie whispered as what appeared to be recognition flickered across her face as she sat up.

"It was mostly for fun," Solos said, his hand tightening around the slender dagger. "Just wanted to see what it would do."

The Titan tilted its head, expression perplexed. His skin, a mixture of many different pink shades, seemed to lighten and deepen in hue every couple of seconds.

"Which one are you?" I asked, rising to my feet. I slipped in front of Josie, who was now on her feet with her blade in hand. "Mo? Curly? Definitely not Larry, because he'd be pissing himself if he was in front of us right now."

The Titan's lip curled. "I am Atlas, Apollyon. I do not know these deities you speak of."

"Atlas?" murmured Deacon. "Oh boy . . ."

Out of the corner of my eye, I saw Luke take the same protective stance in front of Deacon, and for once the pure-blood didn't fight it.

Atlas's sneer turned into a mocking grin. "You know who I am. All of you know who I am. And you know how this will end. Give me what I've come for and I will allow each of you to live. Deny me, and each of you will die."

I sighed. "That's so cliché."

The Titan's all-black gaze slid to me. "You may be the Apollyon and you may be surrounded by demigods, but you cannot defeat me. I am not Hyperion and—"

"I'm not just any demigod. I am *the* Hercules and you are—"

Atlas lifted his hand, and a second later Hercules was flying backward through the air. He slammed into the wall near the staircase, cracking the plaster. "You are nothing to me," Atlas finished as Hercules hit the floor face-first.

"I'm kind of glad you shut him up," Alex said, her body tensing. "But we kind of need him alive."

"Why?" Atlas queried. "So he can continuously lead us to where the remaining demigods are? We knew you would leave. We can wait."

Not surprising. They probably had shades near the University, waiting for us to come out. That was a risk we'd had to take and now we were paying the consequences.

Atlas sniffed the air as he stared at Alex. "You are a demigod, but your *aether* is not as pure. Not like the one cowering behind the staircase." He paused, looking at Josie. "Or this one."

"I'm not a snack," Josie stated, and I smirked. "So stop looking at me like I'm dinner."

"Oh, but dear, that's exactly what you are." Atlas smiled, and it was full-on creepy. "And the rest are completely expendable."

Several things happened at once.

Atlas lifted his arm, fingers widespread. A rush of energy came across the room, aiming straight for Alex and Aiden. Both moved out of the way, spinning out to the sides before it connected. The Titan immediately shifted. The blast of energy cut over to Luke, tossing him up and back into Deacon.

Luke squeezed off several rounds from his Glock, but Atlas twisted and turned wicked fast, dodging each of the bullets. They smacked into the wall harmlessly, and then Atlas was in front of Aiden.

Dipping under Atlas's arm, Aiden sprang up behind him and spun, kicking out, but the Titan was unbelievably fast, more so than Hyperion. He swung back with his arm, catching Aiden across the chest, and up he went, ass over teacup.

And that pissed off Alex.

She rushed the Titan, launching off the ground a foot in front of him. She spun in the air, about to deliver a brutal spin kick.

It never connected.

Atlas twisted around again and caught her leg. He swung her

like a damn baseball bat, throwing her right into Aiden as he regained his footing. They went down in a tumble of arms and legs.

"Holy balls," muttered Solos.

"Fuck getting close." Spinning around, I launched my Covenant dagger at Atlas's head, mostly for a distraction. It worked. The Titan moved to avoid that as I summoned the element of fire. A ball of amber flames formed above my hand. I threw that like a baseball.

A burst of energy rippled from Josie. She'd tapped into fire a second after me, adding another burst of flames to the mix.

Atlas whirled on us. The flames fizzled out before they reached him, as if they had smacked into some kind of force field. "Don't tire yourself out, girl. I've got big plans for you later."

I did not like that.

Neither did Josie.

"Sorry. I'm busy later." A burst of power rippled through the air, washing over my skin, and I could feel *it* inside me, beating at me to get free. A bolt of *akasha* left Josie in a brilliant blueish white bolt of energy. It slammed into Atlas's shoulder, knocking him back a step.

"Ouch," Atlas said, shaking his arm. "That wasn't very nice." He lifted his arm, and suddenly Josie was skidding across the stone floor, her arms wheeling as she tried to gain control of her body, but it was like an invisible hand was dragging her toward Atlas.

Cursing, I shot to the left and snagged her around the waist, throwing her to the floor and breaking the connection. I twisted, taking the brunt of the fall as we landed, her on top. I rolled before Atlas got the upper hand. My knees hit the ground between hers. Our eyes met for a fraction of a second, and then I was in the air. I braced myself for impact.

Hitting the table, I crashed through a potted plant. Soil flew in my face as wood broke under me. I caught myself before I ate stone, landing on my side. I looked up and saw Hercules.

He was on his feet, and he hauled ass across the foyer, his heavy footsteps rattling the table. Slamming his shoulder into the Titan, he tried to bring him down, but that didn't work. Atlas wrapped massive arms around Hercules's chest, lifted *the* demigod up in the air, and then slammed him into the floor, power-driving him down. Stone cracked under their weight.

Atlas rose, spreading his arms wide. "Who's next?"

"Gods." Solos whipped out his Glock and fired several rounds. Like before, the Titan dodged them and headed straight for the Sentinel. Solos tossed the Glock aside, bracing himself for hand-to-hand.

Aiden came out of nowhere, rushing the Titan from behind. He launched into the air and landed on Atlas, hooking his knees at Atlas's hips. Aiden grabbed the Titan's head and twisted sharply. The crack of bone breaking echoed through the room a second before Atlas reached around, grabbing hold of Aiden's shirt. Atlas threw him over his shoulder, sending him flying through the air. Aiden crashed into the floor, rolling several feet before he came to a stop on his back.

"I could've told you that doesn't work," I said, clenching the poisoned blade, trying to figure out how to get close enough to Atlas to use it.

"Thanks," Aiden groaned, rolling onto his side, "for the heads-up."

Luke was the next to go down. He was tossed like a damn football after rushing Atlas. Deacon tapped into the fire element, drawing Atlas's attention as Josie sent another bolt of *akasha* at him from the other side.

I ground down on my jaw, ignoring what felt like a slumbering giant waking up in my chest as I also tapped into *akasha*. Before I could let it go, Atlas smiled again as he lifted his arms. A high keening cry echoed from outside, and then black smoke poured into the house, breaking off into several streams. Shades.

Shades were *everywhere*.

"Holy crap," Josie shrieked as one went straight for her. She dipped and spun around. Stumbling back into the wall, her wide eyes met mine. It was written on her face, how bad this was.

"Gods." Alex hit the ground, narrowly avoiding one of them. "They smell like the River Styx." Rolling onto her side, she used her legs to power back onto her feet. "So freaking gross."

"Keep out of their grasp," Aiden ordered, picking himself back up. "There's nothing we can do about them."

Josie darted to the left, scowling as one grabbed at her long hair. "We need a furie. Like, stat."

Yeah, and like always, those bitches were nowhere to be found when you actually needed them.

It was chaotic, engaging with Atlas while avoiding the shades. One stream of black smoke grabbed hold of Deacon and lifted him all the way up to the ceiling, and that caught Luke and Aiden's attention. They rushed across the atrium, and the tugging in my chest returned as Aiden sent a bolt of *akasha* at the shade. It dropped Deacon.

Right on top of them.

Atlas stalked across the atrium, heading for the stairwell. I shot in from the right. Beyond him, I saw Josie also heading for him. I wanted to warn her back, but we had the poisoned blades. He was halfway to the staircase when Solos came running up from behind Josie.

The Titan whipped around so fast that by the time any of us realized what he was doing, it was too late. He caught Solos by the arm with one hand and then hit him in the chest with the other—no, not hit. His hand went through Solos's chest.

Josie screamed as blood sprayed out from Solos's back.

I skidded to a halt, stunned as Atlas jerked his hand back. Red was everywhere, and in Atlas's hand was something that belonged inside of Solos's chest.

His heart.

Blood drained so quickly from Solos's face as his legs crumpled under him. He folded like a piece of paper. Hit the floor and didn't move. Down. Done. That was it.

"I am so done with this," Atlas said, his hand closing around the organ, destroying it.

All of my restraint broke.

Rage tore through me, ripped me right open. I shouted, the sound echoing through the room, and out of the fury and the grief I reached out, throwing my arms out to the sides. I dropped the poisoned blade as the monster in my chest fully woke up. It recognized all the power in the room—in Alex and Aiden, in Hercules and even in Gable, but especially in Josie. It whispered to me to take. It dug in deep and demanded revenge and promised retribution.

I let the monster take over.

My lips moved and I spoke the words I'd heard before, words that would unlock the ultimate power—words that Alex spoke once before. I didn't understand how this worked. I also didn't care. "Θάρρος."

Courage.

A shock rippled across my body, followed by a wealth of warmth. Determination poured into my chest.

"Δύναμη," I said.

Strength.

Another jolt of power hit me, charging me up. The warmth turned to heat, invading my muscles, breaking them down and rebuilding them rapidly.

Someone shouted, a high-pitched scream. There was a yell, a rougher and heavier gasp.

I kept going as I stepped forward, through the shades circling Atlas. "Απόλυτη εξουσία."

Absolute power.

Amber light radiated through the room. Screams pitched higher as every cell in my body hummed with power. Glyphs appeared on my skin, swirling fast. The shades flew backward, revealing a transfixed Atlas.

I finished it. "Ἀήττητο."

Air punched out of my lungs as static charged the air around me. Cords of light appeared all over the room. One. Two. Then three and four. Five. Six. Seven. The bright luminous cords came from everywhere, slamming into my chest, knocking me back into the wall and then up in the air. Inside of me, power shifted and pulsed. A fire lit me up, hot and cold all at once. Power filled every cell.

My feet were on the floor again, and my head was thrown back. Out of the corners of my eyes I saw bodies withering, but I focused on the source of my rage. Every sense became hyper aware. Vision sharp. The smell of burnt pizza mixed with the metallic tang of blood and the scent of sweat. I heard multiple inhales of breath.

The world was tinted in white.

Fear flickered over the Titan's face. Oh yeah, he knew what he was facing. He knew the end was coming for him, the true end, and there was no escaping it, because *I* was the beginning and *I* was the end.

"No," I said, in a deep and heavy voice I did not recognize as my own. "*I* am done with this."

I summoned *akasha*, but this time it was different. The *aether* sang in my veins and flooded my body. The whitish-tinted amber circled down my arm, crackling and spitting into the air as it powered down my arm.

Atlas tried to move, but it was too late.

Akasha slammed into the Titan, hitting him in the chest, and it kept coming as I prowled forward, keeping up with the intensity, surrounding him with its power. Wisps of smoke hit the air and tiny bursts of light shot out, hitting the shades. The light swallowed and destroyed them.

Atlas was backing away, but one leg gave out and then the other. He hit the floor on his knees, and I smiled as I placed my palm on his face. My chest expanded as I tapped into what was in the Titan, drawing every ounce of *aether* out of him, and what was inside me became a white-hot fire.

The Power retracted.

I jerked my hand back and the whitish-amber light retreated.

Atlas stared up at me, his mouth gaping open. A darkish, shimmery blue blood leaked from his eyes. Underneath his skin, a network of veins became visible, lit from within. The light seeped out, washing over his entire body.

I laughed.

A loud popping sound, like bombs exploding at the same time, echoed through the room, and when the light faded Atlas was nothing more than a scorched spot on the stone floor. I stared down at the spot for several moments until something behind me whimpered.

Slowly, I turned around. There were people on the floor. They were the things that were withering. Things. Insignificant. Moaning. Trying to sit up. Annoying.

I walked toward them, each step purposeful. Something moved to the right of me. I looked. It was big and reaching out to me. Hercules. Gods, I did not like him.

Lifting my hand, I sent him flying backward. My attention zeroed on the dark-haired pure-blood with silvery eyes. He was shielding someone. Blood trickled from his nose.

Oh, yeah, I really did not like him. Couldn't quite grasp why, but I knew I'd be thoroughly pleased if I made him go splat. I lifted my hand.

"Seth! No," a female shouted. The voice was familiar. It did something to me. Distracted me. "Seth!"

A stinging sensation shot across my left forearm, and I spun around, lifting my arm as I summoned *akasha*. It coiled, rushing down my arm.

"Seth," she whispered.

Her voice stopped me, reached in and shook me. The whitish-amber light fizzled out. I looked down and saw blue eyes—Josie. My Josie. And then I saw what she held in her hand. That soft hand trembled, but it was not empty. She clutched the blade. I opened my mouth, but no sound came out. My legs gave out below me, and Josie dropped the stake. I heard it clang off the floor and then I heard nothing.

There *was* nothing.

30

Josie

Dropping the blade, I shot forward and tried to stop Seth's fall. I circled my arms around his waist, but he was too heavy. The toxin had hit him hard, and I couldn't hold his weight. Not when standing and forcing my way to him had leached what remaining energy I had.

I crumpled along with him, hitting the floor on my hip. Pain flared, but I ignored it as Seth's head cracked off the stone floor.

Reaching deep down, I scrabbled up his side and rolled him onto his back. His eyes were closed, dark lashes fanning his golden cheeks. With a shaking hand, I felt his neck for a pulse and then swallowed a cry of relief as I felt it steady under my fingers.

I had no idea what the Pegasus blood would do to him. It could kill mortals. Immobilize Titans and demigods, but the Apollyon? No one had really said what it would do to him.

He was alive.

Out cold, but alive.

Pushing myself up, I sat down and scanned the room. My gaze landed on the blade first. *You will need the toxin, but not for whom*

{ 310 } JENNIFER L. ARMENTROUT

you expect. Medusa's words haunted me. She had known. That woman had known.

And I'd seen the Titan Atlas before.

He'd been in my nightmares. Over and over, he'd been there. That had been him. How? I didn't understand, but he had.

Numb, I lifted my gaze. Deacon was struggling to his feet, along with Luke. Both looked like they'd been blown through a wall. A fine trickle of blood leaked out of Deacon's nose, but he appeared otherwise uninjured. The bruises on Luke's jaw were from fighting Atlas. Hercules was sitting up, his expression absolutely dumbfounded.

"How did he do that?" Alex stumbled to her feet with Aiden's aid, swaying to one side. Both looked okay. "How did he do that?"

I didn't answer, because I didn't know how Seth had tapped into all of us without even touching us.

My gaze finally fell on Solos. "Oh *gods*," I whispered, quickly averting my gaze. What Atlas had whispered in my dream the night before had also been right. *Dig a grave.*

He was . . . I closed my eyes, biting down on my lower lip until I tasted blood. Pain opened in my chest, overshadowing the physical aches that bit and chewed at me.

Solos was gone.

Him falling had tipped Seth over an edge, a very precarious edge I hadn't even realized he'd been teetering on this . . . this entire time.

I was numb, sitting between where Seth had fallen and where Solos lay. This scent of death was different than what followed the shades. This . . . this was heavier, more real.

"Solos," Deacon spoke softly. He'd dropped to his knees beside him. "Oh man. Oh gods, this is . . ." He reached out, but drew his hands back. "This isn't right."

It was never right.

Alex shuffled over to Deacon and her face crumpled a second

before she smacked her hands over her cheeks. She turned slightly, her shoulders tensing, and then, after a handful of moments, she appeared to pull it together. When she turned back around, her expression was devoid of emotion.

"We need to bury him with coins," she whispered. "We need to give him that so he can cross over on the ferry at Styx. Now."

"Agreed." Aiden knelt by Solos, and I saw his fingers move over Solos's face. Oh God, he was closing his eyes. "Gable?"

I'd forgotten all about him.

He crept out from behind the stairs. He hadn't made it farther before everything went crazy. There was no color in his face as he stared at Solos. "We . . . we have a lot of property. There are . . . um, shovels out in the shed, by the pool."

Aiden turned to his brother and Luke. "Go with him. I need you guys to make sure he stays safe."

For once, Deacon didn't argue. With one last look at Solos, he rose and joined Gable. They followed the shaken man toward the kitchen. At the last second, Deacon veered off and hurried into the living room, returning seconds later with a blanket.

"I can't leave him there like that," he explained as he walked up to where Solos lay. Carefully, he draped the blanket over him, covering Solos's face and chest, along with most of his legs.

Then Deacon was gone.

"We need to figure out what to do with Seth." Aiden dragged a hand under his bloodied lip.

I stilled, looking up at him.

"He pulled *aether* from us," Hercules said, sounding like sandpaper had gotten inside his throat. "I was not told he could do that. No one should be able to do that."

I looked back at Seth. The glyphs had now faded, seeping into his skin. His eyes hadn't been amber when he'd faced me. Had the others seen that? They'd been all white, like a god's.

"He didn't just stop Atlas." Aiden clutched a dagger as he neared us. "He . . . he *took out* Atlas. He killed a Titan."

Hercules shook his head back and forth. "That's not possible."

"Looks like it to me." Alex rubbed at her hip and chest as she walked over to the spot where Atlas had stood. The stone was charred. "Looks real possible."

"That means . . ." Aiden trailed off.

"Means what?" I asked, placing my hands on the stone. I pushed up, climbing to my feet. "What does it mean?"

"Only the demigods can kill the Titans, right?" Aiden walked around to stand behind Seth's head. I tensed. "Or entomb them, but no one else except . . ." He didn't finish again, almost like he didn't want to give word to what he feared.

"The only thing that could take out a Titan would be the same thing that could take out one of the Olympians." Alex's face paled. "That would be the God Killer."

Air punched out of my lungs. What had Medusa said? "But that's not possible. You were the God Killer before—well, before you ended up in the Underworld. He's not the God Killer."

Her gaze met mine. "He shouldn't be, but what he just did was the same thing I did to Ares."

"But you're not connected to him, are you?" I reasoned, refusing to believe where everyone was heading with this, refusing to believe that I hadn't heeded a warning given to me.

"Nope." She lifted her hands. "I am not Team Seth right now." I frowned.

"Something hardcore just went down," she continued, gesturing at Seth. "But if he *has* somehow become the God Killer, tripped up some sort of celestial rule, then all the Olympians would be here, right? They showed up immediately after I killed Ares. They wasted no time."

"That's because they knew you were on their side. They knew

you were aware of what most likely would happen. They didn't think you were insane. They fully believe Seth is insane." Hercules took a step back. "If he's the God Killer, they aren't coming anywhere near him. Who would? He could take them out."

"Damn," spat Aiden.

"And why are *we* even here? He can take us out with the snap of his finger," the demigod continued. "Fuck this. We need to blow this joint and—"

"He's not going to take us out." My hands formed fists. "Stop overreacting."

"You don't know that," Hercules replied icily. "None of us do. I say we take one of these nifty daggers and shove in through his—"

"You do that and it will be the last thing you do without being tied up by your own intestines," I warned, a hundred percent serious. "You are not going to harm him."

Herc blinked. "Hell. That's excessive."

"Stabbing him isn't?" I shot back.

Alex stopped several feet from Seth and didn't go any closer. "Dammit. They were . . . they were concerned for a reason."

"What?" I asked, not following.

"Hades warned us before we came up. The Olympians were worried about Seth's . . . his stability. He'd done something before we left Tartarus that had them flipping out," Alex explained, and she winced when she looked over at me. "We didn't say anything, because the Olympians sometimes freak out when someone sneezes too loudly. They wanted us to keep an eye on him."

"That's . . ." I shook my head. "That's wrong."

Alex looked at me and didn't respond, but her expression said it all. It was a cross between pity and understanding.

I opened my mouth to tell them that they should've said something, but then I realized what Seth could've done that had them freaking out. "He fed off me."

That got everyone's attention.

"It was an accident," I explained, my gaze falling once again to where Solos lay. "Things got out of control and he fed on me, stopping before I even knew what was happening. It was right before you guys came here. I didn't know until . . . an hour ago." Had it only been an hour? Felt like days. "It wasn't on purpose." I felt the need to reiterate that. "Doesn't change what he did, but I think . . . I know he's been struggling."

"Damn," Aiden muttered. It looked like he wanted to say more, but changed his mind. "Right now we need to do something with Seth." Aiden was moving to Seth's head. "Before he wakes up."

"I have . . . there's a panic room in the basement." Gable had returned with the boys. I hadn't even heard them. "It's not a hundred percent ready, but it's got walls and a reinforced steel door that will lock."

"That'll work for now." Aiden turned to Hercules. "Grab his feet."

"What about Solos?" Deacon's red-rimmed eyes flicked over to the blanket-shrouded figure. "We need to bury him."

"We will." Luke wrapped an arm around his neck. "But we've got to secure Seth first."

I stepped forward. "Wait. This doesn't feel right."

"I get that it doesn't, especially to you, but we have to do this." Alex looked me straight in the eye. "We really don't know what we're going to be facing when he wakes up, and I hope—no, I *pray*—that he's fine, but we can't take that risk."

I didn't like it.

But I did understand it. Pressing my lips together, I nodded curtly. Everything that happened over that next hour was surreal. I felt oddly detached from it all.

Gable led us down to a semi-finished basement. He'd walked to what appeared to be a normal wall, but hit his hand on the center. A section of the wall separated, swinging open, revealing a room . . . with another room inside of it.

"My mom's husband put a mattress in here to see if it will fit," Gable explained as Seth was carried over and placed on a thin mattress. "I guess they plan on doing this room up also. Bathroom isn't finished, though and . . . none of that matters."

A hand folded around mine, startling me. Luke held my hand. "Come with me."

I dug my feet in.

"I know it's hard." His voice was low. "But we've got to leave him here, at least for right now."

"It doesn't feel right," I told him. "I should be here when he wakes up."

"And if he wakes up not in the right mind, and he does something to accidentally hurt you, what do you think that'll do to him?" Luke reasoned. "It'll make everything worse."

I wasn't sure how anything could get worse at this point, but Luke was right. I let him lead me out of the panic room and up the stairs. I tried not to hear the door shutting behind them.

And then we all went outside, this time with Aiden and Hercules carrying Solos's body to a patch of land south of the landscaped pool. The shovels weren't used. They weren't even necessary, because Alex tapped into the earth element and a deep . . . a deep grave was formed. I realized that Aiden had sent Gable out of the room on purpose. Probably to clear his head, make him feel useful. Smart move.

Solos was placed in the grave and two coins were placed over his eyes. I'd never seen anything like it.

And I didn't cry.

Even though I really wanted to.

The messy ball of emotion pinging around my chest might have been relieved that way, but all I could do was stand there as they moved the dirt back onto the grave.

"He will be awarded a warrior's welcome in Tartarus," Aiden said solemnly, his silver eyes oddly bright. "He will want for nothing."

Staying outside wasn't wise. Neither was going inside, but what other options did we have at this point? Once inside the kitchen, Gable turned off the oven, but there would be no getting rid of that burnt smell. Everyone split before I even realized what was happening, and I was the last to drag myself upstairs. Halfway down the hall, I heard voices—Alex and Aiden.

I should've kept going, but that's not what I did. Creeping to the door, I stopped when I heard them talking in hushed voices.

"I'm going to call Marcus," I heard Alex say.

"And I can summon Apollo and see if we can get Hephaestus to finish a cage," Herc said, sounding surprisingly level-headed. He'd been all business since the Titan had showed up. "That will hold him."

"It held me for a while," Alex spoke. "But I wasn't the God Killer at the time. And I think we all need to accept the fact that Seth has somehow become just that."

I was hung up on the fact they were talking about putting Seth in a cage. An actual legit cage?

"The problem is, will Apollo answer your summons in a timely manner?" Aiden asked. "He pretty much answers when he feels like it, even when it's majorly urgent."

"That *is* a problem." Herc paused. "I can go back to Olympus and retrieve Apollo. Or even Hephaestus."

"What?" Alex demanded, and I wondered if Herc would even return. Didn't sound like he wanted to be anywhere near Seth. "How?"

"I'm not of this realm, and I am able to reenter Olympus . . . under the right circumstances."

"Of course," muttered Alex, and I could almost picture her rolling her eyes. "What are the right circumstances?"

"I need to spill a little of my blood at the highest point of wherever I am, which is convenient since we're on cliffs," he explained.

There was a pause and then Aiden said, "That doesn't sound complicated. You can do it now, before Seth even has a chance to wake up."

My heart dropped.

"Well, I can only do it at the exact moment the sun rises," Hercules added. "Not sure why, but I don't make the rules."

"That's . . ." Alex sighed. "That's at least six hours from now. We have no idea how long the Pegasus blood will work on Seth. Even if it does keep him under long enough to get Hephaestus here, we can't stay here for long. Atlas might be gone, but the other Titans have probably sensed his death. They will be gunning for us."

"Just keep the room guarded and hopefully Hephaestus can fashion us a kennel or something," Hercules advised, and my eyes widened. *A kennel?* "But to be fair, you don't know what he will be like when he awakes. He may not even try to escape. He may be the friendly neighborhood God Killer."

Shocked that Hercules was actually sort of defending Seth, I almost fell over. Those two had not hit it off on the right foot.

"Let's hope that's the case." Weariness clung to Aiden's tone. "But based on previous experience with him, when he goes ape-shit, he goes full-on ape-shit, and it's not a brief thing."

They weren't even going to give Seth a chance. He hadn't gone "ape-shit" for fun. He'd lost it after Solos had died. Anger blasted through me. I pushed away from the wall, about to make my presence known.

"What about Josie?" That was Alex, and I stopped myself, holding my breath. "You really think she's going to leave him in the panic room? Nothing against her, but she . . . she didn't know the Seth we did."

"I don't think she'll do that. She saw how violent he was. She wouldn't put everyone here at risk," Aiden replied. "Besides, we've got Luke watching his room now. She wouldn't hurt Luke, not even to free Seth."

Okay. That was sort of true. I didn't want to hurt anyone who didn't deserve it, but I would hurt someone to protect another. However, I didn't plan on releasing Seth until I knew where he was mentally and emotionally. Things were messy between us right now, but that didn't mean I'd given up on him. Right?

I wasn't sure what to think anymore.

Suddenly exhausted, I crept away from the door and made my way back downstairs before I was discovered. It was strange. The atrium was virtually unblemished, as if nothing had happened there.

As if Solos hadn't lost his life in there.

Drawing in a shallow breath, I forced each step forward. I don't know why I walked into the library. Maybe there was something soothing about being surrounded by books. The familiar scent eased my nerves.

I walked to the couch positioned across from the window and sat down, curling up against the arm. Smoothing my hand over my face, I pushed the hair back from where it had fallen over my eyes.

What had happened?

Gods, I couldn't really process it all.

Everything had changed. Somehow I'd seen this happen. Had Atlas been invading my dreams or . . . or was it something else? Right now, that didn't matter. Solos was gone, here one second and then just *gone*. A tear snuck free, trailing down my cheek. I tried to comfort myself with the knowledge that there was an afterlife. That Solos was ultimately okay. As Aiden had said, Solos would be awarded a warrior's welcome in Tartarus. That didn't make it easier, though. Not really, because death was death, and to me, it was still final.

It was the end.

Sorrow dug deep, hooking itself in with tiny claws that hit bone and muscle. You couldn't cut it out. Grief was there to stay.

And Seth . . . I didn't even know what was up with Seth, who he was going to be when he woke up. The Seth who made horrible mistakes but wanted to do better? The Seth who'd stood in the bedroom, vulnerable and nearly broken as he apologized?

Or the Seth who had leveled all of us, including Atlas? He hadn't just tapped into my *aether*. He'd gotten all of us, something none of us had known he could do, and deep down, I honestly didn't believe Seth had even realized he could do that until he'd done it.

I dropped my hand, curled it against my chest as I drew in a long breath that didn't seem to ease the tightening there.

I'd done the right thing by stopping Seth. I knew that, but was sitting by and keeping him locked up in a room okay? Herc would leave soon, and he would bring back a god who could trap him. Was I wrong for thinking that wasn't the right thing to do? I didn't know.

Right now, more than anything, I needed my . . . my father.

I needed him to do what fathers did. Give me advice. Help me. Get on my side. Support me.

Closing my eyes, I pressed the tips of my fingers under my chin. "Apollo?" I said into the quiet room. Maybe he wouldn't respond to Hercules, but when I'd called his name the night Hyperion had me, he'd come.

Nothing but a soft tick of a nearby clock sounded. I tried again. "Dad?"

And still nothing.

No matter how many times I called his name, Apollo didn't answer. Pressure increased in my chest and more tears snuck free. They kept falling silently, and I squeezed my eyes shut. By the time exhaustion dragged me under, I wasn't sure who I was crying for the most.

31

*J*osie's horrified face was the last thing I saw and the first thing I recalled the moment my eyes peeled wide open and my chest rose sharply.

Holy shit.

I dragged in mouthfuls of air.

What had I done?

The buzz of pure *aether* still sang in my veins, lighting up every nerve ending and filling every cell with light and power. My skin buzzed and my senses were hyper aware.

What in the fuck had I done?

Something had happened to me.

It wasn't just the stolen *aether* charging me up. Every single cell in my body had been reshaped. Raw energy zinged through my veins. A slow smile pulled at my lips as I stretched my neck from left to right. I knew what I was feeling.

I was the beginning and the end.

The God Killer.

My smile spread, but it froze as that knowledge sunk in. How? How was this possible? Immediately, I reached out to see if the bond between Alex and me was strong again, but it was still the same, there, but muted, in the background. That couldn't bode well.

The bright haze of power threatened to drag me in, but the high was tainted—oh gods, it was a bitter joy coursing through my veins. The events before Josie had used that damn poison and knocked me into next week replayed over and over in my head. I didn't need to close my eyes to see Josie's back bow the very second I connected with her and fed. I didn't need to use my fucking imagination to recall how her legs crumpled under her. Or how everyone else's legs gave way as well.

There was no debating this anymore. No pretending that I could stay with Josie and not be with her, because fuck, that obviously hadn't lasted longer than a hot second.

I was not safe.

I was never going to be safe.

Especially when it came to Josie.

Worse yet—gods—the worst thing was the look on Josie's face. She was horrified, but she hadn't been scared. She hadn't looked betrayed, not even when I'd fed on her, not even when I had hurt her.

Frankly, I didn't give a shit about the rest of them, but her?

I sat up, barely aware of the thin mattress that was under me, and swung my legs over the side. Standing, my heart pounded in my chest as I took a step forward. Lifting my gaze, I found a steel-reinforced door. Where in the hell was I? Didn't matter. That door wasn't going to hold me. They had to know that, so either they were incredibly stupid or they had summoned Heph to fashion the same kind of cage that had kept Alex in one place.

But a cage wasn't going to keep me. Not now.

Even if it could, I couldn't let that happen. Because even if I was locked up with no immediate way out, Josie was here.

She would free me.

I knew she would.

And I would destroy her.

Gutted, I knew what I had to do. There was no more fucking around, no more bullshitting myself or Josie, especially not her. I should've done this the day I'd fed off her.

I knew I was on the wrong path, had been on the wrong path since the moment I saw Josie in the stairwell at Radford, but I hadn't done anything about it. Now I would. I would do something about it, even if it pissed off Apollo and the other gods. I'd do it to keep her safe.

Safe from me.

I walked to the door and grasped the knob. Summoning the element of fire, I melted the internal gears. Metal gave way, rendered useless. The steel would've been good if someone was trying to knock the door in, say a mortal, but it didn't stop me. They would've known that, so I knew on the other side there'd have to be a guard.

A distant part of me hoped it was Aiden standing guard, because I would have loved to knock his ass out for shits and giggles, but as I threw the door open, it wasn't him.

Across from the room, Luke pushed off the wall, reaching for the thin icicle-shaped blade. "Shit."

I sprang forward, faster than even he, an extremely well-trained Sentinel, could move. The *power* coursing through me had me feeling off the hook. Spinning, I swiped his legs out from under him. Luke stumbled, letting out another curse as I shot behind him. Whipping around, I folded my arm around his neck from behind. I put pressure, the right amount, on his throat. His hands flew up, fingers digging into my bicep.

"I'm sorry, man." My voice was low, rough. "This isn't personal."

Luke slammed his fist into my arm, but I reached down with my free hand and grabbed the thin blade I knew was dipped in the blood of a Pegasus. Moving lightning quick, I dragged the sharp edge across his forearm.

The result was immediate.

Luke collapsed against me, bones and muscles struck useless by the poison. He would recover. In a few hours.

I pulled him into the cell and gently laid him on the cot, stretching him out. His eyes, full of fury, met mine. His silent, paralyzed glare promised retribution before his eyes drifted shut, giving way to the toxin. I had a feeling he wouldn't be getting the chance.

Still holding the blade, I closed the door behind me and realized that I was in another room, one that was hidden. Hell, they'd dropped me in a panic room in the basement. I almost laughed as I climbed the steps. The house was quiet. I imagined everyone thought I'd be out longer than I was. Not smart. It would be so easy to sneak up on them, especially Deacon. He wouldn't know what had hit him. Alex and Aiden, being demigods, would be harder, but no match now. I could easily—

I shut my eyes, jaw working. My head was a mess, as if there were a hundred voices speaking at once. I needed to get out of there. I headed for the front of the house, but stopped in the middle of the hall. Inhaling deeply, I lifted my gaze to the ceiling I could sense restlessness in one of the bedrooms upstairs, but my attention was drawn to the room in the front—the library. *She* was in there, and the sick thing was, I only knew her exact location because of her *aether*.

It fucking called to me.

It reached inside, wrapped its thready fingers around every muscle fiber and taunted me, lured me. My mouth watered.

Footsteps approached from the kitchen and my head swung sharply in the direction of the opening. Gable stepped out, blond hair disheveled and pants wrinkled.

Bad time for a midnight snack.

Sleep clung to his eyes. "Hey, aren't you—?"

I shot forward, clamped my hand over his mouth. I started to swipe him with the blade, but I didn't know if it would kill him.

So I shifted my hand until his nose and mouth were covered, and I held on until his legs gave out. I caught him and then tossed him over my shoulder. I figured Poseidon wouldn't be happy with how I dumped his kid on the couch, but oh well. Could've been worse.

I could've done a lot worse.

Back out in the hall, I forced myself to keep going toward the front door, but before I even knew what I was doing, I was in front of the library and was opening the door, stepping into the dark room, closing the door behind me.

My heart rate picked up, responding to her proximity, and as I stepped forward, I had no idea if it was because of what coursed through her veins or just because it was her.

It was both.

But it was *her*.

Josie was curled up on the couch, and even in the pale moonlight streaming in from the window above the couch, I could see that she still wore the shorts I'd seen her in last. Her hair was free, falling over the side of her face and over her shoulder, tangling with her curved arm.

So freaking beautiful.

I need to leave.

I walked toward her.

I need to get the hell out of here.

I knelt by her side.

I need to leave her.

I reached out, brushing the tips of my fingers over her lips. They parted on a soft inhale, and a second later she stirred awake. Those thick lashes fluttered, sweeping up and revealing deep blue eyes.

Our gazes collided and locked, and in her eyes, I saw surprise and then—then I saw *relief,* and holy shit, that broke me.

Broke me right apart.

"I'm sorry," I told her, repeating the last thing I'd said to her before the Titans attacked.

"Seth," she whispered, reaching for me.

I don't know if it was the relief I saw in her eyes, even after what I'd done, or the way she reached for me and said my name, as if it was a benediction, but all restraint within me broke.

Common sense dived face-first out the window, and in under a second I was on her.

Rising fast, I clasped the sides of her cheeks and tilted her head back. I kissed her, and there was nothing soft or smooth about it. She jolted in surprise and then grabbed my shoulders, her little nails digging through my shirt and into my skin. I nipped at her bottom lip, and with a soft moan, her mouth opened. I tasted her, drew her in as I dragged my hands down her throat over her arms. I wasn't thinking. There wasn't a part of my damn brain that was catching up to what was happening. Everything was focused on the way she felt, the look in her eyes, and the way she said my name.

I was lost in her.

My fingers brushed the edge of her shirt and I tugged the material, lifting it up. We broke apart long enough to get the damn thing over her head, and then everything else came off in a rush. My shirt. Her shorts. Mine. Then everything else. Nothing was between our hands or our bodies.

Pressing her into the couch, I moved over her and against her. There was no hesitation in Josie. No questions. No putting on the brakes. One of her legs wrapped around mine. Her hands slid down my back, to my ass. She grabbed me, pulling me closer. Our chests crushed together. Her small, hard nipples pressed into me, driving me freaking insane. The room was filled with the breathy sounds of her moans and the rougher ones of mine.

I shouldn't be doing this. It was too risky. My emotions were all over the damn place. No restraint. All it would take is a second to tap into her, to pull from her, to do exactly what the Titans planned to do to her.

But the way she moved, the arching of her hips and how she felt, wet and warm against my length, drove me forward, beyond the point of return. She curled her fingers through my hair as she gripped my arm with the other.

"I love you," she whispered in my ear as I settled between her thighs. "I love you, Seth."

Those words gutted me, cut me right open. I didn't deserve that. I didn't deserve this, but I had to get in her, feel her, one last time, and the memory of this joining was going to have to carry me until the gods laid down their punishment. Reaching down between us, I wrapped my hand around my dick. I groaned as I felt her readiness against the tip. There wasn't a damn thing between us.

I didn't stop.

Josie didn't stop me.

It was foolish. Risky. Fucking idiotic. But as I slid into her, felt every inch with nothing between us, the sensation blew me apart, shot straight to the very core of my being.

Nothing. Nothing had ever felt like this before.

Stopping, I lifted my head and stared down at Josie. Her long neck was exposed, her lips red and swollen, eyes half-open. Her chest rose fast and deep. She smoothed a trembling hand down my chest.

Her touch. I couldn't . . .

I caught her hand, pulling it away from me and pinning it above her head. Her eyes widened as I captured her other hand and drew it above her head, joining it with the other. I kept them there with one hand around her wrists and then gripped her rounded hip.

"Seth," she breathed.

I slammed in to the hilt. Her head kicked back as she made this soft, keening sound that almost made me lose it right there.

Things were frantic.

My body moved against hers, in her, and her arms strained. She wanted to touch me. Gods, Josie loved to touch me, but I held her in place as I thrust into her. I felt her the second before she came. Her hips jerked up, her back arched, and those blue eyes were wide.

Josie's cry was muffled as she bit down on her lip. She broke apart around me, her muscles clenching down, squeezing me, and I exhaled harshly, riding her until she fell back against the couch.

I wasn't done with her.

Pulling out of her, I let go of her wrists and, using my grip on her waist, I flipped her onto her stomach. I moved over her, pressing my chest to her back as I slid my arm under her waist, lifting her hips. I entered her in one stroke, nearly undone by the tightness I felt.

There was no rhythm to how I moved then. My hips pounded into hers, and I kept going, almost as if I was trying to get myself in there so deep there would be no way of extracting me from her, so fucking deep that there was no her, no me, just us. She was so tight, so wet, and so perfect.

Sweat dampened and slicked our skin. The fleshy sounds our bodies made drove me to the brink. Shifting my hand under her, I found the tight bundle of nerves, worked her until she clamped down on me.

Release powered down my spine, raw and all-consuming, blowing my head right off me. Intense. Couldn't breathe around it. Couldn't feel anything else. Only at the very last second, I pulled out and folded my arms around Josie, sealing her body to mine as I came, cradled against her, my face buried in her neck. The world fell away for those precious moments, dropped off and stayed there as our hearts slowed and our bodies relaxed into each other.

"Seth," she murmured, turning her head to the side. A couple of moments passed. "Are you . . . are you okay now?"

I closed my eyes. Everything would be. I spoke, my voice rough. Empty. "Yes."

Josie tensed under me and then she looked over her shoulder. Concern pooled into her gaze. "Seth, we need to talk. They're saying that you're a—"

"Shh," I murmured, shifted us onto our sides, until her back was to my front and my arm around her waist. "I just want to hold you right now. Please? We'll . . . we'll talk later."

She was stiff against me for a moment. "Promise?"

"Promise."

I lied. Add that to the list of fucked-up things I'd done, but she curled into me, pressing her cheek against my chest with both of her hands gripping my arm. Like she was trying to hold me there. Like she already knew on some unconscious level what was happening.

I held her until she fell back asleep.

I held her until I was no longer sure I could walk away.

I held her until it physically fucking hurt to ease her out of my embrace.

Leaning over her, my gaze roamed over her face. My hand shook as I carefully brushed the long, damp strands back from her cheek. I committed every square inch to memory. The natural arch to her brows. The height of her cheeks and the full, pouty bow-shaped lips.

I brushed my lips against her cheek and then again, lower, on her neck, over the faded tag the daimon had given her outside of St. Louis. Then I spoke the three truest words I'd ever spoken and the three words I didn't deserve to utter, to give air, but I said them.

"I love you."

32

Josie

When I opened my eyes, Seth was gone and I was alone in the morning light, lying on my side. I stared at the closed door, wondering if I'd dreamt him. Quite possibly. I'd had some vivid dreams when it came to him, and there was a surreal quality about everything as all my senses came back online.

I looked down at myself.

Considering I was naked under the quilt, I was pretty sure I hadn't dreamt him. And if that hadn't done it, the dampness between my thighs was also a very good indication.

But Seth was gone.

Holding the quilt to my breasts, I sat up, wincing slightly as I moved my legs onto the floor. What we'd done—*he'd* done—on this couch . . . ? Wow. I felt a little shaky.

My clothes were stacked on the floor, as if Seth had folded them for me. Strange. My stomach dipped and twisted as I lifted my gaze again to the library door.

I love you.

His voice echoed in my thoughts. My heart stuttered over itself. He'd never said that before, but I swore I'd heard him. It was too real, his voice too heavy for it to be a part of my imagination, but where was he?

And had he let himself out of the room last night, or had someone else done it? If so, why hadn't they come to get me? Closing my eyes, I swallowed hard, because I knew Seth hadn't been let out on his own. Not after what Herc and everyone were saying. They were planning to summon Hephaestus, and they believed him to be the God Killer.

Seth had gotten himself out.

I just want to hold you.

With a sinking feeling, I grabbed my clothes off the floor and quickly changed back into them since there was no way I was walking through this house with just a thin quilt wrapped around me. I doubted anyone but Seth wanted to see that.

We'll talk later.

Promise?

Promise.

The numb, cold feeling expanded. Things had not been settled between us at all before the Titan appeared. We really needed to talk before, and now it was imperative.

Once in my clothes, I walked over to the door and found that it had been locked. The sinking feeling hit me again. I unlocked the door and stepped out into the brighter hallway. I could hear footsteps upstairs and as I took a step forward, the door at the end of the hall opened.

Alex stepped out, a Covenant dagger in her white-knuckled grip.

The strained set to Alex's face as she stepped into the hall and saw me was like stepping out into icy, winter rain. I knew it. In my bones, I knew it.

"Do you know where he is?" she asked, striding toward me. Every muscle in my body locked up. When I didn't respond, she stopped in front of me. "Aiden just found Luke out of commission in the room we had Seth in, and I found Gable in the same condition in the living room. We can't find Seth."

"Oh God," I whispered, leaning against the wall. I gave a little shake of my head, and it hit me fully then, what I already knew. The intensity behind the way he came to me. The heaviness in his voice. The reason he didn't want to talk then. The softly whispered "I love you." Oh God, what had he done? I lifted my head, meeting her gaze. "He didn't hurt them."

She nodded curtly. "Looks like he got hold of Solos's blade, the one with the Pegasus blood on it. They weren't hurt, but we need to find him. Do you know where he went?"

What I'd said hadn't been a question, but Alex was wary—she had been wary of Seth the moment she set foot on Covenant University soil. So had Aiden, and Seth had seen that. None of that helped him, not when he got lost in his own head.

Pushing off the wall, I stepped around Alex. "He's gone."

"Yes." She turned to me. "He's—"

"He's left." I drew in a breath, but it got stuck and it expanded in my throat. It hurt as emotion crawled up. I took a step forward and stumbled as pressure sliced across my chest. "Oh God."

Seth had really done it.

"Josie?" Alex put a hand on my arm. "Are you okay?"

Stepping away from her, I wheeled around and headed for the front door. Alex was hot on my heels as I reached the door and threw it open. I burst out onto the stone porch, coming to an abrupt halt as I scanned the circular driveway.

One of the vehicles was gone.

My hands fell open at my sides as I slowly shook my head. He'd really left, and with a vehicle he had hours on us, and I doubted he was planning to stay in Southern California.

"Dammit," I heard someone say. Deacon? I had no idea when he'd gotten there. "He's taken the damn SUV."

Something cracked in my chest.

Pivoting around, I walked back into the house and I kept walking, even when Alex called out my name. I needed space. I needed a couple of minutes where I could think. I needed to be alone.

I passed Aiden in the stairwell. He said something, but I didn't really understand him. Climbing the steps, I headed into the bedroom Seth and I were supposed to share. On autopilot, I stripped off the clothes and left them where they fell by the bed. In the bathroom, I cranked on the hot water, waited as steam filled the room. Sliding open the stall door, I stepped under the pelting hot water, arms limp at my sides.

And I stood there for what felt like forever, my head bowed and eyes closed. I stood there until that wave of emotion that had been crawling up my throat finally broke free, burning my eyes. The tears came again and they didn't stop. Not for a very long time.

Everything was a mess and Seth had finally told me he loved me.

Then he had left me.

The mood in the living room was tense, even after Luke had explained that Seth hadn't injured him, had even seemed regretful of his actions. The same with Gable, who was currently holed up in his room. It didn't change the outcome though.

I sat on the couch, beside Alex, as everyone debated what to do next. Alex and Aiden wanted to continue to Canada to retrieve Demeter's daughter and let Herc deal with the runaway Seth issue when he returned. Deacon and Luke were mostly quiet, and no one really asked for my input.

Probably a good thing, because I'd spent the better part of the day absolutely numb and riddled with guilt. I shouldn't have let them put Seth in that room, or at least, not by himself. My instincts had urged me to stay with him, but I'd caved to the advice of others without saying anything. That was weak, and I'd failed him.

I was a pretty big fail when I punched him after he admitted what he done. Granted, he'd deserved that, but when he apologized and when he'd asked me if this was it, I'd said nothing. The only thing I could do at this point was to move forward. Not without him. No. Never without him.

Where could he have gone, and where could he be going? I racked my brain the entire morning and afternoon, latching onto the mystery so I didn't slip into a soul-crushing downward spiral. And I was so close to doing that, wanting nothing more than to throw myself face-first onto the bed and sob until there was nothing left in my body.

"So, you guys are totally okay with letting Herc handle things with Seth?" Deacon asked, leaning against the fireplace I doubted was ever used. "We're just going to forget about him?"

Aiden looked over at him. "We're not forgetting him, but we have to find the rest of the demigods before the Titans do. Atlas might be gone, but the rest aren't."

"I think we need to find Seth," his brother challenged. "We need him when they do come back, especially since he's all kinds of special sauce right now. I don't want to see what happened to . . . to Solos happen to anyone else."

"I don't want that either." Twisting the heavy length of hair in her hands, Alex shook her head. "We need the other demigods to defeat the Titans."

Luke cocked his head to the side. "Agreed, but we need Seth too. We need as much firepower on our side as we can muster, and he has the ultimate power, by the looks of it."

"But . . ." Alex looked over at me, trailing off. Her shoulders tensed and she appeared to choose her words carefully. "I don't think Seth is going to be of a lot of help right now."

Deacon's lips pursed. "You know, I'm just going to address the two-hundred-pound Apollyon God Killer elephant in the room."

His brother arched a brow.

"What you all are not saying is that you think Seth's gone all dark side again, right? That he's hopped up on *aether* and is going to go on a killing binge again, but like a legit, 'kill everything in his path' spree this time. That's what you're not saying," he said, eyes narrowing. "But the thing is, Seth immobilized Luke and Gable, but he didn't hurt them, and you all know damn well, if he'd wanted to hurt them, he would've."

Deacon paused, looking at me. I'd told them earlier that Seth had seen me before he'd left. Of course, I didn't go into details about what we had done, because seriously, that would be a little TMI, but I'd told them that he'd seemed normal. Which was true. Needless to say, Alex and Aiden both had looked at me like they doubted my sanity since I hadn't alerted anyone to the fact Seth was roaming around.

"And he didn't hurt Josie," Deacon continued. "He didn't feed off her. He basically stayed with her until she slept, said goodbye to her, and then left. Does that sound like an out of control, *aether*-sucking killer Apollyon?"

"Try saying that fast," murmured Luke.

"He lost his shit because of what happened to Solos. Can we really blame him for that? None of us were hurt. We need to find him," Deacon stated, his chin lifting. "Before he does turn into that and starts blowing up islands or something."

I stiffened. What had Deacon just said? Blowing up islands?

Holy crappers, the *islands*. I blinked. Would Seth really go home? He hadn't been there since he'd been sent to the Covenant in the UK as a teen, but he'd talked of wanting to go back there. He'd mentioned it once, but to even speak of a place that had been so cold to him, it had to be important. It was a wild guess, completely out there, but it was a very real possibility. His family home was surrounded by nothing by trees and sand. He would be alone there, away from everyone. But would he go that far, halfway around the world? Would he go to that kind of extreme?

Deep down, I just knew he would. Call it intuition, but I just knew I was right.

"I think I know where he's gone." I stood up, thrusting my hands through my hair and then dropping them to my sides. All eyes were on me. "I can find him." Determination filled me. "I'm *going* to find him."

"Where?" Luke asked, attentive.

Glancing around the room, I exhaled slowly. "I think he's gone to the Cyclades Islands."

"What?" Alex frowned.

"That's where he was born, and his home is still there. I can't tell you how I know that. I don't even know, but I just do. He's gone there."

Aiden looked away, his silver eyes flashing as he crossed his arms over his chest. Without saying a thing, I knew he *so* wasn't on board with this plan. Not my problem.

Deacon glanced at Luke, who nodded. "We're in."

His older brother's eyes narrowed. "I don't think that's wise. You saw him. You saw how unstable he is."

"I've also seen how he's been the whole entire time he's been here," Deacon argued. "So I think my decision is *completely* wise."

Alex unfurled her leg, and her shoulders rose with a deep breath. "I'm going to have to agree with Aiden on this."

"Of course you do," muttered Deacon. "I mean, when wouldn't you agree with him?"

Aiden snorted. "Uh, like all the damn time?"

She narrowed her eyes at Aiden and then turned to me. "I know you have seen a . . . a different side to Seth. I get that, but you don't know what he's capable of—"

"And you do?" I fired back without really thinking about it, because of course she knew what he was capable of.

"Yes," she replied quietly, confirming what I already knew. "We all know what he's capable of. You don't. And I'm not trying to be a douche canoe by pointing that out, but it's the truth. Seth can be and is incredibly dangerous, even when he's chill, but now that he's a God Killer most likely jonesing for *aether*? You have no idea how bad it is."

Irritation prickled along the back of my skull, and the rustling of papers on the desk broke the silence. "He's not the same person you knew."

Alex opened her mouth.

"No. He's not, Alex. He's not the Apollyon who was tricked by Lucian and Ares. He's not the same person who got all those people killed. He's not the man who was willing to play second best to another." The room went silent. Crickets could be heard. Alex flinched, but I kept going, my words razor-sharp and clear. "I'm not saying he's all forgiven or that he's perfect. He's not. I know that. But he's Seth. He's not just the sum of only half of what he's done. He's whole and he's not going to be referred to from here on out as the God Killer. That is not who he is. And he needs help, and because I love him—because I'm *in* love with him—I'm going to help him instead of giving up on him." I looked between her and Aiden. "I'm pretty sure that's something you two are familiar with, right? You two didn't give up on each other. Not once."

"Mic drop," murmured Deacon.

Aiden shook his head as he stepped forward, unfolding his arms. "It's not the same thing, Josie."

"It *is* the same thing," his brother challenged, silver eyes brightening. He threw his hands up. "You didn't give up on Alex, and she was legit trying to kill us. None of us did. So why would we give up on Seth?"

Alex pursed her lips as she walked over to where Aiden stood. They stood side by side, a formidable sight. "We're not asking you to give up on him."

"You're not? Because I'm pretty sure you all are totally on board with Herc capturing him. And why would you all want to capture and cage him?" The papers stirred again, and I forced myself to calm down. "If my father or any of the gods truly think he's a threat, they're going to amp up on finding how to . . ." A knot formed in the base of my throat. "They're going to find a way to destroy him. And that's why he would be caged—held until they find a way. That's not just giving up on him, but that's helping them murder him."

"I don't want that," Alex argued, her hands curling into fists at her sides. "I know it's hard to believe, but I care about Seth too."

Heat poured into my chest. I was woman enough to admit I still didn't like hearing that. Nope. Nope. Nope.

"I will always care about him," she added, meeting and holding my gaze. "But we have Titans running around gaining strength, and if they enter Olympus, it's over for all of us. We need to focus on finding the other demigods."

"We need Seth to help defeat them." I was seconds away from stomping my feet. "And you know where Demeter's daughter is. You two can go with Herc and get her. Deacon and Luke can help with finding the other demigods." Stepping back, I fisted my hands until my knuckles ached. "Honestly, I don't care what you end up doing. I don't need your blessing or permission," I told the two demigods. "And if you're smart, you're not going to try to stop me. So either you're going to help me or you're going to stay out of my way."

Luke let out a low whistle and said, "We will do whatever you need us to do. We're not giving up on him."

I waited.

Truth was, Alex and Aiden were both super-strong. They might not be able to stop me, but I wasn't sure. I had more *aether* in me, but they both knew how to use their physical strength a hell of a lot more than I did. I needed them on my side. I needed them to not run to Herc or my father and tell them where Seth might be, but if I couldn't get them . . .

"I will do anything to protect Seth," I warned, my voice low. Both of them looked over at me sharply. Understanding flared in their features. "Anything."

Aiden lifted his chin. "And what if he *is* where you think he is and you find him, and he's not . . . not the same, Josie?"

Cold air drilled into my chest, reminding me so very much of Hyperion's touch. I shuddered. Right now, I couldn't let myself think of that and I wouldn't let myself think of the possibility of Seth being unreachable. I refused to even consider the idea, because I could get to him. I could help him. "That's not what's going to happen, Aiden."

He looked away, a muscle feathering along his jaw. Silence stretched out between us, feeling like an eternity. My shoulders tensed. I fully expected them to argue with me more.

"Okay," Alex said, reaching down and wrapping her hand around Aiden's. He squeezed her hand, and my chest clenched. "We're in."

Deacon smiled.

Beside him, Luke lifted his chin quietly.

Aiden nodded and then lowered his head to Alex's, brushing his lips across her cheek. "You're right," he said after a moment, lifting his silvery gaze to mine. "We owe Seth. We owe him big."

And I exhaled roughly, caught up in a mixture of triumph and exhaustion. I didn't have time for either, because I needed every ounce of strength and determination I had in me. Because I was going after Seth, and I wouldn't rest or give up until he was where he belonged.

Standing beside me.

ACKNOWLEDGEMENTS

A huge thank you to the following people for making the book possible: Kevan Lyon, my agent of awesome; Kate Kaynak for acquiring the Covenant Series all those years ago, which made the Titan Series possible; Rich Storrs for editing through the mess that was my first draft and having the patience to do so; and a huge thank you to the team at Spencer Hill Press. Thank you to K.P Simmons, and to my assistant/BFF Stacey Morgan. A special thank you to Drew Leighty for letting us plaster his face and other parts all over the covers, and for bringing Seth to life. None of this would be possible with you, the reader. Because of you, this book happened. There aren't enough thank yous in the world.

#1 *New York Times* and *USA Today* bestselling author Jennifer L. Armentrout lives in West Virginia. All the rumors you've heard about her state aren't true. Well, mostly. When she's not hard at work writing, she spends her time reading, working out, watching zombie movies, and pretending to write. She shares her home with her husband, his K-9 partner named Diesel, and her hyper Jack Russell, Loki. Her dreams of becoming an author started in algebra class, where she spent her time writing short stories . . . therefore explaining her dismal grades in math. Jennifer writes Adult and Young Adult Urban Fantasy and Romance.

Come find out more at: **www.jenniferarmentrout.com**